Praise for

HISTORY IS ALL YOU LEFT ME

"Adam Silvera knows how to break hearts—at least those belonging to readers of his books . . . *History Is All You Left Me* hits even closer to home [than his debut, *More Happy Than Not*]."
—EntertainmentWeekly.com

"A complex, touching valentine to love and friendship . . . [Silvera] gets the small details of love and loss exactly right. These moments are framed in exquisite prose . . . In this emotionally charged story, Griffin's desire to be honest with himself and others leads the reader to a greater understanding of how it feels to have a conflicted heart."—*The Washington Post*

"Through Griffin, Silvera presents an eloquent, in-depth examination of 'whatever comes next,' of the ways in which the grieving process both isolates people and draws them together."
—*Chicago Tribune*

"Silvera delivers another twisty novel about self-exploration, adolescent relationships and the bond between first loves. *History Is All You Left Me* is a tale for today's youth—one that embraces the essence of time and love."   —*Bookpage*

"Silvera's wrenching sophomore effort . . . is not for the faint of heart . . . A love story for the ages."
—Barnes and Noble Teen Blog

HISTORY
IS ALL YOU
LEFT ME

HISTORY IS ALL YOU LEFT ME

ADAM SILVERA

SOHO
TEEN

Published in the United States by Soho Teen
an imprint of Soho Press, Inc.
227 W 17th Street
New York, NY 10011

Library of Congress Cataloging-in-Publication Data
Silvera, Adam, 1990–
History is all you left me / Adam Silvera.

ISBN 978-1-64129-317-4
eISBN 978-1-61695-693-6

1. Love—Fiction. 2. Grief—Fiction. 3. Obsessive-compulsive
disorder—Fiction. 4. Gays—Fiction.
PZ7.1.S54 Hi 2017 [Fic]—dc23 2016020598

Interior design by Janine Agro, Soho Press, Inc.

Printed in the United States of America

10 9 8 7 6 5 4 3 2 1

For those with history stuck in their heads and hearts.

Shout-outs to Daniel Ehrenhaft, who discovered me,
and Meredith Barnes, who helps everyone find me. Best tag team ever.

INTRODUCTION

Adam Silvera knows I almost never cry at books, which is why I called him as soon as I finished *History Is All You Left Me.*

I was sobbing. I was incoherent.

You're still alive in alternate universes, Theo . . .

I knew this was a story about grief. But it's hard to fully steel yourself for the brutal intimacy of Griffin's second-person narration: this kid, wrecked and aching, speaking directly to his recently deceased first love.

But that's the thing about *History Is All You Left Me,* about Adam's books in general. You *can't* steel yourself. He slips past your defenses—yet he's so present in his own writing, you never really feel alone. It's like being yanked off a cliff by someone who never lets go of your hand.

This freaking book.

Two timelines, one universe. Our hero, Griffin Jennings, is heartbroken and spiraling after his ex-boyfriend's death. But even in the sun-dappled first-love History chapters, Griffin is Griffin. He's observant and thoughtful. He's anxious and uncertain. He's living with obsessions and compulsions that don't always make sense to the people he loves. Griffin is so vividly drawn, it feels impossible that he's fictional—and his story feels so raw and unfiltered, you almost don't notice the mastery of craft behind it.

But that's quintessential Adam Silvera: bold structural choices and meticulous attention to detail, rendered practically invisible by the sheer emotional force of his voice. Who but Adam could so perfectly execute these interconnected timelines? Who could make us believe in a moment as it's happening, and then completely reinvent its meaning ten chapters later? And who but Adam could choreograph it all so subtly that it feels like Griffin just telling his story? *History*'s technical perfection bowls me over every time.

Still, I'm most grateful for *History*'s honesty: for the messy boy whose anxiety feels like it came straight from my brain. For the wildly relatable nerd monologues, and the beautiful confusion of first love. For the unflinching, full-on cliff dive into a sea of raw grief. And for Adam Silvera's unsinkable voice, gripping my hand all the way down.

Love,
Becky Albertalli,
author of *Simon vs. the Homosapiens Agenda*

TODAY
MONDAY, NOVEMBER 20TH, 2016

You're still alive in alternate universes, Theo, but I live in the real world, where this morning you're having an open-casket funeral. I know you're out there, listening. And you should know I'm really pissed because you swore you would never die and yet here we are. It hurts even more because this isn't the first promise you've broken.

I'll break down the details of this promise again. You made it last August. Trust me when I say I'm not talking down to you as I recall this memory, and many others, in great detail. I doubt it'll even surprise you since we always joked about how your brain worked in funny ways. You knew enough meaningless trivia to fill notebooks, but you occasionally slipped on the bigger things, like my birthday this year (May 17th, not the 18th), and you never kept your night classes straight even though I got you a cool planner with zombies on the cover (which you-know-who probably forced you to throw out). I just want you to remember things the way I do. And if bringing up the past annoys you now—as I know it did when you left New York for California—know that I'm sorry, but please don't be mad at me for reliving all of it. History is all you left me.

We made promises to each other on the day I broke up with you so you could do your thing out there in Santa Monica without me holding you back. Some of those promises took bad turns but weren't broken, like how I said I'd never hate you even though you gave me enough reasons to, or how you never stopped being my friend even when your boyfriend asked you to. But on the day we were walking to the post office with Wade to ship your boxes to California, you walked backward into the street and almost got hit by a car. I saw our endgame— to find our way back to each other when the time was right, no matter what—disappear, and I made you promise to always take care of yourself and never die.

"Fine. I'll never die," you said as you hugged me.

If there was a promise you were allowed to break, it wasn't that one, and now I'm forced to approach your casket in one hour to say goodbye to you.

Except it's not going to be goodbye.

I'll always have you here listening. But being face-to-face with you for the first time since July and for the last time ever is going to be impossible, especially given the unwanted company of your boyfriend.

Let's leave his name out of my mouth as long as possible this morning, okay? If I'm going to have any chance of getting through today, tomorrow, and all the days that follow, I think I need to go back to the start, where we were two boys bonding over jigsaw puzzles and falling in love.

It's what comes after you fell out of love with me that it all goes wrong. It's what comes after we broke up that's making me so nervous. Now you can see me, wherever you are. I know you're there, and I know you're watching me, tuned in to my life to piece everything together yourself. It's not just the shameful things I've done that are driving me crazy, Theo. It's because I know I'm not done yet.

HISTORY
SUNDAY, JUNE 8TH, 2014

I'm making history today.

Time is moving faster than this L train, but it's all good since I'm sitting to the left of Theo McIntyre. I've known him since middle school, when he caught my eye at recess. He waved me over and said, "Help me out, Griffin. I'm rebuilding Pompeii." A puzzle of Pompeii made up of one hundred pieces, obviously. I knew nothing of Pompeii at the time; I thought Mount Vesuvius was the hidden lair of some comic book over-lord. Theo's hands had entranced me, sorting the puzzle pieces into groups according to shades before beginning, separating the granite roads from the demolished, ash-coated structures. I helped with the sky, getting the clouds all wrong. We didn't get very far with the puzzle that day, but we've been tight ever since.

Today's outing takes us from Manhattan to Brooklyn to see if the lost treasures in some flea market are as overpriced as everyone says they are. No matter where we are, Brooklyn or Manhattan, a schoolyard or Pompeii, I've planned on changing the game up on Theo on this even-numbered day. I just hope he's down to keep playing.

"At least we have the place to ourselves," I say.

It's almost suspicious how empty the subway car is. But I'm not questioning it. I'm too busy dreaming up what it would be like to always share this space and any other space with this know-it-all who loves cartography, puzzles, video animation, and finding out what makes humans tick. On a crowded train, Theo and I usually squeeze together when we sit, our hips and arms pressed against one another's, and it's a lot like hugging him except I don't have to let go as quickly. It sucks that Theo sits directly across from me now, but at least I get the very awesome view. Blue eyes that find wonder in everything (including train ads for teeth whitening), blond hair that darkens when it's wet, the *Game of Thrones* T-shirt I got him for his birthday back in February.

"It's a lot harder to people-watch without people," Theo says. His eyes lock on me. "There's you, I guess."

"I'm sure there will be some interesting people at the flea market. Like hipsters."

"Hipsters are characters, not people," Theo says.

"Don't hipster-shame. Some of them have real feelings underneath their beanie hats and vintage flannels."

Theo stands and does a bullshit pull-up on the rail; his brain gets him top marks, but his muscles can't carry him as high. He gives up and hops back and forth between the train benches like some underground trapeze artist. I wish he would somersault to my side and stay put. He holds on to the railing and stretches his leg to the opposite bench, and his shirt rises a little so I peek at his exposed skin peripherally while keeping my focus on Theo's grin. It might be my last day to do so.

The train rocks to a stop and we get off, finally.

Manhattan is home and all, so Theo never bad-mouths it, but I know he wishes more of its walls were stained with graffiti like they are here in Brooklyn, bright in the summer sun. Theo points out his favorites on the way to the flea market: a little boy in black and white walking across colorful block letters spelling out DREAM; an empty mirror demanding to find the fairest of them all in a crazy neat cursive that rivals Theo's perfect handwriting; an airplane circling Neptune, which is just fantastical enough that it doesn't give me flying anxiety; knights seated around Earth, like it's their round table. Neither of us have any idea what it's supposed to mean, but it's pretty damn cool.

It's a long, hot walk to the flea market, located by the East River. Theo spots a refreshment truck, and we spend five bucks each on cups of frozen lemonade, except there isn't enough of the sugary slush left so we're forced to chew ice to survive the heat.

Theo stops at a table with *Star Wars* goods. His face scrunches up when he turns to me. "Seventy dollars for that toy lightsaber?"

Theo's inside voice sucks. It's a problem.

The forty-something vendor looks up. "It's a recalled saber," she says flatly. "It's rare and I should be charging more." Her shirt reads PRINCESS LEIA IS NOT THE DAMSEL IN DISTRESS YOU'RE LOOKING FOR.

Theo returns her glare with an easy smile. "Did someone pull an Obi-Wan and cut someone's arm off?"

My knowledge on all things *Star Wars* is pretty limited, and the same goes for Theo's knowledge on all things *Harry Potter*. He's the only sixteen-year-old human I know who isn't caught up on everyone's favorite boy wizard. One night we argued for a solid hour over who would win in a duel between Lord Voldemort and Darth Vader. I'm surprised we're still friends.

"The battery hatch snaps off easily and children can't seem to keep them out of their damn mouths," the woman says. She isn't talking to Theo anymore. She's talking to an equally unhappy dude her age who can't figure out an R2-D2 alarm clock.

"Okay, then." Theo salutes her, and we walk away.

We stroll for a few minutes. (Six, to be exact.) "Are we done here?" I ask. It's hot, and I'm melting, and we've definitely seen that some of the treasures are way pricier than they legally should be.

"Hell no, we're not done," Theo says. "We can't leave empty-handed."

"So buy something."

"Why don't you buy *me* something?"

"You don't need that lightsaber."

"No, stupid, buy me something else."

"It's safe to assume you're buying me something too, right?"

"Seems fair," Theo says. He taps his dangerous watch. It is actually for-real dangerous, as in it's not safe to wear. I'm not even sure how or why it got made, because its sharp sundial hands have scratched unsuspecting people's bodies—mine included—enough times that he should throw it in a fireplace and kill it dead and then sue the manufacturer. He wears it anyway because it's different. "Let's meet at the entrance in twenty minutes. Ready?"

"Go."

Theo dashes away, nearly crashing into a bearded man with a little girl sitting on his shoulders. He is out of sight in seconds. I check the time on my phone—4:18, even minute—and I speed in the opposite direction, into an airy labyrinth full of people's relics for sale. I run past crates of old sneakers, crooked rows of smudged mirrors like a filthy funhouse, poles with floral pashminas that billow from a hidden fan, and buckets of seashells sold in tandem with paintbrushes.

The seashells are kind of cool, I guess, but they don't really scream "Theo!"

A minute or so later, I hit a grid of the market that *does* speak Theo's language. A dream catcher with a willow hoop dyed his favorite shade of green. An entire table of tiny ships inside bottles. He was recently reading up on their intricacies in the hopes of making one himself, except I know he wants his bottle to have a spaceship inside because he always has to put his Theo twist on things.

I still have all the time in the world—if the world only had twelve minutes to offer, at least. It's too bad he's not more of a fantasy fan, because the letter openers here are pretty boss and I'm sort of hoping he's found this table already and will surprise me with one, preferably the one designed like a sword sheath or this one with the bone handle. It's okay because I have all the time in the world . . . Actually, right now, no I don't, because according to my phone, I only have nine minutes, an odd number that's getting me really anxious, so I scratch my palm while running again. I somehow return to a world of more misses. Theo has no current use for breakfast-friendly pots and pans since he's pretty happy eating bowls of cereal with orange juice, and he definitely doesn't need gardening tools unless they come with instructions on how he can grow more video games and computer apps for free.

Then I hit the jackpot.

Puzzles.

I glance at my phone again: six minutes left. I'm no longer anxious; I'm excited. I know from being over at Theo's enough that he doesn't own any of these: a steampunk barn house gliding away on wings built of scraps from a satellite; Santa's sleigh being pulled by dolphins underwater (I don't want to know what's in those wrapped gifts, but I'd also love to hear Theo's guesses); a 3-D puzzle of a soccer ball, and the 3-D part is cool, but the sports part is less cool. I'm not sure where Theo stands on 3-D puzzles, but this doesn't seem like the one "to kick it off"—ha.

Boom, got it. The fourth one in the row on the table: Doomed Pirate Ship. The pirates are being thrown overboard by stormy weather and a raging sea; some try to climb back up, while another hangs from the plank. I know Theo will create a kick-ass story behind this one. The vendor drops the puzzle in a brown plastic bag and even though it costs nine bucks, I just shove a ten into her hands and jet back.

Theo is waiting by the exit, pressed against the wall to hide away in the shade, like a vampire who stayed out too late—too early? I don't blame him. We're both sweating. He looks at his sundial watch. "Two minutes to spare! Let's get the hell out of here before we go up in flames, or, worse, you get sunburn."

On the way back to the subway, the only clue I have of his gift is a box. It's a perfect cube. I have zero guesses as to what it is. Underground we're hidden from the sun, but the mugginess of a crowded platform is unbearable in its own way, like we've set up camp at the top of a volcano and zipped our tent shut. We somehow survive the six-minute wait, and once the train opens its doors, we race to the corner bench and sit before a couple of college-age-looking guys can take the seats for themselves. The air conditioner is on full blast, and I feel more like myself.

"Presents?" Theo asks, pointing at my bag with finger guns.

"You finished shopping first, so you go first," I say, inching my leg a little closer to his so our knees might accidentally touch.

"I'm not sure what kind of logic that is, but okay," Theo says.

He gives me the little box and whatever is inside doesn't weigh that much and slides back and forth as I toss it from hand to hand. I open it and pull out an ornament of none other than Ron Weasley, Harry Potter's best friend.

"What do you think?" Theo asks. "I know he's your favorite character, so you probably already have this, but I thought this one was cool, especially since he's got that seen-better-days roughness going on."

I nod. It's true: this Ron Weasley figurine is a little beat-up, the paint chipped on his red hair and black robe. But he's not my favorite character. It's an easy mistake because Ron is my favorite in the trio—sorry Harry, sorry Hermione—and it's not as if they make ornaments for characters that were only alive and important in one book. But Cedric Diggory is my absolute favorite character in the series, in any book, really. When Cedric died at the end of the Triwizard Tournament, I cried for way longer than I've ever admitted to anyone. Cedric's death is no doubt my most painful loss ever. But it's okay, it's not like I know for sure who Theo's favorite *Star Wars* character is. I want to say Yoda, but that sounds stupid, even to me. It's the thought that counts.

"This is awesome," I say. "And I don't own it already, so thanks." I wonder if the previous owner got over the series and pawned this little guy for fifty cents or something. One man's loss and all that, I guess. "Okay. Your turn." I'm missing the emptiness of the train we rode out, hyperalert that there are nameless spectators watching us exchange gifts and drawing their own conclusions about how we must be dating. It sucks that they're wrong. It double sucks that there's a chance Theo may be too scared to even be my friend after today.

Theo slides the puzzle out of the bag and his eyes widen. "Hell yes. Eight hundred pieces. You have to put this together with me."

"What's the story behind it?"

Theo studies it for a moment. "It's about the impending zombie-pirate apocalypse, obviously."

"Obviously. Tell me, how did the pirates get hit with the virus before anyone else?"

"The zombie virus has always existed, but the scientists knew it was best to keep it as far away from land as possible. They knew humans by nature are stupid and bored and would do something like unleash hell on the world if it meant not having to go to their dead-end jobs on Monday morning. Scientists contained the virus on an island—I'm redacting the name because I can't trust you with this secret, Griff—and they didn't account for the raging storm you see here destroying the island

and releasing the virus until it became airborne, hitting the traveling pirates first. Well, infecting the parrot of Captain Hoyt-Sumner first, who carried the virus onto *The Pillaging Mary.*"

Only then do I lose it and smile. "How the hell are you coming up with these names?"

"I didn't make it up, it's in all the textbooks. Read up on your future's history," Theo says.

"What's the parrot's name?"

"Fulton, but everyone calls her Rot Feathers after she makes all the pirates undead. They later renamed the ship *The Blood-curdling Crawler*, which feels appropriate."

I really want to spend an hour inside his head, climbing all the different whirling clockwork gears.

"These zombie pirates are smart enough to rename their ship?" I ask him. "We're screwed."

"You better be my partner against the zombie pirates," Theo says. "I know how to save us."

Theo launches into different strategies we can employ to survive the apocalypse. We'll need to build a fortress somewhere up high, with cannons and other practical weapons, like military crossbows that shoot flaming arrows. Easy: I almost feel like I can already wield one from all the fantasy books I've read. Apparently, I'll also have to learn how to cook because Theo will be too busy keeping watch twenty-four/seven. He's pretty sure he'll have figured out the key to eternal unrest while the undead are among us—and won't have time to cook or we'll end up dinner ourselves.

"Sound good, Griff?"

"I can't promise the food I cook will even be edible, but desperate times call for desperate measures."

Theo holds out his hand and we shake on it, locking down our roles in the zombie-pirate apocalypse. Touching him gets my heart pounding, fast and heavy.

I let go. "I have to tell you something." The subway car is

rattling and loud, and the curious eyes have drifted. Everyone else is lost in their own worlds.

"There's something I have to tell you, too," Theo says.

"Who goes first?"

"Rock, paper, scissors?"

We both play rock.

"Same time?" Theo suggests.

"I don't think my thing is something to shout at the same time. You can go first."

"Trust me. I'm betting we're both going to say the same thing. It'll be easier this way," Theo says.

I'm not going to keep fighting him on this. Maybe what he has to say is worse than mine, and I won't feel as bad.

"Countdown from three?"

"Four."

Theo half-smiles, then nods. "Four, three, two, one."

"I think I might be crazy," I spit out while he says, "I like you."

Theo blushes, his half smile gone. "Wait, what?" He shifts his body around and stares out the train window, but we're under-ground, so all he'll see is darkness and his reflection. "I thought you were going to say you like me. Are you gay, Griff?"

"Yeah," I admit, for the first time ever, which somehow doesn't have my heart racing or my face heating up. All I know is, I would've lied to anyone else.

"Good. I mean, cool," Theo says. It seems like he's flirting with the idea of making eye contact again before keeping his gaze to the window. "Why were you scared to tell me? That you think you're crazy?"

"Right, that's the second thing. I think I might have OCD."

"Your room is too messy," Theo says.

"It's not about being organized. You know how lately I'm always forcing my way onto everyone's left side? It wasn't like that when we were kids. There's also my counting thing, where I prefer everything to be an even number, with a couple of

exceptions, like one and seven. Volume, the timer on the micro-
wave, how many chapters I read before putting a book down,
even how many examples I use in a sentence. It's distracting,
and I always feel *on*."

Theo nods. "I've felt like this before, too. Maybe not as
intense, but I think it's just a sign of your genius. I'm pretty sure
Nikola Tesla was obsessed with the number three and would
sometimes walk around a block three times before entering a
building. But, Griff, for all we know these compulsions might
just turn out to be little quirks." His blue eyes find my face
again, lit. "We can do some research later!"

Maybe he's right. Maybe I'm not just some delusional kid with
a neck tic who scratches his palms whenever he's nervous, favors
everyone's left side, tugs at his earlobe, and operates in evens.
Maybe it's like autofocusing a camera, where I'm zooming in on
one thing and missing everything else.

"It's been freaking me out a little bit, like I don't know who
I'm going to be in the future. I'm scared something can grow
from this and turn me into a Griffin who's too complicated
for you to be friends with in a few years." I can't believe I'm
unloading all this; it feels surreal, incredible, but I can't stop.
Maybe confessing everything will jinx any illnesses.

Theo scoots closer to me. "I have real things to be worried
about, dude, like if the zombie pirates are going to know how to
use grappling hooks and matchlocks or if they're taking us down
with teeth and nails. You don't scare me, and you'll never be too
complicated for my friendship." Theo pats my knee. His hand
rests there for a solid minute. "And I'm sorry if I forced you to
come out just now—wait, am I the first person you've told?"

I nod, my heart pounding. "You didn't force me. Okay, actually, you did a little, but I wanted to tell you anyway. I just didn't
have the balls or some huge speech. I was also a little scared
I was wrong about my instincts for you. Delusions run on my
mother's side of the family."

"You're not delusional," Theo says. "And you're not crazy."

He reaches for my hand, and it's not for a high five. I know the world hasn't changed, what goes up still has to come down, but the way I see the world has shifted a little to the right, moving forward, and I can now see it the way I've always wanted to. I hope I don't say or do anything that will force the world to shift counterclockwise again.

I squeeze Theo's hand, testing whatever it is we're doing here, and I feel like I'm answering a question I was never brave enough to ask.

"Stick with me here, okay?" Theo says.

"I'm not exactly about to walk off a moving train."

Theo lets go of my hand. I sink in a little, like I've failed him. "I've never told anyone this, but I've been dreaming up alternate universes for a couple of years. You know me, I'm always asking myself 'What if?'" He turns away for a second. "Lately I've been asking myself that more and more. A lot of the what-ifs are fun, but a lot of them are also really personal. Every night before I go to sleep, I find all the notes I've written on scrap paper or on my phone and I archive them in this journal. Dozens and dozens of alternate universes."

The train stops suddenly; passengers leave and others get on, giving us a little more breathing space—but once the doors close, Theo has my full attention again.

"I wrote one on the inside of my arm earlier, during the gift hunt," he continues. "I'm not going to show you yet. No spoilers. But it just reminded me of something. Every universe I've created lately, your face keeps popping up in it. And I thought that if you can't be cool with that, then I wouldn't hate you, but I might need some time for myself until we've had enough distance that I can imagine made-up worlds without you automatically appearing." Theo turns and above his left elbow is his handwriting—not the usual perfection because even *he* can't write on himself neatly—and he holds it closer.

The scrawl reads, *Alternate Universe: I'm dating Griffin Jennings and that's that.*

"I don't know if that makes sense to you at all, but I want that to be real," Theo says, still holding his arm out to me, as if to burn those messy letters into my memory. "If it can't, I understand and I hope we can still figure out how to be best friends. I just can't imagine never taking this shot." He lowers his arm, finally. "You've got to say something now."

I feel like someone has dropkicked me into an alternate universe of awesomeness. I can't believe this is a conversation I'm having, I can't believe I'm legit flirting with Theo and he's flirting back. This universe is clicking with me just fine. I can't tell him all these things, not yet, at least.

"I was going to," I say.

"Okay, but only say something if it's good. If it sucks, shut up."

"I've been freaking out for a while about this same thing, dude. I don't know when I would've manned up and said something, but it wouldn't have beat your bit about the alternate universes. I would've just said I like you."

"Were you going to at least mention how handsome I am?"

"Handsome seems like a strong word, but I would've talked about how you're cool to look at, sure."

"Good to know." I should tell him how much I like the sound of his writing, the words he puts down in his notebooks when he's hunched over his desk; I want to know what they are. I should tell him about the fantasies I've had where the next time I sleep over at his house and we share his bed, that we wouldn't have to use separate comforters and could maybe share one blanket one day without it being weird. I should tell him how fun it is to watch him flip an hourglass over and see if he can complete a massive puzzle by himself, and how I'm always rooting for him to succeed because I know how happy he is when he wins. I should tell him how much I appreciate the way he's been gravitating to my right lately. But I don't say any of this out loud right now because maybe I can admit this to him when it's happening in real time.

"Why today, Theo?"

"The photo Wade took of us yesterday," Theo says.

It hits me that I hadn't once thought of Wade during today's adventure. We're a three-dude squad, but I don't seem to get too anxious of the oddness versus evenness battle there, maybe because we always seem to make it work: it's the universe's one exception. Like yesterday afternoon, at Theo's place we played a *Super Smash Bros.* tournament—Theo and I versus Wade and the computer, teams forged by drawing names from Wade's fitted cap. It was close because Wade's really good with Bowser and the computer level was at its highest, but Theo and I won with Captain Falcon and Zelda. We stood up, victorious, and hugged each other as if we had just won a war against aliens or, even more fitting as of ten minutes ago, a war against the zombie pirates.

Wade had us pose. Theo and I faked our best serious faces, but we failed and cracked up.

"I saw us together and thought enough was enough. I've wanted to be with you for a while now. Wade's pic made it a little more unbearable not to be with you," Theo says.

"I feel the same way, I guess," I say. "What now? How do we lock this down? Probably a kiss or something, but I'm not in the mood." I trip over the last part because, honestly, it's a lie. I decide I'm swearing off lying because telling the truth can bring this kind of happiness, the kind that opens infinite alternate universes. I just really wish I had a piece of gum, but Wade is our squad's gum guy. "Maybe a handshake?"

We shake hands, and neither of us lets go.

"This is cool, but weird," I say.

"Very cool, very weird," Theo says. "But I think we fit, right?"

"No doubt, Theo."

I can't wait to see what happens next.

TODAY
MONDAY, NOVEMBER 20TH, 2016

The alarm clock finally shuts up after ten minutes, but my parents' threats to pop my door open keep coming. Last time they did this, I lost my privacy for two months until my dad finally replaced the lock.

I don't think I ever told you about that; it was after we broke up.

"Griffin!"

"Ten more minutes!" I shout.

"You said that an hour ago," Mom says.

"Six times," Dad adds. "Get dressed."

"I'll be out in ten minutes," I say. "I promise."

The last time I wore a black suit was for your cousin Allen's wedding on Long Island. It was a couple of months after we'd finally started dating, and it was our first formal party, too, if we don't count your sister's baptism. To my relief, Wade—back when we were still close with him—was wrong when he said all gay weddings are like Katy Perry concerts. (I don't think my anxiety could've handled dancing with you for the first time under strobe lights.) When I saw the white roses in the manor's sunroom, I began looking ahead to the day I'd get to wear a black suit as I stood across from you, my hands in yours, ready to say, "You're damn right I do." I didn't know it then, but that was the last time I'd wear a black suit, ever. I'm definitely not dressing up in one now.

I'm going to the funeral as is—okay, not completely as is, because showing up in these thermal pants might offend your grandmother. But I'm not taking off the green hoodie you gave me the afternoon we lost our virginity. I've been wearing it for the past two days—more, exactly fifty hours, though time has been bleeding in places. I wish I never washed the damn hoodie now that you're gone. It no longer smells like your grandmother's old flower shop; it doesn't have the dirt stains from all the times we spent at the park. It's like you've been erased.

I grab two of the four magnetic gryphons you got me two Christmases ago and fix them to the hoodie, one on my collarbone and the other on my heart. It's like the blue one is chasing the green one through the sky.

I stare at the clock, waiting for the next even minute—9:26—and get out of bed. I step directly onto last night's dinner, forgetting I had abandoned the plate down on the floor while I stared up at the ceiling, thinking about all the questions I'm too scared to ask you. But hey, if there's one bright side to your dying, it's that you aren't around to tell me things I don't like hearing.

I'm sorry. That was a dickhead thing to say. I need a condom for my mouth.

As much as I would like to go sit in the bathtub and let the shower rain down on me, I've got to get out of this room. I check the clock on my open laptop and leave once it switches from 9:31 to 9:32.

The hallway is lined with photographs in the cheap frames my aunt gave us last Christmas—the kind of present my mother dismisses as not thoughtful, but since she's so nice, she puts them up anyway. She still drinks out of the Yoda mug you bought her two years ago, no occasion at all, just because. You're always going to be a presence for my parents, even if now they can't see your history on our walls.

I'm hoarding all the photographs and their cheap frames in my room. There are blank spots as I pass: the one of us sitting in your childhood living room on Columbus Avenue, putting together a puzzle of the Empire State Building; us at sixteen/fifteen, you wrapping your arms around my waist after some joke from Wade about boys not being able to hug other boys; you smiling at me from across another park bench as I toasted to my parents' anniversary last year; and my favorites— side-by-side in the same frame—the first was taken by Wade, a blank-faced photo of us doing our damn best to keep our smiles in but failing. The second is of us holding each other and smiling after we came out to our parents at Denise's birthday party.

You were always a fan of the sun glare above your head. "Like a cool, bad-ass angel of destruction," you said. "The angel that gets a blazing sword while you get a harp."

In the living room my parents are already in their jackets, and my dad is holding his baked goods in his lap as they stare at the muted news on TV. Mom sees me first and pops up, which I know is bad on her back, especially on rainy days like today. She hides the pain and approaches me cautiously, unsure which Griffin she's about to get.

"I'm ready," I lie. I'm hungry, I'm drained, I'm over it all, and I'm not ready. But there's a clock on this thing. The service is today. The burial is tomorrow. I don't know what comes after that.

Mom reaches out to me, like I'm some toddler that's supposed to take his first steps into her arms. It's ridiculous. I'm a seventeen-year-old grieving his favorite person. I grab my jacket and turn for the door. "I'll be outside."

When we're all settled in the car, my dad puts on the radio

to fill the silence. I stare outside the window as we stop at a red light, counting pairs for some sanity: two women in jackets, sharing a blue umbrella; two old guys pushing shopping carts out of a market; four beaten-down trees in a community garden; two trash cans piled high with garbage.

The counting brings me some relief, but it's not enough. I drop my right hand to the empty space beside me, imagining your hand on mine. Two hands.

That feels better.

HISTORY
MONDAY, JUNE 9TH, 2014

It's routine after school for Theo, Wade, and me to go to the Barnes & Noble on the Upper West Side to do our homework, but classes are almost over. We browse the shelves instead. Theo was supposed to tell Wade about this new dating thing we're trying out while he and Wade were running laps last period, but he bitched out. I'm not a fan of secrets. Secrets can turn people into liars, and my lying days are behind me.

We wander away from graphic novels and end up in the biography aisle. It is my least favorite section, but here we are because of Wade and Theo.

"I want my own memoir," Theo says.

"Only one person can make that happen," I say.

"I don't have a title yet," Theo says.

"The horror," Wade says, rubbing his eyes again because his new contacts are bothering him. He still looks like himself for the most part—short hair, brown skin, wrinkled shirts—but I think he looks cooler with his glasses. "I'll probably call mine *Wading Through Life*."

Theo fake-yawns. "I can't wait for that laborious read."

Wade flips off Theo. "I'm going to get an iced tea from the café. You guys want?"

"Yeah, actually. My treat though." I give Wade a gift card, leftover from my birthday last month.

"You sure?" Wade asks.

I nod.

Once he's gone, I give Theo the why-didn't-you-tell-Wade-about-us glare, but he turns away, eyes back on the bookshelves.

"How about *Theo McIntyre: Zombie Pirate Slayer*?" I say in the silence.

He smiles, still avoiding my gaze. "But if the zombie-pirate apocalypse doesn't happen, it'll get confused as a fantasy novel. I refuse for my existence to be mistaken as fiction, damn it! Maybe I should keep it simple. How about *Theo: A Memoir*?"

I shake my head. "You're my favorite Theo and all, but you're not the only one."

He turns to me. "You know more Theos? Give me their addresses so I can put an end to this madness." He throws out his hands, like he's ready to karate chop any passing Theos. His fighting stance reminds me of his hipster C-3PO Halloween costume last year. He dressed in a T-shirt resembling the android's body, with gold paint on his face and arms.

"How about *C-Theo-PO*?"

"Nah. Too insignificant. Cool chapter title, maybe." Theo raises an eyebrow and points at me. "I have your title, though. *Griffin on the Left*."

Now I want to kiss him so badly. "It's perfect." I make sure Wade isn't coming, and I pull Theo by his hand, leading him to the next aisle. But I don't act on the kiss because I don't want to rush it or feel like we're doing it behind Wade's back.

"We have to tell Wade, dude," I whisper. "If you want to do it by yourself, that's cool, but if you want to tell him together, that's also cool. But we're not leaving this bookstore until we do so."

"Deal," Theo says, squeezing my hand. "What time does the store close again? I—"

"Whoa," Wade says.

He is standing at the end of the aisle, holding a tray of iced teas. I jerk my hand out of Theo's. "Whoa," he repeats, walking toward us. He's Theo's height, but he seems smaller, the way his shoulders sink. He shakes his head and manages a small smile. "This whole squad business was fun while it lasted."

That's not the reaction I was expecting. "What are you talking about?"

"How long have you two been dating? I knew this was going to happen. You guys doubt my psychic ways, but I called this last year. I just didn't tell anyone."

I don't know what I was expecting. But it wasn't this.

"You had a vision where Griffin and I were hooking up and the world was going to end?" Theo asks. His voice is weirdly high-pitched.

Wade smirks, handing me an iced tea. "Pretty much."

"Your visions are kind of gay," Theo jokes, attempting to get a hold of himself. "You should get that checked out."

I take a sip, attempting to get a hold of myself, too. "Wait. How did you know Theo and I liked each other? Don't say because you're psychic."

"You don't have to be a psychic to have seen this coming. Your chemistry was all over my face." He hesitates. "That came out wrong. Anyway, I'm not going to be some third wheel, guys."

Three is a number I've forgiven since yesterday, but only for our squad. It hopefully won't bother me as much now that Theo and I are together, like our personal unit will count as "one," though I probably shouldn't mention that to Wade. "It's not game over for us. Think of it as a new game, if anything, with new levels and new worlds."

"New obstacles for me if I want to see you guys, and new game modes exclusive to you two," Wade counters.

"You're welcome to join in our exclusive activities," Theo says with a wink.

Wade goes on to list every example of love gone wrong, mainly from comic books: Green Lantern's girlfriend who was killed and had her corpse stuffed in his fridge; Cyclops and Jean Grey, high school sweethearts who keep losing each other to everything the world throws at them; Ant-Man, who douses the Wasp with bug spray, and wow, I didn't realize Ant-Man was so emotionally and physically abusive. A fourth example doesn't follow.

Theo turns to me. "I promise to never bug-spray you, Griff. Do you promise to never bug-spray me?"

"I promise."

Lying, I mouth to Wade so that Theo sees, to make the situation normal, or to try to.

Theo takes his iced tea from the tray. "Are we all good now?"

"Promise me you guys won't destroy the squad when you break up," Wade says. I can tell by his tone he isn't messing around. This is like seventh grade, when Theo and I kept teasing Wade for getting his name trimmed into his fade, and he laughed for a bit but eventually told us to stop.

"Maybe show some faith in us, dude," Theo says quietly. "But sure, I promise we'll be adults if we do break up."

"You're sixteen. You're not an adult," Wade says.

"I'm counting on us being together for a while," Theo says.

I take a deep breath and swear I won't let Wade kill my happy Theo vibes. "I also promise I won't destroy the squad if we break up either. Can we please go back to looking at books?"

Theo gestures for us to come together, and he wraps an arm around both of us. He fake-whispers to Wade, "We have to do a group hug so Griffin doesn't feel left out."

"I hate you both," Wade says.

We all laugh, and like that it's over and there are no more secrets, and I keep smiling longer than anyone else because Theo is betting on us being together for a while. Which is good. It'll give me enough time to come up with the perfect title for his memoir.

TODAY
MONDAY, NOVEMBER 20TH, 2016

I don't want to go in, I don't want to go in. Theo, I don't want to go in, I don't want to go in to say goodbye to you.

The funeral chapel on Eighty-First and Madison looks like toy blocks stacked on one another and weirdly incomplete because it's beige, like they forgot to paint it a real color or thought it'd be inappropriate to do so. I can't believe this is the place your parents chose for your friends and family to say goodbye to you. I don't have another spot in mind, but wherever it would be, it would have some color.

Doesn't matter for me, at least. I'm not going in there.

"Coming in, Griffin?"

"No," I say. "I'm not. I can't."

Mom takes the key out of the ignition and stuffs it into her purse. "We'll sit here until you're ready." She stares straight ahead, where mourners with cups of coffee—no one I recognize—enter the chapel as the hourly bell chimes. I'm okay with missing the ten o'clock mass. I'm not going to be singing or praying my grief away anytime soon. Mom holds out her hand and Dad wraps his own around hers, like usual. My parents' love is straight-up locked down. I'm too numb to feel it right now, but I really owed all my confidence in our own future to them because they'd been together since they were teenagers, too.

Seeing those hands holding each other when I have to imagine yours in mine pisses me off.

I get out of the car and slam the door behind me. The chilly autumn air bites through my jacket and hoodie; breathing in the cold tires out my lungs. The rain isn't coming down hard, but I'm drenched.

My parents abandon the warmth of their busted Toyota and keep to my right, respecting the compulsion you sometimes found fascinating. They remain silent. No fortune-cookie nonsense. I'm lucky to have parents who know when to go to war with me and when to leave me alone in the battlefield.

You're waiting inside. Not you, but you.

I owe you a goodbye.

If you were here, I'd be inside already, which . . . well, the weirdness of you talking me into your own funeral isn't lost on me. You were always a pro at getting me to be brave—to take down the walls that could be taken down, at least. You can't be faulted for my unbreakable compulsions.

At the door I can sense my parents wanting to reach out. I turn and find a couple of other new faces coming toward us. If I don't know them, then they don't know me, and they won't know why it's so hard for me to put my hand on this damn knob and turn it to go inside, because they don't know our history. They might be friends of your parents or neighbors you spoke about but I never met.

The pressure is building, but no one says anything.

I'm pummeling myself to the ground, and I'm drowning without trying to surface, all at once.

I reach for the doorknob. I walk into a space of stale air and grief.

There's a big cutout of your face at the entrance. Your parents chose that awkward photo from your junior-year class pictures, but not the one we agreed was best, the one that was going to be your author photo on your memoir: where your smile was a little on the shy side, and your blue eyes held a hint of mischief. Maybe it wasn't the impression they wanted others to have of you. It's completely lost on me why your parents went ahead and chose it for your funeral. But I won't say anything. Who knows where Russell's and Ellen's heads are these days.

I approach your cutout with my parents shadowing me, offering condolences to God-knows-who. My eyes lock with yours, flat as they may be. I almost talk myself out of it, but I touch the picture, my fingerprints marking your glossy cheek. My fingers trail down to the bronzed card in the bottom center of the frame. I trace each letter:

THEODORE DANIEL MCINTYRE

FEBRUARY 10, 1998—NOVEMBER 13, 2016

"GRIFFIN."

I really don't want to face Wade right now. I haven't been speaking to him as much over the past couple of months, not since everything that went down between you two recently. He tried reaching out several times over the past week, of course, but I never answered the phone or the door. But I turn. Wade is wearing one of the ties you got him a couple of Christmases ago, and he's picking at a scab on his elbow. He's either avoiding my eyes or his contacts are throwing his attention elsewhere. I'm sure he's feeling guilty for not talking to you when he had the chance.

"Sorry for your loss, Griffin," Wade says.

Your former best friend gets that you're *my* loss. That's history right there. "You too," I manage.

I scan the crowd. I'm not surprised the rain didn't affect the huge turnout. I wonder how many of these people have laughed since you died. I'm sure they've smiled at something stupid, like old funny photos in their phones or episodes of some comedy they maybe watched to get your death off their minds. But I want to know if they have busted out laughing so hard their rib cage hurt. I haven't. I'm not mad at any of them if they have. It sucks because I know I'll be alone in my grief for a while. I just want to know when it'll be possible to laugh again. And when it'll be okay.

Wade's gaze finally fixes on me. "You going to talk to Jackson?"

Even after all this time, his name still strikes a nerve with me. "It's not a priority," I say. I should shut up or walk away.

"I know it's different, but he's probably the only other person here who gets what you're going through."

"What they had isn't the same," I say in spite of myself, fighting back tears and screams. I look away again so Wade won't try to comfort me. I see your grandfather holding himself up with his cane, your aunt Clara handing out packages of tissues she probably bought in bulk like everything else, your cousin knitting what looks like a scarf from here, but no sign of your parents. I get it together and ask Wade where they are.

"Russell went out for a smoke," he says. "Been a while. He might be on his fourth by now. And Ellen is already sitting in the front with Denise. With Theo."

She's with your body, not you.

"I'll go find Russell."

"Before you go—"

I head for the door. My parents see me move and come for me as if I'm trying to get out of here for good. I stop when my mom asks me where I'm going, asks if I want to go with her to offer my condolences to Ellen. I don't have it in me this second, though. I try to play dumb and focus on my surroundings instead. I find your uncle Ned in the crowd, reading from the Bible, and catch Aunt Clara busting out her own tissues as she cries with a neighbor I maybe recognize.

But my eyes return to the door in no time.

Your boyfriend is blocking the entrance. He's staring directly at me.

HISTORY
THURSDAY, JUNE 12TH, 2014

Our first date, and we discover it's raining when we get off the train.

"Good news or bad news?" Theo asks.

"Always get the bad news out of the way first. This is New York, remember? Where were you raised?"

"I don't have an umbrella," Theo says.

"And the good news?"

"I'm telling you now."

"Your good news sucks."

If we had time to waste, we'd wait out the storm here at the station. But it's Pop Culture Trivia Night at Bonus Diner, this new diner-slash-arcade, near Union Square, and it begins at six. We haul ass, hating every exposed corner we're forced to wait on before it's our turn to cross the street, and I'm really happy the school year is almost over because there's no way the textbooks in our backpacks are going to be much use to us after this storm.

Damn. The place is roaring with chatter, but there are tables still free. I feel betrayed by how cold it is in here. Indoor places should always be the opposite of the weather outside. No one has ever entered a restaurant on a scorching summer day and gotten pissed at the air-conditioning.

But I'm not letting anything ruin my first date with Theo. I fight through my shivers and register our two-man team. We're seated at table sixteen—good number. I run to the bathroom quickly to try and dry myself with paper towels. I return, tagging Theo out to go and do the same. I survey the room and only then do I feel warmer. We're younger than anyone else here, but I immediately decide all my opponents here are pretty much the coolest people in the universe.

Theo returns, rubbing his hands together. "We're going to destroy them."

He checks out the menu. This is another one of those times where I want to lean in and finally kiss him. I'm not trying to get it over with, but I think not having kissed yet in the few days we've been dating is creating some buildup. But maybe a first kiss without a big moment will speak for itself. Maybe it says, "Hey, I like you when you're not doing anything special."

Before I can even consider leaning in, a hostess whistles and silences everyone in the dining area, even some stragglers at the pool tables and pinball machines nearby. She runs through the rules. There will be twenty questions, all fill-in-the-blank. There will be a minute each to answer them. There will be volunteers walking around the room to make sure no one's cheating. Prize for third place is a book of coupons for a gift shop online. Prize for second place is a replica of the sword and shield from *The Legend of Zelda: Twilight Princess*. The grand prize is a boxed set of the first six *Star Wars* movies, director's-cut edition.

I suddenly, desperately want to win because maybe I'll become just as obsessed as he is, and we can do stuff like host *Star Wars* themed Halloween parties for our friends.

Okay, I need to take a step back and take this relationship one week at a time.

Waitresses and waiters pass out papers and pens as they collect food orders. Once they've cleared the floor, the hostess announces we're beginning in one minute.

Theo turns to me and my heart is trying to headbutt itself out of my chest.

"Question one . . ."

It doesn't take long to see that this evening is mostly about older people who want to get drunk. Within minutes, we're kicking ass. The planet Hoth in *The Empire Strikes Back* was shot where? Norway. (Thanks, Theo.) The writer behind *Toy Story* and *Firefly*? Joss Whedon. The only character on *The Simpsons* with ten fingers? God. The last Harry Potter book was published in . . . ? 2007, but the series actually ended in 1998. (You're welcome, Theo.) Teamwork.

"Final question!"

I'm pretty sure we're nineteen for nineteen, so we can't mess this up.

"Which actor couldn't do the Vulcan salute in 2009's *Star Trek*?"

Theo writes down Zachary Quinto's name and hands our sheet over to the nearest volunteer. "We got this. Get ready for a marathon at my house."

It takes about twenty minutes for the judges to review the answers, when a bell dings. The hostess returns to the front of the room and coughs very dramatically. "I'm pleased to announce there is a tie between two teams! But since we only have one boxed set, we're going to have a live tiebreaker! Can I get one representative from Team Stark-Kirk and one from Team Human-Pirates?"

"Yes!" Theo gets up, and I hope he wins this for us. "You. Up."

"What? No. You go."

"I elect you!"

I pick up the napkin and wave it. "I forfeit."

"Technically, you surrender when you're waving the white flag. It's a small but important difference."

"See? You're smarter. You do it."

"You got this, Griff. I believe in you. Go."

Theo nudges me to the front of the room and retreats once I'm up there. I'm representing us in a trivia contest; this is definitely a bizarre universe. I shake hands with my competitor, a redhead girl in big glasses. It's her against me for the *Star Wars* boxed set. Everyone is quiet, staring at us, excited for the show-down. But my tunnel vision reveals only a smiling Theo and his encouraging thumbs-ups.

"First one to answer correctly wins the grand prize," the hostess says. "Tiebreaker question." She reaches into what looks like an empty mint bowl and retrieves a slip of paper. "From the Harry Potter series, what is Dumbledore's full name?"

A Harry Potter question; I got this. "Albus Percival Brian Wulfric Dumbledore!"

Before the hostess can shake her head, I realize I've gotten it wrong. It's Wulfric before Brian. I gasp with my hand over my mouth. I can't even face Theo. My bespectacled competitor answers the question correctly and receives the roaring applause—the applause I wanted Theo to witness for me. I try to remind myself that this is all silly, and I smile and congratulate her. She is gracious enough to congratulate me too, which makes it a little better.

I walk back to my table with the sword and shield. "I suck."

"Dude, you killed it! I bet you wouldn't have confused those names if you were able to write them down on paper. It's like trying to solve certain math problems without a calculator."

"Which you do all the time."

He shakes his head. "It's not the same thing. You're passionate about this. There's also no way in hell I'd have even gotten Dumbledore's first name."

"You're forced to be nice to me because I just lost," I say.

Theo takes the sword from my hand. "Kneel before the king,

Griff." I look around for the king. "Me, asshole. I'm the king. Who else would be the king? Wade?"

I laugh in spite of myself and get down on one knee, bowing my head as he knights me.

"On this rainy Thursday, I, King Theo of New York City, praise you, Sir Griffin of New York City, for your vast knowledge of fantasy novels I'll never take the time to read myself. And for having the kind of laugh that I like hearing so much I would punch myself over and over if you found it funny."

I rise, still grinning at our own stupidity. Theo twirls the sword between his fingers and swings, but I deflect him with the shield. I keep blocking his attacks. We ignore the waiters asking us to stop playing and eventually run toward the pinball machines, where I finally drop the shield.

"I surrender!" I say. "It's surrender, right? Not forfeit?"

"My work here is done. I have nothing left to teach you, Sir Griffin of New York City." Theo is brandishing his sword, victorious.

I disarm us both as I kiss him, the plastic sword clattering at our feet as he pulls me closer to him.

This feels right, even as our teeth clink. I laugh when we part.

"That's a thing we just did," I say.

"Let's do it more often," Theo says.

TODAY
MONDAY, NOVEMBER 20TH, 2016

Jackson Wright is here, and there's no not talking about him anymore.

There's no denying Jackson and I resemble each other; even Wade joked about it. His hair is a little darker and longer than mine, but still light brown at first look. We're lanky, with bad posture, and we both looked back into your blue eyes with our hazels. You mentioned becoming fixated with the horseshoe-shaped birthmark on his collarbone, much like whenever you traced the "deflated pyramid" on my inner thigh. The big difference between us right now is I'm here at your funeral in your old hoodie and jeans, and he's wearing a suit that's a size too big for him. The suit makes sense, though I'm not sure what an eighteen-year-old in California would do with one.

Here's your history with Jackson as you told it to me: You met him last year on October 29th while walking along the highway. You were on your way to tutor that high-school junior, while Jackson was driving from his mother's house to spend the weekend with his father. The rain surprised you, which doesn't surprise me since you always refused to check the weather app; you prided yourself on adapting to any outside conditions.

Lucky for you, Jackson came to the rescue.

He'd seen you before during this same drive and thought you looked friendly. He was curious about how you existed in California without a car or bike or "some flying carpet." You thought the flying carpet bit was funny. I thought it was uninspired. It's possible I'm programmed to be a dick to anyone interested in you. But really, let's not rule out Jackson's joke sucked because—

I'm letting it go. I'm moving on.

Jackson pulled over and offered you a ride. He was a stranger, but from everything you told me about the impossibly perfect weather in California, it sounds like rain is the first wave of the zombie-pirate apocalypse, so I guess you can't be faulted. Just sucks you were looking for a new partner to aid you in what was supposed to be our alternate universe.

In the car, you and Jackson bonded over films and role-playing games. And the rest is unfortunately history.

First: The phone call on November 7th detailing this new guy in your life. I had hoped your time with Jackson would just be a quick thing, but it stretched to a point where I couldn't deny our own endgame was threatened. I wanted to know exactly what he looked like, what his story was, what your dates were like, what it was about him that mesmerized you.

JACKSON IS BLOCKING THE door. Your dad is trying to reenter the chapel. He has definitely been smoking hard core, and the smell nauseates me instantly, reminding me of all the times he drove us around in his car that stunk of stale cigarettes and air freshener before he finally quit. (Until now.) Your dad doesn't acknowledge Jackson beyond a hand on the shoulder, and while this is sick to admit, it makes me feel good. Jackson *flew* here, but he isn't getting much from the man who taught you how to tie your shoes and ride a bike.

My dad approaches yours. My mom remains close to me.

Wade reappears by my side. I don't know if Wade is nervous over how this is about to go down between Jackson and me or if he's showing me support, but I don't need him right now. I need to do this alone. But right when I'm about to go over to Jackson, your dad and mine step toward me.

"Hey, Russell," I say, twisting my ring finger. It's an antistress trick you taught me, used by people who are afraid of flying—not that I'm ever getting on a plane.

I last spoke with your dad on the phone the day you died, and again the day after, but this is the first time I'm seeing him. He's wearing his reading glasses instead of the horn-rimmed frames he should be, and when he opens his mouth to speak, I notice his teeth have yellowed. He shuts himself up. There's no point asking him how he's doing. I hug him, battling through the invisible cigarette cloud.

"You still think you have it in you to share some words?" Russell murmurs.

I step back and nod. I can't believe I live in a universe where I'm delivering a eulogy for you.

He pats me on the shoulder, like he did Jackson, and walks away to check on Ellen in the service room.

Jackson is making his way toward me, eyes lowered and hands pocketed. My parents and Wade are staring at me. I quietly ask them to give us a minute. I'm not sure if Jackson even wants to talk to me, but it's happening. My mom tells me she'll hold a seat for me. They all leave, and Wade looks over his shoulder as if he's expecting something explosive. There will be no fights at your funeral, I promise.

Suddenly, I'm standing face-to-face with your boyfriend. His left eye is stained red, and he smells like cigarette smoke, too.

"Hey, Griffin," Jackson says.

He says my name like we're friends.

Funny, as I refused to meet him when you brought him here in February for your birthday. No way in hell was I going to go to one of *our* places with *him*. And we didn't exactly check in with each other after you died, not that anyone thought we would. I thought of him, sure, but not so much about how he was doing as I've been wondering what the hell your final moments were like.

He was there with you.

Is it weird to envy him for that, for witnessing something I would never want to see with my own eyes? I have all this history with you, Theo, but he has pieces of your puzzle that would destroy me if I ever had to put them together, and yet I still want them.

"Hey, Jackson," I say. We don't offer each other condolences. Maybe he's waiting for me to do so; he's going to be waiting for a while. "What's wrong with your eye?"

"Popped a blood vessel," Jackson says. "Doctor doesn't know if it's from all the crying or screaming. It'll go away."

I didn't know someone could pop a blood vessel from crying. That's something you would know.

Jackson moves past me to get to your cutout. He doesn't touch your face or trace your nameplate. He rests his forehead against yours—not an even fit, obviously—and closes his eyes.

"I miss you, Theodore," he says.

Using your given name is so unexpectedly intimate, and you weren't about being called that. You thought it made you sound too stiff and presidential. I'm not going to call him out on that. I can't. What if you changed your mind? What if I out myself for truly not knowing who you were before you died?

"How long are you in town for?" I ask. Seems nicer than asking him when the hell he's going to leave.

Jackson turns, shrugs. "I got here last night. I'm thinking about staying another week or two."

I know from you his mother has spent the past few years in a wheelchair, so it's safe to bet she's not here with him.

"You staying with friends?"

You'd mentioned Jackson had "theater friends" at NYU when he visited in February, though I'm not sure you two ever got around to meeting up with them—not with all the time you spent with your family, including the traditional movie-theater outing on your birthday. You must've shared a recliner seat with Jackson; that used to be our throne, Theo.

"I'm staying with the McIntyres," Jackson says.

I'm such an idiot. He smells like cigarette smoke because he was outside with your dad, and he only got the shoulder pat because he's been with them since last night. He must be staying in your room. Of course he is. He's chief curator in the main exhibit of the McIntyre Museum, taking in all the archives of your life. I can see it all: our framed puzzles on your light-blue walls, a bookcase full of sketches you later animated at wicked speed, awards you didn't mind "showing off," your computer station decked out with robot magnets and old *Tetris* cartridges, the golden unicycle wheel you won at that carnival in the Bronx last summer, the plastic bat you used to beat the piñata at Denise's seventh birthday, then saved for the zombie-pirate apocalypse . . .

The outsider is inside the nexus of your life, and I hate it.

"We should probably take our seats," Jackson says. He checks his watch; it's an old one of yours. The way he flashes it is hardly discreet. "The mass is probably starting any minute now."

We walk into the service room together. I switch sides when he walks to my left. He doesn't pay it any mind, going straight for the empty seat in the front beside your mother. Ellen is in full black and silent, resting her head on Russell's shoulder. I'm ready to rage over where Jackson found the nerve to sit next to your parents, when my eyes find your body.

Even seeing it isn't enough to believe it.

You're in a mahogany casket, dressed in a black suit I don't remember you owning. There are tons of flowers placed around you. It reminds me of the summer afternoon you confessed your love of calla lilies, scared to admit it because "flowers aren't manly." When I rambled about my secret obsession with immortality irises after discovering them in some comic, it became a happily manly conversation. Afterward, we'd occasionally visit your grandmother's flower shop before it closed last winter, losing out to all her competitors during the Valentine's Day rush. I process the flowers in the room again, not spotting any calla lilies.

I should've brought some white ones, your favorite. I'm sorry.

I walk toward you even though I know it's not time for that. The minister is about to lead everyone in prayer or sing a hymn, but it's you, Theo, in a box. My vision shakes, my knees tremble. My mom calls for me, and my dad appears at my left side, pulling my arm. I shake him off and switch sides before letting him guide me to our seats on the far left of the room, away from your family and Jackson. The seat is uncomfortable. Too many eyes are on me, so I sink to the carpeted floor, crossing my legs like it's fifth grade all over again.

Father Jeffrey opens with a verse, Matthew 5:4: "Blessed are those who mourn, for they will be comforted."

I guess there *is* something comforting about being in a room with people who love you. But you should've been given more time in this universe. That way, when you were ready to die, you could pack stadiums with people who loved you, not a single room.

There are hymns sung, but not by me. We agreed that I can do a lot of things—like keep up with a car for four blocks before losing my breath or ride a bike with no hands for long stretches of time—but I cannot sing. Jackson is singing, though. I can't make out his voice in the chorus of others, but he's looking at you with a tilted head, like a curious child asking you why you're sleeping in a box.

The eulogies begin, and they're brutal. Your mother is the first one up, and she tries to joke about the nineteen-hour labor she went through with you, before she shuts down and quickly reboots. She tells everyone how she'll miss nursing you back to health whenever you were sick, and how she regrets confiscating your Xbox One after you received a C+ on your earth science midterm. Denise is next. She tells everyone how you two used to have dance parties in the living room, which I never knew, and when she loses it, I snap up from the floor and race toward her because you're in a casket unable to do so yourself, inviting her to sit back down with me.

I'm not surprised your father tells the story about how your first word, "sock," was the first time it clicked with him that you were a little human being that was going to grow up to use all kinds of words to get around the world. Aunt Clara will miss your "funny little movies." Uncle Ned doesn't know who he'll talk to about engines anymore. Wade keeps it quick, too, saying he misses you so much already and apologizes for wronging you. Your neighbor, Simone, is still grateful for the month you went grocery shopping for her after she crushed her leg in a car accident.

Then it's my turn.

Not sure what they want to hear from me.

Maybe they're interested in how our friendship began in middle school over Pompeii. And now I'm supposed to be delivering your eulogy.

I rise, helping Denise up from the floor, too. I encourage her to rejoin your parents, which she does without a fight.

I walk closer to you, your face touched up with makeup, and you don't look like the boy I love. Your body has your features, sure, but you're sort of chalky and very unnatural and it sends a bad chill running up my arms. The bright blue tie they chose for you would've gone beautifully with your open eyes. I slip into the memory of you at your graduation party, superimposing this blue tie over the green one you were wearing to see what it would look like, and then I pull myself out of this reimagining because I can't change our history. I can't begin remembering you wrong.

"One moment," I tell the room.

I walk all the way to you, gripping the frame of your casket. I check my watch, waiting for the next even minute—10:42—and I touch your folded hands. You're cold, I knew you'd be, but holding you after not being able to touch you in so long reminds me of last summer's beach bonfire; the warmth of the glowing fire, our two-man huddle on the sand. But unlike that night, where we promised each other your leaving for college wouldn't ruin us, I'm stuck having one-sided conversations with you as your boyfriend sits behind me. I squeeze your hands, crying a little.

I'm going to tell your friends and family a story about you, okay? I'm not going far.

I let go and turn around.

I step to the center, staring at nothing but shoes and the podium I'm tempted to hide behind.

"I love Theo," I say, choking. I tug at my right earlobe, squeezing it between my thumb and middle finger. "He's been my best friend since I was ten, my favorite person, who was supposed to exist forever. I told him everything, even the things about myself that scared me. Like the time I came out to him as a possible crazy person the same second he told me he was gay . . ." I tell them a bit about how we threw off our straight cloaks two years ago on June 8th, and how it taught me that honesty sometimes leads to happiness.

The memory quickly comes and goes.

I'm crying now, full on, and one hand is pulling at my ear and the other is pressed against my chest. "He made me feel safe from the world, and made me feel safe from myself." My legs are going to give out. "I don't know where to go from here. I don't think any of us do. No one would've ever thrown down money, betting we'd be saying goodbye to Theo so soon, and it's not fair and it's a total nightmare. But we all have mad love for Theo, and history is how we get to keep him."

I make my way back to my spot on the floor, thinking of a thousand more things I want to say. My dad leans over and kisses the top of my head. He tells me I did a good job, but he doesn't know anything. I've said enough to everyone here, but there's still so much I have to tell you.

Father Jeffrey approaches the altar when Jackson hops out of his seat. He steps to the podium.

"Hi everyone, I'm Jackson," he announces in a tight voice. "I was Theo's boyfriend in California."

I can't listen to this.

Except I have to. For sanity's sake I'm going to soldier through this eulogy. You wouldn't want me writing you off or running away. Though it gets me wondering again if you ever told him stories of me, or if you hogged memories of our time together the way you did with him. I don't know which of the two is winning—your eagerness to tell a story about us because not doing so was suffocating, or keeping our history close to your chest like an inside joke you couldn't possibly let anyone else in on.

Jackson is fidgety, tugging at your old watch. "My parents have been divorced since I was fourteen. Even as a kid I could tell they weren't in love. When I finally got my driver's license this year, it was awesome because we didn't have to go through the awkward drop-off where my parents barely said hi to each other. I didn't think I'd find someone I loved while driving between my parents' houses on weekends. I didn't even recognize it was the same guy until the third or fourth time. But one day it was raining, and I saw him on my way to Mom's house, same time as usual, and he didn't have an umbrella. So I pulled over, and he asked me if I often rescued strangers from the rain."

I can hear the words out of your own mouth, Theo. My face heats up.

Jackson smiles to himself, remembering this memory I can already tell is too intimate, more than I ever thought I'd want to know. "I told him I'd seen him while driving several times and he seemed innocent, but better not turn out to be a murderer. Naturally, he found me suspicious for having an idea who he was, so he made a joke and threw his shoulder against the door, like he was trying to bust out."

That sounds like you.

There's some laughter behind me.

"Theo was shivering. He got my SMC sweater from the back-seat—I didn't even offer it to him; he just took it—and he told me he just started classes there, too. I warned him about this creepy professor on campus, and we got to know each other over a fifteen-minute drive. I never told Theo this, but I considered getting lost to spend more time with him. I should've told him."

Jackson pauses.

I'm at war with myself. I'm hating the sadness over you he's owning, but I'm sympathizing with him because it's you he's messed up over. I also wish some of the things I have to tell you were sweet like this and not things that will change the way you see me.

My nails dig into my palm.

"I didn't get a chance to tell him that, but we exchanged numbers and hung out on campus. I did tell him that I was attracted to him at the end of an awesome day we spent together. I did that much." Jackson's lips quiver for a second before it becomes a full-on cry. And, I don't know, it looks more like happy crying. I almost feel compelled to bounce up and hug him or pat his back. I beat on myself as I picture you helpless in the ocean. "Even if I only got to spend that first drive to the planetarium with Theo, he broke me in a way everyone should be lucky to be cracked open at least once. I had the privilege of being destroyed by him until we found a better, real me inside of the person I was pretending to be. I hope I make him proud."

Jackson turns to you. "Thank you, Theodore," he concludes.

He returns to his seat, where he leans forward, holding his stomach and hiding his face with his other hand.

The service comes to a close, which is good for my heart and head, but I would suffer through a thousand more stories about you if there were people here to tell them. Blessed are those who mourn, for they will be comforted.

Tomorrow morning we're burying you.

HISTORY
SUNDAY, JUNE 15TH, 2014

I'm sure I'll sound psychotic if I ever try explaining my growing awareness with even numbers to anyone, even Theo—*especially* Theo—because it's definitely verging on obsessive. When Theo and I were making out at the train station after school on Friday, I found myself counting our kisses. I don't mean like one, two, three, four, and onward, but more like one, two, one, two, one, two to make sure we remained even. And when Theo pulled away at an odd kiss, I'd move back in for another. There are bigger problems than getting to kiss Theo again, but the counting is creeping into the rest of my life, too. Like how today's odd-numbered date is making me a little anxious. How I've now sneezed three times straight and am wishing a fourth would follow.

Oh yeah, I have a cold.

It turns out running through the rain and playing trivia in a very cold diner is both the perfect first date and the perfect recipe to make someone sick. I'm that someone. Theo dodged this bullet, but he's throwing himself back in the crossfire just to keep me company.

"Are we done with the sneezing?" Theo asks.

I'd be really grateful for one more sneeze. "You didn't have to come over!"

We're on the floor of my bedroom, piecing together his zombie-pirate puzzle.

"Yeah, well, I wasn't having much luck with level nineteen of *Tetris* because I couldn't get my brain to stop missing you," Theo says. "I'm not worried about getting sick. I just need you to finish building the plank for *The Bloodcurdling Crawler*, stat."

"I know, I know." I sniff. "I just feel really conflicted because if I build the plank, it means the zombie pirate hanging off of it will climb into the ship and infect the human pirates, or even straight-up kill them." I look at him. "I sort of want to prevent the apocalypse, if that makes sense."

"But if the apocalypse doesn't happen, we won't be the last two dudes in the world charged with rebuilding the population," Theo says.

"You're the dumbest genius if you think that's how reproduction works."

"Oh, I get it. I'm just not going to let that stop us from trying."

I don't know if Theo is smiling because he's imagining us having sex or because he likes making me uncomfortable, but I do know that I don't have the balls to continue this conversation. I collect all the pieces for the plank and put them together like a good little soldier. And damn, now I'm thinking about role-playing where I'm some peon soldier taking orders from Sergeant Theo McIntyre, and when he asks me to drop down and give him one hundred I . . . okay, I have to stop. I adjust the blanket around my shoulders to shield my lap from his eyes.

"You're still cold?" Theo gets up and grabs his green hoodie off the radiator. "Here, it's dry now. There's got to be some scientific study somewhere that proves your boyfriend's sweater will keep you warmer and cure you of any illnesses a lot faster than some Pottery Barn blanket."

"It's actually from Target." I keep the blanket where it is while slipping into Theo's sweater. It smells like his grandmother's flower shop, and it fits me as snugly as it does Theo. "Thanks, dude."

"You look really good in green," Theo says. "Keep it."

"Double thanks, dude."

The puzzle is really a work in progress: the ship has holes in it, as if uninfected humans were wise to the zombie virus and had already begun shooting cannonballs. The ocean—which Theo has charged himself with completing—also has tons of holes, like a series of really deep whirlpools threatening to swallow the ship whole. There's a pirate onboard who's currently headless because Theo has the necessary piece on his side. The sky is dark and broken, my fault, as always. And I only mess it up further when I lean over to give Theo a thank-you kiss, resting my knee on it and accidentally sliding some of the pieces apart. My thank-you kiss was supposed to be a two-off, but Theo pulls me into his lap and locks me in, turning it into something more.

Theo stops, and we breathe. "Do you want to . . . ?"

"Want to . . . what?" This could seriously mean a thousand things: Do I want to put away the puzzle and take our kissing to the bed? Do I want to get completely naked, hurling my boxers across the room and have sex with him? Do I want to keep it simple, maybe let him jerk me off and I do the same for him? Do I want to take a nap because I'm freaking sick and shouldn't be awake, let alone getting physical?

"Don't make me say it," he says.

Theo is blushing. I've made him feel awkward.

"I'm sorry, but if you don't tell me what you want, I'm just going to go ahead and assume you mean crochet a new sweater for you."

"You crochet, Griff?"

"Stop playing cute, Theo."

Theo bites back a smile and shakes his head. "Do you want to practice repopulating the human race?"

"But I'm sick."

"I know. All I ask is that you don't sneeze on me."

I roll off of him because he's on the floor, and we both know from past sleepovers that it's not a comfortable floor to spend the night on. It is how we fell into our system where we both slept in each other's beds, heads facing feet, snuggled up in our own blankets. But we don't have to do that anymore. I stand and close the door, even though my parents are both out shopping for Theo's sister's birthday barbeque this week.

I nod. "Let's practice."

Something I've never considered about my first time: it's the middle of the day. I always thought this was an evening thing, something you do and go to bed afterward, maybe watch some TV if you're not too wiped out. But my parents are supposed to be out for another couple of hours. My mom and dad are both very particular about what they're looking for when they're shopping. Theo and I have enough time to get our act together—maybe even get our act together twice if the first time goes well, or, you know, ends early.

"Do you mind if I close the curtains?" I ask.

"We're on the sixth floor, Griff. I don't think anyone is going to peek in."

"I know, but I think I'll just be a little more comfortable if it's darker."

"You know you're handsome and beautiful, right?"

"I like that you believe that, but I don't want you rethinking it."

"No chance in hell, but whatever you want."

Theo moves over to the bed, sitting on the edge while I turn off the lights and draw the curtains shut. I stand there. Theo is good with words, but he's better with action, he's better with getting things done. It's the part of him that can make it awkward for him to say the word "sex" but be totally coolheaded when the cards are actually on the table. He waves me over with two fingers and his stupid monkeylike, scrunched-up expression that always cracks me up.

I hesitate. "Maybe we should play some music . . ."

"Griffin, we don't have to do this if you'd rather wait."

"No, I want to. I just want some music. Sorry if that's stupid."

I feel weird apologizing, but admitting that I'm trying to make this moment feel special just feels silly. I can't rewind time and take it back. It's been one week since I've been dating Theo, and there's no alternate universe where I can envision myself not feeling embarrassed about our "anniversary." I don't want him to think I'm some loser for paying attention to stuff like that. I used to think it was lame whenever my parents celebrated yearly anniversaries. Look at me now: caring about one week. One week with someone I really like. One week with someone I've been waiting years for. I hope knowing what it's like to spend one year with Theo won't be left to my imagination.

"It's not stupid, Griff."

Theo throws out suggestions, like "Love Shack" for its pure ridiculousness, but we settle on his playlist with scores from action movies.

It's epic.

The music playing on high will hopefully drown out any thoughts that may scare me from going through with this, and the drawn curtains make me feel just invisible enough that I don't have to be self-conscious.

I sit down beside Theo, who immediately holds my hand and kisses me. We lie down. When our shirts finally do come off, it's different from all the times we've gone to the beach, since we never held each other shirtless.

"Should we take off our pants at a countdown from three?"

"How about four?"

Theo smiles. "Right."

"Four . . ."

I unzip his jeans while he untangles the knots of my pajamas.

"Three . . ."

I'm slowly sliding out of my own pajamas, bringing my boxers down too. I wait to make sure Theo is doing the same with his jeans and *Tetris* briefs before I commit. But he's committed, too.

"Two . . . One."

And just like that, we're naked in my bed, our clothes at our feet.

It's weird. It's weird how everything can change in one week. It's weird how we went from best friends figuring out how to confess our feelings for each other to boyfriends. It's weird how Theo was the one who accidentally knocked me off the jungle gym when we were younger, which left a heart-shaped scar on my hip, and now he's able to see and trace the wrinkly scar he's responsible for. It's weird how we used to go into Theo's backpack to grab an extra Xbox controller, and now I'm watching him run across the room naked to grab condoms—which he packed just in case we lost control of ourselves. It's weird how it hurts at first; it's weird how Theo's talking to me to make sure I'm okay feels way better than everything else that's happening. It's weird how we're learning how to do this together, how I don't find myself counting, how I'm able to be here for him and be here for me without distraction, how I forget I have a cold. It's weird how it's nothing like I thought it would be from the countless hours of porn watching I've clocked. It's weird how I can feel his love for me even though that's not a word we're throwing around, and I hope he can feel my love for him, too. It's weird how when we're done it doesn't feel weird at all, how I never want to be invisible when I'm with him, and how I can't believe I ever thought I would doubt this moment in the first place.

"That's a thing that happened," Theo says as he rests his head on my chest.

"It's a weird thing that happened," I say. "Good weird. It's the best kind of weird. The type of weird that should win a medal for how good weird it was."

"What's so good weird about it?"

"Because I got to do this with you." I stare at the ceiling. It could be a starless night sky. "But also because of how I feel. It's like I'm the same me, but not really. Do you feel that way?"

"Nope. I think you said it best: I'm good-weird different." Theo turns over and rests on his stomach. "It took a lot of balls to stop beating around the bush and be fully honest with you, and I want full credit, dammit! I'm a new man! I'm good-weird different!" He pops up, kneeling and pumping his fist into the air. I want to go grab the sword and shield we won the other night and present them to him, but I'm too wiped. I'm remembering I have a cold now. "I'm Theo McIntyre, a dude who just had sex with another dude! A dude who loves another du—" He shuts up, probably wishing he possessed the power to rewind time and undo his words. He gestures around the bed. "Screw it. I love you, Griffin. I'm not even going to pretend that's not what this is. You're not brand-new to me. I've known this for a while. I'm actually happy I outed myself here."

I don't know how to process being someone worthy of being someone's first kiss, of being someone's first date, of being someone's first time, of being someone's first love.

This afternoon wins for its good weirdness.

I smile and it finally comes: sneeze number four. "I'm supposed to be sick. I mean, I'm sick," I say, my throat tickling.

"Say what?"

"Sorry, I, uh. I'm sick. This just seems like a really strange, I mean weird, I mean good-weird day for someone who should be eating soup and sleeping. I wasn't even expecting to see you because I'm sick, but here you are. It's been one week since we've been doing this dating thing, and we just had sex and you're saying you're in love with me and I'm just kind of like, *what.*"

I wonder at what I just said. I'm either doing something very right or very wrong.

Theo laughs and shakes his head. "You're so awkward, Griff. You shouldn't ever be let outside your room. Here's my cue to insert some flirty comment about how I'll lock myself in here with you, but I'm better than that. I think." He lies down next to me, holding my hand. "Please don't go crazy over this. If we want to play dumb over this, we can. I can redo this down the line whenever you're ready."

I drag a finger across his jawline. I have the most honest boyfriend staring back at me. I have no reason to lie to him, and no reason to lie to myself. "You're playing dumb already if you don't think I love you back. But, officially, here it is: I love you, Theo. I love you, dude who had sex with another dude. I love you, dude who is in love with another dude." Four times. I've told Theo I love him four times, and it was easier with each one. I picture each word like a fearless skydiver. An assembly of brave words just dove out of the clouds and landed in my bed.

Theo and I stay there for a little bit longer, but when my mom texts me—asking me how I'm doing and telling me she'll be home soon with hot soup—we know it's time for him to go. There's nothing suspicious about Theo's being here, but we both know things are different now. Love and sex have been added to the recipe of our friendship. We're something new. But, man, Theo and I getting dressed together is a kind of quiet miracle, what people don't even know to dream about until it happens in real time. I try to cling to that dream, to the certainty that everything will feel as infinite as it does now so that our story will be like the high school sweetheart love story my parents have.

"I'll walk you out." I help him put his backpack on, any excuse to touch him some more.

"You say that to all the guys you sleep with, don't you?"

"Only the ones who are stupid enough to love me."

"So, what, ten dudes?"

"You wish it was only ten dudes."

Theo and I kiss for approximately the thousandth time this afternoon, and as he walks out, he says, "See you later. Don't forget that I love you. By the way, in case you were wondering, I still love you. Hey, you rock. Don't change. If you change I might not love you anymore, which is something I do now. I love you times ten."

"If you love me, you won't ever bring math into this again," I say back, rubbing my nose.

Theo keeps muttering "I love you; I love you" while going down the hall, as if those are the only three words in his vocabulary—and before he can turn the corner to the elevator, he stops and holds his hand to his ear.

I mouth the words he's waiting for. I add a "too" to bring the word count to four.

Once I close the door, I miss him. It feels extremely pathetic, but I shake it off because it won't feel that way when Theo and I are together years from now. I feel confident about that. I'm no longer listening to those doubts that make me feel inferior to Theo. And I also believe I'm Theo's first time because he wanted it that way, and not because I was some trial run for someone worthier of him down the line. I don't just believe it; I *know* it.

He said he loves me. I believe that, too. But I want more. I want to *know* it.

SATURDAY, JUNE 21ST, 2014

THEO'S SUMMER COLD—WELL, LET'S keep it real and call it *my* summer cold since it's pretty clear how he got sick—is gone, just in time for Denise's sixth birthday party in Central Park. It's a Disney princess theme. (What else?) Denise and most of her friends are dressed as Elsa, but calling it a *Frozen* party wouldn't be fair to the two Belles and the Mulan in attendance.

"We should've dressed up, too," I say.

"You can't pull off a dress as well as Denise," Theo says.

"I should've forgotten to show up," Wade says, back in his glasses as of this weekend, since his contacts finally became unbearable. He waves at us. "Remember me? Wade Church? The one who agreed to come to this kid's party even though he had something better to do."

Theo turns to me. "Hey, do you hear something? Like a ghost pretending he has better things to do?"

I feel a little guilty laughing, but not enough that I don't. Besides, it's no secret there's tons of bullying in the Theo and Wade friendship. Everyone is used to this by now, me most of all. Sometimes I'm nervous he's going to move on to new friends; I'm not that desperate for an even number in our squad.

"Whatever. Just don't have sex out here or I'm calling the cops."

That's another thing: he references our sex life whenever possible.

"There aren't enough middle fingers in the world, Wade," Theo says. "But for starters . . ." He flips Wade off twice, nods toward me to do the same, which I do. "Here are four."

Wade forces a laugh. "Tag-teaming. Fun."

There's some truth to that. Now that school is out of the way, Theo and I are planning for the summer. We really, really don't want Wade to feel like a third wheel, and it seems like we're failing already. Still, before our summer begins, Theo and I have decided to come out to our parents. And Wade can't roll with us for that. This belongs to the two of us alone.

My mom and dad are sitting with Theo's at the picnic table, eating lunch with some of the other parents. They're laughing and bantering while a horde of Elsas chase Mulan around a tree. I'm a little nervous. More than a little. They're completely oblivious to the missile we're about to fire their way.

"Now seems like a good time," I say.

"Yeah, why not?" Theo turns to Wade. "Okay, kiddo. We're off to go come out to our parents. Have you received any super legit psychic visions on how this will play out?"

Wade shakes his head. "I predict everything will remain perfect in the perfection that is your life, Theo."

"Perfect," Theo says. He throws up a peace sign. "Give us ten minutes. Fifteen if they want to take pictures."

In my head I correct it to sixteen minutes but keep that to myself.

"All right." Wade sits on the ground and pulls out his phone. "Hopefully I can Instagram without those Elsas asking me if I want to build a snowman."

Steeling ourselves, we walk over to the picnic table. We politely interrupt, asking our moms and dads if we can bother them for a second. They follow us to the tree with the birthday balloon tied around it, and we squeeze together in the shade.

"What's up, guys?" Dad asks.

"We want to update you all on something," Theo says. The four of them stare at us, but I stop feeling outnumbered when Theo grabs my hand. "We're dating, and we've decided if you're uncool with it, we're going to live here in the trees." The words tumble out of his mouth in such a rush that it sounds like one long word instead of eighteen separate words.

"No, we said we'd live on the pier," I add.

Theo glances at me. "I'm trying to throw them off. I don't want them finding us if they're not cool with it." He turns his attention back to our parents. "We cool?"

I don't know how everyone else is feeling, but I don't feel cool. I scratch at my palm with my free hand. I felt brave walking over here, and braver when Theo grabbed my hand, but my stomach is turning because we've reached the point of no return. I'm ready to reach for my earlobe when everyone breaks into smiles.

Russell laughs. "That's it? I thought you were trying to leave the party to hang out elsewhere. Poor Wade looks miserable. The answer would've been no, but I'm more than fine with you two dating."

Ellen hooks her arm inside Russell's, patting his shoulder. "Theo, I thought you finally hacked your way into some network you have no business touching and forced Griffin to be your accomplice."

"A likely scenario," Theo says. "Fair."

My mom does this weird shoulder bounce I've never seen her do before, and it might be the happiness of a mom seeing her son dating, but I'm not a fan. "I'm coming in for a hug." She hugs both Theo and I at once. "I didn't think this day would come for years. I'm so excited."

Once my mom backs away to hug Theo's parents, my dad hugs Theo.

"Good choice, Theo," Dad says. Then he comes to me and, yup, another hug. "No more sleepovers, but I'm happy for you both."

The hugging and awkward compliments about how cute we are finally come to an end. I feel lightheaded. Theo and I return to Wade, who's already laughing.

"The hugging quota for sons coming out is maxed out," Wade says.

"Seriously," I say.

Wade stares at his phone. "I guess this is actually happening," he says. "You came out to each other, made out, banged out, and now came out to your parents. You're as out as it gets."

"Thanks for the recap," Theo says.

"I guess I accept this. Get together, guys. Picture time." Wade stands and aims the phone at us.

Theo and I wrap our arms around each other's waists. "Smile or no smile?"

"Smile this time," I say.

All the important people in our lives know about us. Best friend, parents. Theo and I already talked about what comes next. We're pretty sure we'll go public online sometime this summer, but we're not in as big a rush to do so—not anymore. My biggest priority right now is framing the last photo Theo and I took as best friends beside the first photo we've taken as boyfriends.

TODAY
TUESDAY, NOVEMBER 21ST, 2016

You died on an odd day, and we're burying you on one, too.

It's drizzling, but you're tucked away inside your closed casket. The line to place flowers on you is moving, footprints sinking into the muddy grass of the cemetery where we're going to be forced to leave you. I remembered to bring the white calla lilies this time.

We gather in a circle as you're lowered into the ground.

I think about alternate universes as we lay you to rest in this one. There are billions, trillions, existing all at once: one where we never broke up and you stayed in New York, one out of reach from oceans that have it in for you, one where we *both* moved to California for school, one where you quit school and left animation and Jackson behind because you missed me so much, one where we met halfway somewhere because you wanted me not only to be your future but to help you find it, one where we're the sole survivors of the zombie-pirate apocalypse . . . countless more where things are right, maybe with some touches of wrong. But in them all, you and I are more than history. I have to believe these universes exist; it's the only way to manage the suffering here. Alternate versions of me are perfectly happy with alternate versions of you, because you're alive. Alternate Theos all honor the promise you made never to die (not even at the hands of a zombie pirate).

But you're being lowered into a hole. Your parents and Denise are freaking out. Jackson is crying, and his shoulders shift left to right, like he's looking for someone—*you*—to cry on, until reality kicks his ass, too. Wade is standing with my parents, embraced by my mom. And I'm somehow on my knees. I was standing a minute ago, rocking back and forth, crying for my favorite person to bust out of the casket and hug me. I look up, and Jackson's eyes find mine. For a second, it almost feels like we're about to race into the hole to join you. Being buried alive has got to be better than whatever comes next.

This is the moment of the end. This is where we give up hope on reversing time, where we abandon finding a cure to death, where we live in this Theo-less universe, where we say goodbye.

But I can't. It is goodbye for most, but not for me. Never me.

HISTORY
THURSDAY, JULY 17TH, 2014

Our Squad Day was long overdue. We chilled at the High Line, the coolest park in the city. Central Park is fine and all, but it can't really compete against an aerial urban railroad. There was tons of foot traffic along the gravel walkway, but the three of us managed to find this great spot on the grass, overlooking the Hudson River. We put together a puzzle of a chained dragon— something we would have done before Theo and me. We decide to walk back uptown, catching the sun falling lower and lower as we pass buildings, and as we get closer to home, I remember my mission. I wanted to wait until we were alone, but why shouldn't Wade hear this, too?

"Still coming with me to buy condoms?" I ask Theo. It's my first time buying them, and if Theo knows what's good for him, he'll go with me.

"You would need to find me a one-way ticket to an alternate universe where you walk around naked twenty-four/seven for me to miss this," Theo says.

Wade struggles to find his voice and spits out, "Just say yes next time." He shakes his head and starts walking off. "You guys have fun with that."

Theo runs ahead and blocks him. "No, no. You don't want to feel like a third wheel, right? Come on, be a bro that helps his other bros buy condoms."

I help Theo drag Wade into the Duane Reade by my building. Wade is shaking his head, but we're all laughing like idiots as we make our way to the family-planning aisle—straight to the wall of condoms. My family plan: don't start a family the next time we have sex. But condoms are only 98 percent effective, so who knows?

"You got to love the options," Theo says, beaming at our possibilities and Wade's discomfort. "I can't help but think of horses and gladiator sandals with Trojan. Magnum sounds kick-ass, like it's going to come with a bazooka. Casanova is trying too hard to be suave, I think. Suave comes before sex, not during it." Theo picks up a small black box. "What about this one? They're spelling skin with a *y*." He picks up a blue box. "Or we can go classic. Not sure why anyone would want classic when you can have Trojan's Fire and Ice condoms."

I raise my hand. "I'll go with boring classic if it means my dick won't simultaneously burn and freeze."

"Fair."

"How about Durex?" Wade suggests, gamely trying to get into the spirit of things. He's never had sex before, but both Theo and I know he came close a couple of times during our freshman year. "Does that make you think about ponies or rocket launchers?"

"It's horses and bazookas, but no." Theo takes the Durex condoms from Wade and pats his back. "Thanks, man."

We enter the line. I'm not laughing anymore. I really wish they had self-checkout here because buying condoms may be the most awkward legal transaction ever. It's weird to be looked at as someone sexually, I don't know why. It even felt a little weird for Theo to see me that way, and he's not some random cashier. It's rare I see the same cashiers here, so I really shouldn't care; I might as well be buying these condoms on the other side of the world in a country I never plan on visiting again. But it still feels like this purchase comes with a spotlight. I grab some impulse-buy candy in the hopes of dimming the glare.

"Just be cool," Theo says. "You're not buying drugs."

He's right. I'm going to be cool. I'm *not* buying drugs. I'm not even buying alcohol, where I have to be twenty-one. Buying condoms is totally normal. It's something enough guys are doing because there are options, which means it's a thriving business, which means there are multiple companies trying to convince us theirs is the best, which means we have everyone—including myself, in this moment, sort of—to thank for not only helping to keep the world a safe place, but for making sure it doesn't become too overpopulated.

"Griffin. Hey."

No way.

I freeze at the sound of my dad's voice. He's right behind us. I honestly think I'd rather be caught masturbating.

Wade laughs a little to himself, probably because this is going to be painfully humiliating. He slow-claps. "Bet you're regretting bringing me here."

There's no being cool about this. The only thing that could make this worse is if I turn and see that my dad is also buying condoms. I know my parents still have sex, because I'm not an idiot, I know they're not just watching Netflix or going to sleep early when they wish me good night around 8 P.M. I turn and he's holding shaving razors and boxes of cereal. The cereal reminds me of being a kid and eating breakfast in front of the TV during Saturday-morning cartoons. I'll never be *that* innocent again.

"Hey, Dad."

He nods at Theo and Wade. "How was the High Line, guys?" He spots the condoms in my hands, which are poorly hidden behind the gummy worms. "Oh." He's trying to say something.

His arms are sort of all over the place, like a robot being turned on for the first time.

I desperately want a superpower right now. Maybe mind control so I could wipe my dad's memory clean and then force him to turn around and get the hell out of here. I'd settle for invisibility, though.

"Protection is good," Dad says. "You can't get pregnant, but there are other dangers."

At this point I'd even take the power to set myself aflame, anything.

I put down the condoms in a bowl for dollar chocolates. "Nope, not doing this," I mumble. "Let's forget this ever happened, Dad. Come on, guys." We try leaving the aisle, but my dad cuts ahead of us.

"Wait. We should be able to talk about this. This doesn't have to be embarrassing," Dad says.

"This doesn't have to happen in a Duane Reade line either . . ."

Knowing we have no choice but to follow him, the four of us end up hiding out in the aisle with all the shower products. Theo and I are standing side by side. We turn to Wade, who's grinning and won't take a hint and leave. Of course not. He finally has the upper hand.

"Your mom and I were thinking about sitting down with you soon to talk about this stuff—to talk about sex. Let's call it what it is. Sex. We figured you two might be thinking about this at some point . . ." Dad stops himself. "Wait. Have you both already . . . ?"

My face is on fire; maybe my superpower wish to burst into flames is coming true. "We have," I say.

Dad sucks in his upper lip, which he normally does whenever he's nervous he might say the wrong thing if he speaks too quickly. He looks directly at me. "Was that your first time?"

"Yup."

"Good choice," Dad says, turning red. "That came out wrong. Sorry, Theo. I'm trying to say sex means more when it's with someone you care about."

I know my dad had sex a couple of times before meeting my mom—I forget why it came up a couple of years ago, but it did—and it's good to hear he feels this way. It just sucks that I have to be reminded of it right now, when all I wanted to do was buy condoms with my boyfriend and our best friend.

This silence is painful and awkward. Endless, too.

Theo points at a bottle behind my dad. "Hey, a shampoo that doubles as a conditioner."

"Groundbreaking product, Theo!" Wade laughs. I can't blame him for how much he's loving this.

"I know you don't need some birds-and-bees talk," Dad continues. "Birds and birds? Maybe it's bees and bees? I'm not sure if the bird or the bee is the boy in that idiom." He gets lost trying to figure that out for a second before returning to earth. "I don't know all the mechanics of same-sex sex, but I've been researching different forums lately, and I'm around to talk if you have any questions. Both of you."

Researching? Jesus. "Okay," I say, my eyes now glued to the scuffed linoleum floor. "Thanks, Dad."

"Thanks, Gregor," Theo says.

"Anytime," Dad says.

Never again, please.

"I'm going to do you both a solid right now," Dad says.

Maybe he's going to do some Jedi mind trick to make everyone here forget this interaction ever happened. He gets back in line, grabs the condoms out of the bowl of chocolates, holds them up for us to see, approaches the cashier, and puts the condoms, cereal, and razors on the counter. I look around the store because I can't bear to watch. I spot rat poisoning and the wheels of my superhero origin story begin spinning; I'll drink some and will suddenly have the ability to become a tiny rat at will—a rat that doesn't need condoms, a rat that can avoid the awkwardness of his father buying condoms for him.

Theo and I bolt for the exit. Wade strolls after us, beaming.

Outside, Dad offers me the plastic bag with our condoms, then switches to Theo before I can take it from him, then switches back to me, then back to Theo. I snatch the bag from him when it comes back my way.

"You coming home soon?" Dad asks.

I nod, staring at the ground again. "Probably not going to make eye contact with you for at least a decade."

"Sounds fair. I'll see you later. Good night, Theo."

"Good night, Gregor."

He walks off.

Wade slow-claps again. "Good going, guys. Do you think your dad is trying to figure out who's the top and who's the bottom yet?"

"Shut up," Theo says.

I grab Theo's arm, and the three of us walk in the complete opposite direction of my father. "I know it's really early, but do you think I can move in with you? I'm never going back home. Unless your parents are going to hit you with a 'bees and bees' conversation sometime soon, too."

"Nah, I got that birds and bees conversation when I was ten," Theo says.

"I guess they didn't suspect you only needed the bees talk, right? Or is it birds? Damn, my dad had a point there," I say.

"Doesn't matter. I like birds and bees."

I grab Theo's wrist and brake. "Come on, it's me. You don't have to keep up the act about the birds . . . or bees . . . damn it, you don't have to fake interest in girls anymore."

"I'm not faking interest," Theo says. "I'm pretty sure I'm bisexual."

"Why didn't you tell me?"

"I thought you knew. I had crushes and stuff, though I guess I talked about that stuff more with Wade."

Wade's smile has vanished. He's stone-faced now, which is actually great because I might flip out if he laughed at Theo and me about this. Getting caught by my dad while we're buying condoms is one thing; feeling my relationship threatened is another.

"I figured those crushes were covers," I say in the silence. I did the same thing he did; I thought girls were cool and everything, but I didn't think I actually had the right heart to date them.

"Well, they weren't." Theo looks genuinely puzzled. "I'm sorry you got the truth mixed up. Why does it even matter? I'm dating *you*, Griff."

I glance at Wade, but he's glued to his phone. I don't like that I didn't know this essential truth about Theo. I know there's more to him than I can ever capture and keep close to me, like his fleeting thoughts or his conversations with other people, but this is bigger. It's so central to his heart, one of my favorite things about him—the way he loves me, the way he loves his parents and sister, the way he loves the squad, the way he loves discovering life's mysteries and solving them.

This flips everything around, right?

I let go of his wrist. "It's stupid, but it feels like more competition." I feel like I'm going up against the entire world, that there's no way I'm the absolute best fit for him on this planet. I at least thought I'd be able to see a new guy swooping in, but now I have to be suspicious of everyone. I have things I don't want to know but have to know. "What's your type? Girlwise."

"I don't know what kind of girls I like, Griffin, because I think my type is just good people, period." His voice softens. "I'm sorry we never had a real conversation about this, but trust me that this isn't something all that serious in my head. It's not keeping me up at night because I'm happy with you, and I'm not counting on someone better coming along." Theo grabs my hands. There's no lightness to his voice, only conviction. "Please don't feel threatened."

He kisses my cheek.

I believe him, in this moment, but it's what can happen in the future that chokes me a little. I'm not going to say anything, though. Being paranoid can't possibly take me anywhere good.

I kiss his cheek.

"Was that supposed to be a fight?" Wade asks. He doesn't even bother to look up from his phone, but I appreciate his being here to lighten the mood. "Not enough blood."

We walk in silence for a bit.

"Griff?" Theo says finally.

"Yeah?"

"Two important things going forward."

"What's up?"

"One: We only order condoms online from here on out. Two: We're definitely never using those condoms your father bought us."

TODAY
THURSDAY, NOVEMBER 24TH, 2016

I thought nothing could beat the weirdness of last year's Thanksgiving. You were supposed to fly back to New York to bounce between our families' dinners. It was our tradition. Instead, you stayed out in California and joined Jackson's family for the night. Your parents were bummed, Denise was bummed, Wade was bummed, I was bummed; we were all really freaking bummed because it was the first time we were going to see you since August. But we didn't give you shit for it because you said you really needed to concentrate on homework—specifically your animation, the one about the warrior fishermen catching dragon eggs in a volcano, which you ultimately abandoned anyway.

My entire Thanksgiving was spent at my aunt's apartment, wondering if you were liking Jackson's family, why you were becoming so obsessed with Jackson himself. It wasn't a comfortable headspace. Suffocating, actually, but you were alive and still the endgame. I'd go back in time for those problems.

My aunt's apartment is hell-hot like usual. "Happy Thanksgiving, Rosie."

I'll never forget the first time you met Rosie, confusing her for a slimmer version of my mother, who was heavier at the time, congratulating her on all her lost weight, which everyone found funny, even Mom. Rosie may be half a decade older than my mom, but she's been consistently going to the gym, and I think I can even feel some abs coming in as we hug.

"Happy Thanksgiving, Griffin," she says, squeezing me. She tries to look me in the eye but I completely detach, so she greets my parents, giving my mom a kiss. Their sisterhood has always made me want a sibling. Grieving would probably feel a little less lonely if I could turn to someone my own age, maybe a little older and wiser and scarred from battles I'm fighting for the first time. Maybe I wouldn't have done the things I've done.

The kitchen smells like cornbread and gravy (for the mashed potatoes you obsessed over); there's turkey, stuffing, mac'n'cheese I won't ever touch, yellow rice, and then I'm hit with the sweetness of the cranberry sauce. I throw off my jacket, but the kitchen is still baking me alive because I'm in your hoodie, so I make my way out into the living room. My little cousins charge me, trying to climb my legs. I don't have smiles for them. I can barely even get their names straight because I see them so rarely. They live upstate and their names all begin with *R*, an insane tradition that is eventually going to lead to kids named Rasputin or Raiden from *Mortal Kombat*. I soldier through the hugs and sympathies from my older cousins, but my grandma is the one who really wears me out.

"Griffin, come sit," she requests, patting the air because there's nowhere beside her I can actually sit. I crouch, letting her take my hand with both of hers.

She turns ninety this December. I lost you at eighteen. She lived a life as a military mechanic, a manager at a pharmacy, a great-grandmother, a wife to a man I never met and later to a man I never liked. You lived a life as a genius, an honors student with a promising future, a first love to me, and then a boyfriend to Jackson. She lived a lot in her life, but you got cut off before we could set things right.

"How is your eye doing?" Grandma asks. She's probably remembering that time my classmate Jolene accidentally elbowed me in the eye—in sixth grade. There's dementia for you. My cousins sometimes crack jokes because nothing's funnier to them than someone's mind abandoning them and taking on a life of its own.

"My eye is good, Grandma," I say. "Much better. How are you doing? How's Primo?" Her brown-bellied, yellow canary got sick a little while ago.

"Have you prayed today?"

"I prayed this morning," I lie. Lying about prayer would've felt a lot more sinful if I ever believed in God, but well, those thoughts are better suited for someone with reasons to believe in the miracle of resurrection.

I glance at Davis, the ten-year-old soccer-obsessed cousin who was grossed out when he caught us kissing. He's hogging the TV Grandma could be using to watch one of her shows. Only then can I go in a corner and power down. I see her empty glass, another exit strategy. "Do you want more water?"

"I already have water. Where is Theo? I want to watch one of his movies."

Grandma is really fond of your animations. I think her favorite is the forty-second clip of the spider chasing that one red ant. When it reaches its posse, together they form that super ant that scares the spider away. It's possible she just really admired the flowers you put in the background. I could probably pull up some of your animations for her, the ones I have on my phone—except "Griffin on the Left," that's for my eyes only—but I don't have it in me to watch the videos myself. I need my phone, anyway, to hear your voice.

"Theo can't make it," I say. I'm sure my mom or aunt told her you died. She's forgotten already, but I'm going to let it go instead of repeating it back to her. I like that she thinks you're alive. "I'm going to get you more water, Grandma."

I kick Davis off the TV, task him with getting his great-grand-mother some more water, and I retreat into Rosie's room, where I hide underneath the coats on her bed.

Putting a song on repeat used to drive you crazy. I could never shake certain lyrics or beats out of my head until I listened to the song for a week straight, sometimes two. You hated the sound of your own voice recorded even more, and I'm sorry you have to hear it again as I play your last voice mail on repeat: "*Hey, Griff, sorry I missed your call. I was out and my phone was off . . . you sound like you're walking the plank. If* The Walking Dead *pirates didn't already chase you off, call me back and let me know you're okay. Bye, man.*"

I really like this message because there is no mention of Jackson, even though he was probably the reason you were out. Also because you called me Griff, not Griffin—like you got used to doing whenever Jackson was around.

I press PLAY again.

I'm on my thirty-eighth listening this session when someone pats my ankles. I hadn't even noticed they were sticking out over the edge of the bed. I'm tempted to just kick the hand away, but I come out from underneath the coats and see my dad.

"Dinner is ready. *Thanksgiving* dinner, which comes once a year. Don't bank on seeing cornbread again for another year."

What an awful pitch for Thanksgiving—the fuck do I care about cornbread? Has he completely forgotten the reason I'm hiding from the family I'm usually so excited to see?

But I get up and head out into the living room. Pretty much everyone already has their food on a plate, standing in a circle against the walls while the kids are on the floor sitting cross-legged or on their knees. Right: prayer first, then food. My mom has pre-pared me a plate because apparently when someone's grieving, they revert back to an age where they have to hold someone's hand to cross the street, ask permission to stay over at a friend's house, probably require a nightlight, and can't serve themselves dinner. I thank her before I have a condom-over-mouth-worthy outburst, and step over Reynaldo—I think—to stand between the busted stereo and a potted plant in desperate need of water.

Rosie throws a towel over her shoulder and claps, like we're about to huddle together and she's going to coach us through our dinner. "Who wants to lead us in prayer?" She turns to her three grown kids: Richie, the eldest, who was always too in his head over work to ever connect with you; Ronnie, who didn't bring the latest love of his life to dinner this year; and Remy, who's always been my least favorite. Not because he's the third kid or how his name doesn't quite fit with his brothers', but because he used to talk shit about us behind your back, which I never told you about because his antigay nonsense is his nonsense.

None of them volunteer. My dad takes a step forward.

Rosie claps. "Whoa, first-timer. Take it away, Gregor."

The turkey leg I'm sure Dad pushed women and children out of the way for almost rolls off his plate when he gestures out to the family, inviting us to hold hands. But we're all holding food, some of us drinks. He realizes his error, chuckling. Remy is to my right, and he surely wasn't going to hold my hand anyway. His son, Ralph—an old man's name—is to my left, so this is all for the best.

"Dear God, thank you for bringing our family together for another year of good food and good company, but mainly good food . . ." He pauses, actually pauses expecting laughter. Grandma, my mom, Rosie, and a couple of my older cousins indulge him with a chuckle, but none of the younger ones do; the ego-soothing instinct isn't quite programmed in them just yet. "A friendly face our family has grown to know well over the years is absent tonight, unfortunately. We all—Griffin especially—miss him dearly, and will continue praying for his family."

I might freak out or throw up or throw up and freak out, Theo.

Dad pauses and takes a deep breath. "God, we ask you to keep our family safe for another year, and thank you for our blessings. Amen."

In the choruses of "amen," I sink against the wall, resting my arm on the rim of the pot. Whatever food I thought I was going to be able to manage before will not be happening. I think again of your family, especially Denise. I can't even imagine what it must look like over there, what it must be like to be a family that others are specifically—and pointlessly—praying for on Thanksgiving. And then there's Jackson, possibly tacked on at their table, camping out in their home. I don't think it's parasitic, but even *I've* kept my distance. They have enough wounds without tending to someone else's pain, too.

"Griffin, Griffin," Grandma calls me from across the room, her voice just loud enough to reach me, despite my cousins' nearby conversation about football. "Where is Theo? I cooked the mashed potatoes."

She didn't cook the mashed potatoes; Rosie used her recipe. And you really do love her recipe, but you were also hooked on potatoes in general. I never understood how you could eat an entire diner dinner of mashed potatoes, one baked potato, and French fries with a random green apple on the side. But you did it. You did it every time.

"Theo can't make it, Grandma," I say. "I'll let him know he missed out on your mashed potatoes."

"You'll let him know?" Remy asks. "Oh brother."

"Don't," Rosie warns.

Grandma is trying to ask me a question, but the younger cousins are shushing her; the little instigators want to see something go down. When I try getting up, Dad braces me and keeps me on the floor while Mom grabs my hand, squeezing it. Remy sniffs. "Come on, already. He dated the guy for what, a year?"

"I've known him for seven years," I answer through my teeth, scratching the hell out of my free palm because I'm so nervous about the person he's dragging out of me.

"You're too obsessed. Get over him and do something for yourself." Remy's tone isn't even confrontational. It's as if he's just simply stating this, like we're the kind of friends who swap advice.

I rise, pushing my dad's hand away, but he keeps a hold on me. "I'm not going to hit him," I lie, shaking him and my mom off. Remy is six years older than me and I give a grand total of zero shits. I know you're not about me getting into fights, and not just because I *can't* fight, but you're not here to calm me down or hold me back. "You don't get it, you don't—" I turn to everyone in the room, searching for someone who *does* get it, but no one here has been through this. "Everything I did for him I did for me, too, because it made *me* happy to see him happy. That's not obsession, you dickhead, it's love."

He's embarrassed, his cheeks flushed. Rosie looks pretty ashamed herself for creating such an asshole.

"Except he was dating someone else," Remy says. "Get over it. He did."

Theo, you're about to have some company, and I'm sorry it's not someone more worthy of you.

I lunge at the bastard—I hear the gasps of my mom and Rosie, some cheers from some younger cousins, screams from others—and my dad catches me before I can snuff him, dragging me back toward the kitchen while Remy laughs.

"We're going home, Griffin, it's going to be okay," Dad says, no longer manhandling me because I'm pissed but hugging me because I'm crying.

SAFE TO SAY NEXT Thanksgiving will be spent at home, or maybe at whatever college accepts a guy who plans on doing zero work for the rest of his senior year.

My parents are sitting in front of the living room TV, eating leftovers—does it count as leftovers if it's food they never got to dig into in the first place?—and I'm back in my room. I'm stretched across my bed when my phone rings. I'm expecting it to be Wade, but it's your mom. The last time she called was to tell me you died.

It's close to eleven, which makes me even more nervous to pick up. "Hello?"

"Hi. It's Ellen. I'm sorry to call so late."

"It's okay. How was your—" I'll pass on asking about dinner. It's probably one of the few nightmares she stands a chance at putting behind her. "How are you doing?"

"It's impossible, Griffin. I am constantly . . . It's lovely hearing your voice," she says. "I'm getting ready to try and get some rest, actually. But I wanted to check in and see if you would be okay with me giving you Jackson's number. He wanted to call you but I thought it would be better for you to reach out if you felt up to it."

I almost ask her why Jackson wants to talk to me, but she's already wasted enough time being a middleman. "That's okay," I say. "Is he up?"

"He's wide-awake. West Coast time," Ellen answers before a long pause. I'm wondering if she's nervous about what will happen if Jackson and I talk.

"I'll give him a call and let you get some rest. If there's anything I can do, like watch Denise or go grocery shopping for you, I'm more than happy to," I say.

"Thanks, Griffin. You're sweet. I'll let you know. Have a good night."

"Good night."

I hang up, and Ellen texts me Jackson's info.

I stare at the seven numbers following Jackson's California area code. I press CALL before reasoning can beat loneliness. This, this moment right here, is the sudden switch from same-old-same-old to crazy intensity. I sit up and press my hand to my heart, counting with its rhythm. "One, two. One, two. One, two. One, two. One, two . . .

"Hello?"

". . . One, two," I finish. He interrupted me at an odd count—we're not off to a good start. "It's Griffin."

"Hey," Jackson says. It's quiet for a bit, and I can hear him breathing—short, quiet breaths you probably heard while he was sleeping. "Thanks for calling."

I nod like he can see me. "Everything all right?"

"No," Jackson says. "No point pretending anything is all right. No pressure, but are you doing anything tonight? I know this is a little weird. Yeah, it's weird. But I wanted to throw it out there. I could really stand to get out of the house."

I'm not sure how I would answer this for myself. I only know what you would want me to do. "I think Theo would like that," I say. It's true. I know Jackson and I playing nice will make you happy, especially since we never got that right when you were alive. But agreeing to this still makes me nauseated.

"You're right," Jackson says. "He would've."

"I can meet you at Theo's. Give me twenty minutes."

"Okay. I'll see you in a bit."

"See you." I hang up.

Our conversation was three minutes and two seconds long. Better.

I force myself out of bed. Maybe something good will come from talking to Jackson. No one gets it, Theo. The guidance counselor assures me I'll heal with time. My cousin thinks I'm too young to be in love. Wade doesn't know anything *about* love. My parents thought I was in good-enough condition to go to dinner instead of letting me hide in bed underneath my covers. I know that's not healthy; I'm not stupid. But you and I had plans. We didn't have a map to reach our destination, and your detour with Jackson left me very lost. Still, I held hope we'd find our way back to each other. And then you died, and now I'm left wandering around with zero sense of direction. Talking to someone else who's lost might help.

I throw my navy peacoat over your hoodie. I slip into some dark jeans and the worn-out, scuffed-up boots you bought me for my birthday this year—our inside joke on how stupid it feels to buy boots during May when it's sneaker weather. Even though your call wishing me a happy birthday came a day late, the boots arrived on my birthday and they're my favorite. Thanks again, Theo.

My dad is fading when I walk out into the living room. He snaps awake when he sees me out of the corner of his eye. My mom is already asleep on the couch's armrest, her feet tucked between my dad's legs. He pats her knee.

"I'm sleeping here," she murmurs. She throws a sweater over her face and is a goner.

"Where are you going?" Dad asks. "It's almost eleven thirty."

"I'm meeting with—" I almost say your name. Whenever I was staying out late on weekends or non-school nights, all I had to do was tell my parents I was with you and I was home free. But I catch myself. "Jackson. I need to get out for a bit. He does, too."

Dad lifts my mom's leg off his lap and gets up from the couch, covering her with a decent blanket. "Did he call you?"

"Ellen gave me his number because he wanted to talk to me, so I called him."

I can tell he's surprised, if not concerned. "Want me to drive you guys somewhere? It's supposed to snow again any minute now."

"I'm in the mood for a walk, Dad. Is that okay?"

"Your phone is charged?"

I nod.

Dad hugs me. He makes me promise I'll call him if I want to be picked up, and that I'll answer whenever he calls. Yes, yes, yes, yes . . .

You're going to watch me hang out with Jackson one-on-one. It feels unusual, something unrepeatable in one lifetime, like you're on a rooftop with your two favorite people to watch Halley's Comet streak across the sky. Except there's no way you would've ever been able to have Jackson and me in the same place, not even for a comet. Instead, I'll be walking the streets where we lived with someone who isn't you, someone who was in love with you, too. Isn't this the best of both worlds for someone who was torn between two boys?

HISTORY
FRIDAY, SEPTEMBER 26TH, 2014

I have no guesses as to why the guidance counselor wants to meet up with Theo at the end of the day. I bump into Wade between classes, and he has no clue, either. He shrugs it off and says we'll find out later, but it makes me feel small not knowing. Theo is happy, right?

It's hard enough faking interest in seventh-period earth science. I need to know these differences between igneous, sedimentary, and metamorphic rocks and other stuff for weekly quizzes and Regents exams, but I swear I paid attention to 2 percent of this afternoon's class. I was too anxious for Theo's news. Once the final bell rings, I completely skip going to my locker and head straight to Theo's, and I'm relieved seeing him there already.

"Hey," I say, kissing him on the cheek. Everyone knows we're dating, and it hasn't been a big deal. A lot of our classmates spread throughout sophomore and junior year assumed we were dating back when we were still just best friends, and the freshmen crack that code easily because Theo and I arrive most mornings holding hands. It's been really cool that our deans don't give a damn. "What's going on? We're not waiting for Wade."

"Clearly not," Theo says, smiling. "I'm sorry for the suspense."

"I've been totally fine," I joke, loosening my tie.

"Right." Theo stops unloading his bag and leans against his locker, a picture of us on the inside, pinned by a *Tetris* sticker. "The guidance counselor called me in to talk to me about early admission. Spoiler alert: I have kick-ass grades across the board. I'm even beating out some seniors this month in my AP classes. Ms. Haft even used the word 'wunderkind,' and it took all my will not to propose right then and there."

"Wow. Uh, what has to happen for you to get in?"

"They want me to write an essay before November first to submit to colleges," Theo says. "Ms. Haft thinks I should apply to Harvard, but I really like the animation program at Santa Monica College. I have to talk to my parents about where their finances are. Dude, I could be in California by this time next year." He closes his eyes while he leans his head against his locker, smiling and lost in this dream where he's free of me. "Isn't this awesome?"

I'm not giving my face a chance to betray me, so I hug him before he can open his eyes. "You deserve this, Theo. I'll help out any way I can." I hope that's not an empty offer for both our sakes.

I'm scared, though. The possibility of Theo's moving across the country sort of feels like it could be the beginning of the end. I was already nervous about what was going to happen to us when I enter my senior year as he begins college. Now there's a chance he'll be two years ahead of me. It doesn't feel promising. I can't beat these paranoid feelings out of my head.

I back away, and he's beaming. His face lights up in the same way when a trailer comes on for a new movie he's really excited about. He has this preview in his head, and he can't wait to see if it's everything he's daydreaming about.

I smile for him. But it's a lie. I'm not happy.

TODAY
THURSDAY, NOVEMBER 24TH, 2016

Now would be a good time to retreat to our zombie-apocalypse bunker, because the end of the world is here: I'm on my way to your house to pick up the person who stole you from me.

I don't hate Jackson, Theo. But I don't have to be his friend. The only reason I was even friendly when I met him was because I couldn't be an asshole. I couldn't ever look like I was against him or wanted to sabotage your relationship. When we had our eventual reunion, you would be able to see how my love for you trumped my own happiness. But now—as vulnerable or pathetic as this sounds—Jackson is someone I'm turning to. I'm not strong enough to suffer alone.

It's snowing a little and freezing, and the cold air bites at my exposed neck, ears, and my hands when I pull out my phone to text Jackson: I'm two songs away.

I delete the text and in its place send, I'm like six minutes away.

Jackson wouldn't have understood the first text; I'd only send that to you. I'm not confusing him for you, but I'm walking the usual route to reach your block. In the time it's taking me to fight against the wind, to pass the supermarket with bikes chained to parking meters, the car rental place, the bagel spot that is stingy with their jelly, and the pet shop with the lights currently off, I've heard "Love Minus Zero/No Limit" by Bob Dylan twice. You knew how to measure my distance in songs. Jackson doesn't.

This block is legit memory lane for me, and the sudden force of it is almost too much. The spot in the street by the post office where you almost got hit by the car, leading to your broken promise of never dying; your neighbor's stoop where we sat and cried after breaking up, wiping our tears with sleeves and each other's hands; the front step leading into your lobby that you always forgot about, stubbing your toe at least twice; the sidewalk where we played Frisbee, waiting for the mailman to bring your letter of acceptance; the many times we got locked out, but most especially that week after we discovered sex and couldn't get into your empty apartment; how after you moved to California I would sometimes find my lovesick self standing in front of the intercom, wishing I could press 2B and summon you down here into my arms.

I'm not going upstairs. I'd never make it out of there. I can't even get myself to go into the lobby.

I text Jackson: I'm downstairs. And cold.

Within a couple of minutes, Jackson comes rushing toward the front door, pulling a coat on top of a lighter jacket. Maybe that jacket is one he uses for those supernatural rainy days in California, days where he pulls over on the highway for life-changing boys like you.

That wasn't called for. Condom-over-mouth: I know the drill, Theo.

"Hey," I say, throwing a what's-up nod. Jackson is a foot away, already shivering, and I almost lean in for a half-hug situation but pull back.

"Hey." Jackson zippers his coat and tugs a hat down over his head, some hair sticking out from the sides. "Sorry, I couldn't find my other glove upstairs." He slides one glove on and sticks his bare hand inside his coat pocket.

I would've drop-kicked you if you returned to New York with this can't-soldier-through-the-cold attitude.

"Where are we off to?" he asks.

"Not sure," I say. "Follow me."

For a while I take in nothing but cars honking, the slosh of melting snow, the occasional passersby on their phones. I glance to my right, and Jackson has fallen behind, side by side with my shadow cast from a building's beaming sensor lights. He spins, walking backward to dodge the wind. I switch from my straightforward left to his backward left. But then he flips around and I swap back to my original spot while he holds his scarf in front of his face. I'm sure I dizzied you with that dance, Theo, but Jackson has no idea what the hell is happening. We turn a corner where we're protected a little better from the heavier winds.

"How was dinner?" I ask him. I figure hearing it from him won't be even a tenth as painful as hearing it from Ellen or Russell or, worse, Denise.

"Not great," Jackson says. "They didn't want to sit at the table. We set up base in the living room and ordered some Chinese food. Denise put on the Disney channel, but I don't think she was watching. I offered to bake some cornbread or brownies, but no one was really interested."

"Denise didn't want to help bake?"

"No," he says.

It's even worse than I thought.

Jackson stops in front of a shuttered deli, jump-starts again, getting a little ahead of me as if he has any clue where we should go. I speed-walk and catch up, which, given the same length of our long legs, is a bit of a race, but I win; it's nice winning against him.

"I shouldn't have been there tonight," he says. "I don't belong."

No, he doesn't. He's that blue W-shaped piece of the Celestial Sky puzzle you and I fought over, the one I kept trying to fit into the wrong spot despite your insistence. In the puzzle that is your house, Jackson doesn't have a space carved out for him.

"I feel really guilty that Theo spent his last Thanksgiving with me."

He *should* feel guilty. If you had known that was going to be your last Thanksgiving, I know you would've come home, even if it meant carting Jackson with you like luggage full of shiny new video games—ones you'd play for a while before your interest eventually faded because you missed the classics.

You and I have always been good about letting things go, especially things that are out of our control. I could probably throw some memories his way to prove this, but I'm hoarding them.

I remind myself that just because someone is forgiving, it doesn't make asking for forgiveness easy. Remember that, Theo.

"Nothing you can do about it now," I say after a minute.

I brace myself against another assault of cold air, the snow in my face. I hide my hands in my sleeves, folding my arms across my chest to keep my coat close. I stop walking when Jackson falls out of vision. He tucks his gloved fist in his pocket and holds his bare hand open in front of him. It seems backward at first, but I remember doing this as a kid. This must be Jackson's first real snowfall, and he smiles when he catches some. He closes his hand, crushing the snowflakes; wipes it on his jeans afterward; and steps toward me.

"Can I tell you a Theo story?" Jackson asks. He's speaking with the urgency of someone who's been locked up inside his home all day, dying for human interaction, an urgency I understand.

Part of me wants to say yes, the other part is screaming, *Hell no.*

"I don't want this to be weird, Griffin," Jackson says. "We should be able to talk about Theo. If that's impossible, we can part ways tonight and never see each other again. I'm sure that's what everyone is betting will happen anyway." He sounds sort of sad when he says it. He's also one hundred percent right. "But I think we can be better than that."

It's true. I know it is. It's why I'm out here in the freezing cold on Thanksgiving night. You would want us to keep your memory alive. I didn't think there was a chance in hell that this person—the person who asked you to stop being friends with me—would suggest a relationship of our own. I don't know if I can stand hearing about your happiness with him, but maybe it'll help me understand you better. Maybe it'll help me add pieces to the puzzle of your life. Time for a test run.

"What's your Theo story?"

Jackson crouches, picking up snow and forging a snowball—maybe his first, I don't know, since there's been snow on the ground since before your funeral—and he throws it at the wall. "Theo freaked out after I told him I'd never touched snow before. It's kind of a lie because there's a photo of me as a kid making a snow angel by the Brooklyn Bridge, but I don't actually remember any of that. Theo was hoping it would snow when we came for his birthday, just so he could see me . . ." He stops himself.

"So he could witness your first snow," I say.

I get it. It's like when you finally introduced me to the original *Star Wars* trilogy one weekend. Watching Jedi battles was fun, and imagining myself wielding a dual lightsaber was badass, too, but my favorite moment by far was the smile on your face after pressing PLAY on your laptop. You turned to me like I was supposed to have already formed a glowing opinion, when all I'd seen were big yellow words info-dumping me.

Here's where it gets tricky. Jackson's story hurts, but only because I've experienced that same happiness before.

"Follow me," I say. I know where we're going now. I lead him toward Lincoln Center. I have my own story to share.

When I had you here, walking this walk with me, we held hands like no one would ever think there was anything off about it. We straggled to enjoy as much time away from parental supervision as possible, even when our socks were wet and our toes were cold. With Jackson, I hurry. Soon we're at the entrance, walking across the wide, brightly lit steps. The elegant plaza and columns and grand banners promoting the latest ballet always reminded me of a setting I'd find in a fantasy novel—I told you that the first time we came here as a couple. I gravitate toward the Revson Fountain. I'd always called it the "big fountain" before you came along with your specifics. I know the flowing jets of water and lights are off because it's winter, but there's still a wrongness to it all, like the fountain has died and been abandoned.

"I'm going to go ahead and guess you and Theo came here and made wishes," Jackson says.

For that brief moment I forgot Jackson was here. I'm about to break down and cry in front of him. I shiver, not from cold, and step away. He's not someone I want a hug from.

"Yeah, we made wishes. And the whole thing is kind of bullshit." I flip off the fountain. "Look, there are so many coins in here. People actually thought their spare change could buy them stuff, like actual riches or something else. We're all suckers."

Jackson stares at the water. "I always thought it was more religion than fantasy," he says. "Ignore everyone throwing in money for more money. Everyone else is praying. Throwing a coin into a fountain is a little less disappointing than praying in some church. You go straight to the Big Man's house, you expect results."

I turn to him. "Question: How the hell can you believe in God? After Theo?"

Jackson shrugs. "I don't spend my Sundays at church, but I've always taken to the idea of bigger plans. I had big plans with Theo—now I don't. There's got to be something to take away from this. I refuse to believe he died pointlessly."

"Theo didn't die so you could personally learn some big lesson on life." I can feel my face getting hot.

Jackson comes closer to me, and I take a step back because I'm shaking harder and he should be nervous about being left alone with me. "That's not what I'm saying, Griffin. That would be a complete waste. I know that; you know that. I'm just not going to give God the silent treatment because I'm pissed off Theo is dead. Theo believed in God."

"I don't need you to tell me what Theo believed in," I snap. I'm sorry, Theo. I should apologize to him, not just to you. "Sorry, I'm . . . I'm in a bad place and . . ." I don't understand why he would be talking to God for comfort when he could be talking to you. "I should have known this, but being back here without Theo sucks."

"Yeah. It's one of the reasons I'm not excited to go back home." Jackson turns back to the fountain. "I know it's taboo to share, but what would you wish for?"

"I know you're more interested in what Theo would wish for," I say.

"That would require resurrection," Jackson says.

"I guess it's not *that* taboo to share," I say. Some of my wishes would also require a resurrection to come true.

I tell Jackson some of the things I wished for, like your mom's good health when she had that breast cancer scare. How I wanted you so badly to have a scholarship so your parents would have more money in their pockets to fly you back and forth to New York whenever you missed home. I don't tell Jackson about some of the other wishes I made, like on this past New Year's Eve, where I cried so hard I couldn't breathe because I was wishing you would call at midnight and tell me you missed me and loved me and would come back to me and be mine again someday soon.

"That was really nice of you," Jackson says. "Selfless."

"I only ever wanted the best for him," I say. I'm not sure I believe I was the best fit for you, Theo, but I do think I was better than Jackson.

Jackson digs around his coat pocket, pulls out a handful of change, closes his eyes, mouths something, and tosses all the coins into the fountain.

I'm not asking him what he wished for.

He steps side to side, his shoes sloshing, rubbing his arms. "It's cold," he says.

I can barely survive another minute of this myself. I'm ready to call it a night, but I don't have much to look forward to alone in my room. "It's also late. If you want, you can come back to my place for a bit to talk."

"You don't have to do that," Jackson says. "Maybe there's a coffee shop open?"

"My dad is awake, and he'll feel a lot more comfortable going to sleep if I'm home," I say. "But if you think it's weird, it's okay."

"No, I want to keep talking. Let's go. Should we take a cab, though? I'm not sure I can survive a walk."

I'd give your West Coast boy shit for not toughing it out, but a ride sounds nice. We head uptown along the curb, heading in the direction of my building as we wait for an empty cab in the dead of night. One finally pulls over beside us after a bit. Jackson jumps in first, warming up behind the driver—on what will be my left side if I get in. I consider settling into the right side, just angling my body so I'm facing him, but I'm already clawing at my numb palm, so I race around the other side and open the door.

"Stealing your seat," I tell him.

He shifts to the right and I get inside. If he's confused or troubled, he doesn't show it. How much did you tell him about me, Theo? Does he know about my OCD? He closes the door on his side as I do mine. I give the driver my address and we're there in eight minutes. I pay in cash and we get out, running into my building.

It was 2011 when you came over to my house for the first time. Your parents were spending the day with Denise at her classmate's birthday party. They didn't want you home alone. Your parents called mine, and I got really excited when my dad told me you were coming over for a few hours because we were on summer break and it was harder to hang. You brought over a puzzle of a medieval castle while we watched X-Men DVDs. As we put it together we made our own plans to see each other again soon—assuming my parents were cool with me running wild with you, of course—and I could feel how much you missed me too, and it was cool, even if we never said it.

But bringing Jackson home is something completely different.

The outside of my building looks sort of fancy, but as we go inside, I can't help but notice things I never paid attention to before: the lack of a doorman; chipped paint on the dark-blue railings; the smudges of fingerprints on the elevator buttons, no one employed by the superintendent to wipe them clean daily; the yellowed stain on the hallway carpet. I'm hoping Jackson doesn't see them. It's stupid because I know I go to a private school and get healthy monthly allowances, but I hate that Jackson will compare the awesomeness of your building to mine and feel sure that you were always above someone like me.

We reach my door. Jackson leans against the wall.

I unlock the door and peek in, finding my dad asleep with my mom on the couch, the TV still on. It'll be hard to have a conversation with Jackson in the living room with them there. We tiptoe inside and head straight to my bedroom, and Jackson closes the door behind us.

"I swear my parents have their own room," I say. "My mom just likes sleeping on the couch from time to time."

Jackson doesn't reply. He takes in my room, starting with the framed photos of you on my bed. Outside, stories of you with him can prick and stab me. But here in my room, where memories of you are leaping off the bed and shelves and walls and desk, we're on my turf. I can use our history as a weapon if I want to. Except I don't. I'm not going to take your death out on him, especially not with you watching.

I can't watch him.

Jackson moves over to my bed, hovering over the photos

before finally picking up the one of you smiling at me from the bench. "What was the occasion?" he asks quietly.

"My parents' anniversary, couple Aprils ago," I say. "They've been together since they were seventeen, I think. I don't know, my dad claims sixteen and my mom says seventeen, but I think they're counting different anniversaries, if you get what I'm saying." I shouldn't look at that photo with Jackson here because I might crack, but I miss seeing your smile outside my memory, so I join him. "That was a chill afternoon."

"Your parents have a good marriage?"

"Yeah, they're great. I get confused sometimes when I walk into a room and find them talking and laughing. I figured they would've said everything that's to be said by now, you know? Nope. They never shut the hell up, and I love it." Only then do I realize he's asking because of his own parents.

Jackson sits down on my desk chair, shrugging in his big coat. He glances up at me, clearly bummed out, then looks back at the wedding anniversary photo. "I'm not even going to pretend you haven't had the same dreams as me. I know you loved Theo like that, too."

Love. I love you; this isn't a past-tense love.

He doesn't wait for me to say anything before he goes on. "But people don't take me seriously, like I'm not allowed to be destroyed over Theo and love because I'm not even old enough to legally drink. My dad actually had the balls to tell me I have the rest of my life to fall in love again."

"Sounds like you need to skip some weekend visits when you're back home."

Jackson sneers. "He won't notice or care. He works for the airline, so it'll free up his weekend to either stay in another city and meet women at bars or—sorry, I'll shut up." Not entirely sure what he's apologizing for, but he's always saying sorry for something, right? Now he's staring at me. "Do you feel defeated, too? It reminds me of this race I was in where I was in the lead and fell and busted my knee, and everything I was running toward was done."

I hope this isn't his sly way of telling me he thinks he was winning you over. If there was ever a time for him to be apologizing over something, it's now. "I was running the same race, Jackson. And you weren't in the lead."

"I wasn't talking about you, I swear. I just never counted myself worthy enough to score a dude like Theo. That's what I meant about being in the lead," Jackson says.

I avoid his eyes. "Sorry."

"I get it. You and Theo grew up together and were each other's firsts for pretty much everything. But you do get that I loved him, too, right? And he loved me, even though I sometimes had trouble believing it because of you. I don't know why it matters so much to me, but I wish you wouldn't write off what he and I had, especially since every couple has to start somewhere. You just beat me to the punch."

I think I'm supposed to say something here. But I can't.

"You're pissed, aren't you? Look, talk to me. Whenever Theo and I were disagreeing about something, we always talked it out immediately. If we let it build up, it would turn into something far worse than it had to be. Please talk to me, Griffin," Jackson says.

Shutting up and shutting down have always been what I do best during confrontation. You called me out on that. Still, I'm trying much harder than usual not to say something unforgivable. It's *your* forgiveness I'm gunning for here. Keeping my mouth shut about my problems with you is something I planned on being better at when we got together, especially after you told me how talking through stuff was working for you and Jackson. It's not that I didn't want to resolve any issues; I just didn't want to do it in the heat of the moment, when there was a chance I'd say something undercooked and hurtful.

But you threw some blows Jackson's way, too.

In the early months of your relationship, you turned to me whenever you two were fighting. Jackson didn't like how close we were, how you never let him cut me out of your life. Since I couldn't say anything bad about Jackson, I was forced to tell you to give it time, that everything would iron itself out. And every time you called me back, I hoped it was to tell me how you and Jackson broke up, how it wasn't ultimately about the fights but because of how much you still love and miss me. But without fail, the calls always went the route of, "We worked it out, just like you said. Thanks for hearing me out, Griff."

I sit down on my bed. I have no idea what to say now.

Jackson stands, zipping up his jacket. "I'm going to go." He walks toward my bedroom door. "I'm sorry I bothered you with all this." He stops and shoots me this disappointed look, not too different from the one I'd find on your face when I was camping out in my silent zone. "I'm sorry I tried, Griffin. I really thought you would get it."

Whether I like it or not, I have to speak up. Jackson also has history with you. I'm sure you both had inside jokes, favorite spots, pictures that will sting me but might be worth seeing to see your face again, stories that may introduce me to who you were out in California. There's a side of you I never saw. Jackson not only knew that side, he loved you for it.

"Don't go," I say. "You're right. We love the same guy, and it's weird, and he would want us to talk anyway, even about the stuff I don't want to hear or the things I'd rather keep to myself." I get up from my bed and go to my closet. I pull out the air mattress, the one my parents bought for the rare occasions they allowed you to sleep over after we started dating—not that we used it. "You should stay. It's gross outside. Maybe we can have a do-over tomorrow morning."

He hesitates. "You sure?"

I unroll the air mattress on the opposite side of my room, away from my bed. "Yeah, it's cool." I pull my phone charger out of the outlet, throwing it onto my bed, and plug in the air pump. It's noisy and might wake up my parents, but there's no way around that. It's a quarter to one, and I'm ready to pass out after I get to listen to your voice mail.

"Thanks, Griffin," he says quietly.

"No problem. I can get you something to wear." Out of habit I reach for your drawer and pull it open. I freeze for a second, taking in your four T-shirts, two pairs of pajamas, gym shorts—even though you hate the gym—socks, a Monopoly onesie you brought over as a joke, and a hoodie. I'm never dressing Jackson in your clothes. I close your drawer and open one of mine, tossing out a long-sleeved shirt I've outgrown and pajamas onto the air mattress. "Do you want some water?"

"If you don't mind, thanks."

I leave my room, pee, brush my teeth, tiptoe around the kitchen while getting two glasses of water, and return to find Jackson in my clothes. I hand him his glass. I'm still thrown off by his presence—this guy I've wanted nothing to do with—by how he is actually spending the night in a room where I did everything with you from sleeping to sex, playing video games to putting together puzzles, fighting and trading weird kisses, bad karaoke and slow dancing to no music—this place of being ourselves and being each other's, and so much in between and everything else.

I grab him a comforter from the closet, a pillow from my bed. It's all stuff only I used, not what you used; those stay with me. I'm left with three pillows, so I toss him a second without explaining why.

"I'm passing out," I say, switching off the light. Jackson is hit with a slant of moonlight. "Bathroom is to the left of my room if you need it."

"Thanks," Jackson whispers, like I'm already sleeping. "Good night."

I roll into bed, still in my jeans and your hoodie, and turn my back on him. I hug your pillow to my chest and rest my face where you used to rest yours. My phone is dying, but I connect my headphones and press PLAY on your voice mail, over and over.

In the middle of the fourth listening, Jackson calls out to me.

"Griffin? Sorry, Griffin, you awake?"

"Yeah?" I stare at the wall.

"Thanks for giving me a shot. I see now why Theo never shut up about you."

I don't respond. But I put the phone down. I press my face deeper into the pillow, squeezing my eyes shut, and I do my damn best to fall asleep, but my ear tugging and need to cry keep me awake. You kept me alive when we were apart. I promise I'll always do the same for you.

JACKSON'S CRYING WAKES ME up. He's trying to suppress it, but it keeps slipping out. He sounds a lot like me the past few days, how I'd give in to the grief but make sure I wasn't loud enough to draw attention from those who think words will make me feel better. I can't turn around because if the bed creaks, he'll know I'm awake. I don't know how to comfort this outsider.

Jackson, like me, loves you. Also like me, he is stuck in this universe without you. I know what you'd say: there are limitless alternate universes. Is there one where you've decided to watch over Jackson from the afterlife? No, that's wrong. Even Jackson said you were always talking about me. I refuse to believe I'm living in a universe where you're not even with me in death. I refuse to believe that you're hurting for him right now as he cries, tilting your telescope a little bit to the left to find me wide awake, not doing anything to comfort him. You must think I'm the worst human ever, and I swear I'm not. I've made some mistakes, sure, and if you've already caught on, I'm sorry, but I can't reverse time and undo them. You'll have to forgive me.

That's assuming you're in this universe, that you're watching, Theo.

HISTORY
FRIDAY, OCTOBER 31ST, 2014

The haunted mansion jigsaw puzzle I'm piecing together with Wade on Theo's bedroom floor is really coming together. I'm not sure if this is good or bad. It's a two-hundred-piece puzzle we're spending time on instead of partying with everyone else on Halloween.

Wade looks up, holding the piece needed to crown the ghost king, tapping it against the shattered windows of the mansion. He's dressed as Doctor Who. "Hey, Theo? Would you mind hurrying the hell up?" he asks. "How often does Halloween land on a Friday?"

"More so than it lands on Friday the thirteenth," Theo says without missing a beat. He's not even fully dressed up yet. He's still at his computer, reworking his early-admissions essay.

"I was eleven when I said that," I moan. "Let it go."

I love Theo, but I also really love Halloween. There's a party in Brooklyn with fog machines and karaoke and a deejay and, above all, a costume contest we're all trying to get to, but Theo's essay is due at midnight. He was going to submit it at 7:00 until he made the big mistake of reading it one last time. Turns out he no longer believes in everything he spent the past month writing about. Now it's 9:45—odd minute—and we're still here in his fog-less, karaoke-less, deejay-less room.

At least there are costumes. No one here is really a fan of *Doctor Who*. But Wade is wearing this tweedy jacket, red bowtie, matching fedora, and carrying around some wandlike stick—all because of Shania, the party's host, a big *Doctor Who* fan and Wade's latest crush. Since Wade doesn't care about the character, a bet has started up. Every time Wade is called "black Doctor Who," Theo owes Wade a dollar.

Of course, Theo and I are in the greatest getups this universe has ever seen: zombie pirates. It's a tribute to our relationship, obviously, but it's also just stupid, goofy fun. Tonight I'm Griffy the shipmate, who was slain by One-Eyed Theo the Bloody—except Theo still doesn't have a single drop of fake blood on him that didn't come from hugging me.

"How much more time do you need?" Wade asks. "I'm sure your essay is fine."

"If I were shooting for 'fine' we would've been out the door a week ago," Theo says, spinning away from his laptop to glare at us. "Everything could change if I get everything right here, okay?" He rarely gets this fed up. In his eyes there are few emergencies in the world worth freaking out over. "I would have to be really dumb to think I'm the smartest dude out here. There are so many candidates more qualified than me, and I'm not counting on them screwing up their essays for me to get in. I have to be the best." He hides his face in his hands. "Sorry. You guys should probably head out without me."

Wade glances at me, silently asking if we should leave.

"You go ahead," I tell him. "Good luck with Shania."

"Good luck with the essay, Theo," Wade says. "I'll send you the black Doctor Who bill."

Once he bounces, I kneel in front Theo, taking his hands in mine. I see his eyes are red. My own eyes widen. "What's going on?" This is the closest I've ever seen him come to crying.

"It's the changes, Griff. I now have it in my head that I want to be in college by next year. I know it's not all good things if I get accepted. It's a year away, and I already know I'm going to miss you so hard." Theo sinks to the floor with me, wraps my arm around his shoulders, and rests his face against my chest. "You know I love you."

"I love you, too."

"I love the idea of college, too. I hope that doesn't break us. I just always sort of thought high school was this game with scores that don't matter, but I'm wrong. The right people are paying attention. In some alternate universe where I didn't get off on being top of the class, I probably would've slacked and missed out on this opportunity."

"But you didn't miss it," I point out. "You're rewriting this thing for the fourth time because you care so much about it."

"If I don't get accepted, it's going to feel like a huge blow."

"That's a lot of pressure, Theo. It's pressure you weren't counting on being under for another year," I remind him. I massage his arm and take a deep breath. It's never been easy finding the right words to comfort someone so brilliant. "You're not just someone with good grades, Theo." I wait for him to correct me with something cute like "astronomically amazing grades" or "the greatest grades in all the land," but he doesn't have it in him right now. "You're not someone that just memorizes facts for exams and forgets them the next day. You don't just have lucky guesses in pop quizzes. You bring textbooks with you into the shower. Basically, you're a really weird superhero."

He forces a smile. "One day, Batman is going to take off his mask and, boom, it'll be me."

"Robin is hotter, but I'll settle."

Theo looks up at me and I lean forward and kiss him.

"How'd I do?" I ask. "With the pep talk?"

"I'm motivated," Theo says. "And feeling guilty you're not out there enjoying your favorite holiday. Get out of here."

I pull off my eye patch and throw it across the room. "That thing is itchy anyway." I stand, pulling him up with me. "You're taking a two-minute recess before diving back into the essay." Theo seems a little anxious, but he's okay with giving me two minutes in exchange for my Halloween. "My parents taught me these kisses when I was younger."

I lean in to his face, like I'm going in for a kiss, but I brush his eyelashes against mine and wait for him to do the same. "That's a butterfly kiss."

"Kind of tickles," Theo says.

I bump his forehead with mine a couple of times. "That's a caveman kiss."

"I didn't know cave people were so romantic."

I rub his nose against mine, not stopping until Theo mimics me. "That's an Eskimo kiss." I want a fourth kiss now, something special like these. "My parents only taught me three, but I'll figure out another now . . . uh . . ." I look out the window where the streets are alive and undead from Halloween. "Here's a zombie kiss." I nibble on his cheek, growling. I bust out laughing when Theo returns his own zombie kiss.

"I like the zombie kiss best," Theo says. "Screw college, let's have sex instead."

"Your parents and Denise are here."

"Screw them too."

I smile. "Nope. I'm helping you with your essay. Come on." I point to his desk chair and he sighs. But he can't sit still and starts pacing.

The question is simple: What creation are you proudest of?

Theo had originally wanted to talk up some of his animation videos, but tonight he changed his mind; he's super proud of his alternate universes. Together we look through his journal. We're standing by the window, but I'm not even the slightest bit distracted by all the Harry Potters and slutty dinosaurs walking the streets. Theo is practically walking me through his brain, a tour of his imagination, and we're both lost in it, lost in why this universe we live in beats the rest. We're two zombie pirates who aren't leaving the ship to feed on brains, but there's definitely a greater voyage ahead.

Anyway, we always have next Halloween.

TODAY
FRIDAY, NOVEMBER 25TH, 2016

Good morning, Theo. Sorry I shut down on you last night. I couldn't shake off that haunting suspicion you're hovering over Jackson instead of me. It was like some itch speeding around my body, always a second too late from scratching it dead. Don't roll your eyes, but I did some soul searching. I dug deep into our history and remembered all our good times and the happy memories that would've eventually brought you back to me in life. I no longer believe I'm in this alone, talking to myself.

I am still questioning how often you're looking around for Jackson, though.

Jackson.

I haven't forgotten he's here. His crying stirred a tornado of sympathy and rage in me, and while I remained firm against the force of that grief, I am definitely battered. I should've turned around to see if he'd worn himself out and fallen asleep or lay awake staring at walls like me, but I couldn't bring myself to do it.

Jackson was right: yesterday was a bad start for him and me. I don't even know what it's the start of. Thankfully there's no school today, so I don't have to spend this morning fighting with my parents to let me stay home or zombie-walking between classes when they send me anyway. Jackson and I will use the time attempting a do-over for you.

I sit up when my phone flashes 8:02. When I turn, Jackson isn't in bed. The comforter is flat on the air mattress, Jackson's clothes are on the floor, but he's not here. I leave my room to see if he's in the bathroom showering or something and find the bathroom door wide open. I hear the loud clatter of my mom's laptop keys. You always joked with her about it, accusing her of trying to look busy so she wouldn't have to answer your probing questions about what she was like as a teen.

In the living room, I find Mom at the dining room table with Jackson, who's sitting in your seat. I wonder if Mom told him it was your seat or if he felt drawn to the seat because of you. Maybe it's a total coincidence.

"I'm sorry about that," Mom is saying. At first I think she's apologizing to me, but she closes her laptop and looks up at Jackson. "Some clients didn't get the notice I'm supposed to be email-free today. So, you're skipping the rest of your semester?"

"My professors have been understanding, but I don't have it in me," Jackson says.

"Same," I say, joining them at the table. I sit opposite of Jackson, like I normally did whenever it was you in that seat, and I keep my eyes on the bagel in front of him. "Except no one's giving me a time-out, so I'm pretty much going to fail everything."

"There's still time to turn everything around," Mom says gently.

She goes on about conversations she's had with my teachers about extra credit and issuing me hall passes so I can run to my guidance counselor's office whenever. But she loses me when I look up. I'm reregistering why Jackson Wright is here, in my apartment, in my clothes.

In a lot of ways, Jackson is a clone of me. Our hazel eyes are strained from sleeplessness and crying, framed with pale black bags darker than the ones I got last summer from when we spent an entire week playing Xbox games online until morning. His bagel has barely been touched, and I bet he's also been eating just enough lately to shut up his growling stomach. He's also unable to operate through schoolwork and everything else life demands; he loves you and you loved him.

"Griffin? Griffin?" Mom grabs my hand and squeezes.

"Sorry." I slide my hand out from under hers. "Got lost in my head again." I hide my hand under the table so Jackson doesn't see me scratching my palm.

"No need to apologize." My mom stands and picks up her laptop. "I'm going to go wake up your father."

I don't know when he made his way over to the bedroom, but hopefully my mom catches him up on why Jackson is here.

"How'd you sleep?" I ask him. Playing dumb is another form of lying, I know.

Jackson shrugs and avoids my eyes. "You know."

I don't know if he means *you know how it is* or *you know damn well I didn't sleep very well,* but I'm not investigating further.

"Have you spoken to Russell or Ellen?"

"I called Ellen an hour ago. It sounds like they're all relaxing this morning." Jackson picks up his bagel and looks like he's about to spin it like a quarter before looking up at me with flushed cheeks; maybe this is something he does at home or did with you. "Thanks again for letting me stay last night. I thought about heading back out this morning to give you your space, but your mom was awake when I came out here to call Ellen."

"Did she recognize you from the funeral?" And the playing dumb continues, because my mom is admittedly pretty familiar with photos of Jackson. I showed her the online album you made of you two. I wanted her to tell me I'm not crazy for seeing a resemblance between him and me.

"She did, yeah," Jackson says, and cringes a little. "There's no denying she was really surprised to see me."

I imagine she was as shocked as all the funeral attendees who witnessed two boys at your funeral, their awkward competitiveness, each delivering a eulogy about the love of his life. Until this morning my mom had never seen another boy coming out of my bedroom who wasn't you. "My bad. I should've left her a note on the whiteboard so she knew you were here."

"She played it cool," Jackson says. He leans toward me and lowers his voice. "I got to ask you something. Please answer honestly. I wouldn't ask something if I didn't think I could handle it. All right?"

He's going to ask something crazy intimate about you, Theo; I can feel it. Maybe he's bold enough to ask about our first time or why I broke up with you.

"Do you hate me?" Jackson blurts out. "I know we don't know each other. But I get it if you hate or hated me. I guess I want to know where we stand without Theo."

This breakfast is even weirder than the first breakfast you forgot me—the one a few weeks after we broke up, where you didn't send me a picture of what you were eating with some pretentious caption. Your pictures always had a 90 percent chance of making me smile and feel okay about actually getting out of bed. But Jackson Wright in my living room, asking me if I hate him? That is definitely stranger.

I'm about to try and answer him, when my parents walk out of their room together.

"Gregor, this is Jackson," Mom says.

Jackson stands and holds out his hand. Every second Dad doesn't shake it, I feel guiltier and guiltier for being the source of his resistance, with all my hating and crying. He finally gives in, probably remembering he's an adult who must put that ahead of being a father when another kid is involved—especially a kid who must already be uncomfortable as hell in our house.

"Morning," Dad says. He quickly moves to the couch. "How long are you in town for?"

"I'm flying back on Monday," Jackson says, standing. "I should actually make my way back over to Theo's house now." He tries to take his plate to the kitchen sink, but my mom intercepts him, the way she always intercepted you. He turns to both my parents. "Thank you for breakfast and for being cool with me staying over."

He walks back to my room and I follow him, leaning against the threshold.

"You good?" I ask.

Jackson sits on the air mattress, his head hanging low as he flips his phone around in his palms like one of those finger-sized skateboards. "Are *you* good?"

"Of course not."

"Same here."

Jackson puts his phone down, folds his comforter, picks his clothes up from the floor, and heads to the bathroom without a word.

I twist open the air mattress's nozzle, staring while it deflates, the piercing whistle quieting down as the bed folds into itself. I throw everything in the closet, including the pillow he slept on. I'm drained. I would be game for a nap. I owe him another shot, though. I know it.

Jackson returns from the bathroom and hands me the clothes he slept in. "Thanks again for letting me crash, Griffin. I'm going to hail a cab."

"Save your money," I say, pretty unaware what his cash situation is, though I'm going to go ahead and guess average. "I can walk you there." I grab my peacoat to throw over your hoodie.

"Isn't it really cold outside?"

"Probably not that bad." I check the temperature on my phone's app. "Okay, it's pretty cold out, but I'm sure you could use some fresh air too." I pull on my boots and grab my phone and keys. "Especially if you're just going to stay in the apartment all weekend."

"You're right. Thanks, Griffin." He gets suited up in his jacket and single glove. I'm tempted to look for an extra pair of gloves, but he's already hurrying for the door. In the living room he waves at my parents; you would know better, but I can't tell if his wave is halfhearted or hesitant. "Thanks again for breakfast, Mrs. and Mr. Jennings. I hope you both have a nice weekend."

I never gave him my last name. I'm guessing you did or Facebook told him. But I catch a glimpse of what you must have seen, and not just from his manners. He's definitely got that pull-over-to-rescue-a-boy-from-the-rain heart.

"Have a safe flight home." My dad doesn't get up from the couch; he barely looks up from his laptop. He's undoubtedly playing one of those puzzle games you got him into so he could keep his mind sharp on days off and weekends. "Where are you going, Griffin?"

"I'm going to walk him back to Theo's." I'll always call it your place, even if you never spent a single dollar on rent, even if you're not physically living there anymore. "I want to go for a walk anyway."

Neither of my parents will protest. They're well aware the alternative will be me camping out in my room, listening to your voice mail on continuous loop.

"Sounds good. Call us if your plans change." Mom gets off her laptop and comes over to shake Jackson's hand. "I'm sorry again for . . ." She cuts herself off, her eyes darting around. I really hope she wasn't about to call you Jackson's loss—*again.* "Good luck deciding what you'll do about school."

I lead the way out without saying anything.

Jackson follows me down the staircase, and I don't know if he can sense my shift in attitude, but I need to get my act together before that final step so I don't take it out on him—*again.* I hate that word right now, and probably always will, since it's been tagged with this very moment of betrayal and disappointment; this kind of haunting is why people have to watch what they say and what they do. I hit the last step and am still carrying this ugliness on me, and I can't shake it off of me any more than I can shake off my grief or shame. I'm like a coin constantly flipping—heads, tails, heads, tails, heads, tails, heads, tails—like someone tossed me into the air to settle something once and for all but didn't catch me, and now I'm falling into an abyss, unable to see what will come up when I land.

I hide my hand in my jacket pocket. I scratch my palm in peace.

I'm tempted to take Jackson down my usual route to your house, but it'll stir too many memories.

"Let's pop a left," I say, turning away from the supermarket and car rental place at the last second. "You have friends in New York, right?"

"Sort of. My pals Anika and Veronika are studying theater at NYU. We went to high school together back home, but it's one of those friendships where distance ruins everything." Jackson shrugs. "I miss them, but I can see online they're doing just fine without me."

"How close were you three?"

"We've been tight since freshman year. It was the first meeting for the Dungeons & Dragons club and we wanted to join, but I could tell they were as hesitant as I was about what that would mean for our high school status. I don't know, we were being fourteen, I guess."

So: Jackson is one of those eighteen-year-olds who speaks about being fourteen like it was ten lifetimes ago. I bet you found that charming.

"By junior year we got over all that nonsense, but since Anika's ex-boyfriend was in the Dungeons & Dragons club, we formed our own after-school club at Anika's house and made up our own game, Cages & Chimaeras. Theo even . . ."

You *what?*

"Theo what?" I ask out loud.

"Theo got to play the game with Anika and Veronika in February when we were here."

I didn't know this. I wanted to hang out with you, of course, but there's no way I was willing to suffer through watching you hold Jackson's hand or laugh at his jokes. I nod politely, which Jackson completely misses because he's not looking at me.

"Why don't you reach out while you're here?" I ask.

"Anika and Veronika are both home for Thanksgiving. I think they're coming back the day I leave, which sucks. They wanted to Skype chat, but . . ." He shuts himself up again. I'm ready to challenge him again to tell me more, but he stops. We're in front of the window of Game Express—my favorite video game store. You have to admit that even though you were always more of a GameStop loyalist, Game Express never let you down, because of the discounts. "Are you cool with going in here for a minute or two?"

"Yeah, let's go."

I can find you in there.

The warmth inside feels good. I don't recognize the young woman behind the counter, and I would definitely remember someone with blue-streaked hair and yellow contacts: a demon vibe. It's really cool. But I shouldn't be surprised about new faces. I haven't been here since earlier this summer, and even that visit wasn't for very long.

"They have a lot of Game Boy stuff," Jackson muses. He picks up a couple of bargain games from a bucket, dropping them back in a second later.

"Yeah, it's great."

There's nothing I want to buy, so I just follow Jackson around as he tours the store—my favorite, not yours—for the first time. At least I think he's never been here before. I don't know why you would've walked with Jackson over here in the winter unless you were trying to bump into me and mess with my head or make me miss you more. Let me shut up or you'll think I'm back to my old paranoid self. I swear I've improved. I swear I have a better grip on reality these days.

Jackson spends a lot of time with the Xbox games. He checks out a racing game, a fighting game, and a spy game before moving on.

I stop him. "Anything else here catching your eye?"

"Not really."

"I was counting the games you looked at and you stopped at three . . ."

"Okay." He's confused.

"I have this thing with numbers. I prefer things to be done in evens."

"I didn't even hear you counting."

"I was counting in my head. I'm always counting in my head. Sometimes I don't even realize it, but I know I am." I know how this sounds, and I want to be able to tell him and the rest of the world that it's okay, that we don't have to get caught up on odd occurrences like this, but I know it won't be okay—if I can control something for my sanity, I want to give myself that relief. "Three makes me really anxious in ways that one doesn't because things often come in ones, so three marks the first odd number where I'm always anticipating a fourth whatever. I can't focus otherwise."

Jackson nods and picks up some discounted Halo sequel. It doesn't feel as natural as the first three games he reviewed so I'm tempted to ask him to check out two more games. That way I'll have two sets of three, and I can clock out of this moment with a glowing six, but I accept it and move on.

"Thanks," I say.

If he's judging me, I can't read it on him. I don't believe he has that ugliness inside of him, truthfully, unlike some of my classmates these past few months—you know nothing about this—as my compulsions worsened.

"Anytime," Jackson says. He continues cruising the aisles, and every now and again I catch him glancing at me; it's possible I've ruined his browsing experience by making him extra conscious of doing everything in even numbers. But maybe not. He seems relaxed here, like he's ditched his grief at the door, unaware it will continue stalking him the moment we leave. His peace reminds me of you on the floor in front of a puzzle.

We wander over to a display of classics. Your weight pins me down even more when I see those cartridges lined up. I never owned any of these consoles, but you were obsessed: the first PlayStation and Nintendo, Sega Genesis, the short-lived Dreamcast, and a bulky Game Boy that couldn't possibly fit in anyone's pocket. I smile in spite of myself at the dusty glass shelves, remembering times I played some of them with you or watched you kick ass while I did homework: *Pac-Man*, *Space Invaders*, *Earthworm Jim*, *Sonic*, *Mortal Kombat*, *Batman*, on and on.

"It's like a flea market," Jackson says.

"Except not." I point to a NOT FOR SALE sign. "I like that it's just a shrine."

"Bonus points for it not being in a museum."

I spot a cartridge on a lower shelf. *Tetris*. I sit on my knees. Jackson crouches and joins me.

"His favorite," Jackson says.

The comment doesn't bother me the way others have because you playing *Tetris* isn't a very intimate detail. Hell, even your teachers knew about your *Tetris* addiction from all the times they confiscated your phone during class. Jackson presses his hand against the case. Maybe he's forgotten I'm there, here, right next to him.

I have a story for Jackson.

"Did Theo ever tell you about *Mac: The Family Curse*?"

"No."

"He hated it so much. I mean *most* people would hate it. But he thought it would be perfect because it was this game where you get around doing physics-based puzzles. But there were so many glitches that Theo charged himself with going back to the store to buy out all the copies so no one else had to suffer through it. I bet him two dollars he wouldn't do it. I lost."

Jackson laughs a little, which is awesome because this was basically a forty-dollar joke on you—well, thirty-eight-dollar joke, since you made two bucks back.

"He ranted about the game for days. Sometimes I would wake up to a text about something else he hated about it or found illogical." I'm smiling again, and this time I'm smiling *with* him, which is a nice little recess from confusion and heartache and guilt and unhappiness. It's the kind of relief I felt whenever I was stuck home sick, missing your face and voice, and then you would call me the second school was over and I would feel whole again. I would give everything to be able to play *Tetris* with you right now. Knowing I can't rips away the moment and banishes me back to this empty universe.

"I'll wait for you outside," I tell Jackson.

I get up and leave so quickly I'm sure the blue-haired cashier thinks I probably pocketed a Yoshi key chain or something. The cold air bites my face, a useless zombie kiss. Jackson joins me a few seconds later, empty-handed. If he was planning on shopping—shitty timing to buy a game, if so—I totally ruined that for him.

"I'm sorry I made you talk about him," he says. "I didn't know that story. It's weird, but it's cool to learn something new about him instead of remembering all our good times, you know?"

"It's good to talk about him," I agree. "It always is." But it sucks that I'm talking about you, and to you, and that you can't talk back—something Jackson will be going back to California not ever knowing. "I know talking about Theo keeps him alive. But that doesn't make it any less hard that he isn't walking around here, keeping *himself* alive."

Jackson nods and pockets his hands, shivering. That's all. He's staring at me the same way that I'm staring at him—in misery.

I won't lie to him about how I'm sure this will get better, and he doesn't try consoling me with any of that nonsense, either. I move to his left and lead us back toward your house.

"HERE WE ARE."

He stands in front of the door, waiting to be buzzed in without having even looked at the intercom. So I guess he was used to getting let in when he stayed here in February. I press 2B for him while he bounces up and down. He's either warming himself up or really has to pee, not that he would've said so during our completely silent walk over here.

"Who is it?" Ellen calls down through the speaker.

Jackson answers for himself and adds my name. Ellen buzzes us in.

"I wasn't actually planning on going up," I tell Jackson. "I just wanted to walk you back."

"Don't you want to see everyone?"

"Of course I do, especially Denise. But, I don't know, I want to respect their grieving period too and not move in on their space." I've thought about this a lot, but I never planned on telling Jackson, the ghost who's haunting your home right now. "I didn't mean that as a shot against you. I know your options were pretty limited, especially with your friends back home this week."

"Can I be honest with you?" Jackson says. He moves deeper into the lobby, avoiding the chill that keeps creeping in through the front door. "It'd be nice to have you up there with me, even just for a few minutes."

He's a puzzle piece that doesn't fit. And he knows it.

I can only imagine your face if I said no to Jackson right now; I'm sure it would look a lot like the face you made the last time I saw you. But I don't want to think about that; forget I brought it up. That's taboo.

"Let's go up," I tell Jackson.

I barely register Jackson thanking me. Up the staircase we go toward your apartment, and I don't want to be here; it's too soon. It will always be too soon. Time doesn't heal all wounds. We both know that's bullshit; it comes from people who have nothing comforting or original to say. But I wonder if others keep up with this lie because they don't want to speak the harsh truth. The wound never closes and the pain remains, always piercing, always burning, always suffocating, always bleeding.

Ellen greets us at the door. She isn't waving with her fingers like usual. It might have something to do with how it isn't you and me returning from a movie, but instead two boys who love you. "Good morning."

"Morning," Jackson says, slipping past her.

"Morning, Ellen." I step inside, hugging her once she closes the door. She hugs me back; it's the first time we've held each other since losing you. In this one hug I no longer feel like she is disappointed in me for breaking up with you, that she still sees me as her other son. In that instant, I'm glad I let Jackson convince me to be here.

Ellen takes me by the arm. "Let me make you boys some iced tea."

I'll say it long after the zombie pirates have won: anyone who rejects your mother's iced tea—even during winter—hates happiness. I follow her into the kitchen and everything looks the same, except for the addition of a round table by the window. Jackson sits first. I grab four glasses—an extra for Denise—to distract myself from trying to figure out what happened to the old (perfectly fine) table, and wondering if this new one has been here for so long that Ellen wouldn't even consider it new anymore. I sit beside Jackson, and Ellen begins her routine, slicing fresh lemons for us.

"Theo would've wanted all of this, right?" Ellen says quietly. "Did you have a good evening?"

"It was good," Jackson says.

I don't know what else to add. I hear the tinkle of piano keys off in the living room. "That Denise playing?"

"Should be." Ellen peeks into the next room while stirring the iced tea. "Good, Russell is with her. My sister forwarded some article to me on Wednesday or Tuesday . . . the days are scrambled; it doesn't matter. She sent me an article about distracting children from their grief by forcing them to stick to their routines." She pours us iced tea. "It's worth a shot."

"Totally." My routines calm me down when they're not turning me inside out.

Ellen checks her watch. "We're taking her to her friend Mitali's house in a little bit." Without another word, she ducks out into the living room.

I remember Mitali. She's the fast-talker. Your parents hosted that detective birthday party for her, years ago. Mitali and Denise and a bunch of other girls whose names even I don't remember insisted on being called "grown-up detectives" instead of "kid detectives" and took it way too seriously, but we played along. You were the murder victim in the living room, surrounded by "yellow crime scene tape"—*cough*, party streamers, *cough*—until you got up for a water break while they were investigating their latest clue in Denise's bedroom. Big mistake. Mitali rushed out and said you were cheating. The best part: she accused me of being a bad doctor for being wrong about your being dead. I wish you were cheating at death this time, too.

I down the iced tea and place my glass in the sink. Jackson and I follow Ellen into the living room. On the couch are folded blankets and a pillow. Maybe staying in your bed was too much, and Jackson camped out there. I don't ask him.

Ellen crouches beside Denise, who is sitting on the piano bench with Russell, and grabs her hand in both of hers. "We have to head out in a bit. Mitali's father said he's making the apple pie you love. Do you want help pick out something cute to wear?"

"I can dress myself," Denise says. Her voice is flat. She pulls her hands out of your mother's, swings off the bench, sees me, turns away, and returns for a double take and her eyes widen. "Griffin!" She charges toward me and hugs me around my waist; I don't think I fully registered at the funeral how freaking big she's getting.

"What's up, Dee?"

"What are you doing here?"

The answer is awkward, but I owe it to your sister to tell the truth. "Jackson stayed over at my house last night, and I walked him back over here."

Denise's face scrunches up, and she looks back and forth between Jackson and me. "I thought you two hated each other."

Something you said to me once: *The world should stop lying to kids because they're always brutally honest with us.*

"Denise!" Ellen scolds.

"Denise, geez," Russell says.

Her cheeks flush. I hate that she's embarrassed over this.

"Griffin and I just haven't had a chance to be friends yet," Jackson says. I feel like he's talking down to her a little bit; don't you? I don't think he means to, but maybe he hasn't spent enough time around kids. More importantly, he doesn't deny her claim. He really thinks I hate him, and even though I don't want to set him on fire or curse him to die a thousand deaths, I'm not sure he's wrong.

"Yeah." That's the best I got.

Then Ellen forces Denise to get ready for apple pie and play-time with her chatty friend, who is bound to go on and on about typical nine-year-old stuff that she can't possibly care about any-more. Losing you is going to be her express ticket to adulthood, I bet.

I sit on the couch, fighting away the memories, keeping my eyes off your closed door straight ahead. Russell is sitting on the edge of the piano bench, his face in his hands. I don't know what to say, so I bring up the routines because talking about normalcy seems, well, normal.

"Yeah. The *routines*," Russell growls. "I'm sure Virginia will send El another psychobabble article on the drive over to Mitali's, and we'll drop everything to try that out." He gets up and pulls a pack of cigarettes out of his bathrobe pocket. "Could you let El know I'll be outside by the car?"

I've never seen Russell bounce so quickly. He doesn't seem to remember or care he's in a bathrobe.

It's only a couple of minutes before Ellen and Denise emerge from the bedroom, dressed in new clothes for the playdate. Ellen's eyes dart around with the same intensity as on those mornings she would drive us to the arcade in New Rock and you were still in the shower. "Where's Russell?"

Jackson points with his thumb toward the front door. "Stepped out."

"He said he'll be by the car," I add.

If Ellen is trying to mask her annoyance, she's failing. She takes a deep breath and tosses a ring of keys onto the couch between Jackson and me. "You boys know where everything is. Griffin, you're welcome to hang around, of course. Jackson, if you step out, don't forget the keys. We should be back in a couple of hours."

Denise gives me a hug and Jackson a high five on her way out.

"I won't hang around long," I tell Jackson once we're alone.

"I'm not kicking you out," Jackson says.

"I know." I definitely don't plan on being here when your parents and sister return; it's just too much on them, you know. "It's hard being here . . . I don't know how the hell you're doing it."

"Without choice," Jackson answers.

"Right. It's good that you were here." I mean that.

"No way was I going to miss his funeral," Jackson says.

I get up and go toward your bedroom door. I'm pretty damn aware you won't be on the other side, hunched over your desk, drafting a rough sketch of a universe you hope to bring to life in an animation. I'm still tempted to knock anyway.

"I haven't gone inside," Jackson says.

I turn away from your door. "What? I thought you were sleeping there."

"Hell no. Would you have been able to?"

I've imagined this scenario before and find myself in your bed, always. But I missed being in your room with you long before you died.

"Have you seen his parents in there?"

"Russell a couple times, yeah."

"Did anyone say they didn't want you in there?"

Jackson shakes his head.

I turn back to the door and grab the doorknob. "I'm going in. You can do what you want, but I—"

"I'll go with you," Jackson says. I feel his fast footsteps on the floor.

He stands to my left, but instead of releasing the doorknob and switching sides, I close the space between me and the door so he's no longer directly beside me. I'm even closer to you now. I turn the doorknob. Here we are, at the main exhibit of the McIntyre Museum.

I want to tell you what it's like being surrounded by these light-blue walls again. Our framed puzzles are still there: the astronaut waiting for the train, my favorite; the map of Brazil, which was brutal but fun to piece together; an open suitcase containing another suitcase piled high with Russian nesting dolls; and Pompeii, our very first. If I had to take a shot at describing what it's like, I would call it my resurrection.

But this wonder, this second life, is short-lived. All the air is squeezed out of me when I see photos of you and Jackson on the windowsill beside your bed. Right where our photos used to be. Your arm is wrapped around Jackson's shoulder in one, and your smile is really wide; it's an image I'm familiar with, of course, which is why it feels so out of place. I turn away from the window before the other photos stab me, before I flip out on Jackson, demanding to know if he made you take our pictures down. But I only find more foreign objects. Next to the graphic novels I gave you is a boxed set of four mass-market thrillers. I don't know if it's a gift from Jackson or completely unrelated. The dream catcher on the floor is new too, and I don't know if it's from some special event with Jackson, like the Batman figure I got designed with your face, which is still perched on top of your bookcase.

I don't want to ask Jackson anything. I was wrong before. I don't want to be clued in to your life without me. I can't do this. I run out, almost tripping over myself. Jackson is calling for me, but I can't be with him right now, so I charge out of your apartment and down the stairs.

Thank God I never took off my jacket because it's freezing out here. I stop running at the corner, shaking. I look to the sky, squinting at the sun between the clouds, before closing my eyes to see your face in my memory more clearly.

But the you I'm remembering isn't the same you I found upstairs in your room.

You were finally able to speak back to me, Theo, and I don't like everything you had to say.

I'M BEAT DOWN BY the time I walk through the front door. One of the lessons I've learned over and over since our breakup and your death is how the pain becomes physical. My body aches. I'm so drained, you would think it was like the time we rode our bikes around Central Park for three laps—the number still bothers me—and we powered up that steep hill. My stomach tightened, my legs burned, my arms were sore, and my throat was dry. I'm just as ready for a nap now as I was then.

I go straight for my room, ignoring my mom as she closes her laptop and calls for me. She shouts for my dad to let him know I'm home, but alone time means only you and me. Not Mom, not Dad. I walk into my room, close my door, and throw myself on my bed, too drained even to cry. I hope you don't think this means I'm grieving you any less. Blame it on my body. I'm burrowing into our pillows when my door opens. True to my idiot nature, I forgot something key in the game of warding off unwanted people: the lock. I wish I could vanish into one of my alternate universes right now.

"Did Jackson get back okay?" Mom asks.

"Yeah, Jackson is back at Theo's, where he's grieving *his* loss," I say, turning around and sitting up. "You were ready to call Theo Jackson's loss again, weren't you?"

She nods, like I actually needed her to confirm what was what. "You both loved him, Griffin. I'm not pretending his pain isn't there, too."

"Nope, that's Dad's job," I say.

"What did your father do?" Mom asks.

Dad stays quiet, probably debating whether or not he's going to arm up and go to battle with me.

"He made Jackson really uncomfortable . . . like, even *I* wasn't that cold to him," I say. I can only imagine being outside my state, outside my *time zone*, in the home of someone who tried to make an enemy out of me, feeling unwelcome and helpless.

"Cut it out, Griffin," Dad snaps. His tone reminds me of when I would get into trouble as a kid over little things, like trying to sneak into their bedroom to scare my mom while she was working, or yelling fake words over and over for attention. "You can't be pissed at your mother for being too nice to that guy and pissed at me for being too cold to him."

"So you admit you were cold to him?" I snap back.

"I won't deny it; I wasn't very welcoming. But that's because I know my son. I don't believe you're actually upset at your mother or me. We won't fight you if you don't fight us. What does Wade call us? Team Griffin?"

"The Griffin Squad," I correct.

"The Griffin Squad," Dad repeats. "We know seeing Jackson can't be easy, but you soldiered through it anyway. I hope it's helped you out in some way. If not, he's gone and you never have to see him again. But we're here for you and want to know what you need from us."

"I do need something," I say.

"What?" Mom asks.

"Space. Please give me some space. I'm really tired." I can't cry. I can't fight.

Dad begins protesting, but Mom shuts him up, thankfully. They're out in no time, and I find enough energy to close the door behind them, locking it this time. I get back in bed and crawl under my covers, expecting to fall asleep instantly. Of course I don't. Considering the week and year and month and life I've been having, I'm stupid to think I'd even be lucky with the small things.

HISTORY
THURSDAY, DECEMBER 25TH, 2014

This is the first year the squad isn't doing Secret Santa. We usually pull names out of Wade's fitted hat, but now that Theo and I are dating, there was no way we weren't going to get each other gifts on the side if one of us drew Wade's name. It's the kind of stuff that makes our relationship unfair to our friendship with Wade. We broke tradition, which Wade seemed a little bummed about, but he snapped out of it when he realized he'd be getting an extra gift.

Having already spent the morning and afternoons with our own families, it's nice to kick back in Wade's bedroom. We're listening to his jazz playlist on his new speakers. Theo holds out his phone and clicks on my name.

"Check out your new contact photo."

It's the photo I texted him this morning of me standing beside my Christmas tree, holding the Ron Weasley ornament he got me on the day our history began. It's wild how two seasons later, I'm still blushing because of this guy.

Wade must see it, because he distributes the presents Theo and I left underneath the mini Christmas tree when we first arrived.

Theo and I agreed at the beginning of the month that our presents had to be "thoughtfully random." It basically just meant I couldn't buy him a puzzle and he couldn't buy me anything Harry Potter–centric, which sucks because I got zero Harry Potter–related gifts this year for the first time since I don't know when. A key chain would've been appreciated. The gift Theo got me, a small box wrapped in emerald-green paper, makes me wonder if I put too much thought into my gift for him. Mine is in a big box.

We look at each other nervously.

We go in a circle, pushing Wade to go first.

Wade starts with mine, which is this little-known novel, *The Adventures of the Courtesan and Golem*. It's a dark comedy about a barren prostitute who steals a potion from her sorcerer client to create a child and ends up bringing a golem to life.

"I have no idea if it's good," I say, holding up my hands. "But you were dropping hints recently you'd be interested in giving fiction another shot if something different crossed your way. If you know more books like this, you need to stop hogging them and share."

Wade smiles. "Thanks a lot, Griff."

"Griffin," Theo coughs out. He insists on being the only person besides my dad who calls me Griff.

"Control freak," Wade coughs back. He shakes his head and scans the back cover. "This sounds up my alley. I'm not sure what that says about me, but I'm in. Thanks, *Griffin*." He opens Theo's present: a dozen different ties. There's also a note telling him to step up his wardrobe game. "Wardrobe is about to be on point. Thanks, Theodore McIntyre. Is it okay if I call you that, Theodore McIntyre?"

"Theo will do," Theo says, smiling. They fist-bump.

"Your turn," I tell Theo.

"Bastard."

Theo opens Wade's gift: an illustrated cocktail recipe collection.

"Once your early admission is approved, I want you to know how to underage-drink responsibly," Wade says.

Theo and I laugh.

Then Theo slides my gift for him a little closer. I really wish this moment could be private. You don't have to be dating someone to tell if they don't like a gift. Unless someone here is secretly and exceptionally good at hiding their bullshit, I like to think we all have pretty good bullshit detectors. He torments me by tearing open the wrapping slowly, but joke's on him: there's still an ordinary box he has to get through, too. Once he breaks that open with his keys, he pulls out a bust of Batman. It takes him a second to see that it's not Bruce Wayne's face staring back at him. It's his own, thanks to this website I found that puts people's faces on action figures and dolls.

Theo laughs so hard he falls over. I'm close to collapsing with him out of relief.

"I don't get it," Wade says.

"On Halloween Theo joked one day Batman would take off his mask and we'd see it was him all along," I say. We were shooting for "thoughtfully random," and I hit that mark. Bull's-eye.

Once Theo recovers and gives me a thank-you kiss, he props Batman-Theo beside him and gestures toward my gifts. "Open Wade's first."

"Yes, sir."

"Disclaimer," Wade says. "It's sort of a couples thing, but I think you're more likely to freak out over it, Griffin. But don't mistake this as me being okay with you two being super-inseparable. I just had this idea and couldn't shake it."

I tear open the wrapping paper, and all I see is the back of a frame, but when I flip it over I see my face and Theo's face. Together. Not like a mirror, but sort of. Different parts of our features are blended together to create one face: his blue eye, my hazel; the small string of freckles along his nose, my bump on the bridge; his bottom lip, my upper; his blondish eyebrow, my dark one. It's a portrait and a puzzle.

My hand actually shakes a little at the thoughtfulness of this. "Wade, wow. Thanks so much." I toss the picture in Theo's lap and hug the hell out of Wade, probably for the first time ever, then sit back beside Theo. "I'm going to hang it up as soon as I get home."

"Figured you would. Let's see what Theo got you."

"The best for last, of course," Theo says. "Drumroll, please!"

We all sit still for a few seconds before banging on the floor with our fists. There's weight to the small box. I tear open the wrapping, and it's a little treasure chest. "Please tell me there are mini zombie pirates inside," I say. Theo shrugs. I unlock the chest and inside there are four winged figurines with a little note.

"'A compulsion of gryphons?'" I read with a smile.

"Thoughtfully random, right?" Theo is crazy excited. "Gryphons because of your name, obviously. Those little bastards are hard to find, by the way, but I found one with Wade in a thrift shop and ordered the other three online."

I examine them, stopping when I see a little plate on one's back. "What's this?"

"Collective nouns just never make sense. A murder of crows, a smack of jellyfish, a business of parrots. Nonsense. Straight-up nonsense. I made up a compulsion of gryphons for you. Compulsion works because you have those little quirks and because I made magnetic clips out of the gryphons so they're bound together." Theo hands me another plate from his pocket and demonstrates by placing it inside my shirt and tossing a gryphon at it so it's magnetized there. "Do I win Christmas? The point of Christmas is winning it, right?"

"You both win Christmas," I say.

"Good answer," Wade says.

"So-so answer," Theo says.

I put all the plates inside my shirt, magnetizing all the gryphons. I don't tell them I was lying. They didn't win Christmas. I did. How could I not? There's a compulsion of gryphons soaring around my heart.

WEDNESDAY, DECEMBER 31ST, 2014

IF I'D SAT DOWN with a psychic last January and she hit me with some prediction on how I'd begin dating Theo in June, I would've spent my year staging an elaborate mission to steal back my ten dollars. Even if psychics are real, I don't think I would've survived the anticipation. Sometimes it's okay to be surprised. It's going to sound stupid, and I wouldn't ever say this out loud, but the way Theo and I came out to each other was sort of like getting caught in a thunderstorm. Storms can suck when they're knocking out power and ripping apart houses, no doubt. But other times the thunder is a soundtrack to something unpredictable, something that gets our hearts racing and wakes us up. If someone had warned me about the weather, I might have freaked out and stayed inside.

But I didn't.

It's New Year's Eve, a few minutes till midnight. The party my parents are throwing in the living room for their friends and favorite neighbors is busy enough that no one has noticed how Theo and I have slipped into my room with glasses of champagne.

"Cheers," Theo says.

"Cheers."

We clink glasses and swallow our first sips of champagne. It's dry, crisp, and sour—exactly as the bottle advertised. We don't close my door. In the event my parents *do* realize we've gone missing, I don't want them thinking we're having sex, especially if there's any chance it'll lead to another awkward talk with my dad. But it's about to be midnight, and we'll want to be alone for a few reasons.

I place my champagne down on my dresser and turn the TV on so we don't miss the countdown. Four minutes until 2015.

"We're going to kick next year's ass, right?"

"Maybe we don't kick next year's ass, bully," Theo says, throwing on his best serious face. "Maybe we invite it into our homes and take it out to dinner?" He cracks. "Nah, we're kicking next year's ass." Theo places his glass down, too. He comes into my arms, holding me tight. He rests his chin on my shoulder for a few moments before snuggling his forehead against my neck, flesh on flesh.

The countdown is beginning, and the freezing crowd in Times Square is a chorus carrying us into January. My chest is tightening.

"Four," I say.

"Three," Theo says.

"Two."

"One."

"Happy New Year." I shake my head in disbelief, marveling at the guy in front of me. It's New Year's, and I get to hold someone, and I get to be held. I get to kiss someone, and I get to be kissed. We kiss while "Auld Lang Syne" plays in the background, and I keep it together for as long as possible, but then I break and I'm crying.

"Griff, what's up?"

"This song gets me sometimes." I close my eyes. I'm a little embarrassed to be crying in front of him. "I love you, Theo."

"I love me, too."

"Be serious for two seconds. I'm crying."

"Okay. One, two . . ."

"I take it back."

"I love you more, Griffin," Theo says, pulling me closer to him. "I'm blown away by how happy you make me. Thank you for being there for me when I'm stupid enough to think I'd rather be alone."

When Theo gets into Santa Monica College—and he will because he's Theo—it'll be tough, but I apparently blow him away with how happy I make him. I won't drop that ball.

I can't predict what will happen this year, but I'm okay with more thunderstorms.

TODAY
SUNDAY, NOVEMBER 27TH, 2016

I'm going to call him, okay?

I owe Jackson that, and I owe you that.

I sit on a bike railing, my feet swinging. It's cold and getting dark, but it's the only place where I'm certain of privacy since my parents are constantly in my space. I wait for the time to change, and once it's 8:34, I hit CALL on Jackson's nameless number. I might create a contact profile for him after this. He picks up after the fourth ring, dangerously close to the fifth.

"Griffin," Jackson says. There's water spraying in the background.

"Bad time?"

"I answer and make calls in the shower all the time," Jackson says.

"Any phone casualties?"

"A couple," Jackson admits, and I wonder if he's as surprised by the lightness in his voice as I am. Maybe he's even relieved to talk about something that won't get him crying. "Did you get my text yesterday? I'm not sure if it went through or not but I—"

"I got it," I interrupt. "I actually thought we should talk before you bounce. Unless you're showering because you have some-where else to be . . ."

"I don't," Jackson says. "I'm only showering because I have nothing else to do. Denise and her parents already went to bed." It's weird to hear Jackson refer to Russell and Ellen as *Denise's* parents, not yours. "Did you want to come over? I'm sure Russell and Ellen won't mind."

"Dry up and get dressed," I say. "There's an entrance to Cen-tral Park on West Seventy-Second. It's not that far from Theo's, but if you get lost, use the map on your phone."

"What time?"

I almost tell him I'll be there in six songs. "I should be there in twenty minutes. See you then."

I hang up, wondering if I've actually given him enough time to finish off his shower, properly dry himself so he doesn't return to California with a killer cold, get dressed, track down his second glove, and find me at the park. If he's late, he's late. I've spent a lot of the past year waiting—mostly for you. Here's hoping Jackson actually shows up.

I WAS GOOD ON time getting to the park. Jackson, on the other hand, is not. I'm staying warm holding the two coconut hot choco-lates from the café, each with four pumps of caramel syrup. You always claimed this was your genius concoction, like you were some mad scientist. These coconut hot chocolates were must-haves during fall and winter, like the Spider-Man Popsicles were during spring and summer.

I keep an eye out for Jackson, left to right, right to left. I sip from my cup and finally spot him jogging across the street toward me. His jacket isn't zipped up, and his hands are buried in his pockets.

"I got lost, sorry," Jackson says.

"It's okay. I should've picked you up." I hand him his drink. "Here, it's a drink Theo invented. It's nothing too weird, just coconut hot chocolate with caramel. Have you had it?" *Please no, please no.*

Jackson shakes his head. He cradles the cup, warming his hands, and stares at it.

"Theo also talked about making his own Theo smoothie, but he never got around to it."

I expect him to comment. He nods and doesn't say anything; I don't know if he's unimpressed or lost in his head. He looks around. "I've been here before, back in February."

I should've guessed. In the second month of the year, he was here with you. In the second-to-last month of the year, he's here with me. I will never wrap my head around how a single moment can keep throwing our lives around. I feel like a rock being skipped through the ocean—pain, relief, pain again, relief again, eventually destined to sink.

"Did Theo do his troll impression when you guys went through the tunnels here?" I ask.

"Not here in New York, but he did back home. We have these tunnels that start at the side, go beneath the street, and take you up to the beach," Jackson says.

If I remember right, the troll impressions started because of your mother. She'd pick you and Wade up from elementary school—before I was in the picture—and when it was nice out, she'd walk you both through the park and tell you stories about the trolls that live on the bridges and in the tunnels in the park, threatening to eat children that ran away from home. I'm really surprised you weren't more of a fantasy-genre fan, considering your mom's imagination.

"I can take you down the path Theo would've taken you," I say. "But I won't do the voices. I suck at the voices."

"I'd like that," Jackson says. "I know Theo really wanted me to 'meet' the New York trolls, but we had to meet up with my friends one night and we never got around to it."

I don't like that he bummed you out, that he disappointed

you. I don't like that you saw such a future with him that you were okay with that disappointment, that there would be more time for you two. I don't like that he trusted this future with you, either. I don't like how threatened he still makes me feel. I don't like how unfair I am to him. I don't like that I'm likely bumming you out with my jealousy. I don't like that I'm disappointing you with my nonsense.

I shake all of this off. There's no point getting upset with you for sharing your childhood with Jackson.

I walk into the park and Jackson follows. It's a good chance to get some air, and for me to clear it. "I'm sorry I ditched the other day. I thought being in Theo's room again would feel like being in a museum, but I couldn't get it out of my head that he's dead."

"More mausoleum than museum, right?"

"Exactly."

I'm weirdly self-conscious about the mounds of dirty snow and scattered trash. It must seem ugly to someone who lives in the land of beaches and perpetual sun, of seagulls and dolphins. It's like a guest has showed up to my home uninvited, without giving me a chance to clean my room. I've felt this way before, even without Jackson by my side. In January and February, right before you and Jackson came here, I thought I was suffering from seasonal affective disorder like the rest of New York. Maybe I was a little—it was find-a-way-to-put-two-coats-on brutal weather here—but mostly it was knowing you were happy and undisturbed in a sunny place, in a different time zone, likely throwing back a smoothie, with someone who wasn't me.

"I want to keep it real with you, Jackson," I tell that someone now. I hope he believes the unbelievable thing I have to say, because it's one hundred percent true. "I don't hate you. I thought I did, seriously. But I only hated your relationship with Theo. I didn't think you were going to be someone he actually

brought back to New York to meet his family and friends." I
consider stopping at one of these benches, even though they're
wet from melted snow, but if Jackson doesn't sit beside me I'll
be forced to face him during this confession. "I hate that you
also have history with Theo. And I hate that you were building
a future with him."

I can't tell you the last time I've been this honest.

You're my favorite human ever, but I really, really can't tell
you, Theo.

Jackson stops walking. "You know I don't hate you either,
right?"

I stop too, but I don't face him. I look everywhere but at him,
counting: eight bars on the sewer grate; six piles of dead, crusty
leaves that make the shape of a frown; two lit lampposts (I make
a mental note to myself to find a second broken lamppost to
account for the broken one up ahead); two adults approaching
. . . and I'm guessing *they* aren't in the midst of the impossible
situation Jackson and I are now miraculously confronting—
maybe even embracing.

"You wanted Theo to stop talking to me." I don't mean it as
an accusation. This is a legit conversation, guy to guy, broken
heart to broken heart. It doesn't do me any good to make everything a showdown; it doesn't make me a winner.

"Well, I hated your history with Theo, too," Jackson confesses. "I hated how often your relationship with him made me
question if we would actually survive. You know, I wasn't actually
supposed to come with him to New York in February. My mom's
birthday was the day before, and we always spend it together.
Breakfast at her favorite diner, then a movie, then back to the
diner for lunch, then another movie, then back to the diner for
dinner, then another movie, then back to the diner for milk-
shakes, and finally a movie at home."

I almost interrupt to tell him how much I appreciate his
mother's symmetry—four movies, four trips to the diner—but

shut up and let him go on. I never once got the impression he wasn't always a part of your visit home.

"But I blew her off because I knew Theo would be here and that he would see you." Jackson lowers his head. Now I look at him. "It's the whole out of sight, out of mind business. I swore if I didn't take that trip with him, it was a sure bet Theo would call me and tell me you two were getting back together."

I'm ready to turn away when he catches my eye.

"I thought maybe next year Theo would be able to join me and my mom for the celebration." He shrugs, which I know he doesn't mean as a dismissal. He's doing that thing I've done before where I try to shrink my own feelings, try to make my problems sound smaller to others because sometimes people just don't get it. But I do, and he should know that.

The first troll tunnel is just ahead. We continue standing there.

We don't hate each other. We shouldn't hate each other's histories, either.

I can't shake away all of those feelings. Not immediately, at least. I doubt Jackson can either, especially here in Central Park, where I'm acting as a guide on a tour you should be leading. Our situation is like some rigged card game, and the hand the universe laid out for us is made entirely of jesters; we're some cosmic joke. But maybe we don't have to fold so easily. Maybe we can keep playing the game and make kings of ourselves, in spite of it all.

I step to Jackson, look him in his strained eyes, one still redder than the other because of that popped vessel. I hug the hell out of him. I hug him for *him*, because he knows firsthand how love and heartbreak can turn someone crazy and suspicious. I hug him for you, so you'll be proud of me for doing the right thing instead of turning my back on him like I did the other night. I hug him for myself because his brutal honesty is somehow saving me from feeling worthless and defeated. I hug him for all of us because we're no longer forces battling against one another.

"We're finally doing something right," I say, taking a step away from him.

"Too bad we couldn't be this mature when he was alive," Jackson says. "Maybe we would've gotten there eventually."

I nod. "I hate that we complicated his life the way we did . . . and I hate that maybe it would've gotten to a point where Theo would've felt forced to say goodbye to me or you—or even both of us since we couldn't get along."

It's one of many reasons I'm sorry, Theo.

"Yeah." That's all Jackson can say.

I pat him on the shoulder and turn away, inviting him to follow me. The stories I'll tell him about you are good for him to hear and good for me to talk about. It's okay that he's not as forthcoming tonight. I sort of like being in the pilot's seat, flying us through the skies I know. I think Jackson and I risk crashing if he's in total control.

"THIS IS A BETTER send-off than I was betting on," Jackson says on our way out, through the very exit where you and I once took turns pissing, late at night, keeping watch for each other. "I didn't even think I'd get to see you again. I wanted the chance to say sorry for trying to cut Theo out of your life."

I know I have plenty to apologize for too, but something deeper is clawing at me. "Do you have to leave tomorrow?"

You heard that right, Theo: I, Griffin No-Middle-Name Jennings, have asked my former nemesis, Jackson Wright, if he can stay in New York.

"I can't impose on Theo's family anymore. They need their space," Jackson says.

"Stay with us," I counter. "It's not like you have school to worry about."

"I'm not sure your father would be cool with that," Jackson says.

"He will be. I'm sorry he was a dick to you. He was just being overly loyal to me." Unlike my mom, who wasn't being loyal enough. But she's in the right. I know that.

"My flight is already booked, though," Jackson says.

"Your father works for the airline. Don't you get free flights?"

"Well . . . yeah."

"Look, if you want to go back home, I'm not stopping you. But if you want an escape, I'm giving you a chance."

"No, it's not that I don't want to stay, but—"

"I'm so ready to shoot down this next excuse."

"I have a question, not an excuse."

"You want to know why I want you to stay, right?"

"Exactly."

"You're the only person who gets what I'm going through, what we're going through. Theo's family is grieving harder than us, no contest. But we lost him too, and I feel like people are surprised that I haven't just moved on already. I don't know if that's the same for you. I don't really care about those people anyway. I have zero intention to forget about Theo, ever. If some genie popped up and was like, 'Hey, you want to use one of your wishes to forget Theo ever existed and cure your heartbreak?' I would probably make two wishes and then kick the genie in his nuts for saying something that stupid."

"You really wouldn't use your third wish?" Jackson asks.

I shake my head. Unless I was guaranteed another go at the genie so I could have a total of six wishes, I wouldn't ever use my third wish, even if it left me in the company of that asshole genie forever. "My point is, you get me and I get you," I tell him. "I think we can help each other through this, and, even better than that, I think we can legit help each other heal. You game?"

He smiles, but he looks shaky in the cold lamplight. "I would have to be an idiot to reject healing. You're right that going back home would really suck right now. It'd be so lonely, and I'd see Theo everywhere." He pauses. "Are you sure about this?"

I see you everywhere now, too. I'm hoping talking to Jackson about you might help lessen the pain, though. It'll definitely help with the loneliness.

"I'm sure."

We're closer to my house, so Jackson and I head straight there with a plan to get his stuff tomorrow when I get back from school. As we approach my building, I quietly say, "I'm sorry for everything, too."

MONDAY, NOVEMBER 28TH, 2016

JACKSON CAN'T SLEEP EITHER. It's been almost a week since your funeral, so it's probably fair to stop blaming his sleeplessness on West Coast time. No one can sleep because you're keeping us awake: me, Jackson, your mom, your dad, your sister, Wade probably. It's 6 A.M. and even though I should do my damn best to at least get a power nap in since I have to get ready for school in an hour, Jackson and I chill by the closed window and watch a plane sail across the dark skies.

"It's been two weeks," I say. Two weeks since you've been gone.

"I know," Jackson says. He moves away from the window and settles into the air mattress.

I keep watching the plane. Jackson should be at the airport now, getting ready for his 8 A.M. flight back home, back in time as he gains three more hours in his life. But instead he's here for me to talk to, and, unlike you, Jackson can talk back.

MY DAD PULLS UP right in front of your building. I let Jackson know I'll see him after school. He's tired as hell. I'm no monster; I considered letting him stay over while I'm out, but all our stuff is there, yours and mine. I don't think Jackson is going to rob me; the only thing he's ever stolen from me is you, and you were fair game. But I don't want Jackson touching my things or your things when I'm awake, figuring out the history without me there to inform it.

It's dead silent in the car after we drop Jackson off. If Dad doesn't say anything to me by the second red light, I'll listen to music instead. The second red light comes in no time, and I'm putting on my headphones to listen to Lily Allen's cover of "Somewhere Only We Know," when Dad catches my eyes in the rearview mirror. He speaks up. "How well do you know Jackson?"

I'm not sure what to make of my dad's strange tone. "I know Theo trusted him," I say, letting the headphones dangle. "I do, too."

"How old is he?"

"He's eighteen." Until Thursday, at least, when he turns nineteen.

You'll never be nineteen. You're stuck.

Then the floodgates open, and Dad lets me have it: I was wrong to encourage Jackson to skip his flight; I was wrong to invite Jackson to camp out in my room, especially without talking to him and Mom first; I was wrong to be at the park late last night, especially when fewer police are patrolling this season (I have no idea where that fact comes from, but whatever); I was wrong, and am wrong, to act so irrationally.

"I know you miss Theo, but—"

I put on my headphones and blast my song really loud.

ZOMBIES HAVE BEEN ON the brain today, so to speak. (Not the zombie pirates who will rule us one day, sadly.)

I've taken many zombie forms throughout high school. There were the brain-dead days when I'd been up very late cramming for a midterm. The same was true after all-night video game sessions or phone calls with you. I would zombie-creep through the halls, unable to pass any tests or even come up with a good lie as to why I didn't do my homework, whereas you remained at the top of your game. Then there's the kind of zombie I've become now: the one who has lost everything—his brain, his heart, his light, his direction. He wanders the world, bumping into this, tripping over that, but keeps going and going. That is life after death.

Today I'm the zombie standing in front of your old locker, as if it's some underground bunker where I'll find you alive.

But I know better.

You're dead, and I'm the worst kind of alive.

I GET HOME BEFORE Jackson's cab arrives. I can't kick him out every day I go to school, but I can't exactly hide you when he's in my room, either. I look around in a daze. I can box up the things that are really personal and exclusive to me, like the letters you would write me every month on our we-finally-got-together anniversary. Or the drawing you gave me on the one-month anniversary of the first time we had sex. The generosity you endowed both of us with is too damn funny not to frame, but too damn crude to share. There are a lot of little things that I would never share with anyone, especially not Jackson. Maybe back at a time when I wanted to make him feel jealous, but not now. There's some history he doesn't need shoved in his face.

Luckily the apartment is empty. I pack up everything I can find in a single box and seal it shut with duct tape. Not to be extra distrustful, but I don't think it's a good idea to leave it in my bedroom closet, where I've invited Jackson to help himself if he needs stuff like new sheets, so I take it out to the hallway closet. My eyes fall on a shoebox: things I took out of my room a couple of days after you died. Those items still have no business being in my space, so I drop the new box on top of it and close the closet door.

Jackson sends me a text; he is pulling up any second. I get

downstairs in time to see him exiting the cab with a single gym bag. I was expecting him to have a rolling suitcase, but I forget he's a kid like me, who was only supposed to be here for a few days.

As we go upstairs, Jackson tells me how your parents were weird when he told them he decided to stay with me. I don't know if they're suspicious of me, which wouldn't make sense. They're completely unaware that the most dangerous thing about me is my capability to lie, and that didn't start until the end of our relationship. But I'm cutting back on the lies— trust me. Being brutally honest is a freedom I never expected. Maybe your parents were weird because of how unlikely a . . . I don't know what word to use here because *pairing* sounds too romantic and *friendship* sounds too strong. You would know the word. Whatever Jackson and I are, it's unlikely. But at the end of the day, however concerned your parents may be, they did not invite Jackson to continue staying with them, so here he is.

"What did your parents say?" I ask.

"My dad is okay with getting me another ticket when I'm ready to go home. My mom isn't a fan of me ditching school for the rest of the semester, but she trusts I know what's best for me," Jackson says, dropping his gym bag by my desk.

I let out a grim laugh. "I wonder what that's like. I got hit with a lecture on my way to school." I go through my clothes, sorting extra button-ups, T-shirts, jeans, and boxers I don't mind Jackson borrowing.

"Yeah, Gregor didn't seem thrilled I was spending time here."

"No, it's more that he's annoyed I did this behind his back. Whatever." I hand him the clothes, more than he will likely wear, enough that if I cleared a drawer for him, I could fill it. I throw myself onto my bed and toss him my TV remote. "My nap during algebra got interrupted, so I'm going to shut my eyes for a bit. Feel free to watch whatever you want or read or sleep or whatever. You're almost nineteen, you'll figure it out."

"Thanks," Jackson says quietly.

I'm tempted to ask him if he's okay, but you know me when I'm passing out; I sleep-talk, half listening, half inside a dream, and I make zero sense. This is not the best time to have a serious conversation, as I suspect he may want to have. I don't even have the energy to put on my headphones and play your voice mail, but the sound of the TV brings me some comfort, some familiarity. I haven't touched it since you died because people shouldn't be watching TV when the person they love is dead. But now as I drift off, it reminds me of marathons we enjoyed, movies we hated, TV shows we watched weekly, documentaries that kept us awake, action films that bored us, and the meaning-less background noise it provided so we could make out and do other stuff uninterrupted.

It really sucks you're not sleeping beside me. Mostly because it would've been nice to know if I am actually falling asleep with a smile on my face, or if I'm loopy and imagining it.

IT FEELS ODD THAT Jackson is now part of us, right? Odd in the number, yeah, but I mean odd-odd; strange, unexpected. It's everything you would've liked when you were still here to kick it with us. You can see, Jackson and me are growing up because of you. I hope this doesn't sound like your death has fixed our lives; I hated when Jackson said that, I hate myself for even hinting at it. Anyway, the three of us are skipping dinner with my parents tonight because I still want some space to cool down after my dad's takedown. I hate feeling like a naughty kid.

Besides, now that I'm a little more myself, I want Jackson and me to have some one-on-one time (you excluded, well, included, of course). Specifically, I want to know what was with him when I fell asleep—best nap all week—that made him a little more distant. We sit on the air mattress with our bowls of pasta and he's scrolling through the movie queue.

"What are you in the mood for?"

"Whatever you want."

Jackson puts on the second *Terminator* movie, but after twenty minutes of fidgeting and looking around the room, it's pretty clear we're not paying attention.

"You still watching this?" I ask.

"Not really," Jackson says.

"Because it's garbage?"

"I have Theo on the mind," Jackson says.

"I was going to ask. Did I say something earlier?"

"You mentioned my birthday. Theo and I had plans back home. We were going to take surfing lessons and check out this exhibit and end up at the beach. It's weird how I won't be home for my birthday, and I won't be with him, and . . . I must sound like a broken record."

I shake my head. "I'm sure together we sound like a concert of broken records. If you're still around, maybe you can meet up with your friends. They should be back in the city by then, right? Maybe your birthday can be the hang-out you need. If that doesn't work out, I'm here for randomness."

He sighs. "Thanks, Griffin. I haven't even thought about Anika and Veronika, honestly. I'll reach out over the next day or so. I'll definitely need a distraction that day."

I get it. Even when you were alive, events you missed felt wrong when they finally rolled around. I had to turn to people who didn't matter as much to me, which sucked. Having a plan isn't always a guarantee.

It's been two weeks since you died, and one week since Jackson and I delivered our eulogies. Like I said, odd.

HISTORY
WEDNESDAY, MARCH 25TH, 2015

I don't think my quirks are actually quirks.

It's not quirky to be ready for my birthday in May because I'll finally stop being fifteen for the next three hundred and sixty-six days (leap year!). It's not quirky to blame anything bad that happens in March because it's the third month of the year. It's not quirky to risk how much I'm eating if it means an odd amount of meals that day. It's not quirky to list examples in my head and get frustrated when I can't come up with enough options to make it even.

It's not just the numbers thing, obviously. I'm a magnet to everyone's left side and I don't know why. It can all be disruptive, but as long as everyone is in the right place and every number is balanced, I'm really good. Seven doesn't bother me as much, but maybe that's because I was born on the seventeenth. Maybe it's just because seven is a kick-ass number. Maybe I'm making a bigger deal out of this than it really is.

Maybe my quirks actually *are* quirks.

Maybe I'm taking it out on myself because these little quirks Theo finds cute aren't enough to get him to stay.

Back in January, Theo was accepted for early admission to Santa Monica College.

We're sitting on his living-room floor, me to Theo's left, obviously, while he opens up the latest delivery from his future home. Russell records this unboxing on his phone to later add to the "Big Theo Moments" folder he has on his computer. Theo pulls out an SMC fitted cap, an SMC T-shirt, and an SMC hoodie.

I can't possibly feel panicky because Theo's pulled out three items, right? That doesn't make sense. I know why I'm losing my breath: it's because every time I think Theo might reconsider and stay here in New York for another year, something like this pops up—an email or a letter or a padded envelope or, now, a swag box. I know he's already got one foot out the door.

Theo puts on the cap and winks at me. "The SMC heads sure know how to seduce a guy, right?"

Alternate universe idea: Theo and I are living together in a huge house overflowing with hats because I bought him a new one every day to get him to stay.

SUNDAY, MAY 17TH, 2015

MAYBE I PUT TOO much pressure on my birthday. There are only a few hours left, and it's not the memorable day I was counting down to, even though all the right pieces were in place: I woke up to a video from a shirtless Theo for my eyes only; my parents gave me three hundred and fifty dollars (I returned ten dollars under the guise of a thank-you tip for bringing me into this world, but really I just wanted a number that felt more even); I hung out with Theo and Wade at Bonus where Theo and I kissed for the first time, and we played several rounds of pinball and air hockey; I got some great gifts and I haven't even gotten Theo's yet, but my favorite so far is the Cedric Diggory key chain Wade got me.

And now I'm walking around Union Square with the guy I

really love, while he holds my hand and whistles the *Star Wars* theme song.

But all I can think about is how Theo will be gone this fall.

I won't have him with me for the first day of school, walks in September, for a couples costume for Halloween, for side-by-side studying for midterms in November, for preholiday craziness in December, for his birthday, for my *next* birthday. We won't have those days or every little and big moment in between once he's gone. I have him now, and I still can't throw on a smile that doesn't feel like a lie. But at least I can lie if it makes him happy.

"Today's been incredible," I say. "Thanks for throwing all this together."

Theo took charge of my birthday. I don't know if it's because he loves me or because he feels guilty for leaving, but he signed up for the job and saw it through. I had my doubts. He's been spending a lot of his weeknights and weekends downloading new computer programs to prepare for SMC life. I have to keep reminding myself that he's not always putting his brain before his heart. More importantly, it's not a bad thing when he does.

He leads me to a bench. We sit, watching two women play chess on crates nearby.

"Griffin, I got to let you in on something," he says.

"What's up?" This already doesn't feel good.

"I know you," Theo says. "Like, a little bit. We've been dating for almost a year, and we go way back. Fifth grade. I know something's up. You're supposed to be able to talk to me when something's up. If you don't, the Bad Boyfriend Council will show up at my house and give me a demerit."

"What happens when you get too many demerits?"

"I'll be sentenced to an entire month without masturbation or sex. You got to save me here," Theo pleads. "You're not okay, are you?"

I keep my eyes on the chess game, on the perfectly even number of squares. "I'm going to miss you," I tell him, which is true. "I know we still have the entire summer to look forward to, but what's going to happen once you move to California? We'll see each other on holidays?"

"That isn't enough for you?"

"I'm scared it's not going to be enough for you," I admit. "You're going to meet some guy, or girl, and, yeah, maybe you'll be friends at first, but it's just going to get you missing something physical. I don't think Skype-Griffin is going to be enough for you."

"Will Skype-Griffin love Skype-Theo? He better, because Skype-Theo is planning on loving the hell out of Skype-Griffin, even if he can't kiss him."

He's gotten me to smile. Screw everyone who hates public displays of affection, because I have to get my kisses in before I become Skype-Griffin.

"You feel better?" he asks.

"I'm sorry I didn't say anything sooner."

"It's okay. Just don't forget about the assholes over at the Bad Boyfriend Council who would force celibacy on a seventeen-year-old with a cute boyfriend." Theo pulls his phone out of his pocket. "Speaking of, I should probably give you your birthday present. It's not done, but I promise you, I have every intention of finishing it."

He pulls up a video and presses PLAY. It's an animation. There is a compulsion of gryphons flying across the side. The one with feathers my favorite shade of blue is on the right until he torpedoes to the left. The narrative of one gryphon moving to the left of three gryphons would make zero sense to anyone else, but it means everything to me. It means he pays attention to the way I move, to my favorite color. It's only fourteen seconds long and probably counts more as a clip than it does a video, but I know how much time goes into a single frame, and that's time he took away from himself for me. This clip means my favorite human loves me.

"I swear I'm going to add more to it," Theo says, probably feeling shitty because I keep staring at him without telling him how much I love it. "I have some ideas, but I don't want to spoil it for you. Do you like it?"

I throw myself at him, and damn it, I'm not letting go.

SATURDAY, JUNE 27TH, 2015

AFTER A MORNING OF feeding and naming ducks in Central Park (Daffy was an asshole who wouldn't share) and an afternoon eating ice cream at the High Line, I follow Theo back into his apartment—right as his family, my parents, and Wade shout, *"Surprise!"*

He turns to me. I play-punch him in the chest.

"Surprise, Theo," I say.

"I have no idea what's going on," he says to the room. "Good job, everyone."

"It's a surprise party," Denise shouts, smiling widely enough that I notice she lost that wobbly tooth in the bottom row.

"You, little lady, are a genius," Theo says. "But why am I having a surprise party?"

His mother steps over and sweeps him into a hug, rocking with him. "It's your graduation party. Griffin's idea."

Theo steps back and turns to me.

"It sucks that you have to wait four more years to graduate," I say.

Theo claps his hands urgently. "I'm going to need to ask everyone to go home so I can have the entire place alone with my boyfriend." There are a couple of laughs but mainly just blushing and wide-eyed looks from our parents. "Please leave all the gifts." He looks around. "Wait. There aren't any gifts? New mission! Please leave and go buy me something nice and return in a couple of hours. Thank you."

No one leaves to buy Theo gifts.

His parents offer him a sip of celebratory wine, maybe half believing it might actually be his first sip, but he passes once he sees me holding a green graduation cap I bought off some graduating senior earlier this month. Theo lowers his head and lets me crown him. Everyone stops what they're doing to get photos of Theo in his cap. Russell encourages our squad to get together for what he calls a "family photo." I wonder how much of a family we'll be once it's just Wade and me and Theo is in California, but right now we're at our tightest since Theo and I came out.

"You're a mind reader," Theo tells me.

"Not really," I admit. "A lot of your confusion about whether you should stay or go had to do with not seeing high school through until graduation. You never got your glory."

"And now I'm saying peace out before I can be declared valedictorian of my year," Theo says, as if graduating school a year early isn't a bigger win. "I'm sure Suzanne Banks will get it now, but she'll always be salutatorian in my heart."

"Check your pillow."

"Is something there?"

"If Wade is good at favors, there should be."

"It's there," Wade says.

Wade and I follow Theo into his room where he rushes to pick up the fake diploma I created for him:

THEODORE DANIEL MCINTYRE

VALEDICTORIAN AND

THE MOST BADASS HUMAN IN THE UNIVERSE

TODAY
THURSDAY, DECEMBER 1ST, 2016

Once Jackson gets off the phone with his mother, I'll wish him a happy birthday. It's five in the morning in Santa Monica, but I'm not surprised that Ms. Lane is the kind of mother who wakes up this early to call her son on his birthday. I'm impressed she beat me to the punch, considering Jackson was sleeping six feet away from me.

I sit up in bed, thinking about how December is kicking off with a few firsts. It's the first month you're not alive, which also means we're approaching one whole month without you. It's Jackson's first time celebrating his birthday in New York, away from his parents. It's the first snow day from school—a cancellation we were happy to receive last night from the school board even though I hate blizzards.

I, uh, need a fourth first . . .

Okay, okay.

I'm having trouble. Help me out here, Theo. You used to be so good at helping me even things out. I'm trying to guess what you would say right now. I look around the room, which you always advised was a good place to start. Most times you'd save me from the landslides of panic; I feel one bouldering through me now.

I don't know if I'm imagining it or not, but my heart is speeding up faster than usual. I'm desperate for anything, sort of like when two people are having an awkward silence and everything would be slightly better if someone said something . . .

I got it! Today is the first time I will go out into the snow and play as a present to Jackson.

Damn it. You should've reminded me I'm meeting Jackson's friends later for the first time; you know we have dinner plans. I can't get it out of my head now; it's clicked as a fifth, registered itself in my head. I need a sixth first now. I'm in a good place if I think up something else after the sixth since I'll hit a seventh and maybe even an eighth, and, wow, if I hit all those, I will be pretty close to ten firsts today. Hitting that record is tempting.

I can't.

My heart is rioting, my chest is tightening, my throat is swallowing nothing, and my fingernails are going to war against my palm.

Jackson notices. But he's in the middle of pulling on his second sock, and he stops. He moves the phone away from his mouth and asks me if I'm okay.

"Put your other sock on, please," I say.

"I have to call you back, Mom." Jackson hangs up on his mother and immediately pulls on his other sock. I need the balance of two socks on two feet almost as much as I need a sixth first.

My face gets hot, or maybe it's been hot for a while. I don't know, I don't know. I'm burning everywhere. The heat spreads down to my shoulders and down to my elbows and down to my wrists and down to my thighs and down to my knees and down to my toes. I want to undress and cry a little because I can't focus on what I should be focusing on—the next and last first—because all I can think about is how you're not here to help me and how Jackson will never understand what it's like to live in a head like mine, to be powerless against these impulses.

Jackson, with both socks on, approaches and crouches before me, almost like I'm strapped to explosives and may self-destruct any second now. "Griffin, what is it?" He adjusts himself to be on the other side of my right knee. "Is it an angle thing?"

I found my sixth first: today is the first morning I'm allowing Jackson to help me find sanity. He's been helping me out with grief. I push him away when it comes to my compulsions. You've been there for me since pretty much the beginning, and I've turned to you. It's hard to control something that has control over me. No one understands, but it's freeing to let someone else in to try.

"I'm okay." I wipe my forehead with the back of my head. "I got stuck in my head."

"Was it an angle thing? How can I help you next time?"

His thoughtfulness reminds me of you.

"It was a counting thing. Let's drop it for now because I've spent enough time in my head already." That's the nature of having a brain that spins, I guess. I know brains aren't supposed to spin—minds can, not the actual brains themselves. But there's a lot going on in my head I don't understand and may never understand, and it seems silly to cling to the idea that my brain is this fleshy thing that stays in its place, this thing that behaves like other brains.

"I'm sorry," Jackson says.

"Not your fault," I lie. I can't let it slip that this particular train of thought derailed because of him; he's the source of counting these firsts.

I've imagined many easier lives in alternate universes—somewhere Jackson no longer exists and some where he never existed in the first place—but I never counted on living in a universe where Jackson is a welcome and helpful addition to my life. I would've never predicted a universe where I'm actually careful about how Jackson feels.

I get up from bed and look out the window. The blizzard is

going strong and is expected to reach four feet today, maybe six by Sunday. "You sure you still want a snow day?"

"I'm sure," he says. "I want to send my parents photos of me in the snow."

I'm betting Jackson's father won't call until closer to noon, though I'm hoping he'll prove me wrong. Until then, we'll keep blaming it on work. Maybe he's up in the air and unable to call. Maybe he's surprising his son by visiting New York to see him. I have my doubts on that one. I hope Jackson isn't counting on it, either.

"It's your day," I say. We're definitely waiting until the snow isn't pounding down like this, but I am determined to honor his wishes. "How are you feeling about seeing Anika and Veronika?"

"I'd be surprised if that still happens," Jackson says, still staring out the window like it's the last time it'll ever snow. "Veronika is always looking for excuses to cancel. She hates leaving the house. I'm sure she cancels everything now that weather is a factor."

"No wonder you and Theo couldn't risk being late the night he wanted to take you to the park," I say.

I think this was really mature of me to bring that up, by the way. You owe me a high five.

"Exactly," Jackson says.

"We should have a back-up plan, just in case." My heart isn't trying to blast its way out of my chest anymore. Helping Jackson out is rescuing me from my own head. "Think of it as a snow-day plan for your snow-day birthday plans. What else would you want to do? Something you can only do in New York?"

"Theo used to talk about the High Line," Jackson says.

I move away from the window so Jackson doesn't see me blushing. I am blushing, right? My face is burning again. I wonder if you brought up my name when you mentioned the High Line, if you told him how we would buy lemonades and laugh at the ice vendor who was sneakily eating Popsicles when she thought nobody was looking. Maybe you avoided telling him about how we would hold hands and create stories about the lives of the people we could see working in offices. Maybe you left me out completely so you wouldn't hurt his feelings.

"If your friends suck, we will go to the High Line," I promise. It's been a while since I've been there. "Jackson?"

"Yeah?"

"Happy birthday, by the way."

Jackson finally looks away from the window and smiles. There's no mistaking the sadness in his smile, like maybe he was hoping to find you when he turned around. But when someone is grieving, a genuine smile is a small victory in the big battle. "Thanks, Griffin."

I don't mean to speak for you, but I know you'll feel better having these words of yours thrown out into the universe. "And a happy birthday from Theo, too."

Jackson is a little surprised, but his smile doesn't break—no sadder, no happier. Sometimes neutrality is a victory, too.

"WHAT'S A COLDER WORD for freezing?" Jackson asks, bundled from head to toe in my dad's coat, hat, gloves, and the scarf I forced on him.

"Fucking freezing?"

Jackson nods. "It's fucking freezing. I'm not sure I really want a snowman best friend anymore."

I smooth out the snowman's base. "Nope. No backing out. We didn't work this hard on his ass to give up now."

"Maybe we should make it a snowwoman," Jackson suggests through chattering teeth. "You only see snowwomen when it's a family in need of a mother for the children. But whenever it's one snowperson, everyone automatically makes it a snowman."

"Revolutionary snowwoman it is! Some snowperson will write sonnets about you," I say. I cup the snow and begin molding the snowwoman's breasts. "That's some Theo thinking of yours, by the way. We didn't get much play in the snow because I'm not a big fan, but I think if I did it anyway, Theo would've had the lightbulb moment to create a snowwoman just because."

"I can't think of a better person to channel," Jackson says over the howling winds. There's no smile this time.

He and I build and build, convincing ourselves not to go back inside and take a break to warm up because it'll be too brutal to come back outside. The snowwoman's breasts look more like cones, but I move on to her head because Jackson and I are not exactly teenage boys obsessed with breasts. The snowwoman's head isn't proportionate to her body, just like her body isn't proportionate to her leg ball.

"She needs a face now," Jackson says.

I feel guilty for two reasons. The first is because I should've done this with you and not put it off because I assumed we'd have all the time in the world once we got back together. I also feel guilty because I wouldn't have been able to be as happy about this as Jackson is.

"I'll find her a face." My teeth are chattering. I walk around for a little bit, grateful to have my knees and legs out of the wet snow. I go into the trashcan, collecting items—well, let's call it what it is, *garbage*—that can be useful in giving the snowwoman a face. I return and drop our options, everything colorful against the white snow.

Jackson immediately reaches for the shard of dark green glass from a broken Heineken bottle.

"Really? Are you about to shank her?" I take the glass from Jackson and give the snowwoman her smile—well, smirk.

"Not bad," Jackson admits.

"Don't doubt my vision again."

Jackson uses the filthy green top from a water bottle as the snowwoman's nose. I empty out a popcorn bag, using handfuls for clustered eyes and the bag as really flat hair.

"She's beautiful," Jackson says, laughing a little.

"Beautiful in the sense that she's made of nothing but snow and garbage, right?"

"Yeah, I wouldn't date her," Jackson says.

"Not your type?"

"I like my snowwomen with carrot noses and vanilla wafer eyes," Jackson says.

I laugh a little, surprising myself. I can't say I'll miss the snow-woman when she's nothing but popcorn in a puddle—I'm obviously going to throw the shard of glass away before ditching her—but this was a nice recess from everything. Maybe that's what Jackson is: a recess from everything, even though he's got a foot in everything, too. I guess I could say he's freedom.

Did you think of Jackson as freedom?

IT DOESN'T MATTER HOW long I've lived in New York, but every now and again someone suggests a restaurant that's been around forever but whose existence still surprises me. I know the city is big, but wow. I can only imagine how shocked I would've been if I had gone out to Los Angeles. Anika is apparently a fan of Spotlight Diner, across the street from Washington Square Park and the NYU dorms. It's a little more downtown than I'm used to these days, but it's a guarantee that Jackson's birthday isn't doomed—Anika and Veronika's chances of actually showing up are way higher since we're so close to where they live. If they do ditch, Jackson and I can go to the High Line, which is either a twenty-minute walk or quick cab away. (If I can find a cab, then a cab it is.)

Jackson is sitting on my right, of course. Directly across from our booth is a mirror. I've got to say, the gray dress shirt Jackson is borrowing from me doesn't look bad on him. I'm not going that far and saying it looks good, because it's just as baggy on him as it is on me, but he's somehow managing not to look like he's living out of someone else's closet. It's probably too late to gift it to him for his birthday, right? Nothing would be better than the old "If you like it, you can keep it" trick.

"Anything else I should know about Anika and Veronika?" I ask him. I've gotten some basics but not the intimate stuff, nothing like the topics I should avoid or things that might offend them. I've been ambushed in the past that way, and it sucked.

"Yeah, anything else he should know?" a girl cackles beside me.

I glance up. I recognize Anika and Veronika from the photos on Jackson's phone, but he really needs a phone with better camera quality. These two are I'm-forgetting-I'm-gay stunning. They both have dark skin and are dressed like sisters in their denim tops, but that's where their physical similarities end. Anika has long braided hair and a lean, muscular frame—probably from running track. Veronika's hair is shaved and she's got piercings in her nose, left eyebrow, ears, and the corner of her lower lip.

"Happy birthday!" Anika says.

Veronika cheers.

Jackson slides out of the booth and tries to hug Anika first, but Veronika sneaks in, squeezing his midriff.

"I'm so happy you made it," he says.

"I wouldn't miss it for the apocalypse," Veronika says.

"For the thousandth time this week, that doesn't make sense. Retire it," Anika says, shoving Veronika out of the way to hug Jackson. "You're basically admitting you're otherwise open to watching the world burn."

"For the thousandth time this week, the world often sucks and I can either burn with my eyes closed or watch it all turn to ash for a hot second," Veronika says. She settles into the booth without saying anything to me.

Anika waves Veronika off and turns to me. "Griffin, right? I'm Anika."

"Hi." I stand and shake her hand before falling back into my seat.

"The other woman," Veronika says. "So to speak."

I'm not the other. I was the first.

"She's kidding," Anika says with a dark look at her friend, sliding in beside her. "She's not funny, but she's kidding."

I'm not laughing, and I won't fake laugh.

Jackson sits back down slowly, as if he's suddenly unsure if this was a good idea. But his smile doesn't waver. "It's really good to see you both. How was Thanksgiving? How have classes been? What's going on?"

He's only asked three questions and before I can jump in to nudge him to ask a fourth, Anika and Veronika fire off answers.

"Thanksgiving was weird without you. No one ate my mom's cranberry stuffing," Veronika pipes up, casually reading the menu.

"But everyone understands why you weren't there," Anika adds.

"My mom sends her condolences, obviously."

"How are you do—"

"Classes are okay," Veronika interrupts. "We're partying a lot with the theater crew. We're not failing any classes yet either, so that's a plus. NYU is putting together a production of what's basically a hipster version of *Peter Pan*. Anika and I are going to go head-to-head for Wendy, even though she can no doubt steal the role of Captain Hook from this dude Jeremy if she wanted."

Anika stops the waiter. "Hi, could we get some waters? And a muzzle for this one?" The waiter steps away. "You're talking ten times too much."

I would say twenty times too much. I don't understand how Jackson can miss someone so self-absorbed and insensitive. I also don't believe you actually enjoyed playing card games with this girl. Anika seems chill, no doubt. But there's no way you left your hang-out with Veronika and turned to Jackson and said, "I love her! Let's be sure to do that again!"

"I'm just excited," Veronika says. "I haven't seen Jack in a while."

"Jackson," he corrects. "Only Theo calls—called me that."

Besides my dad, you're the only one I let call me Griff. Jackson and I both gave you that intimacy. You're gone, and so are Griff and Jack, dead with you.

"There's no way I could've known that," Veronika says.

"Maybe if you actually showed up to our Skype dates you would," Jackson says. He doesn't sound angry, just disappointed. I'm not sure if Jackson is the angry type. I'm still learning.

"Listen, Jackson . . . Is it okay if I call you Jackson?" Veronika leans forward. "You could've moved out here with us. You decided to stay back home and go to school—"

"Go to a school where there are better programs for me," Jackson interrupts.

"Let's not do this," Anika says. She turns to me, apologetic.

"Animation isn't that bad out here. I know a guy who loves it," Veronika says.

"Good for him. I don't want to attend a school where animation class isn't that bad. I'm sorry my school didn't offer productions of hipster *Wizard of Oz*—"

"*Peter Pan*," Veronika corrects.

"—but I respected you moving out here to do what was best for you. I knew you and Anika would get closer once you started rooming together, but I didn't think I would be so squeezed out."

Veronika glances out the window, as if bored. "I'm surprised you noticed anything, considering you were *always* with Theo."

I don't like where this is going. Someone's going to say something stupid, something unforgivable. I'm still anxious from the three questions Jackson asked that pretty much started this mess. I'm openly scratching my palms on the table, hoping Jackson will notice and cease fire. But he doesn't even acknowledge the waiter, who comes by to take our order and just as quickly steps away so as not to get caught up in the cross fire.

"Theo was always there for me," Jackson says.

Veronika claps. "Good going on Theo, then! You both were in the same city. I stopped making as much of an effort with our Skype dates and texting you back once your relationship with Theo hyper-drove into this serious thing we couldn't possibly understand but were simply expected to. I get it. I was with you during all your rejections and heartbreak in high school, and you picked up some cute guy on the highway and it was magical and totally worth blogging about. I get the obsession, but don't pin this all on me. You're at fault too, Jackson."

He blinks at her. "You have no interest in actually being friends, do you? Don't pity me because of Theo." His voice cracks; mine would roar.

Veronika shakes her head. "There's no pity. Don't try and twist this into me hating you because I didn't love your boyfriend as much as you did. I'm sad for you, of course, but I didn't know the guy. We played cards once, and it was nothing but inside jokes between you two."

There are so many emotions rocketing through me during this ping-pong: jealousy over and curiosity about the inside jokes (even though we have our own, probably ten times as many); rage for how she's making you sound so insignificant; sympathy for Jackson, who, like me, is grieving and, also like me, could really go for friends who didn't act like assholes during this particular time; confusion as to why Anika hasn't shut this down and how everything could spiral out of control so quickly.

"I was making him feel welcome and comfortable," Jackson says.

"That was *our* job," Veronika says, rolling her eyes. "You didn't trust us to try and get to know him. You hogged him to yourself. We honestly felt like you only felt obligated to hang with us because you were in town."

Jackson turns to Anika. "You thought this way, too? With everything she's saying?"

"God no, definitely not everything she's saying." Anika shakes her head, then shrugs. "But I agree with a lot of it. I love you, Jackson, but you put this relationship before everyone and everything else. I'm not mad at you. College and distance will do that to people. But we've had a lot going on over here, too, before Theo . . . We've had a lot going on and we felt weird not being able to tell you. But honestly, we couldn't risk your not putting in the friend time it would ask of you. There would be no coming back from that."

"Let's drop it," Veronika says. "Let's just keep texting over who's seen the latest episode of whatever dumb show we're all bingeing on and keep our tragedies to ourselves."

Now I'm positive that I don't like where this is going, has already gone. I'm fidgety; I scratch and scratch my palms. I try to relax the tic in my neck, rotating it like usual, but it's traveling down to my shoulders and spine, so I'm doing all sorts of stretches. I flick my wrists, weirdly tense as if I've been up late writing essays; I crack all my knuckles and even double-check to make sure they're all cracked. I'm discomfort personified.

"Definitely don't tell me if it's about your recent breakup with the latest love of your life," Jackson says. "I saw your status switch from In a Relationship to Single on Facebook; I'm all caught up there. At least he's still alive."

"Jackson, don't," Anika says.

Veronika's face twists in a way I would've never assumed possible from all the deliriously happy photos I saw of her online. "Did my Facebook status mention I broke up with the latest love of my life because of the abortion I had to have? Did my Facebook status tell you all about how I wasn't ready to be a mom and he wasn't ready to be a dad and how we agreed this was a bad time, that we would go to the clinic together and he would hold my hand through this? Did my Facebook status tell you he didn't show up and hasn't responded to any of my texts? My texts certainly weren't very nice, but the campus psychologist I've been seeing to deal with my guilt seems to think they were fair." Veronika gets up. Her eyes are wide and she's trembling. Anika clears out of her way. "I didn't wish you any ill," she says, leaning over the table. "I know you must've been hurting in ways I don't know, but even when Theo was still alive, I lost a part of myself and lost a little person who was growing inside of me and was going to look like me. You will never get to be Uncle Jackson. I'll never get to be this kid's mom. Next time you see my relationship status change on Facebook, maybe check in and ask me if I'm okay."

Before any of us can say a word, Veronika whirls and runs out into the night. There's silence, a blast of wintry air. The door closes behind her.

"I had no . . ." Jackson is crying and, damn, I'm almost there with him.

It's fair to say he had no idea, but it's also fair to admit he could've known. I see myself in him more than ever right now; it's almost as if we're made of the same messed-up clockwork, ticking and ticking out of balance.

"She'll punch me if I chase after her, right?"

"Is a punch really the worst thing that can happen to you right now?" Anika asks him.

Jackson's head drops.

"If you're not going to go after her, I should," Anika says. She leans over and gives Jackson a quick hug. "Let me know when you're leaving town. We should try and . . . well, not do *this* again, but we should catch up." She waves to me. "I'm sorry we didn't get to talk more." She rests her hand on Jackson's shoulder. "Happy birthday." She rushes off.

"I suck," Jackson says. He wipes his eyes with his sleeve.

The waiter cautiously steps over. "Are you two going to order?"

I tell him we're going to leave and apologize for the holdup. I leave a ten and usher Jackson out. I'm relieved my anxiety is going away, probably because I'm freezing to death once we're back outside. I have to force Jackson's arms back into my dad's coat while he's crossing the street, heading in the complete opposite direction from the train station.

"I'm the worst," Jackson says. "I had no idea, but I could've called."

"You don't suck," I tell him. "That whole thing sucked. We will never know what she's going through. But she also has no idea what *we're* going through. This isn't some competition about who gets to be more upset." Damn, grief is complicated enough without wondering how someone else is handling their own shade of it.

"Which way is the High Line?" he asks, sniffling. His nose is already red.

I respect Jackson's silence as we walk toward Tenth Avenue. I try to convince Jackson to let us take a cab, but whenever I stop to hail one, he keeps going. If he's reacting like this for offending his friend, I can only imagine what happened when he lost hold of you in the ocean.

I still can't bring myself to ask him about that day. Your death is proof that I shouldn't blindly trust these false promises of more years and months and weeks and tomorrows and hours and minutes just because I'm young. And I know Jackson is the only person who can fill in the blanks for me on the afternoon you drowned; he's the only one who can delete all the horrific things I've imagined once and for all. If Jackson goes, those answers will be gone forever. But I still can't get myself to go there, to press him on what it was like to be by your side when you died, what it was like to watch the lifeguard try and pump oxygen into your corpse.

Honestly, Theo, I'm scared the truth might actually be more painful than my imagination.

Jackson is shivering and hugging his chest by the time we make it to the High Line, but if his legs are as stiff as mine, he's soldiering through, following me up the stairs to the top. I've never seen the High Line during winter. I wish Jackson could see the train tracks, but there's a pretty cool quality to the white-dusted potted plants and snow-covered wooden seats.

I hope in your lifetime you once managed to stroll through here during winter, even though I think you would've told me if you had.

Jackson doesn't seem to appreciate the wonder, or to care about being up here at all. He walks straight to the railing and stares down at the traffic. The wind hurts; it's a lot colder up here than down on the streets.

"I should've stopped Veronika, right? I should've apologized and cried with her and asked her how she's doing," Jackson says. I can barely make him out over the wind. "I would've done that a year ago, a month ago. I don't buy into everything she said about me being too obsessed with Theo. But I do feel really damaged without him. I keep pushing people away . . . I let her go. Do you feel that way, too?"

"One hundred percent." I stare at the traffic with him. If drivers could see their ridiculousness from our vantage point, there would be so much less honking, so many fewer snarls. "Did Theo talk about how he stopped speaking to Wade?" I ask him.

Jackson shakes his head. "Not much. It happened over the summer, right?"

"Yeah."

"Theo stopped bringing you both up around that time," Jackson says. "He could tell it made me uncomfortable. I'm sorry."

I nod. It's so damn cold. I really wish we were having this con-versation indoors. "I get it. There were times it felt like he was trying to avoid saying your name, too."

What a mess you've left behind, Theo. The mess isn't your fault, it's mine and Jackson's, but man. This is dirty business here.

"All I know is they got into an argument," Jackson says. "Why did you stop talking to him?"

"Loyalty to Theo," I say. "And now that I can turn to Wade, I don't. I think we're pushing people away because if we can't have Theo, we don't want anyone else."

"But I'm letting you in. I wasn't counting on that."

"We're both fading from ourselves, I think."

We're exactly what I hated in Veronika not even an hour ago. He doesn't agree or disagree.

I grab Jackson's arm and drag him away from the railing, the moon to our backs. We hurry down the stairs and dive into the first available cab, our bodies shaking and teeth chattering. The driver has the heater up as high as it will go, and it's either very weak or my body was minutes away from turning into an ice block.

"How can I make this right, Griffin?"

There are no easy answers here. This won't be as simple as an apology. Jackson and I are broken, in desperate need of repair, but the only mechanic we're interested in seeing is our favorite person—and you're clocked out forever.

"I don't think we're in a good place to try and fix friendships right now in our current state," I answer. I'm honestly not sure if this is some lie to make it easier or an unfortunate truth, but it's where I stand. "Maybe if we keep letting things crash and burn, everything else is bound to fall back in place."

Or maybe the fire will grow.

HISTORY
WEDNESDAY, AUGUST 26TH, 2015

Once we're sure his parents aren't coming back upstairs, just in case they forgot their car keys or wallets or something, Theo and I throw off our clothes as if they're on fire. We jump into bed. This is the last time we're going to be naked together for months, and I'm not going to let these boxes of his folded clothes and belongings ruin that. We've been dating long enough that whenever we do have time to sneak some sex in, we don't usually spend that much time kissing, but this afternoon is different. Theo is kissing with force and hunger, and everything about this feels very final to me. I lock my arms around him, like a wrestler grappling an opponent, and I never want to let him go because I know what has to happen next.

Friday, August 28th, 2015
I'm quiet as Theo, Wade, and I walk to the post office to ship Theo's four boxes to California. Theo's flight is tonight and already I can't keep it together. If I open my mouth, I'm not sure what will come out. Theo and Wade seem fine though, talking about the second *Avengers* movie instead of using this time to reminisce. They'll regret it later; I already am.

The post office is another block down, just across the street.

"I'd Hulk-smash you right now if it gave me the ability to run like Quicksilver to California," Theo tells Wade. "I could even race my packages there."

"What the hell? Why can't you Hulk-smash some stranger?" Wade asks.

Theo laughs. "Pulverize some nameless citizen? That's not the Captain America spirit. He can't be your favorite character anymore. Your new favorite is Daredevil, the Ben Affleck version." He steps off the curb, turning around to see Wade's face.

"I'm going to miss your bullying—dude, watch—"

A car honks its horn and Theo stops walking backward in the street.

"Theo, move!" I scream.

Theo turns around and sees the car. He bullets forward toward the post office, tripping over the boxes he's dropped, falling flat on the street. The car swerves with a screech at the last moment, nearly hitting Wade and me, and brakes at the corner. The driver gets out. He's in a rage, shouting at Theo for being reckless and stupid, but I block out everything he's saying. All that exists is Theo. I run and kneel beside him. He's staring up at me, but I don't think he really sees me.

I hug him, reassuring him over and over he's okay, reassuring *myself* over and over he's okay. He's okay, he's okay, he's okay, he's okay.

He's going to be okay. And I'm going to have to be okay too.

I help Theo up while Wade talks the driver down, convincing him to back off, to get back in his car and forget the whole thing. I lead Theo to the post office, where we both lean against the wall by the entrance, sinking to the ground. I grab his hand and rest my head against his shoulder.

I should tell him I love him, or how I don't know what I would've done if that car ran him down. But I don't. "I think we should break up, Theo."

Theo jerks but doesn't let go of my hand; he's snapped out of his shock. "What?"

"I've been thinking about this the past couple of days. I'm scared I'm going to be holding you back somehow," I say.

"You're not," Theo says. "That's ridiculous."

"I can't risk it. I can't risk getting in your way."

"You're not in my way, Griff. You're the reason I even got my essay done."

That's not true, and he knows it. He would've gotten it done without me. I'm not the reason he qualified for early admission in the first place. That's all him and his brain.

"Everything is going to change when we're not in each other's faces, you know it. I'm not saying we should stop being friends. I want everything to make sense and there's something not right with . . ." I can't do this. "There's something not right with trying to play the long-distance game for two years."

"So you don't love me anymore, Griff?"

We haven't looked each other in the eye this entire conversation. I'm staring at the cigarette butts on the curb. Wade has the common sense to hang out by the mailbox on the corner and leave us alone.

I shake my head against Theo's shoulder. "It's the opposite." My throat tightens. "You're screwed because I'm never going to *stop* loving you. I'm counting on us getting back together when our lives fit better. You're endgame for me. But you have to promise me you're not going to be stupid and walk into traffic. Don't die at all. Okay?"

"Fine. I'll never die," Theo says, hugging me closer to him.

"I mean it. Promise me."

"I promise you: I'll never die."

I sit up and turn his head to mine, kissing him and squeezing his hand. I'm doing the right thing. He's going to focus on himself and figure out the life he wants and hopefully I'm in that picture. I'm going to be okay.

Theo's crying a little and initiates our kisses: the butterfly kiss; the caveman kiss, one where we stay pressed against each other's forehead way longer than usual; the Eskimo kiss, which breaks me and makes me start crying too; and finally the zombie kiss.

"I'm eating your tears," Theo says, laughing. "Gross."

I laugh with him. I really hope I'm right, how this is best for him. It would suck if this is the last time we're ever going to be this close to each other. It already sucks how I'm breaking my own heart for his happiness.

But if he's happy, I'm happy. Right?

TODAY
THURSDAY, DECEMBER 8TH, 2016

I'm sitting on someone's right during free period.

My breaths are tightening. I'm so itchy it's as if an army of ants is launching an assault on my body. I want to scream, but I'm in the library, the place of mandatory silence, a freak-out-free zone. It's one more thing I can't control. I try and keep calm by scratching my palm, but the whole thing is ridiculous. I can't bury my anxiety deep in my hand, like a dog and his used-up bone in a backyard.

I thought this seat was a better spot than the other last seat available, which is to the left of Wade. I don't know the guy next to me, but the more and more I try to avoid Wade's eyes as he peeks at me from across the room, the more and more I get to know the guy a little better, like how he hums songs I don't know and nibbles on his pen cap. These little facts are enough to turn him into a capital p Person, a Person who's on my left, a Person who should be on my right.

I have to ask him to switch seats. It's what I should've done in the first place. I know myself. I should've known that the more and more I push thoughts about Wade and his own grief aside and how guilty I feel he's suffering alone, the more and more I was going to zoom in on someone else. I lean over, which feels bizarre. I really wish you or Jackson were here right now to distract me from all of this.

"Hey. Can we switch seats?"

The pen cap falls out of the guy's mouth. "What?"

"Can we trade seats?" I'm eager to get this resolved, eager to be where I belong, eager to get these antlike itches off of me, eager to get my temperature back down, eager to be out of Wade's sight, eager to be invisible.

He points to a phone connected to an outlet. "My phone is charging."

"You can leave it there."

"Yeah, right."

"No one's trying to steal your phone."

"Says you."

"Are you a freshman?"

"Sophomore."

That explains his arrogance. "Just give me your seat."

"Why?"

I shouldn't have to explain my compulsion to him. But he has what I want. But he's a stranger who knows nothing about me. But maybe he won't be such an asshole if I gave him the chance to understand. But maybe people should be kind without reason.

"It's personal," I say.

"I personally want to keep an eye on my phone," he says.

I stand and kick my seat back, losing control of myself in this controlled environment. "You're not even supposed to have your phone on you!"

The sophomore leans back, surprised, maybe a little frightened. The new librarian approaches with caution. She doesn't know I'm not normally some troublemaker, and I doubt she's going to know how to handle me, either.

"See, now we're both going to get written up," I tell the

sophomore. I bet you anything I'm sitting to his left in detention.

Then I see Wade rushing toward me, his backpack and textbooks abandoned at his desk. I'm catching fire. The librarian is about to say something, but Wade jumps in between us.

"I'm sorry about him," Wade says, and his apology makes it sound like he's sorry for my entire existence. "He's grieving right now."

The librarian's eyes widen. She nods in understanding about who I am. I wonder how she knows. I'm not close with her, but on the other hand, I would've bet everything that for the past few days, I've stunk of grief and looked like a poster boy for depression.

"I understand and I'm sorry for your loss, but you have to keep it down in the library or—"

"We're going right now." Wade grabs me by the shoulders and steers me out into the hall. I take a deep breath, ready to cry.

I shake him off. "Don't touch me."

"How are you doing? You don't answer any texts or calls."

"Take a hint then."

"I'm not going to back off, knowing the state you're in," Wade says. He rubs his eyes. "I knew Theo, too—for longer than you—but okay. You're not being fair treating me like I fucking held Theo's head underwater and—"

I turn left and run. If I don't run, this hallway will become a crime scene. He shouts his apology for that unbelievably dickheaded thing he just said, but I keep going. Wade has never been good with words, but now I can't get this visual out of my head of you, out in the ocean, being drowned by the person you trusted the most before I came around.

I'm getting the hell out of here—off this floor, out of this building. I almost trip going down the stairs, and I half-wish I did and broke my neck. I'm sorry; that's not okay to say. You know I would never give up on life like that, especially knowing yours was stolen. I would never just press a button and power myself down.

I run to my locker.

Remembering my combination is hard, but my fingers turn the dial and do their thing. I grab my coat and slam the locker shut, charging to a side entrance. The dean is coming down the stairs.

"No running, Griffin!"

I don't stop. I rush past her and push open the door. She calls for me, chasing after me with no jacket or sweater, but I lose her quickly. I run through the street, almost slipping because of the slush, and I run into the train station and text my dad to let him know I'm coming home and never going back to that place.

This all happened because someone was sitting on my left.

WE'RE ALL GATHERED IN the living room, discussing what went down at school. Jackson is sitting to my right, as it should be, and my parents are sitting across from us on the chairs they dragged over from the dining-room table. Everyone has calmed down, myself included. I wasn't surprised to learn from Jackson that my mom was freaking out after she got the call from my dad telling him I ditched.

"You're staying home from school tomorrow with me," my mom says. She's trying to make eye contact with me, but I continue staring at the TV, even though it's off. "You're too vulnerable in that environment right now."

"I don't want to go back next week either," I say. I'm done pretending anything I do in class actually matters for my future. I could ace all my classes like you did and complete all my homework assignments and still find myself the victim of a random and fatal accident. If you knew you were going to die young, would you have spent as much time studying, Theo? I'd bet two dollars you would have, actually. But we're different. I can't even sit on someone's right without having a panic attack.

"Okay. We can see how you're feeling on Monday," Mom says.

Dad nods. He looks worried, not that I can blame him. "We understand how hard it is being somewhere where you spent so much time with Theo," he says. He's right, but school isn't the only place where I spent so much time with you. He turns to my mom. "Maybe next semester we can get Griff transferred to another school. Fresh start."

"This isn't some out of sight, out of mind thing," I say. "It's Theo."

Jackson nods. "Transferring is too easy. I've thought about it too, but it feels wrong. Like I'm trying to forget him."

My parents look at each other. They've always had a way of wordlessly consulting. They're honestly both good cops. The closest my dad has ever come to playing bad cop was when he shrugged Jackson off after meeting him, but now it's my mom's turn. "Jackson, would you mind if we speak to Griffin alone for a second? We need to talk to him about something sensitive."

"Whatever you're going to tell me I'm just going to tell him," I say.

"It's okay," Jackson says. "It's a family meeting, I get it. Sorry." He gets up and heads straight into my room, closing the door behind him.

"That wasn't called for," I say.

Mom looks at me. "We've been very accommodating, but I'm honestly not sure if Jackson's being here is what's best for you right now," she says. "You're going through a huge loss—"

"Jackson is the only one who understands," I interrupt.

"—and it might be time for Jackson to go home to give you a more stable environment. More importantly, we need you to see a real therapist." She stands and takes Jackson's seat, *your* seat, beside me. My parents rarely falter on this left versus right business, thankfully; you never did, either. "If Jackson's presence is affecting your compulsions, it's a problem. Regardless, you need to see a therapist and psychiatrist soon."

I can't tell them that I'll be fine, that there's really nothing wrong with me. I hate even recognizing myself as wrong. But I also doubt words and exposure therapy will make the compulsions stop. I think it'll be the opposite, like seeing a psychiatrist will only drag the compulsions more into focus. The real problem is that my parents are too *normal* to understand this.

"You can't make me," I say. And I know I have them there. There's no way they can punish me any more than I already punish myself.

"Therapy isn't a bad thing, or anything to be ashamed of," Mom says. She reaches for me.

"Then you go." I shake her hand away and go to my room. If she wants to go see a "mental health professional" and report back on how I'm supposed to be doing according to the seven stages of grief or whatever bullshit they'll feed her, she can be my guest. I don't need that in my life any more than I do Wade's telling me everything about you I already know.

I just need you and Jackson.

I close the door behind me and throw myself onto my bed.

Jackson is sitting on the air mattress, texting someone. "They want me to go, don't they?" I don't answer him, which says everything. "It's okay. Don't get mad at them. It's probably for the best, anyway. It's like we said out there, that we have to face Theo, wherever he is. We can't hide from him."

"But Theo *lived* in New York," I say. I sit up. I can't believe my parents have made Jackson so uncomfortable he's ready to go. "Sending me to a different school isn't going to change that."

"But I don't live here," Jackson says quietly. "Theo isn't here for me the way he is for you." He wobbles from the center of the deflating air mattress to the edge and sits with his elbows on his knees. "I already texted my dad, and he's looking into getting me a ticket this weekend. It might be hard because of the snow and cancellations, but we'll see."

So that's it, then. Once he's gone, I know I'm going to end up back in that black hole of worthlessness. I can already feel his support being sucked away. I lie back down and stare up at the ceiling.

Jackson fills the silence with a list of everything he's been missing back home anyway, always in pairs because, like you, he's grown hyperconscious of my needs. He misses his mom (a lot) and dad (a little); his dog and the runs they go on; his bedroom, your dorm room; his school halls and classrooms (not enough to resume classes, though); his car and driving in general; the sun and sleeveless shirts; iced coffee and popsicles; digging his toes into the grass at the park and into the sand at the beach.

"I would miss all that stuff, too," I say, even though a lot of it is alien to me, closer to an alternate universe you'd create than my reality. I don't know what it's like to have the freedom of a parent-free space like a dorm room where you could've come over without us feeling like there was a spotlight on what we were doing. I don't know anything about getting behind the wheel of my own car—or any car—and deciding my own path, wasting as much gas as I want because it's gas I bought with my own money. I don't even know what it's like to have a dog. But I can't fault Jackson for missing the things I do get, like my toes in the grass; drinking iced tea; the heat I feel on my arms and the back of my neck when I'm in a tank top; and even something as annoying as shielding my eyes from the sun, because I'll take brightness and sweat over darkness and chills anytime.

Jackson takes a deep breath. "It's almost been one month . . ."

I know.

"This is for the best. It may sound stupid, but I want to be back home on that day," Jackson says.

I envy him so much. He gets to go back to his land of sunshine, where in spite of the pain, good memories of you will greet him. I'm doomed to freezing weather that will keep me trapped in my room, alone with impulsive thoughts I don't want to act on. I almost joke how it'll be nice to have my room back to myself, how I hated competing for shower time with him anyway, but they're lies. Jackson is not my enemy. He's filled cold silences with warm stories, even if those stories sometimes hit too close and burned me.

Jackson gets up and approaches my bed. "Can I sit?"

I've been really good about not letting him on my bed; he's never asked, I've never invited. He's always chilled on the bedside chair or the air mattress. But I'm vulnerable, so without moving an inch from my current position, I turn my eyes away from the ceiling to his and say yes.

He sits down at the edge of my bed, not pushing his luck by getting too comfortable.

"Thanks for letting me stay here, Griffin. Seriously. I still feel broken—that's not your fault, that sounds bad—but I don't feel like a million different pieces anymore. I'm never expecting to feel whole again. I don't think you are either. I hate the idea of leaving you here alone." He shuts up, and his silence isn't the same silence I'm okay with, the one where he and I don't have to say anything and are just cool with someone being around. "Are you going to be okay?"

That's when it comes to me. Out of nowhere, like those genius epiphanies you had all the time, I'm possessed with brilliance. "I'll go with you. You can show me what Theo's life was like out there. We could keep each other company on the thirteenth." Saying these words out loud, I feel like I'm flying right out of that black hole.

"Would your parents let you go?"

"I can work it out with them. Are you cool with me going with you?"

"Absolutely." Jackson smiles. "Let me text my dad."

He pulls out his phone, but I throw my arms around his neck, and his arms wrap around my waist. I should pull away, but I don't.

FRIDAY, DECEMBER 9TH, 2016

"I'VE MISSED FAMILY HANG-OUTS since the divorce," Jackson tells my parents over dinner—his "farewell dinner," as my dad put it. We're buttering them up now in the hopes they'll let me go with him on Monday. "This is back before my parents took shots at each other, obviously, but for the most part it was cool catching them up about my day. I think I've missed home-cooked meals even more, though. The steak tacos really lived up to their glory, Mr. Jennings."

"Glad to hear," my dad says, wiping his mouth clean of salsa. "But seriously, call me Gregor."

"You got it, Gregor."

"Thank you again for understanding, Jackson," Mom says. "It's been wonderful having you around the house. It truly isn't personal. We just want Griffin back on track, and the same for you as well."

Jackson nods. "I can't thank you all enough for letting me camp out here. It's time for me to figure out my next moves at home, too."

I'm scratching my palms. "I want to go with him for a couple of days. It's almost one month since Theo died, and I want to be in California with Jackson for it. It's not like I'm going back to school right now and—"

"Your time off isn't a vacation," Mom interrupts.

"I wouldn't call grieving Theo a vacation."

"I'm sorry. That's not what I meant, but I'm sorry. But your recess from classes has been suggested so you can relax somewhere familiar. You've never been to California," Mom says.

I know a lot about California from everything you've told me, from everything Jackson has told me. I know from my own research, when I was considering going to college out there to be reunited with you. I know from common sense.

"Have you outgrown your fear of flying?" Dad asks. "If you had a panic attack in your library, we can't trust you to be okay up in the air for several hours."

I'm about to suggest I take a sleeping pill, when more excuses come my way. They can't afford a plane ticket on such short notice, especially given the money they're saving for my therapy sessions. They don't care that Jackson's dad has already booked us both tickets. Neither of them can take off work right now to accompany me, like I'm some kid on a field trip in need of a chaperone instead of a seventeen-year-old who would be staying with Jackson's mom.

"I'm not comfortable with this," Mom says.

"Me either," Dad says.

"Well, I'll be uncomfortable here once Jackson leaves," I say. I don't get how they haven't seen a difference in me. I've been able to watch a little TV without feeling guilty for not grieving and crying. I'm in a place again where I can imagine myself laughing again, *really* laughing, with tears in my eyes and everything. Besides, I want to see your dorm room, your favorite places, the places you avoided. I even want to visit the beach where you died. "I really want to see what Theo's life was like out there. I swear I'll give therapy a shot if you let me go."

Mom grabs my hand. "Therapy has to come first, Griffin. We don't like trying to pressure you into this, but we all have to face the truth here: you need to see someone professionally. You'll be able to visit Jackson in California when you're feeling better. I'm sorry." She releases me and begins clearing the table.

I was delusional to think they'd let me go. But at least I asked.

It would've been nice to leave with their permission.
Oh well.

SATURDAY, DECEMBER 10TH, 2016

IN THE CEMETERY, JACKSON and I pass a lot of elaborate headstones carved from rocks of different colors, their sharp angles poking out like the skeleton limbs buried beneath them. Maybe the families wanted to throw down as much money as possible to get the best headstone in the catalogue, one final splurge on the one they lost. Even though your headstone is pretty standard—flat-faced, gray, only knee-high—to me it stands out better than all the others, almost as if it would glow in the dark. I want to kneel before it, but then I realize I'm stepping on you. This is the closest we've been physically since November 21st, when we buried you. I don't want to think about the state of your body under this frozen dirt. But I can't help it.

"This feels right," Jackson says. "Thanks for bringing me here. I can't think of a better way to spend my last weekend in New York."

"Do you think you'll ever come back?" I ask him. "Maybe to make things right with Veronika and visit Anika?" I still can't believe Anika never made time to talk things out with Jackson; there's no way he could've known about Veronika's abortion. If these are his friends, maybe he needs new ones. Maybe that's me. Maybe that's why he was drawn to you.

"Yeah. I would want to see you, too," Jackson says.

There's a flash of warmth in my face before the cold wind chews it away. "It's weird, right? Us. Not bad-weird anymore, but still weird when you think about how much time we spent trying *not* to be friends."

"Every morning I wake up without Theo, I think about how

strange it is that I'm waking up in your room. It always takes a second to click, no offense."

"None taken. I'm the same way. I want to ask you something. And you can't lie to me or avoid answering because we're pretty much standing on Theo right now and that's deeper than swearing on a Bible."

"Shoot." Jackson doesn't even stop to consider this like I would've.

"Did you worry Theo would ever break up with you and get back together with me?"

"Competing against his first love was so impossible sometimes," Jackson says. "I know Theo would never cheat on me, but if he were going to do it, I know it would've been with you."

You never told him what happened when you were here in June without him, did you? Sorry, that's taboo. Even now.

Jackson bounces a little to warm up. "If it's any consolation, I don't think I would've had it in me to be his friend if we'd broken up. I would've wanted him in my life, but I wouldn't have been able to stand it. I would've said goodbye. I don't know how you survived this."

I'm not sure I actually *did* survive it. Look at me now, Theo: I'm about to run away from home and get on a plane, two things that had never crossed my mind to do. Maybe I will need therapy when I get back. I'm shattered and empty. I'm loyal to the end, but that's the heart of my problem and may soon be Jackson's too: when exactly is the end?

SUNDAY, DECEMBER 11TH, 2016

JACKSON IS FOLDING HIS clothes, packing for the flight tomorrow. "Are you sure you want to go? There's no turning around once the plane takes off."

He's whispering, but I almost panic that my parents will

overhear us. Then I remember they're both napping—or having sex, whatever—in their bedroom. "I'm definitely going. You're more scared of them than I am."

Jackson puts his shirts in his bag. "I don't want to piss them off. I like them."

"If you snitch on me, I'll end you," I say.

"Not snitching. I really want you out there with me. It's the only reason I'm not completely freaking out right now."

I'm not freaking out, either, and I'm not sure why. Maybe because I'm committed. I'll have to lie in the worst way possible and scare the shit out of my parents to get out there, but I'll call them the second Jackson and I land, so they know I'm safe. I'll fly home on Wednesday and I'll be punished forever, but it's worth it. I have to see how you lived.

The doorbell rings.

"Let me get that." I rush out of bed and open the door to find Wade standing there with an aluminum tray; I can smell cupcakes. He baked them for my birthday this year. I can see one of the ties you bought him peeking out from underneath his coat.

"Sorry to stop by unannounced," Wade says. "You weren't answering my texts and I wanted to see how you were doing, since Thursday . . ."

His voice trails off.

Jackson comes out of my room with an empty glass on his way to the kitchen. He waves. "Wade, hey. How's it going?"

Wade's eyes narrow. He turns away from Jackson and back to me. "What the hell is going on?" He's quiet, but the question sinks in as if he shouted it. "You won't talk to me but you're hanging out with the guy that made your life hell?"

My lips feel dry. "Things have changed," I say. I want to close the door on him.

Wade closes his eyes, fighting back tears, and shakes his head. "Clearly. You're no longer suffering alone, unlike me. Real nice, Griffin. You're so fucking selfish."

I should tell Wade about the trip. But he might react the same way as my parents. I can't risk this for him.

I *am* selfish.

Wade drops the tray at my feet. "Hope you both enjoy." He storms away and slams the door behind him, the noise echoing through the hallway.

I can't chase after him, Theo. I have to get ready. I have a flight to catch.

MONDAY, DECEMBER 12TH, 2016

CAN YOU BELIEVE IT, Theo? I'm in an airplane, ready to take off.

I'm going to California with Jackson, and I'm fighting back a freak-out. I have to keep it together before I get kicked off. Before I prove my parents right that I'm probably not in the best state to be doing this.

I'm not a fan of what I had to do. Jackson hates it too, but it didn't stop him from pulling the cab over a couple of blocks away after he said goodbye to me and my family, so I could join him. I only have a small backpack with me. My parents think it's full of books and notebooks for a fake trip to the coffee shop to work on make-up assignments. It's actually stuffed with shirts, underwear, a phone charger, and a toothbrush. I have the other essentials in my wallet—cash, starter debit card, ID, ticket.

I hope *you'll* also forgive me for lying. I'm doing it for you.

We're in row fourteen and I'm seat number one. Good row number, okay seat number. But this panic attack has been crawling my way since we arrived at the airport. I didn't count on all the lines and the brief flight delay. I try buckling my seat-belt, but it's different than car seatbelts, and Jackson assists me without asking, which startles me for a second because he's so close to my dick. But within seconds he's done and I'm fastened in; I can't help but feel as if he's trapped me here, like a strait-jacket.

"How are you doing?" Jackson asks.

I shake my head and twist my ring finger, the trick you taught me.

Jackson reaches into his backpack and pulls out a copy of last month's *Entertainment Weekly*. "This'll help you take your mind off of it."

I go straight for the movie reviews, but in no time a flight attendant calls for our attention and delivers all sorts of safety instructions about where to find oxygen masks and how to locate exit doors. Jackson is reading his own magazine, which annoys me a little because he's responsible for me on this flight. "Do you have this memorized?"

He answers me by quoting the flight attendant and mimicking her movements. "I've flown a few times," Jackson says. "We're going to be okay."

Within minutes the plane is moving down the runway and it feels like driving down the highway. Except cars don't pick up speed the way this planes does; cars never make me so nervous that I grab the door handle the way I'm gripping the armrest. Cars don't shake violently like this. Cars definitely don't lift at the front and take off into the air.

Jackson's hand rests on top of mine, hesitantly. I don't pull away, and his hand expands, holding mine. "How are you feeling?"

The plane swerves left and I'm certain this is it; we're going to crash. I look out the window during this shift and it's sad how this plane didn't even get high enough to make the people in the freezing city below seem small, like ants in the snow. The plane finds its center. The captain announces our flight will be a little over five hours and that attendants will be around shortly with refreshments.

"That's it?" I ask.

"That's it," Jackson says, releasing my hand.

My heart is still thumping. "Were you ever scared to fly?"

"It's probably better for me to answer this after we land."

"We're already up in the air. Whatever is going to happen is going to happen," I say.

"You're not going to parachute out of here?" Jackson asks.

"I have no idea how to get out of this seatbelt. I'm not going anywhere."

"I still get really nervous, and I'm not sure when that will stop," he admits. "It's weird, because my dad is a pilot. Or maybe that's the reason. I'm always a little on edge. This may sound selfish or horrible, but the only time I felt sort of ready for any tragedy was when I was with Theo."

"Was he brave on planes?"

I'm asking Jackson to tell me something about you I don't know while I'm flying. What a day, huh?

"Theo was funny. He's the reason I buy magazines for flights instead of watching a movie or something. He would go through all the features, stuff like 'Who Wore It Best?' and would owe himself a dollar every time he was able to guess the right actor or actress for the celebrity crossword puzzles."

I might cry. This isn't a bad cry. This isn't one of my I-never-got-to-do-this-with-you cries, I swear. It's one of my I-might-have-a-laugh-attack-if-I-keep-thinking-of-this cries, which are good. I'm hit with a realization: the Theo you were with him isn't the Theo you were with me, and maybe that's okay. I've been so desperate to know who you were becoming, I never stopped to think about how everything that made you my favorite person could've changed. Maybe you didn't outgrow me; you just became someone else. It doesn't make me want to know the new you any less, but it makes me feel a little less worthless.

"That's really funny," I say, picturing you hovering over crossword puzzles the same way you did jigsaw puzzles, except with a few bucks fanned out before you and rewarding-slash-deducting from yourself every time you got something right. "So being with Theo is the only time you felt safe?"

"Not safe. Comforted. Knowing I'd be able to hold Theo's hand or hug him if anything happened, comforted me. I knew I wouldn't be leaving Theo behind if I died alone."

It's screwed up, but it makes sense. "Then Theo drowned in front of you." The words just pop out of my mouth. It's the first time I've said it out loud, and it shocks him too. He tenses up and tucks his hands between his legs, squeezing them tight, like he's locking them away. Even as we're on our way to celebrate how you lived and to visit the beach where you died, we haven't crossed this line yet.

You left us alone. Your death made us each a piece in this awkward puzzle that doesn't completely come together, but it's enough to make out the image: two boys in love with someone who is never coming back.

I shouldn't have brought this up. It was a shitty thing to say to Jackson. He has to live with how he wasn't able to save you. I was lucky enough to be spared that tragedy.

We're pretty quiet for the next five hours. I even get a couple of brief naps in. When the plane slows and dips down, I jerk upright, tensing. Then the pilot announces we've begun our descent and to make sure our seatbelts are on. Jackson side-eyes me and laughs.

"Don't forget: we're *supposed* to be going down at this part," Jackson says.

"If I hate this I'm walking home."

"I'll walk with you."

I bravely look out the window as the plane slows and lowers—in little drops I wish were smoother, but who cares as long as we land. Once we're lower than the clouds, I see a city washed in sunlight. I can even make out a beach in the distance. The plane safely touches down on the landing strip and bullets toward the airport with incredible speed, roaring. I'm thrown forward a little. And then it's over. We're gently rolling toward the gate.

"You flew!" Jackson says.

"I flew," I breathe.

My life has changed. I can't take back my first flight any more than I can take back losing my virginity to you, any more than I can take back the things I would love to undo. Possibilities are wheeling through my mind rapidly. If I can fly here for you, where will I go for me?

IT'S ALMOST FIFTY DEGREES in California this morning—I've gone back in time by three hours—so I roll down my window because I welcome anything above New York's twenty degrees (with a wind chill that makes it feel like ten). I'm on the left in the cab, as I should be, taking in the sights—mainly other cars—as we exit the freeway and enter Santa Monica.

I have one missed call from my mom and a couple of texts from both of my parents, asking me how the homework is coming along and how I'm doing. I feel a wave of nauseating dread, even though I knew all along what would happen.

"Let me get this over with," I tell Jackson.

"Good luck."

I almost ask him to put on headphones so he doesn't have to hear my mom's deafening scream when she learns I'm three thousand miles away.

I swipe the number.

"One second, Griffin," Mom answers, and she tells whoever she's with that she needs a minute. "Sorry. There you go. How are you doing?"

"I have to tell you something, and you're going to be really upset," I say.

"What's going on . . . Griffin, please tell me that you're not in California," Mom says. Her voice is calmer than I expected. But there's also an edge that's totally unfamiliar.

"I'm in California," I say. "I'm sorry. I really wanted to be out of there, and I'll do whatever you want when I get back, therapy and whatever else, but I—"

"You are coming home today!"

There she is, the mom I know; the mom you knew, too.

"Do not leave that airport," she goes on. "Stay there—"

"I'm coming home on Wednesday morning," I interrupt. "I'll give you all the flight details."

"That's not happening. I'm flying out there and—"

"Fine. Fly out here. But I'm still not leaving until Wednesday. Tomorrow Jackson and I are celebrating Theo's life," I say. It's a struggle to keep my voice even. "I'll send you Jackson's mom's phone number along with my flight info. You can call her."

Jackson texts me his mom's number.

"How will I know I'm talking to Jackson's mom?" she cries. "It could be some woman on the streets you paid twenty dollars. How can I possibly trust you anymore? Have you called your father yet? Wait. He didn't know, did he?"

"No, I called you first."

"You lied to us." She sounds so disappointed. "You tricked us."

"I know. I know, and I'm so sorry, but I had to—"

"I'm at work right now," she interrupts. "Send me Jackson's mom's number and pick up when I call you." Finally her voice softens. "Are you okay? How was the flight?"

"I'm okay. I didn't freak out. Jackson took care of me."

Mom breathes into the phone. "Pick up when I call you next."

"Okay. I love you, Mom."

There's an excruciating pause. "I love you, too." She hangs up.

"Yikes." I avoid Jackson's eyes as I send in a flurry all of the relevant information to both my parents. My dad texts me a minute later, asking for both of Jackson's parents' addresses, which Jackson types out for him.

Jackson hands me back my phone. He offers a tentative grin. "Well, how are you liking California?"

I laugh. "Not the best twenty minutes of my life, but not the worst, either," I say.

"Let's improve that. What do you want to do today?"

I look out the window and hope I don't get sent home. Jackson's parents could tip the scale in that direction. "I don't know. Your call."

When I imagined myself moving to California, I always thought the first thing you and I would do together would be hitting up the beach. It's an obvious thing to do, but it's such a one-eighty from what we're used to back in New York. But that was in an alternate universe. I don't have any direction of my own out here in this one.

Twenty minutes later, the taxi drops us off on a street corner. The air feels different, buoyant, like I can float on a breeze that smells like ocean and seaweed. I adjust my backpack on my shoulder. I missed the sun, but I'm already wishing I had sunglasses. Instead I shield my eyes with your bunched up hoodie.

Jackson pays the cab driver and points down the block at a light orange one-story house between two sand-colored houses. Considering it's the only house with a ramp and railings leading to the front door, it's what I would've guessed it was. The house looks worn and a little battered, like it's weathered a fierce storm, but I love it. I can sense history pulsating from it.

"Is this your childhood home?" I ask.

Jackson shakes his head. "When my parents split, everything else did too. My dad got his apartment in Culver City, and Mom stayed here in Santa Monica. Mom's feels like the closest to home, but I really miss where I grew up. It would've been cool to show you and Theo that house, but this one's not so bad."

Yeah, having a house is definitely not so bad. Not to mention the free flights he gets from a father who could probably easily afford every trip if he had to. I'm not about to call him out on any of that, of course—especially since you told me you did already. You were around him so much that bursts of Jackson's privilege never bothered you. You cracked a couple of jokes Jackson never found too much truth in, but it reached a boiling point when he wanted you to skip work to hang out with him. "Some of us need jobs to afford the museum," you told him, and a fight broke out. The fight wasn't enough to break you up, though.

Jackson finds his keys inside his backpack and unlocks the front door.

"Mom, we're here!" He looks around, crouching over expectantly, and fast little footsteps come charging our way. With a name like Chloe, I expected her to be a really beautiful golden retriever, but she's a black collie. Her tail wags as she gets her ass scratched by Jackson.

"I'm in the kitchen!" comes his mom's voice.

I step toward Chloe and she runs out from underneath Jackson's hand and backs away from us.

"You're too tall to walk up on her like that. Get down here with me," Jackson says.

I crouch beside Jackson. He makes kissing sounds and says Chloe's name in this funny voice that sounds like a stoned Mickey Mouse. I guess Chloe trusts Mickey Mouse on pot, because she comes over and lets us both pet her. In addition to the ass scratch, Chloe likes being pet roughly on her head.

Jackson throws his stuff on the couch and I do the same. The place feels very spare, not as elaborate as I was expecting. Maybe there isn't so much history, after all. Or maybe it's history that they don't want to show off. I understand that now. They've been living here long enough that they should have more furniture, shouldn't they?

I follow Jackson into the kitchen, where his mother is sitting at the dining-room table in her wheelchair. Ms. Lane is typing one-handed while she holds up a piece of mail. I've never seen pictures of his father, but Jackson is a younger version of his mother, no doubt. He bends over and kisses her on the cheek, then hugs her.

"I'm happy you're home," Ms. Lane says, hugging Jackson so hard she drops her piece of mail.

I rush over and pick it up for her, handing it to her when they part. "Hi. I'm Griffin."

She smiles up at me warmly. "It's great to meet you, Griffin. Thank you so much for hosting Jackson. I know it meant so much to him to be with friends," Ms. Lane says. Then she shakes her phone and her face grows somber. "There's a bounty out for your head, by the way." She turns to her son. "You could've warned me that your guest was a runaway."

"I'm sorry," Jackson says. "You're still okay with him staying, right?"

"Give your mother a call," Ms. Lane says to me, sounding weary and resigned. "She's coming around to the idea as long as you both stay here and not the dorm."

Relief floods through me. That was the final hurdle. I know a shitstorm of trouble is still waiting for me when I get back, but I'm clear to be in California until Wednesday, for you, with Jackson. "Okay. Will do."

"My condolences, by the way," Ms. Lane adds. "I understand you and Theo were very close."

"Thank you."

She nods. "Have a seat."

I wonder where you sat whenever you visited. I go for the seat to the left of Jackson, obviously.

"How was flying, Griffin? First time, right?"

I glance between them. "Jackson kept me sane." I haven't met someone's parents at this level of face time since yours, and it feels really weird. "I think it'll take a few more flights before I really get used to it, but it wasn't the worst thing. Going home to that weather is going to really suck."

"Ah, if I could go anywhere right now, it would be New York during the winter. I miss coats and walking down the street and my toes numbing because of the slush. Traveling has been admittedly frustrating since the accident. Rolling through the streets of New York would be difficult."

I don't ask about the accident that landed her in the wheelchair, even though she seems like she'd be open to talking about it. Jackson never told me. It still feels like her story to offer and not one I should ask just because I'm curious. It's a lot like when people at school were asking around to hear how you died. Just because people are curious doesn't give them the right to an answer.

"I like your setup here," I say. "Your house is awesome, too."

"It's home," Ms. Lane says.

I want to study Jackson's reaction, but I don't want to give him away in case he hasn't talked about this discomfort with his mother. I would be a little surprised since they seem so close, but you and I were close and that didn't stop me from withholding stuff to protect your heart. Maybe that's what's happening here.

She turns to me. "I hope I'm not out of line, but Jackson mentioned you're also taking a break from school at the moment. Something happened at school?"

It spills out of me. I'm not sure why, maybe because it's so exhausting to bottle it all up, but I tell Ms. Lane everything. I let her know about all about my compulsions, their rules, and how they rule me. I let her know about the freak-out where I bolted from the library and got home and threw off my uniform and banished it to my closet. I let her know about how my parents want me to commit to therapy outside of my guidance counselor. I let her know how helpful her son has been for my recovery.

Ms. Lane smiles briefly, proud of the son she raised, of the boy you loved—even if she doesn't approve of how he handled my surprise visit. She wheels over to the refrigerator and pulls out a strawberry birthday cake shaped like the letter *J*. Jackson is smiling so wide, kind of kidlike, and I'm not sure I'll ever get over how surprising it is to see happiness in someone who's lost someone they love.

Ms. Lane bursts into "Happy Birthday" by herself, but I jump in midway—again, surprising—and what's even more surprising is when Jackson jumps in and sings happy birthday in his own honor. We're all laughing by the end . . . and man, Theo, I really wish you were here to add your voice to the chorus.

THE LATEST SHOCKING THING to happen in *this* universe, the one I live in, not one you created: I'm walking into Jackson Wright's bedroom with my bag, to stay the night. I'm tempted to ask him everything you've ever done in this room, like where you studied if you ever studied here, or if you ever sat on the ledge of his window when you talked on the phone, like you did in my room. But that could lead to something too intimate, something that will cross a line.

His walls are rust-orange, a shade that might look red when sunlight isn't pouring through his white-framed windows. I'm pretty sure the gigantic bed in the center of the room is king-size. What goes without question is I've never seen any bed piled high with a mountain of clothes like his is. I notice his closet door and dresser drawers are wide open; packing for a trip while grieving must suck. There's a little bed in the corner, which I'm guessing is for Chloe and not guests like me. There are bookshelves with very few books but plenty of card games and their expansion packs.

"This is it," Jackson says, tossing his bags onto the floor. "Bedroom one of two. What do you think?"

There are five movie posters on the wall from classic films, but I've only seen *Edward Scissorhands* (which I hated). The other four—*The Goonies, The Shining, Scream, A Nightmare on Elm Street*—I haven't, so when I group them like that, it's not bad. Still, the fifth movie poster haunts me. "Guess I'll be sleeping in the living room."

"Why? There's plenty of room on the bed . . ."

"Once you move every article of clothing you own? I have

a thing against *Edward Scissorhands.*" I'm actually not entirely making excuses for my OCD; that poster is seriously creepy, and so was the movie.

"What is this thing you have against my favorite Johnny Depp movie?"

"I saw it as a kid and it scared the shit out of me. I had a nightmare he came to my school cafeteria in a straitjacket and wanted to cut me," I confess.

"But he's in a straitjacket."

"First off, anyone approaching me in a straitjacket is scary enough. Let's factor in the fact that Edward has blades for hands, and what you're left with is ten-year-old Griffin so scared his parents had to give the DVD away to a neighbor because he couldn't stand having it in the house." I point at the poster. "And now I'm faced with my enemy again, twenty times bigger than the DVD case."

"We should watch it again while you're here."

"I will leave today if you think that's going to happen."

Jackson walks over to this little desk he has in the corner. "How are you going to unlock the door if you're in a strait-jacket?"

"Not funny."

"You're right, I'm sorry." Jackson raises one hand up in sur-render. Then he quickly reveals the other from behind his back, holding a pair of scissors and clipping at air. He takes a step toward me and laughs before he can get too close—too close to my raised fist, that is. He puts the scissors back down on the desk. "Truce?"

"Truce." I put my bag down beside his. "This room is huge." Twice the size of mine, I would guess.

"Yeah, out of the three bedrooms, my mom let me take the master bedroom. I guess she didn't see any reason to be in the room meant for two parents. I also think she wanted me to have some victory after the divorce, so big room it is,"

Jackson says, opening his window as Chloe comes in and settles herself into her bed.

I walk around, spotting the same photo of you and Jackson on his desk that was in your room where ours used to be. Jackson folds some of his clothes. I help him out until I notice some writing on the wall in the corner of the room. I walk over and it's faded, but I can make it out: *THEODORE + JACK*. His name is in your handwriting and yours is in his.

"What's this?" I don't mean for my tone to be so accusatory.

Jackson stops balling up some socks. "We did that after our first fight. And yeah, we were fighting about you."

He tells me the story; it's the first I'm hearing of this. You and Jackson were hanging out in Venice Beach after classes. You were both mimicking the lifts and flips the other muscular guys were doing, and you were failing spectacularly. In the middle of Jackson's cartwheel, I called you and you answered. Jackson thought you were going to tell me you'd call me back, but you sat down in the sand and kept talking.

"It bothered me so much," Jackson said. "But I couldn't say anything bad about you. I refused to say anything at all after he finally got off the phone twenty minutes later. Theo hated that silence."

What you don't understand, Theo, is silence is sometimes better than someone speaking before they're ready. That is how lies slip out.

"I drove us back here so I could give him back his stuff, and I was going to break up with him. Anika didn't believe me when I told her that, but I was serious. I didn't want to keep competing against his past. Theo told me to stop being so silent and tell him what's wrong. I told him it was you. He grabbed a marker and said he was going to prove his allegiance."

Jackson closes the shades and turns off the lights. *THEODORE + JACK* comes alive, glowing ocean blue in the dark. I can only imagine how bright the words will become when it's actually pitch-black out. I feel something unpleasant stir inside me.

"He had no idea it was an old glow-in-the-dark marker Veronika left behind. He said if I actually cared about him, I would write his name down. I got down there with him and did it." Jackson stares at your names, his voice softening. "Then he said he loved me. First time. I said it back."

I don't say anything. My silence is crushing. You used to tell me about all these fights, fights I used to find happiness in, but you never told me this one ended the way it did; you never told me about this one at all.

"We need to get out of here," I hear myself say. "If I'm going to be in trouble in California, I'm going to make the most of it. Where can we go? What can we go do? Anything."

"How about a drive?" Jackson asks, flipping on the light so that your names fade instantly.

"Good battle plan," I say.

But very little planning actually goes into this mini road trip. Jackson doesn't swap out his sneakers for sandals to be more Californian (or at least what I understand Californians to be like); he doesn't pack a cooler with sandwiches and water bottles; and he doesn't grab suntan lotion in case we end up outside longer than expected. He tells Ms. Lane we're heading out for a drive, but that's it. Jackson takes me outside to the connecting garage, where a black Toyota Camry is waiting for him. Jackson gets into the driver's seat and so I automatically go to the back, sitting in the center, opposite the rearview mirror, where some sort of spy pen is dangling.

"You don't want to sit shotgun?" Jackson asks. "Oh. Wait, so how does that work? Do you never sit in the front?"

"I'll sit in the front when I learn how to drive or move to London," I say. Or if I manage to break out of this compulsion, but let's be realistic: here I come, London.

"Noted."

Jackson presses a button and all four windows are automatically lowered. That ocean breeze fills the car. He pulls out of the garage, the gate shutting behind him, turns sharply right, and sets off down the road, wind flying into my face in the most relaxing way possible. I'm about to shout to ask Jackson where we're going first, when he turns on the radio, blasting the first pop-heavy station that comes on.

Before I know it, he's beautifully singing this terrible song about pregaming on a Friday night. He drives with one arm resting on the window frame and occasionally throws his head back with closed eyes to carry a tune I would slaughter if I dared to lose myself in a moment like he does. But it's fun for me, watching him sing, just like it was fun watching you sing in the car with your parents or in your bedroom. I look to the front passenger seat, imagining you sitting on Jackson's right, singing with him. I picture you turning around to find me, reaching a hand back here to shake my shoulder until I sang with you.

There's an alternate universe where we're a crew of three, so tight and unbreakable we don't need a fourth to even it out for me. Where a fourth would only be trouble. Jackson drives, you're sitting shotgun, I'm yelling at you both to turn up the volume when our anthem comes on, and we all sing so loudly the radio doesn't stand a chance against our slightly off-key, comfortable chorus. But that's not a universe any of us lives in, unfortunately.

HISTORY
FRIDAY, SEPTEMBER 18TH, 2015

It's been a little difficult keeping up with these Skype dates because of Theo's college schedule and the time zone difference, but we're managing. On Fridays he's free from class by two, and we're able to chat around four, once I'm home from school. But we only have an hour to do so because of his tutoring gig.

I call the moment I'm home, and he answers immediately.

"You're late," laptop-screen-sized Theo says.

"By two minutes," I say.

"You've screwed yourself out of two minutes with me. And . . ." Theo holds up the care package I mailed him earlier this week. "That's two extra minutes I've had to wait to open whatever this is! Is it you? Are you in the box?" He shakes the box, and I sway back and forth.

"Open it!"

His roommate Manuel, shirtless as usual, pops up behind Theo as he opens the box. "Hey, man." He waves to me before asking Theo if he can see what's in the package.

"Is it safe?" Theo asks.

"It's not a flipbook of me undressing."

"Damn it. Now that you've put that idea in my head, whatever is in here will be inferior. You are your own downfall, okay?" Theo opens the box anyway, of course, and pulls out two adult coloring books—one of *Star Wars*, the other of *X-Men*—and a pirate bobblehead. "Okay, the bobblehead is pretty awesome."

Manuel takes the *X-Men* coloring book. "Theo, man, a coloring book isn't going to help you fit in here."

"I'll start giving a shit when you start wearing shirts." Theo snatches the coloring book back. "Thanks, Griff."

Theo and I talk enough that I wouldn't ever say we're *not* catching up. His schedule for school and tutoring can be pretty demanding, but he always makes time for these Skype dates. Part of me knows we shouldn't be calling them dates since we're not technically dating anymore, but we're still pretty affectionate to each other, and it's clear neither of us is trying to move on. Knowing he loves me is the one thing keeping me from going completely insane without him.

THURSDAY, OCTOBER 29TH, 2015

THEO IS TWENTY MINUTES late for our Skype call, so I shoot him a text. The message gets delivered, but he doesn't reply back immediately. I know he had his tutoring session this afternoon—this junior at a local high school is apparently summer school–bound if Theo can't help him turn his grades around—but whenever he stays late, he always lets me know so I'm not sitting in front of my laptop like some pathetic, lovesick asshole.

Like right now.

Except I am a pathetic, lovesick asshole, dressed up like Han Solo because I wanted to surprise Theo with a sneak peek of my Halloween costume. Maybe he's still walking home and doesn't want to get his phone wet. He mentioned it was raining pretty bad earlier.

SATURDAY, OCTOBER 31ST, 2015

"IT'S CRAZY HOW ONE year ago today, you were helping me out with the essay that got me here," Theo says, already dressed for Halloween minus the Wolverine claws he's pulling on this second. "Everything can change overnight."

"I wouldn't call a year overnight, but yeah. You being out there is my fault," I say, putting Han Solo's pistol to my head. "I should've let you submit your first essay."

"I probably would've still gotten in," Theo says.

I frown at the screen. "I don't remember that arrogance last year when we missed the party. College going to your head?" I'm joking. At least I think I am.

"Like I said, everything can change overnight. Anyway, sorry that today is a bit of a drive-by Skype hang-out. The party is off-campus, but I hear the Jell-O shots will give me whiplash."

"Is that a good thing?"

"We'll see."

I feel like he's choosing Jell-O over me, but I let it go because I know he's choosing socializing and fun for his sanity. There are only so many times someone can talk to his ex-boyfriend slash best friend via Skype and not want more. I always forget all about more in these moments, but it's possible it's not enough for him.

"It's all good," I say. "I have to run out and see Wade soon anyway. Have you spoken to him recently?"

Theo's eyebrows meet. "It's been a couple of days since I texted with Wade, but I haven't heard back."

"I'll tell him to hit you back today."

Theo flexes his hand and his plastic claws—six total—look kick-ass. "Don't worry about it, Han." He winks. The door knocks and he hops up. "And there goes Manuel without his damn key again. One sec." Theo gets up and shouts as he gets closer to the door. "You shouldn't dress *down* as Tarzan if it means you won't have a pocket for your—Oh. Hey."

"Surprise!" I don't know this voice, and I'm not sure Theo does either.

"Hey," Theo greets.

"Yellow is a good look on you," the guy says. "And it's an even better fit."

Theo doesn't respond.

"Is this a bad time?"

I'm overhearing something I feel isn't my business, but I'm not logging out.

"No, I'm on a Skype hang-out. I just got to say bye to my friend. Wait out here a minute?"

Theo closes the door and returns, blushing. "Sorry, that's my friend Jackson. He's my ride tonight. I should head out."

"Yeah."

"You still going to be around tomorrow for a chat?"

"Yeah."

"Okay, Griffin. Be safe out there. May the Force be with you."

"You too, Theo. Good night." I don't remind him that Han Solo didn't believe in the Force, at least not at first. He clenches his fist and throws on a smile I'm not really buying before logging out.

I sort of don't want to go out anymore.

I can't get it out of my head that Theo called it a Skype hang-out and not a Skype date. Or that I was just his "friend" and nothing more.

SATURDAY, NOVEMBER 7TH, 2015

ANOTHER SATURDAY, ANOTHER SKYPE call. Theo is telling me all about this pinball arcade he visited last night with Manuel—along with that Jackson guy from Halloween and a couple of other freshmen. I don't think I should be reading between the lines here because all I can make out is a warning for me to brace myself. I've known Theo for years; I can tell when he's about to lead into a big speech about some change. And I don't get the feeling it's going to be as good as when he grabbed my hand on the train and told me his feelings for me.

"Who won?"

"Manuel," Theo says. "Dude is a beast. It's one of the few things that can get him to throw on a shirt and hang with everyone."

"Sounds like you got a squad growing out there."

"Nothing like you guys," Theo says. "You know how it goes. You go to school with some people and then you never talk to them again." He catches himself. "Not going to happen to you two. I swear."

But it's already happening. Wade and Theo got into one of their little fights again—no one's owning up to what it's about, probably because it's that stupid—so I'm Theo's only real link to the squad. Even then, Wade and I hardly count as a squad. Theo is our glue, our center.

"Jackson is cool, though. There, uh . . . there might be something going on there with him," Theo says. Now he's completely avoiding eye contact. He is confessing something I've suspected since Halloween. But suspicion isn't enough to stop the room from spinning. Suspicion isn't the same as confirmation. "I don't know. It's still early."

"Cool," I lie. It's a small lie, but I know even then the lies will grow as long as Theo's time with Jackson does.

"I've been wanting to talk to you about this for about a week. It's just really confusing, because I know I'm not over you. But I like hanging out with Jackson," Theo says. Hearing Jackson's name is suffocating, only I can't show any weakness, because Theo is now looking at me. "I want us to be able to talk about this, Griff. You're still my favorite person. You're extremely important to me, but if you don't want to hear any of this, I can't get mad at you. What are you thinking?"

I nod like everything's okay. Even my movements are lies. "Of course I want to be here for you, Theo. Look, we're not dating. I broke up with you because I imagined that this might happen. You're not doing anything wrong." Except spitting in the face of everything we were by moving on two months later. "How'd you guys meet?"

"It was actually on that day where I was late to our Skype chat. It was raining and Jackson pulled over and offered to give me a lift. He gave me a shirt from the back to dry off with, and it was an SMC shirt. We got to talking and we met up that night in the lounge to keep talking." There's a lightness to his voice, relief from getting this off his chest. "I think you'd like him, actually."

I fake a smile. "You tend to have good taste," I joke instead of screaming. "So you really weren't expecting Jackson on Halloween?"

"Not at all," Theo says, almost in one breath. "I wanted to talk to you."

"What did he dress up as?"

"Cyclops," Theo answers. "He grew up with a Wolverine and Cyclops fantasy, so we thought it would be funny."

I don't see how it's funny to do a couples costume thing when you're not dating someone, but okay. "Hey, I actually have to call Wade back," I lie. "But you should text me a photo from Halloween if you have any. I want to see what this guy looks like." It's probably the most honest thing I've said.

"Will do. We still good for our call tomorrow?"

"Yeah." There's no fucking way I'm ever having another video chat with him as long as Jackson is in his life. I put on an okay show tonight, but my face is bound to betray me. Only phone chats from here on out, where he won't be able to see me dealing with any of my tics. "Don't forget to send that photo. See you, Theo."

Theo takes a deep breath, his head shaking a little. "Later, Griff."

I log out.

I stare at my phone, waiting for this picture.

I don't know why I'm doing this to myself. Every word he said felt like a brick to the face. He's not trying to hurt me; I trust he loves me enough to never intentionally destroy me. But once a brick is thrown, it's out of his hands and it's up to me to dodge it. If I duck, Theo will think I'm not strong enough to withstand the pain. He may be right.

I wonder if Jackson will look like I imagine, which is everything I'm not: lean, with a surfer's tan; hair more golden than Theo's; unreal blue eyes some crush would be poetic about; roll-out-of-bed stubble that looks intentional.

My phone buzzes and there are two attachments. I click them open before I can change my mind. The first is of Jackson, alone, sitting on some floor somewhere. He's not what I was expecting at all. He reminds me of myself. We have the same complexion, same dark hair, same long legs, and same smirk. Theo found himself a Griffin clone. I'll throw money down that Theo walks on Jackson's right.

I check out the second photo, this one of Wolverine-Theo with his arm thrown over Cyclops-Jackson's shoulders, and both of them are smiling.

The weird thing is, I actually feel better. I don't think I'm out of the running here. If I have to let Theo throw bricks at me in order to keep him in my life, I don't have to let them hit me.

I can catch them.

THURSDAY, DECEMBER 31ST, 2015

LAST YEAR ON NEW Year's Eve, I thought a lot of nonsense about storms being awesome. Then an actual storm brought Theo and Jackson together. I also didn't really account for lightning, which feels like it's struck over and over.

Lightning hit when Theo got his acceptance letter.

Lightning hit when Theo packed up his room.

Lightning hit when Theo moved away.

Lightning hit when Theo met Jackson.

There's nothing I can do but allow myself to keep getting struck. Even if I stop talking to Theo, that won't help with my imagination. It doesn't help tonight, when I'm trying to force myself to fall asleep early because I know there's no chance Theo will pull himself away from Jackson to call me at midnight, my time. I can't stand to be awake at the exact moment hours from now when he's kissing Jackson in a completely different time zone.

Theo will finally be visiting for his birthday, so if I can be strong until February, if I can keep bouncing up whenever lightning strikes, there's a chance I can win him back.

TODAY
MONDAY, DECEMBER 12TH, 2016

Jackson pulls into the parking lot of a church. I should remind Jackson where I stand on this God character, but this place is beautiful. I'm practically sticking out of the window to admire the sand-beige bricks and sunlight glinting in the stained-glass windows. You never mentioned going to services with Jackson, but I guess I wouldn't be surprised if you did. I'm trying to be respectful here, but my feelings on faith at the moment are the same feelings I have for the church itself—beautiful and promising on the outside, but possibly disappointing on the inside.

I won't share any of these nonbeliever thoughts with Jackson. He's clearly here with a purpose, maybe to pray for you, wherever you are.

Jackson gets out of the car and I do the same. It's so nice out here and I feel weird thinking it, but it's nicer to grieve during a winter in California than back in New York, where the weather makes life miserable enough. He's already helped me by letting me run away with him.

"Get in the driver's seat," Jackson says.

"Say what?"

"I'm teaching you how to drive." Jackson goes toward the passenger's seat.

"Wait. You're not here to pray?"

"No, we're using the parking lot. It's a Monday afternoon. Not exactly a busy time."

I start to laugh. "Get the hell out of here."

"Damn it, Griffin, language."

I can't believe I'm doing this, but why not? I get in the front seat; Jackson sits shotgun. He buckles up quickly like there's a chance I will send us gunning into the church in the next moment or two. Being in the driver's seat is odd. It's been a couple of years since I even sat shotgun.

Jackson instructs me on where to place my hands, and I call him out for being a bad role model when he was driving—his left arm was out the window. He teaches me everything there is to know about the mirrors and turning and signs and even etiquette, as if I'll be tailgating someone momentarily.

I get started. It's exhilarating, even at fifteen miles per hour. It feels a lot like the arcade games we would race in, except it would be really bad for both Jackson and me if I drive us off a bridge right now, because we probably won't respawn. Jackson encourages me to move a little bit faster, which, of course, nerves my foot into stepping on the pedal a little too hard, so I hit the brakes and Jackson's head flings forward. I'm surprised it's still attached to his shoulders and not flipping through the windshield. In this church lot, I will go ahead and say God bless the person who invented seatbelts.

Jackson doesn't kick me out of the driver's seat. He laughs it off and coaches me to keep going and not to freak out.

It takes a few minutes, but I start to get the hang of it. I'm driving in circles like a pro. It's freeing to be in the driver's seat, to decide if I'll go left or right, forward or reverse. It's freeing to be in control.

• • •

JACKSON DIDN'T FORCE ME to drive us on the highway—a good thing; otherwise we probably wouldn't have arrived at your college in one piece. The student housing building seemed bigger and nicer in the pictures on the school's website and the photos you texted me, but in person it's a little drab. Maybe that's another reason you liked staying over at Jackson's so much, with his friendly dog and even friendlier mother.

It's weird seeing students in hoodies in warm weather like this. There must be some California phenomena where residents mistake sixty-degree temperatures as cold. You've done this yourself. Back in December or January, I can't really remember, we were on the phone and you mentioned needing to run back to your dorm room to grab your hoodie because it was a little chilly. Meanwhile, I was dealing with a winter that felt very subzero. I was wearing sweaters underneath my coat but forgot my gloves, so holding the phone was brutal on my fingers. It was a good-enough excuse to get off the phone. You sounded too happily Californian and unfamiliar. I'm okay with admitting that now.

Jackson parks and immediately a couple of girls come charging toward him, offering him their condolences and telling him how much they miss you. A lump lodges itself in my throat; I should have expected this. He keeps turning to me, and I don't know if he's trying to introduce me to these girls or if he wants me to come up with an excuse to rescue him from this, but more students join the crowd and keep us apart.

I recover quickly. This is both a show of how loved you were and of how deeply connected you and Jackson were. Jackson looks like he's about to cry now, though. I'm catching snippets of memories, all clamoring to be heard at once:

"So funny, like, I spat out my margarita laughing the first night we hung out."

"He was so cool about letting me cheat off his homework if I loaned him video games. He was mad chill."

"I thought I was the king at chess until I went up against him."

"I went over to see if he could fix my TV remote and I had the greatest four-hour chat with him."

They miss you. They might have even been your friends.

I grab Jackson's shoulder and pull him away, mumbling that I have to steal him away for something. Jackson is shaking, and I wrap my arm around his shoulders. Everyone quiets. They watch us walk toward the building, and they must be confused as hell, possibly mistaking my friendship for intimacy—but the only thing I care about is making sure Jackson doesn't collapse, especially not before we go into your room to pack up your belongings. At least we've figured out a way to turn my running away into something constructive. Even my parents approve. We have to decide what's okay for Jackson to keep and what should be sent back to your family.

Jackson leads me through the halls. The endless doors are identical, except for some with the occasional flyer or decoration, but Jackson never loses his way. There are still times where I get confused getting home if I go a different route or get too lost in my head or whatever song I'm listening to. But Jackson could probably find his way to your room blindfolded. I know it's West 10 from all the mail I sent you—but if I'd somehow forgotten and was here without Jackson, it would've been easy to figure out by what's outside: bouquets of flowers, candles, and mourning notes taped to the door.

The lump returns. I can't read what people say about you; it hurts too much. Jackson and I aren't the only ones hurting. I don't know when you gave Jackson a key to your room, but he unlocks it and lets us in, and we're careful to step over the flowers.

"Here we are." Jackson's voice is shaky. "It feels like a ghost town."

I only know this room through photos you and Jackson posted on social media at the beginning of this semester because you were celebrating being roommate-free for sophomore year. On your desk is your laptop, your iPhone dock-slash-charging station, the pirate bobblehead and coloring books I sent you in my first and last care package, and a *Star Wars* mug with pens inside. The single bed is unmade. It's so small, and whenever Jackson slept over, you two must've been forced to really push up against each other so no one fell off the edge. I have no idea when you and Jackson had sex for the first time, but the first time you casually mentioned it to me was a couple of months after you were already dating him, a little joke as if you were testing the waters to see if I would laugh. I did, but I knew you could tell it hurt me, because you never brought it up again. Either that or you and Jackson stopped having sex, which, let's be real . . . I know you.

"I'll be back in a minute. I'm going to go get a couple of boxes," Jackson says softly, leaving me alone.

I hate that you're not resting in that bed right now, asleep, or with your headphones, listening to a song you would recommend to me. I go to your desk and pick up the pirate bobblehead. I flick his cutlass, watching him shake his head around and smiling the biggest smile. It's as if he's the sole surviving pirate who didn't get infected by the zombie virus, who's now in possession of maps to everyone else's buried treasures, setting sail to collect them all. I keep flicking and flicking until Jackson returns.

"Do you care if . . . do you care if I keep this pirate?" I ask him. I know I got it for you, but I don't know if Jackson has a connection to it too; weeks ago I wouldn't have even asked.

"That's yours," Jackson says, setting down some boxes.

"Thanks. Theo and I had this ongoing joke about pirates." I sit down on the bed, still flicking away in twos.

"The zombie-pirate apocalypse, right? He told me about it."

The pirate turns me into a kid—a crying, confused kid. Jackson sits beside me, wrapping his arm around my shoulder.

I bounce the pirate across my leg, like he's walking the plank, and send him diving into the ocean, into Jackson's lap. Jackson winces and laughs a little while pulling me closer. It's unsettling how nice the body contact is. I wonder if he's feeling the same way. I shift a little, hoping to burrow into his side a little more closely, but he lets go of me completely, possibly mistaking my movement for discomfort.

Maybe he's not feeling the same comfort I was. Maybe I was pushing myself past a line I shouldn't be crossing.

We work on packing your room up. Jackson packs away shirts and jeans I don't recognize into one box; I clear out your desk and drop it all into the second box. It's a task that takes a little less than twenty minutes and no more than two boxes.

I'm still crying a little when we're done. I can't believe your entire life out here could be stored away in two boxes.

I CAN'T EVEN PRETEND I'm tired because of jetlag like any other guy crossing time zones for the first time. It's only day one of the Theo Tour, but it's exhausting me in ways I didn't predict. Jackson is the same, obviously. He's been quiet since we got on the highway. He completely ignored my backseat-driver request to turn on the music to try and cheer him up.

The spy pen on his rearview mirror catches my attention again, so I ask him where he got it, even though I suspect it's from you.

"Seventeenth birthday present from my dad," Jackson answers, taking a second to look at it before returning his focus to the road. "He knows I got over birthday presents somewhere around thirteen or fourteen, but he still picked this up for me at an airport in Chicago anyway because I was really into spies as a kid. I lied to Theo last year and told him his collector's edition Daredevil action figure was my favorite gift ever, but it's actually this spy pen."

I'm sure the action figure was a close second, Theo.

"That's actually really awesome," I say. "No offense to him, but that's not what I would expect based on everything I know about him. I know he's generous with free flights and stuff, but this is different."

"Exactly," Jackson says. "That's why I got over birthdays, I think. I kept getting all these presents from my mom and dad, and every time it felt like they were buying me. I got the master bedroom and my car from my mom. I got a really nice laptop from my dad. Then my dad picks up this spy pen, which is basically just a flashlight that can also write in invisible ink, but it reminds me of when I was a kid and my parents worked together to create missions for me with fun codes to crack."

I let this all sink in. "You're happy they split though, right?"

"Yeah, they hate each other. But something as small as creating spy games for my entertainment reminds me of the teammates they could've been."

"If you're going to tell me you keep it on your rearview mirror so you can always look back on those times, I will punch you in the dick."

Jackson laughs. "Don't punch my dick. I'm not that philosophical. I keep it on my rearview mirror because it will get lost anywhere else. Besides, with all the back and forth, the car is really my only constant thing."

"You're dangerously close to the edge of philosophical bullshit."

"Okay, fine, fine. I keep it in my car at all times because I sometimes have a thought so private I need to whip out the pen and get it off my chest, but with invisible ink so no one will ever read it."

I raise my fist, like I'm about to smash it down on his dick. "I know how invisible ink works. Try again."

"I never know when I might need a flashlight?"

I lower my fist. "Better."

He smiles and I catch myself smiling too in the mirror.

Without warning, Jackson pulls over on the highway, an intersection running alongside a cliff, and switches off the ignition. I don't know why my mind jumps to the worst thing possible without any substantial evidence to support it, but I turn around expecting to find a cop car behind us even though Jackson's driving is perfectly fine, if you ignore all the times he closes his eyes to sing or takes his hands off the wheel. The severity on Jackson's face would suggest as much, but he snaps off his seatbelt, turns to me, and says, "This is roughly the spot where I met Theo."

I have no words. I'm numb.

I get out of the car, and Jackson does the same. I feel really out of it until I step on something metallic, the crunch knocking me out of my daze, and I see it's just a Pepsi can someone likely threw out a car window. The ground is beautiful; it's this mixture of dirt and sand, and if I had to describe it for someone back home, I'd say it's like the baseball field in Central Park. But when you met Jackson, it would've been dark and wet, maybe even muddy. It's weird, but I somehow wish your footsteps survived untouched, like in cement, so I could step where you stepped. But I don't need it. I no longer need to study every inch of your path that led you to climbing into his car on that rainy day—I finally see what you saw in him.

"Did you guys ever come back here?" Maybe that's too intimate to ask, but it's safe to assume. You and I loved riding the L train together, always wondering if whatever car we were in was the exact car where our own history began, the prologue to what should've been an epic love story.

"Once a month," Jackson says.

"Why only once?"

"We'd save it for anniversaries," Jackson says. "I know celebrating every month is stupid, but it really meant a lot to me. Theo was my first serious relationship, and I wanted everything

to have meaning, especially after how worthless I felt with my ex.
I definitely had to be the one to remind him of the date, but he
was always happy to entertain me."

You and I celebrated anniversaries too. They were also my
idea, but that faded after seven months—at least until our first
year, and even then we didn't really do anything special. We
would acknowledge it, take a moment to jokingly appreciate
surviving each other, and move on. I thought everything we *did*
was special, even something as simple as an afternoon with an
adult coloring book.

"Theo was accommodating that way," I say.

I can picture it, you and Jackson sitting on one of these
boulders watching traffic, or even just standing and holding
each other. I really wish I knew how to be truly happy for you
when you were alive. When you brought Jackson to New York, I
should've been more open to meeting him.

"You drive by here a lot, right? Do you think you're going to
pull over all the time? Save it for anniversary days? Or change
your route completely?"

"I'm sure I'll come on random days too."

"Even when you're dating someone new?"

Jackson's face scrunches up and his hands raise, like he's carrying sand and letting it slip between his fingers, and ultimately
shrugs. "I don't know. I'm not thinking about dating anyone
else right now. Are you?"

"Hell no. But I haven't been thinking about that for a while
now. I know everyone keeps reminding us that we're young and
we have the rest of our lives ahead of us, which I always thought
was stupid. Someone could drop an anchor off this cliff and kill
us right now."

"Maybe if we were living in a cartoon," Jackson says.

"I'm seventeen and you're nineteen. I'm not saying we have
to go on dates right now, but we should be open to someone
new eventually, right? Theo is gone and more than anything, I

want someone to tell me when it's okay for us to let someone else in."

Jackson shakes his head. "I'm not thinking about moving on right now," he says. There's something in his voice that I can't interpret, but both guesses make me feel shitty. The first is that he's judging me for throwing this out there, for trying to have this conversation. The last is he believes I should've moved on a while ago because you and I weren't even dating when you died. I hope that's not what he's thinking. Love doesn't begin and end with some online status.

I drop it.

I let him know I'll wait for him in the car so he can have a minute alone out here in the space you shared. In the backseat, I rest my arm on one of your boxes and observe Jackson from the window. He's not crying, and, what's more notable to me, he's not talking to himself, which means he's not talking to you, either. I wonder when that will start.

Jackson returns to the car after a few minutes. "I'm ready to head back. You cool with that?"

"Yeah."

We drive in an awkward silence. I know I should fill these silences with explanations instead of letting them drag on, but I don't have the energy to explain where I was coming from when I said we'd eventually have to move on. All I know is you wouldn't want us crying over you forever. Right?

I HANG UP WITH my mom just as we pull into Jackson's garage. I assure her for the fourth time that once I get home, I'll honor my promise and go to therapy.

I gained three hours today—I wish it were four, of course—but it's been so draining that I'm paying the price for it now. I'm exhausted. But I have no regrets, other than wishing I'd documented our day on Instagram or Facebook. I haven't touched those accounts since a couple of days after you died.

Jackson must've trained Chloe right, because she isn't barking when we enter the house, just wagging her tail with tired enthusiasm; she's already over my newness. He immediately throws all the clothes off his bed and onto the floor, including the shirts we folded and socks we balled up.

"You're more than welcome to sleep in the bed with me. It's big enough, obviously." He gestures at his king-size mattress. It's definitely big enough so that we wouldn't touch. Maybe he even played a game with you, rolling over to you, bumping into you and laughing until your lips found each other's . . . and I'll black out everything from there.

This is making me feel a way.

I don't know how Jackson truly feels about this. He's probably being nice but might actually prefer if I slept on the floor with Chloe, which is pretty much the treatment he received at my house. To take it to another level, I don't know how you'll feel about this, if you'll see it as some sort of betrayal. It only makes me think about how all our families would react to this, and whether or not they would be happy to see my friendship with Jackson has grown so much that I would feel comfortable sleeping in a bed with him, or if they would mistake it for something it's not.

To top it off and even it out, I don't know if I'm feeling okay with this idea because I trust Jackson is a good guy who won't pull anything that'll make this uncomfortable, because I trust Jackson doesn't have any feelings in him to make me suspicious of this simple invitation, or if I'm feeling okay with this because I'm truly lonely and miss sleeping in a bed with someone—because I missing sleeping in a bed with you. Sleeping in a bed you've slept in next to someone you've slept with might be the next best thing for both Jackson and me.

"Are you sure you don't want me sleeping down here with Chloe?"

"Chloe sleeps alone," Jackson says.

"Sucks for Chloe."

"No, Chloe gets action. She just sends all her hookups back to their respective doghouses once the deed is done."

"Poor guys."

"You're assuming Chloe plays it straight."

Jackson closes the window because all sorts of bugs have been known to sneak in during the middle of the night, not that they make it very far throughout the rest of the house before Chloe hunts them down and eats them. In a flash, Jackson unbuckles his pants, his jeans drop to his ankles, and he kicks his way out of them. I'm expecting him to pull on some pajamas over his slightly hairy legs and somewhat revealing gray boxers, but he sits on top of his covers like this shouldn't be surprising to me even though I've only seen him going to bed in my sweatpants the past few nights. Jackson counts the pillows, throwing one off the bed so only four remain. It fills me with warmth that he's making the bed safe for me. He sets his phone to charge, uses a remote to turn on his air conditioner, and lies down.

I wonder if this is his routine.

I walk to the opposite side of the bed, to the left side. "Did Theo sleep here or where you are?"

Jackson knows where I'm coming from with this. "He originally only slept here," he says, patting the side he's on. "He never admitted it, but I think it was something left over from you. But one night he fell asleep on that side and changed."

You used to joke I ruined you because you would find yourself wandering to everyone's right, not just mine. But Jackson somehow fixed you. I press a hand on this side of the bed where you once woke up feeling differently, and I sit down, hoping Jackson can somehow fix me, too. The cold air fills the room. Soon I'm under a light sheet, the comforter at my feet if I need it. Jackson turns off the light and the whirlwind of discomfort I was anticipating never hits me. It doesn't feel right, but it doesn't feel wrong either.

What hasn't changed is how much I like noise when I go to sleep, something that started when I was a kid. My parents originally thought I only wanted the TV on so I could keep watching cartoons instead of going to sleep, but I truly just wanted noise to drown out everything happening outside my window.

"Bore me to sleep with a story," I say.

Jackson laughs. He launches right in with how whenever Anika and Veronika stayed over during high school, they would play their card game, talk shit about the latest person they couldn't stand, have heart-to-hearts that always surprised them and sometimes made things awkward, and would always end in three-way spooning. He asks me about the good days with you and Wade. I push all the bad stuff away, remembering fun times, like relay races in middle school and funny things like Wade's aversion to eating snacks shaped like animals and the way he quickly steps onto an escalator as if it's going to suddenly change its speed. Jackson tells me how much he misses his friends, but I can't get myself to admit that about Wade.

It's after midnight, officially the thirteenth. Jackson must know it too, but neither of us brings it up. You know Jackson and I would sacrifice so much to have you lying here between us, but I'm learning there should be some times I put you to rest for a little bit instead of obsessing about you every day. Or I'm trying. I don't know what will be left of me if love and grief can't bring you back to life. Maybe I need to be brought back to life, too.

TUESDAY, DECEMBER 13TH, 2016

IT'S BEEN ONE MONTH since the universe lost you. One month since you woke up in the morning. One month since you opened a book. One month since you ate a meal. One month since you keyed a text message. One month since you went for a walk.

One month since you held a hand. One month since you kissed your boyfriend. One month since you thought of a future that's not happening. One month since you maybe dreamed up your own alternate universes.

It's been one month since you died.

It's been one month since you lived.

"WHAT DID THEO DO on his last day?"

Jackson and I haven't spoken much today. To each other, at least. We had a fairly quiet breakfast with Ms. Lane—scrambled eggs and sausage links. Anika called Jackson because she remembered the date, and the two caught up for a little bit. I called your family and spoke with Denise for a bit, relieved your parents let her stay home from school today. I guess they've cut back on their whole stick-to-a-routine business. Jackson and I have only spoken about little things, like what time we need to get to the pier, but nothing bigger than that. But once Jackson pulls into the beachside parking lot, the gleaming sand and Pacific Ocean straight ahead of us, all my silence turns into curiosity, and all my curiosity refuses to hold back.

I want to know everything about the day you died.

Jackson doesn't answer me.

We get out of the car. Jackson kicks off his sneakers, leaving them in the front seat, his little life hack to keep sand out of his shoes. ("You can't get sand in your shoes if your shoes never touch the sand," he told me yesterday.) I do the same, leaving my socks behind too, and my feet are burning against the asphalt, so I hop over to a patch of grass as if I'm walking on hot coals. Jackson doesn't seem to be as distressed as I am.

The sky is the same blue as yesterday, nothing magical or noteworthy going on there. But the Santa Monica Pier grabs my attention, its Ferris wheel standing tall.

"We went on the Ferris wheel for the first time together," Jackson says, as if reading my mind. "Both of us. I don't hate heights as much as Theo did, but we promised to get through it together." He pulls out his phone and I remove the sunglasses Jackson loaned me so I can clearly see the photo of you two sitting in a Ferris wheel car, making fake-scared faces. The clouds look so close to you both, it's as if you could've brought one back down with you.

You had a first on the day you died, too, something you did to feel braver and something you were supposed to be able to reflect on when something else scared you.

"We felt untouchable after that," Jackson says. He throws his phone into the front seat and locks up.

He walks past me and I follow, stepping over a guardrail and onto the sand. He's not running toward the ocean, childlike—not that I was expecting him to do so—but there is a charge in his step, which I wasn't expecting. This is the place where you drowned, the place where Jackson watched you drown—there's no way in hell I could ever hurl myself into this like he is.

We walk past a family of three spread out on a towel. The father is reading from a tablet, the mother is filling out a crossword puzzle, and the little girl—who I'm considering the tip of this odd triangle, her parents balancing her out from bottom angles—is building a sand castle and in desperate need of more sunscreen. I hope her parents will grab her if she wanders away, that they won't let her get too far, that they'll be there to pull her out of the waves.

Jackson and I reach the edge of the wet sand. He looks around, crying, his hands trying to speak for him but constantly falling back to his sides.

"I don't even know the spot where it happened, Griffin," he manages, his voice strained. "When accidents happen, people know where to leave flowers, but not me. Everything happened so quickly. All I know is the lifeguards weren't close enough. And I, I . . . I wasn't fast enough."

He walks into the ocean, and I go with him. A small wave

brushes my ankles and toes, sending chills up my legs, and I almost retreat, wishing my feet were burning against asphalt again. But I stay with Jackson.

You once shared a really weird speculation about water with me. It was when you first got out here and I actually thought you must've been stoned. You said every single molecule in all bodies of water—ocean and lake, shower and sink—has a story and reason for existence. You always thought there was more to the world, but this idea about water didn't feel very conversation-worthy before. What was I supposed to say when you thought a drop from your showerhead was about to fall directly into your drain, missing you completely, and head out on its way toward a greater purpose than cleaning you? College kids smoke weed; everyone knows that. This is what I felt like saying.

But as I stand here in the ocean that stole you away from us, I wonder if any molecule here witnessed your death, if any water splashing against my legs filled your throat as you struggled to breathe.

I wade in deeper, knee-high, and my jeans tense against my legs. I crouch, crying now, too, and punch the water again and again. Punching water hurts. But I don't stop, even after I'm drenched, even after Jackson calls my name, even after I howl, even after a wave surprises me and takes me under, though now I'm fighting the ocean to release me as I tumble underneath, panicking.

I know I'm not that deep, but I don't know which way is up, I've never been able to keep my eyes open underwater. The ocean gets heavier, pinning me down—no, it's sucking me up, and it's Jackson, not the ocean. I inhale a deep breath, spitting out water, and Jackson hugs me and I hug him back.

"What the hell were you doing?"

I lost my sunglasses when I was taken under, and the sun is piercing. I try telling him about your damn water molecules and wanting to fight them all, but I keep crying and crying, knowing what I felt under there for a few seconds is nothing compared to what you experienced when your arms and legs couldn't fight anymore, when your panic probably got the best of you, when you breathed in water, when your brain shut you down. Thinking of this terrifies me, but I know I'm safe with Jackson— you could've been too if he were in here with you.

"Why weren't you swimming with Theo?" My question comes out in a cough and sounds more accusatory than I mean it to, and Jackson freezes. We're inches away from each other. It's still hard to make out his face because my eyes are irritated and the sun is attacking my vision. "I'm not blaming you."

"I know," Jackson says quietly. "Theo wanted to go in alone. He had just gotten off the phone and wanted a minute to himself. I stayed at the beach with our stuff, and Theo went deeper than he should've."

It isn't Jackson's fault.

My rage dies down. My body is registering how ice-cold this water is, even after I've made rounds underneath it. I also officially hate the ocean because it can't be trusted with any of our lives. I was right to protect my sand castles from the ocean as a kid. Screw this. I hold Jackson's bare arm and force him out of the water with me.

I take off my shirt and drop face-first into the sand, feeling the sun on my back and shoulders instantly. It's not burning me alive like it should be. Instead it actually feels kind of relaxing. Or maybe that's just because I'm back on dry land.

"I'm sorry," Jackson says, sitting beside me, staring out into the surf. I almost ask if he's talking to you or me, when I remember he doesn't talk to you like I do. "I should've been in there with him. I could've saved him. Everyone's lives would've been so much better."

My hand flies out toward Jackson's as if his hand were some deus ex machina button that could blow up every zombie pirate in a single blast. "You're not single-handedly responsible for

Theo, okay? You didn't force him out there, and you made every effort you could to bring him back."

Jackson nods, but I'm not sure any of this is actually comforting him. The fact is that I feel just as powerless now as he did then.

I'VE BEEN BLINDSIDED INTO watching *Edward Scissorhands* tonight with Jackson; I'm blaming my yes on our vulnerable state. I always thought you'd be here with me when I finally took on this childhood fear, ready to pause the film if I needed a second. I never thought I'd be watching it in Los Angeles with another guy who loves you, especially not while wearing his shorts. I would've preferred sitting outside, watching the sky burn in yellow-orange and pinkish-red clouds.

It turns out this film isn't as terrifying as I remembered it to be. Sure, it's creepy because Edward has scissors for hands and scars all over his pale face, but how scary can the guy be when he's trimming a bush into a dinosaur and giving dogs haircuts?

"The film score may have had something to do with it, too," I tell Jackson, sitting cross-legged with a pillow on my lap.

"I'm not sure who composed it," Jackson says, pulling out his phone.

"Danny Elfman."

Jackson nods when his search comes through. "Yup."

"Suck it, Google," I say. "Did you ever hear Theo say that?"

"Yup. It was like a cowboy match with him to see if he could answer something before I could draw my phone and look it up. Theo would've kicked ass at Jeopardy."

I turn away from the movie. Jackson gets what it was like to be with you so much, I could hug him. "I bought him the Jeopardy video game, which was a huge mistake. I felt like the hugest idiot whenever we played."

"You're not an idiot."

I shake that off. "Did you ever feel smart around him?"

"No, and I'm older. I probably felt worse than you did."

That age stuff is stupid and almost cost you and me our friendship, but I get where he's coming from. "Theo was never trying to be superior about it, which I loved. He was just so excited to be learning everything to the point that it sometimes felt like he didn't have enough room in his head to remember the little things . . . and a couple of bigger things. It's weird how all the information Theo spent downloading into his stupid beautiful brain is now gone."

I nod, the happiness between us gone, as well. I turn back to the movie, but I'm not watching.

"He left all his knowledge with us," Jackson says. "Some of it. I can't really remember all of it. But the stuff I do know will probably never come up in real life, fun facts basically. Like how the Hoover Dam was built to last two thousand years. And how in the Middle Ages, cats were shoved into sacks and thrown into bonfires and hurled off church towers because they were associated with witchcraft. He also got me hooked on tons of older songs, like 'All Out of Love' and '(They Long to Be) Close to You.'" Jackson goes through his phone and plays "Come Sail Away," cranking it up. "This is one of my favorites."

"Mine too."

Jackson inches toward me, very close. "Okay, please don't punch me, but I want to show you something Theo taught me."

"Why would I punch you?"

"Because I'm about to be really close to your face, and you might think this is inappropriate, in which case, punch me. Okay?"

Jackson gets on his knees and tells me to do the same. He puts his hands on my waist and leans in, but not toward my lips. "This is a butterfly kiss." I tense up as he brushes his eyelashes against mine. "This is a caveman kiss." He bumps his forehead against mine, gently. I'm shaking a little. "This is an

Eskimo kiss." He rubs his nose against mine with closed eyes, expecting me to do the same, but I'm scared of what I will do if I move. "And this is a zombie kiss." Jackson nibbles on my cheek, doing a very stupid growl. He stares into my eyes afterward and smiles. He's pretty happy he shared something so intimate with me.

He doesn't know that I know all of this.

You taught him something personal to me. You taught him a routine I had with my parents as a kid. You taught him something I never thought I would share with anyone else until you came along. You taught him a kiss I personally created for us when I grew up needing a fourth.

I get it.

People are complicated puzzles, always trying to piece together a complete picture, but sometimes we get it wrong and sometimes we're left unfinished. Sometimes that's for the best. Some pieces can't be forced into a puzzle, or at least they shouldn't be, because they won't make sense.

Like Jackson and me on this odd day, or any day.

I grab Jackson by the back of his neck and kiss him—not a butterfly kiss, not a caveman kiss, not an Eskimo kiss, not a zombie kiss—a straight-up kiss where my tongue finds its way into his mouth and his massages mine back. Jackson wrenches away from my lips, looks me in the eyes with confusion, but I'm not sure I find regret there. He takes a deep breath and flies back toward me. Jackson kisses me with the same aggression I surprised him with.

His fingers rake my lower back as he pulls me so close to him our chests are pressed together, hearts hammering against one another. I push him backward, and he probably thinks I'm done, that I've come to my senses or something, but I take off my shirt and send it sailing across the room. I'm used to seeing a smile when reaching this stage in bed, a smile because someone is excited to be doing this with me, but Jackson must be struggling with this, except not enough that he can stop himself from pulling off his own shirt and dropping it on the bed.

"Where are your condoms?"

Jackson manages to reach into his bedside drawer.

"Should I turn off the lights?"

"Nope."

I want you to watch me have sex with your boyfriend.

This is someone who's grieving over you, another human with his own human feelings who shouldn't be used as a weapon against you. But I'm a human too, with my own human feelings. You used our intimate history to create a future with someone else, and that's a thousand times worse.

You used our love against me. Now I'm using your love against you.

WHEN WE'RE DONE, SWEATING despite his shitty air conditioner, I stare up at the ceiling. Jackson does the same.

I'm naked with Jackson in Jackson's bed in Jackson's bedroom in Jackson's home in Jackson's state in Jackson's time zone.

I want the lights off more than anything right now.

If there's anything I want more, it's for you to go away. I spent so much of my time being loyal to you, even when we weren't dating, because I thought we had our endgame plan. Look where that loyalty got me. I'm stuck here trying to figure out my next move. What I've now learned is, going forward, I have to be careful whom I trust with my heart. I have to be suspicious that someone will use the love I give and carry it over to someone else.

You did this to me.

History is nothing. It can be recycled or thrown away completely. It isn't this sacred treasure chest I mistook it to be. We were something, but history isn't enough to keep something alive forever. You're not the best friend and love of my life I've spent this past month mourning, and missing long before that.

I don't want to talk to you anymore.

WEDNESDAY, DECEMBER 14TH, 2016

WHOSE DOG IS BARKING?

It takes a minute for everything to click, but I know I'm in Jackson's bed where we had sex last night. Wow, I had sex with him while Chloe was in the room. There's something wrong about that scenario. I don't know, it's like having sex in a room where a baby is sleeping, except there's no way his dog slept through that. I'm facing the wall with the poster for *The Goonies*.

Another difference: there are no arms wrapped around me like whenever I woke up next to that asshole, Theo.

I slowly turn. Jackson is also at the very edge of the bed, an entire island of space between us. Neither of us had cuddling on the brain.

"Are you awake?" Jackson asks.

"Yeah," I say, wishing I had a piece of gum. It sucks I can't run out of here and hop on a plane to escape all of this, because my flight isn't until this afternoon. But nothing about my life has been easy lately, and maybe that's how it should be. I turn as Jackson is sitting up, and I register Jackson is dressed—completely different clothes than yesterday, thankfully. I'm still one hundred percent naked, so I cover up my entire body with the sheet I slept in, suddenly insecure of everything.

"I didn't get any sleep last night. Maybe five minutes," Jackson says. "Probably six minutes," he corrects.

I slept. I know because the last thing I remember is turning away from the ceiling and squeezing my eyes shut after promising Theo I was done talking to him.

"It didn't mean anything," I spit out. It sounds harsher than I intend, but that's me since Theo died, rough around the edges, and his betrayal has only made me sharper. It sucks for Jackson that the tip of my sword is at his throat—poor wording considering last night's event—but Jackson isn't at fault because he didn't actually steal Theo away from me. Theo was simply over me. "Right?"

Jackson nods strongly, like the pirate bobblehead I put in Jackson's car's cup holder on our way back to his place the other night.

"You're completely right. It was a weird day. Being back at that beach really twisted me."

"We were vulnerable," I say, which is a half lie. He was hurting because of how much he misses Theo, and I was trying to hurt Theo.

"Exactly."

"I'm going to get dressed," I say.

Jackson turns away. I had no problems being naked around Theo. It's not as if Jackson has a six-pack, but I don't feel that comfortable around him, sort of like when I was a kid and would keep my shirt on at the beach around my friends. I find my underwear on the floor next to my sad-looking condom. I get completely dressed in ten seconds and throw the condom in his trashcan. I tell Jackson to put *Edward Scissorhands* back on so I can see how it ends, while I go brush my teeth. But all I end up doing when I get to the bathroom is sitting on his mother's shower bench and crying while the water in the sink runs.

"I'M OKAY, DAD."

"I'm not buying it," Dad says. His bullshit detector has improved tenfold ever since it failed him on Monday morning when I flew out here.

I've been 90 percent honest about what Jackson and I have been up to the past couple of days, but he can tell something else went down besides watching movies and driving around town. I don't know how to tell him Theo dicked me over and how I did something unforgivable in return.

"I know. Things aren't awesome right now, okay? I promise I'll tell you both everything when I get home tonight."

"That's all I wanted to hear."

"How everything sucks?"

"No, honesty. We'll both be at the airport ready to pick you up," Dad says. "Don't change your mind last minute and fly to some other country."

I hear footsteps in the hallway, so I tell my dad I have to go and will text before I board. I hang up and sit down on the bed as Jackson, wearing nothing but boxers and a towel around his shoulders, enters the room. He doesn't say anything to me. Last night has undone the friendship we'd started, but maybe once I get home and we have space between us again, we can salvage some of it.

Jackson kneels before me and his hazel eyes lock with mine. He kisses me and I give in so easily, I don't push him off. His hand goes under my shirt and finds my shoulder, squeezing, before coming right back out to untie my shorts' drawstring. I massage his sides, still a little wet. He climbs into my lap and kisses me again, this time rougher, not nearly in control of himself like he was the first time we did this.

I pull away because despite Theo's betrayal, I'd rather feel nothing than shame, but Jackson keeps coming for me. "Jackson, stop."

He backs off, rolling off of me and onto the bed. His eyes are red. "I miss him so much. I never deserved him. I'm not the guy he thought I was. I fucked up."

"We both did."

"No, not about last night. I didn't want to ruin your trip, but . . ." Jackson is crying, and I'm terrified of whatever it is he's about to say. I have no theories. "I didn't go . . . I didn't go into the ocean to save Theo like I said I did. I ran to get a lifeguard instead because I was scared I would drown too, and . . . I didn't want to die but I was really fast, I swear, I just couldn't risk . . ."

Jackson is the reason Theo broke his promise to never die.

"You fucking coward," I whisper, and I don't know how it doesn't come out as a shout. "You let Theo . . ." I'm getting louder, speaking through my teeth as tears blind me. "You let Theo die." I jump up from the bed, squeezing my eyes and fists shut. "I would've risked my life for him!"

"You can't know that, Griffin. Not until you're facing a moment like that."

"I would've *never* stood by and watched Theo die!"

Jackson jumps up and he holds my arms. I don't know if he's trying to stop me from shaking or keep me from walking out, but I break out of his grip and punch him in the face, which surprises both of us, and then I punch him in the face again, which only surprises him. Nothing could surprise me right now. I feel as if I'm watching myself from a distance.

Jackson's nose is bleeding. He looks up at me, shaking his head. "You're the one who sent him into the ocean in the first place! He was listening to one of your voice mails and needed alone time. Don't blame this all on me."

I'm so dizzy I almost confuse the blood on my hands as my own. The last message I ever left Theo was telling him we had to talk about that taboo thing we promised we'd never talk about . . .

Jackson may not have saved Theo, but I'm the one who killed him.

I run out of Jackson's house in my socks. I don't know if I should go back or forward, left or right. I go left because that's my default. My options suck because I'm not in my city, where I can run home and wait in my bed. Moments later I throw up on the clean sidewalk, and no surprise again: I don't feel any better.

WHEN I FIND MY way back to Jackson's, he stays out in the living room while I pack—well, shove all my clothes back into my backpack and collect my things. I get a text telling me my cab is outside. I'm in a daze when I say goodbye to Ms. Lane, shaking her hand, and thank her with a smile no one could ever believe is legit. I put on my backpack and head to the door, where Jackson is standing.

"Griffin. Do you want me to drive you? I can—"

I pictured this moment on my walk back here, where I would speed past him as if he's no one, but I stop at the door. I don't know if I want to punch him two more times or hug him goodbye and apologize for being such a horrible human being. But I can't let him off the hook. So all I do is look him in the eye and hope he never forgets the face of someone he helped break beyond repair. Someone he tried fixing out of guilt.

I keep moving and get into the cab. I don't turn back to look at Jackson. I lower the windows and take in the smells one final time because I will never return. Thinking about home is what helps me through the slow crawl of the airport—the faces I can turn to once I'm back, the only faces I can trust.

The plane takes off on schedule. The heights and helplessness don't bother me this time around. There are some strong winds, and when the plane sways unexpectedly, it feels like my heart drops to my stomach. But I don't freak out or wish Jackson or anyone is here beside me. I just stare out the window, wondering what it would be like to have this view if the plane actually crashed.

FRIDAY, DECEMBER 16TH, 2016

I'M GOING TO THERAPY this morning because a promise is a promise. And unlike some others, I want to honor mine. I leave my gryphon pins inside the drawer with the rest of Theo's belongings and change into one of my own sweaters instead of his hoodie. My dad is accompanying me to my first session, to be there for me. I suspect he also wants to make sure there's zero chance I'll hop on a plane and never come back.

"Shotgun, Griff?" Dad asks as we get into the car.

"I'm good," I lie. He should know better than to ask me to sit on his right on the very morning we're going to see someone about my compulsions. He's still angry with me, not that I blame him.

I stretch out in the backseat and cover my face with my peacoat. Theo used to get concerned whenever I slept with the comforter over my head, like I was going to suffocate by the time he woke up next to me. I didn't get to wake up next to Theo too often—not romantically, at least, since we had plenty of sleepovers—but the times we did get to catch each other's eyes opening were great. But I won't dwell on them. He moved on.

I have to do the same.

Twenty minutes or so later, the car stops. I hear my dad's seatbelt click and retreat back into its metallic reel. My jacket slides off of me. "Wake up, we're here . . ." He looks me dead in the eye, and I turn around, hiding my face against the backrest. "Griffin, it's okay to cry."

I snatch my jacket back, putting it on as I get out of the car. I walk toward the boxy clinic, which looks less like a serious institution and more like a daycare for future criminals currently still in diapers—gray bricks, garden-green window frames, and a dark blue door with sunrays painted around the knob. I don't get what they're going for, but I wish my parents' insurance offered more than this.

As I walk in, I determine the best spot for me in the waiting room. I go for the chair on the wall opposite the entrance because the desk clerk and offices are all to my right from this position. Spread out on the table are bullshit tabloid magazines. A mother-type sitting next to the potted plant is reading a newspaper. There were a couple of times I tried getting into the newspaper after Theo and I broke up, because of something he said while we were dating: "Some people know a lot about a little, others know a little about a lot."

I wanted to be more like him, someone who knew a little about a lot, so our conversations would never lose steam, so we could learn what makes this universe tick together. Pointless.

Dad walks in and heads straight for the counter, glancing my way like I'm someone who cut in front of him in line. I've seen his frustration a lot since getting home. I keep resisting his good guy–ness because I don't deserve it, and that pisses him off. Dad signs me in and sits quietly next to me, to my right, picking up some magazine and flipping past pages of celebrity gossip and who wore the dress better until he finds the film reviews.

"Maybe we can go see a movie this weekend? Invite Wade?"

"No thanks," I tell Dad.

The secretary peeks over her counter. "Griffin Jennings?"

She waves me toward an open door. Thankfully Theo is no longer around, because I wouldn't want him following me into this appointment. Therapy is supposed to be private, and it's hard to be fully open with a stranger as it is, let alone with my ex-boyfriend watching my every move.

I let myself in, closing the door behind me. "I'm Griffin," I say.

The doctor comes out from around the desk. He has this otherworldly, wise-man thing going for him, with the streaks of gray in his jet-black hair and sideburns. His light-orange eyeglass frames are so distracting, I'm tempted to ask him to take them off, but striking him blind won't do me any favors this session. He's here to listen, and he's here to rewire me.

"Good morning, Griffin. I'm Dr. Anderson, but feel free to call me Peter."

There are five letters in Peter. I'm going to keep it formal with him.

Dr. Anderson invites me to have a seat wherever I'm comfortable.

I'm the compass arrow, trying to find my true north. There's a blue chair, which is inviting, as well as a deep-green couch, which was Theo's favorite color. Dr. Anderson sits in front of his desk with excellent posture. That spot is great because I consider that direction to be true north since it's *his* office. I stand between the chair and couch, torn. "I'm going to stand for a bit," I decide.

Dr. Anderson shifts to the edge of his seat. "Perfectly fine. Should I join you?"

"No." He's a few inches taller than me and is intimidating enough.

"Shall we begin? Care for a glass of water?"

His desire to make me comfortable is only making me anxious. I want to be able to talk to him because I have no one else, but I can already feel an itch in the center of my palm. "Let's just do this."

Dr. Anderson relaxes back into his seat. "Your parents have filled me in on everything you've been going through lately," he says gently. "I'd love to hear everything from you."

This is impossible because they don't know everything. They don't know I played a role in Theo's death, and they don't know everything I've been up to since breaking up with him. My face warms up. I scratch at my palm and pull at my earlobe. I turn away from Dr. Anderson, staring at the wall so he's now to my right. I want to punch all the stupid certificates that supposedly credit him with powers to heal me. I want to tear the clock away that's simultaneously crawling and rushing me.

This is not going to help. Dr. Anderson has as many true powers as a street magician. He's just a dude with card tricks and hidden wires.

But I know I've been lying to myself, too. I know Theo is still out there, watching me. He's followed me into his room, and this can't be how he finds everything out.

I have to tell him myself.

SATURDAY, DECEMBER 17TH, 2016

I'M READY TO TALK again, Theo.

I should say sorry for giving you the silent treatment, but we can both agree that's the last thing I should be apologizing for right now. I have no words for what I learned on Wednesday. But words never even brought you back to me when you were alive. Words are actually what sent you walking into the Pacific Ocean. You have to know I'm sorry for being the reason you're no longer part of this universe, for being the reason you will never get to experience the future you were working so hard for, for being the reason you will never get to employ any of your genius strategies against the damn zombie pirates, and for being the reason everyone will grieve until they're dead themselves.

But there's something else you should know. It's time I use my words for good and stop twisting them just because I regret the truth.

HISTORY
WEDNESDAY, FEBRUARY 10TH, 2016

"I'm not going."

I throw my textbooks in my locker, one by one, take out my peacoat, and slam the door shut. Several students glance at me as if there's a bubble above my head that will tell them why I'm so pissed and hurt, but they keep moving so they can get home and watch Netflix and dick around on Facebook. But Wade isn't leaving my side.

"We haven't seen him in, what, five or six months?" Wade says. "It's his birthday."

"And he brought his new boyfriend here to spend it with him." I spent the past month excited about Theo coming home for his birthday, but a couple of days ago, he dropped the Jackson bomb over text. "He doesn't want me there," I say. Theo doesn't want me, period. I walk away, putting on my coat and hat.

"*You* broke up with *him*," Wade says.

"He wasn't supposed to move on the next day with some me-knockoff," I say.

"I thought it was two months," Wade says. "And you guys aren't clones."

"We had a plan and he's . . . I don't care." I leave through the side entrance, the cold biting at my face immediately. I hope Californian Jackson is having a rough time out here.

Wade follows me outside without his coat and jumps in my way. "I swear you're going to regret this."

"Get back inside." I try to walk around him, but he's persistent.

"You both swore to me you wouldn't let your relationship get in the way of our squad, remember?"

I remember. I remember being that idiot. "Take it up with Theo."

"Well, I'm still going to the dinner." Wade shivers and shakes his head. "At least give him a call later, okay? I know you'll both feel better if you at least talk."

"Okay." I can do that. "Seriously, get back inside. I'll see you tomorrow." We fist-bump and Wade finally lets me pass him, just in time so I can cry without him seeing me.

THE PUZZLE PORTRAIT OF Theo and me, the one Wade gave me two Christmases ago, sits in my lap. I'll never understand how time can make a moment feel as close as yesterday and as far as years.

So I call Theo, remembering all the good things about Theo during our friendship and relationship, like how thoughtful he's always been and how he's always made me feel safe. If I focus on all the times he's messed up since he met Jackson, I'll just be an asshole, which he doesn't need from me, especially not on his birthday.

"Hello?" He's upset.

"Hey," I say. "Happy birthday." I want to ask how dinner is, but common sense shuts me up.

"Thanks."

"I'm sorry I couldn't make it out tonight," I say. I do regret not going—maybe Wade is psychic after all—but I also know it was the right move.

"Same," Theo says. "You think you'll be able to hang out tomorrow? I really want to see you."

Maybe our relationship isn't such a blip in his eyes after all. "Yeah, Wade and I can—" I shut up when I hear Jackson and Ellen laughing in the background. Bonding has never made me feel so nauseous before. "Hey, I have to go. But enjoy the rest of your night, okay?"

"Griff, wait, what happened?"

"I'll talk to you tomorrow, Theo. Happy birthday."

"Talk to me, I—"

I hang up and throw the puzzle portrait across the room. It doesn't seem right that it remains intact.

TUESDAY, MAY 17TH, 2016

"MAYBE THEO DIED," WADE tells me over the phone.

"That's not funny," I say.

A couple of hours ago, around ten my time, Theo uploaded a filtered photo on Instagram of himself with Jackson, both of them wearing shades and too much sunscreen on their foreheads, playing chess at the beach. It's safe to assume the game was earlier, but I don't know what else Theo has been doing with his day that he can't call and wish me a happy birthday.

I know this isn't some revenge nonsense left over from February when I didn't go to his birthday dinner. We talked that one out; he gets that I wasn't ready to meet Jackson.

"You still haven't opened his present?" Wade asks.

"Nope."

I've opened every other present today except the one the UPS guy dropped off this afternoon. It arrived right as I got home from school. My parents got me some new video games and an envelope of gift cards. Wade baked me a dozen cupcakes, and

I haven't tried any of them yet, though I lied and told Wade they're great.

"Your birthday is over in a couple of minutes," he says.

I didn't need that reminder. "Yeah. I'm going to open it now. I'll talk to you at school tomorrow."

"I got to wait until tomorrow?"

"I doubt it'll be worth the wait."

"Better not be."

"Thanks again for the cupcakes."

"Happy birthday, Griffin. See you tomorrow."

It's weird seeing Theo's dorm address on the package instead of his Manhattan address. I grab a pen and stab my way into the box. I pull out a pair of navy boots with black laces and a card.

The card reads:

> *Happy birthday, Griff. I saw these and thought of you immedi-*
> *ately. You'll look cooler than everyone else out here.*
> *Your best friend in the apocalypse,*
> *Theo.*
> *P.S.: Wear these EVERYWHERE because the post office here*
> *sucks. EVERYWHERE, I SAY, EVERYWHERE.*

It's a great gift and I will wear the boots everywhere, but I don't know how I can count on him to be my best friend during the apocalypse when he can't even call me on my birthday. There's still another two minutes.

I'm sure he'll come through. Right?

THURSDAY, JUNE 30TH, 2016

EVERYTHING FEELS WRONG. I'M hugging Theo for the first time since last August. I have both arms wrapped around him, with my chin pressed deep in his shoulder, and he's hugging me like I'm his uncle, not best friend slash first love. *Theo* feels wrong.

He looks wrong too. He's come home with a slight tan I didn't really expect because of all the filtered photos he uploads. I don't want him to look unhappy, but I don't like how airy he seems, like life has finally made sense now that he left.

"It's great seeing you guys," Theo says, hugging Wade a lot more intimately than he does me. It's not like Jackson is here and can see us; he's vacationing with his father this week in Cancun. I'd be surprised if it's actually for "father-son bonding" and not a guilt trip.

"You too," I say, burying my hands in my pockets.

"It's been a minute," Wade says.

Theo sees the boots he got me for my birthday, the toes scratched from how often I wear them. "The boots!"

"I'm wearing them everywhere, as requested," I say.

"Good going on messing up his birthday," Wade says.

"Honest mistake," Theo says. "It's weird thinking of Griffin being born on an odd-numbered day. At least I got the shoe size right!"

WHY CAN'T THEO'S COMING home ever be simple? Even though Jackson isn't here with him this time, I still feel his presence all afternoon. Theo avoids saying his name so he doesn't set me off. Don't get me wrong, I prefer it this way, but whenever Theo's about to talk about him, he turns to me and changes the subject, like I should feel guilty. He's also checking his phone constantly, answering Jackson's texts immediately. I can't wait until we're underground on our way to Brooklyn for randomness so his California me-knockoff can't reach him.

On our way to the train station, Wade brings up colleges. "I don't think I could be away from home that long. I'm probably going to stick around here in the city next fall."

"It's not the worst thing," Theo says.

It's not the worst thing because he's found himself paradise, whereas the rest of us are stuck here missing him, alone. "I'm definitely applying to SMC," I say.

Theo nods. "If that's what you want you totally should." Now he sounds like a fucking guidance counselor.

"Of course it's what I want," I say. I almost remind him it's what we both want, but I promised Wade I wouldn't make today about Theo and me. I have no idea what I want to study in college, but I know Theo and I only stand a chance at repairing our relationship if we're closer.

On the 4 train to Union Square, Theo and Wade talk about Netflix shows. I feel invisible and voiceless. I'm sitting opposite of Theo and Wade, and they're both laughing away like it's totally normal how Theo and I don't fit anymore. It reminds me of the early years of our friendship, when Theo and Wade were the best of friends and *I* was the odd man out, this add-on they were auditioning for their squad. I'm shrinking back into an eleven-year-old desperate to prove himself, desperate to show Theo I could be really helpful when he's putting together puzzles, desperate to be caught up on all the latest cinematic scores so Wade would think I was cool.

Screw this.

We get off at Union Square, and while we're waiting for the L train, I stand between the two of them, getting in Theo's face.

"We need to talk."

"Griff . . ."

I turn to Wade. "I need ten minutes with him. Alone." Wade tries protesting, but I grab Theo's hand and drag him down the platform, stopping underneath the staircase. "Okay, we need to cut the shit here for ten minutes. Can you do that? Can you give me complete honesty for ten minutes, and then we can go back to playing dumb?"

Theo looks like he might cry. He pulls out his phone. I'm about to remind him there's no service down here—he hasn't been in California that long that he could possibly have forgotten this already—but he sets a timer for ten minutes and starts it.

I wouldn't have set a timer. I want an entire life where I'm honest with him without repercussions, but since I offered ten minutes, I'll take what I can get. "Are we still endgame?"

Theo nods, shakes his head, shrugs, and freezes. "I don't know."

"Do you know if you still love me? Or have I been completely delusional about everything between us?"

"You're not delusional," Theo says. "I do love you. But I love Jackson too." It's the first time he's told me he loves him. I filled in that blank myself, but it's still more painful even than the first time he told me they had sex. "I don't know what to do. You broke up with me, Griff. We kept talking, but I didn't know what your goal actually was. I thought maybe you were over me. Jackson was there, and I liked him."

I nod. My body is on fire. "Should I bow out?"

"No, no. I mean. I don't know. It's not fair for me to make you wait," Theo says.

"Will it suck for you if you know I'm not here waiting for you?"

"Yeah." Theo nods. "I know that's selfish, but you want the truth."

It is selfish.

An express train on the other side of the station rockets past us, keeping us quiet and staring at each other. I'm tempted to grab his hand again, this time to hold it, but I feel rejected before I even reach out. When the train passes, Theo asks me if there's someone else.

"Of course not."

"You don't have to lie if there is. I would get it."

"I don't lie to you," I say. "Let's say I move to California for school. What happens then? Do you break up with Jackson?"

"Probably."

I haven't loved a possibility like this in so long. I've been loyal to my love for him, and if I can hold on for a little bit longer, we might get our endgame after all. Theo is willing to throw away everything he has with his convenient boyfriend, who was "there."

"Okay. I miss you so much," I say.

"I miss you too," Theo says. "I keep walking to Jackson's right. There have been times I expect to see you, and it's like a punch to the face."

He holds out his hand for me and I take it, of course, but I don't expect him to pull me in for a kiss. I doubt kissing me was part of Theo's agenda today. It doesn't matter. Kissing is what we do for the next few minutes until the timer blares its alarm in his pocket, vibrating against my leg. I don't want to stop, but Theo lets go of my hand and backs away.

"That's all taboo, right?"

"Yeah. We're back to playing dumb now, Theo."

Theo walks around the staircase to find Wade. I follow him, feeling a lot like I did on my birthday—sad but also a little victorious because he sent me a gift. When the L train arrives, I imagine it being the same train where Theo and I first came out to each other.

THURSDAY, AUGUST 11TH, 2016

IT'S BEEN A PRETTY lonely summer. Theo was only here for two weeks. But there were more than a few times I couldn't stomach hanging out with him because of how often Jackson would text and call. Wade kept busy with parties and job hunts, but now he seems adrift, too, trying to salvage what's left of freedom before we enter our senior year. I'm counting down the days until I'm out in California with Theo. Granted, a part of me isn't counting on actually *being* with Theo when I get there. I'm not that unrealistic.

Now Wade and I are sitting on Wade's bedroom floor. We're bouncing his handball back and forth, listening to the *Iron Man* soundtrack.

"You still feel like breaking up was the right move for me?" I ask him.

"Yeah," Wade says. "I know you don't feel that way."

He's right. I've asked myself that same question over and over, every morning when I wake up without a text from Theo, every night when I go to bed wishing I could video chat him to say good night, and my answer is never yes. Not when I'm being honest with myself.

"I'm not stupid to think so," I say.

"I never said you were. But it's been a year, right? You got to do you."

"He's just killing time with Jackson," I say, bouncing the handball back his way. I shouldn't be talking about this, but I'm cracking. "Theo said we'd get back together once I was out there in California."

"When did he say that?" Wade throws the ball behind him on the bed.

I know I shouldn't, but I can't help it; I have to talk with *someone*. I tell Wade everything Theo and I agreed is taboo. He'd probably be really upset at me for betraying his confidence— even though it's Wade—but I'm alone here. Theo can at least forget about me in the meantime. I'm crying when I finish spilling because I'm not sure I can go another year of Theo not loving me the way I know he can.

"Theo is an asshole to make you wait," Wade says. His voice is harsh, not the usual joking way he bullies Theo to his face or talks about him behind his back to me.

I shake my head and get a grip on myself. "It's my fault. I broke up with Theo . . . I broke up with Theo before he could break up with me." It's the first time I've said the truth out loud. I'm sabotaging my trust with Theo and my trust with myself because being brutally honest is the relief I've needed since last year. "I didn't think he could keep loving me. I thought it was better if I just killed it dead before he did. This way, I can say I controlled our outcome. Except he said he's still in love with me."

In some weird way I wish I was the one who almost got hit by a car last summer so Theo could have had that flash moment where he has to picture life without me. Maybe I'd be able to "do me" the way Wade thinks I should.

Wade scoots closer to me. "You're not complicated. Theo became stupid. He's a genius academically, but he's become a gigantic idiot when it comes to dealing with you." He takes a deep breath. "I have to tell you something. Theo got a single room for his sophomore year so he can have more private time with Jackson. I don't think Jackson is going anywhere anytime soon."

I stare at Wade's bed. My heart pounds. I can hear construction outside in the hallway, the TV his mom left on before leaving to play dominoes with friends. Theo is moving on because I was insecure. "I shouldn't have doubted him."

"Stop blaming yourself, dude." Wade pats my shoulder. "I was there from the start. You did everything. Hell, you maybe did too much. That's a good thing! If Theo wants to throw that away, you need to throw him away."

"That's your best friend," I say.

Wade shakes his head. "Doesn't matter. Theo shouldn't have asked you to wait around for him, like you're some backup plan."

"He admitted it was selfish."

Wade looks into my eyes. "Stop defending him, Griffin. And stop putting him on some throne. Theo's messing up is his fault, not yours."

He pulls me into a hug, which is rare. But I need it. I hug him back. Then he kisses me, which is unimaginable.

I don't know what's happening, and I don't know why I haven't stopped it. I don't have feelings for Wade, never have, and not just because I thought he was straight. But I haven't been kissed like this since June, and that was a secret stolen kiss with Theo, which we never talked about again. It's different, too. I never thought I would ever kiss anyone who wasn't Theo. I never thought some kisses come with different rhythms. Wade is slower than Theo, but it works.

I like it.

At that moment, I stop kissing Wade. He's Theo's best friend. "What the hell?" I gasp, backing off.

Wade doesn't apologize. He stares at me, probably expecting me to punch him or to run away. He's no longer the same Wade I grew up with and this dizzies me, even more so than the news of Theo getting the single room so he can pretty much live with Jackson. I wouldn't have known this without Wade, the only person who's really been by my side since this breakup. I can't count on Theo.

So I kiss Wade again. I kiss him *because* he's Theo's best friend.

I have a thousand questions, but I don't need a single answer right now. There's only the urgency to prove to Wade that I am complicated, that I'm the real idiot who does idiot things and that's why Theo doesn't want me. If I'm as good as Wade thinks I am, then it wouldn't make sense for Theo to jump into bed so quickly with someone else.

I take off my shirt and pull off Wade's too. I climb on top of Wade and he sinks to the floor, flat on his back, and I kiss him a lot like Theo kissed me the last afternoon we had sex. It's not long before we make it into his bed, completely undressing ourselves, and Wade confesses this is his first time—across the board. I take the lead. I close my eyes the entire time.

It doesn't last long. But it has rerouted everything.

I get dressed in a hurry. I can't look at Wade on my way out; I ignore him as he asks me to stay so we can talk this out. I've had many destructive urges like this over the past year, but I figured if I ever did give in to one, it would be with a stranger, not with someone who's been sitting front row in my life the past few years.

I want to tell Theo, but I know I can't. There's no coming back from a betrayal like this, not ever.

WEDNESDAY, AUGUST 31ST, 2016

I KEEP DIGGING AND digging. Theo is never going to take me back. Not after he learns I've had sex with Wade five times already. The first time took both of us by surprise; the second took Wade by surprise, when I appeared at his front door, pissed off because Theo posted a photo of Jackson on Instagram. The third time was because I stupidly went on Jackson's Facebook page and his three most recent profile pictures all included Theo. The fourth time was because I found the "Griffin on the Left" clip Theo made for my birthday two years ago and was disappointed in myself for believing he'd actually finish it. Most recently was because I was broken and lonely and only felt whole when I was losing myself with him.

But now Wade is holding out for the sixth time.

"You don't talk to me anymore," Wade says. "And you know there's a lot to talk about."

I've never asked Wade how long he's known he's gay or bisexual or curious or whatever. Big talks haven't really been part of the plan. I come over, I do something I wish I could black out, and I go home wondering if I'll ever have the nerve to drop this bomb on Theo.

"Let's talk afterward." I lean in and reach for his zipper, but he catches my hand and backs up.

"You said that last time," Wade says.

I consider walking out, but then I might lose my only friend.

It hasn't felt like friendship lately, or even friendship with benefits—just benefits. I can't use him the same way Theo is taking advantage of me. "You're right." I get up, moving over to his spinning chair. "I'm sorry. It's really easy to get caught up in my own bullshit lately."

"I get it." His tone is nicer than I deserve. It makes me angry; why, I don't know.

"So." I spin around in the chair. "Why didn't you tell us you're gay?"

"I don't really care about titles right now, but Theo actually knew. I told him last year," Wade says.

I stop spinning. "Were Theo and I dating? Where was I?"

"The afternoon you had me distract Theo while you hunted down a graduation cap for his surprise party. I kept it real with him because I wanted to know how he knew which feelings to trust." Wade bounces the ball against the wall, keeping his eyes off of me.

"But why didn't you tell me?" Not being in on something from our squad makes me feel like the third wheel I was when I first started hanging out with them, the third wheel Wade was terrified of becoming after Theo and I came out.

"I didn't want to make a big deal out of it. You and Theo made big deals about everything, and that's not me." Wade misses his next catch, and the ball rolls under the bed. He gives up and sits down on the floor. "You confused me too. I really wanted what you and Theo had, and I wanted it with you. Don't worry, I'm not in love with you."

This wasn't actually a concern of mine. If anything, it's another reminder how unloved I am these days, but I keep that to myself.

"It's been really hard watching you so hurt," Wade says. "I wanted to make you feel better, and it was risky, so I made a move. I didn't expect it to get so far."

"Me either."

I hope he isn't trying to start something up with me. I love Theo way too much to fake interest in someone else. Sex is one thing to cover up, but I can't bullshit love. "You cool with it? Being gay or bi or whatever?"

"You and Theo made it look pretty cool. You guys were like bros that kiss and have sex. That sounds wrong, but you know what I mean." Wade rolls his eyes at himself, fighting back a yawn. "I wish it was as easy as you and Theo made it look. But I got freaked out along the way and didn't know what would happen if I got rejected. I didn't want to screw up our friendship."

I'm tempted to respond to his honesty with some of my own, how I'm only engaging with him sexually to get back at Theo, even though I'm not sure that's a gun I ever want to shoot. Wade would be stupid not to suspect this, but there's a huge difference between suspecting someone has a gun and finding one pointed at you. He doesn't deserve or need to be hurt. He deserves a hell of a lot better.

Maybe he and I can still be friends. But that's as far as we can go with this. Nothing else—except hopefully that sixth time in bed.

THURSDAY, SEPTEMBER 8TH, 2016

I'M PLAYING ZOMBIE LASER tag with the wrong person. Wade wanted to play laser tag for his birthday, but I wasn't counting on his selecting the zombie game. I didn't know this existed; otherwise, I would've treated Theo to it for his birthday or for date night. That doesn't matter, though; I'm not letting it ruin my night or, more importantly, Wade's night.

We run around the arena with our team, using our sci-fi-looking blasters and bows and foam-tipped arrows to take out the glow-in-the-dark zombies slithering and growling against the walls. We stay close, our arms pressed against each

other, and I feel so trained for this battle from all our imagined zombie-pirate apocalypse scenarios. We end up in a
lab, when a zombie pops out of a locker and our entire team
unloads their magazines of lasers into this poor son of a bitch.
But when four zombies flank us from every exit, I spin around
with the laser blaster like a maniac.

A zombie scratches at Wade, who's too busy laughing at me
to notice. He only collapses when he finally registers what's
going on.

I let the zombies get me too. I'm not fighting this battle
without Wade.

My heart rate settles down as Wade and I exit from where
we started, pass all the blood-streaked corridors and through
the destroyed fences. We're both sweaty, catching our breath. It
triggers memories of having sex with Wade. I wonder if it does
the same thing for him. We've been really good about not doing
that anymore.

We go to our shared locker, grab our phones and wallets,
and go to their burger joint and buy overpriced bottles of water.
Wade's phone vibrates. It's Theo trying to FaceTime him. Wade
screens the call.

"You can answer it," I say. It's not like Theo and I aren't
talking.

"I'm having fun with you," Wade says. "I can hit him up later."

I'm a little relieved, honestly. And I'm having fun with
Wade, too.

SATURDAY, SEPTEMBER 24TH, 2016

WADE AND I ARE crouching on the sidewalk, checking out the discounted books on the blanket by the curb. There's absolutely zero
chance of me focusing on reading anything after Theo's call an
hour ago: Jackson wants us to stop talking, for good. Maybe Theo

broke our taboo rule—like I did—and finally told Jackson about our kiss and promises. All I know is Theo told Jackson he's not kicking me out of his life. That didn't go over well with anyone.

"Theo is trying to do the right thing," I tell Wade, who's been really upset since the call.

Wade drops a book with a Greyhound bus on the cover. "You're smarter than this, Griffin. There's going to come a time when keeping you happy is no longer the right thing. He's going to choose Jackson."

I stand. Crowds are continuing into Times Square, so I turn the other way and walk off. Wade chases me down, but he's not apologizing for saying the wrong thing like he normally does.

He stops me, gripping my shoulders and staring into my eyes. It's intense, and whenever I try looking away, Wade shifts himself back into focus. "Stop getting pissed because I'm the only one keeping it real with you. You need to move on. It doesn't have to be me or anyone, but you're going to drive yourself insane waiting around for him. I hate watching this."

I want to break out of his grip and push him away, but I know he's the only one here for me.

"Why do you care so much?"

"You're such an idiot. I've always cared." Wade reaches into my jacket pocket and pulls out the Cedric Diggory key chain he got me for my birthday last year, dangling the keys in front of my face. "You were never paying attention." He forces the keys into my hand, closing his own around mine. "I was never going to make a move on you because of Theo, but I still wanted you happy. The key chain of your favorite Harry Potter character. That collage of you and Theo." His narrowed eyes are watering. "I wanted to make one of you and me, but I respected you guys as friends."

Focusing on Theo these past few years has prevented me from truly appreciating Wade's role in my life. He's not just some third wheel who claims to be psychic. He doesn't just say the wrong thing at the wrong times. He's a capital *p* Person who speaks the truth and looks out for everyone's future, sometimes before his own.

Wade lets go of me and my heart continues speeding. "I'm done with Theo. It's almost been a year and that asshole still has you waiting for a phone call. It's not right."

"I can't get rid of him," I say. "He wants me in his life, and I can't do that to him." I don't break eye contact with him. "I don't want you to go either. I want to be more for you, but it's going to take time. Can you give me that?"

"Can you actually try?"

"I will."

I have to be careful with him. Wade is a Person and I don't want to play with his head the way Theo has played with mine. Believing in hope hasn't gotten me far, and I don't want it to hold Wade back either.

SUNDAY, NOVEMBER 13TH, 2016

WADE AND I ARE in bed, legs tangled in one another's, and we're eating tortilla chips. The heater is blasting and movie scores are playing in the background of our conversation about attractive Avengers.

"I'm not a huge fan of any of the Bruce Banners," I say, scooping a chip into the bowl of salsa. I'm extra careful not to drip because Wade will freak and try to clean the blanket immediately. "Thor is pretty damn awesome to look at, but I'm feeling pretty loyal to the Captain."

"Can I be Team Captain America and Team Black Widow?"

"Of course."

"Okay. Can I be Team Captain America and Team Black Widow and Team Tony Stark?"

"You need a fourth," I say.

"Right. Team Captain America, Team Black Widow, Team Tony Stark, and Team Griffin."

I bite back a smile. "You're not playing the game right. I'm not an Avenger." He's about to counter, but I interrupt him. "You should've come out sooner. We could've had squad chats like this."

That vision doesn't feel wrong: talking about dudes with Theo and Wade, as normal as a group of straight guys talking about which girls they like. Maybe this kind of talk is what Theo was hoping for when he brought Jackson around earlier this year. It was never going to make sense for me in the place I was in. Things are different now.

"Screw Captain America, screw Black Widow, and screw Tony Stark and all his money. I want to be Team Griffin," Wade says. "When are we giving that a shot?"

That vision of Wade and me doesn't feel wrong either. A little blurry, yeah, because I definitely still have feelings for Theo, but they're not as strong as they used to be. Moving on feels weird. Moving on with someone who used to be Theo and mine's third wheel feels even weirder. Things have changed over the past couple of months. I've spent less time hanging out with Wade because Theo indirectly sent me running there and more because it's where I want to be.

"I want to talk to Theo about it first," I say. I have a lot I need to get off my chest. Some of it includes Wade, but not all of it. "You cool with that?"

Wade nods, untangling his legs. "I can wait another day."

We hang out for a little bit longer before I slip on my new winter boots—it felt weird wearing the ones Theo bought me—and kiss Wade at the door. "I'll call you later."

"You better or I'm off Team Griffin."

I WALK AROUND MY bedroom, knowing I'm pretty much saying goodbye to the future I've been imagining for myself for the past couple of years. I don't feel super confident in a future with Wade just yet, and there's a chance I never will, but I'm not feeling as hopeless. Theo is with Jackson, and I'm going to try things out with Wade. If Theo and I are meant to get back together, then it'll happen in its own way. But I'm not waiting anymore. Wade was right.

I call Theo and it goes to voice mail. "Hey, Theo, it's Griff. I sort of need to talk to you about something big. It's not about us, I swear. That's a little bit of a lie, it involves us a little, but not what you think. Anyway. Call me back."

TODAY
SATURDAY, DECEMBER 17TH, 2016

There it is, Theo.

I was hiding history from you. Maybe this blindsided you. Maybe you suspected this all along. But here's what I bet you didn't count on, because it took me by surprise, too: I see myself falling in love with Wade. It's a twist in our own love story that has my head spinning and my heart pounding. I thought I would use him as revenge for you moving on, but I never thought I would be actually moving on too.

I wanted to do this right by being honest with you the way you were with me when Jackson entered your life. Please believe me when I tell you now that I'd actually found the strength to officially shelve our endgame plan when you missed my call.

You died four hours later.

When I got the news, I didn't cry just because it meant we'd never get to be in love again, but also because my best friend would no longer share this universe with me. I don't know what you would've thought of me with Wade, but it doesn't matter now. I was in love and love died and the pain you've left isn't pain I can see myself having the strength to face again.

But this doesn't stop me from entering Wade's building. This doesn't stop me from hoping he'll be home and hoping he won't turn me away. I get into the elevator and it's miraculously going nonstop between the ground level and the twenty-seventh floor, but it still somehow feels like it's taking forever, even longer than the time the three of us got stuck on the seventeenth floor for the longest twenty minutes of our lives.

It's weird to think about how much has changed and gotten messy, almost as if our friendship was a one-thousand-piece puzzle being put together by a one-year-old who got everything wrong. Sometimes this universe feels like an alternate, but maybe you already knew that.

I step out of the elevator, and if I was thinking about changing my mind and running home, I've lost my chance. Wade walks out of his apartment carrying a garbage bag in each hand. He's wearing nothing but his bright orange basketball shorts and white ankle socks. My heart drops, like I'm back in the elevator and the cables have snapped. It's not just because his body is beautiful without the abs he desperately wants or the way his eyes narrow whenever I surprise him, like he's trying to find me without his glasses. For the first time since you've died, I'm admitting to myself how much I really missed this guy and how strange it's going to be to only be friends.

It's you all over again.

"Griffin."

The chills running through are not like the kind that come from a cold winter evening like this one. They can only come from someone calling out the name of a person they love.

"Your socks," I say.

Wade looks down at his socks. "My socks?"

"They're going to get dirty," I say.

I close the space between us, doing my damn best to fight away this hollowing urge to hug him. I reach out for the bags, brushing my cold fingers against his warm knuckles for a quick, unbearable second, and I carry the bags to the other end of the hallway, smelling the clinking beer bottles, and drop them down the garbage chute. I'm expecting to find Wade waiting for me by his door—if he hasn't ignored me or told me to go away by now, I trust he won't at all—and he's walking toward me, stepping through the puddles of melted snow my boots have left.

"Your socks," I say again.

I think he's going to kiss me. I don't have a single muscle left in me to push him away, but instead he wraps his arms around my neck and presses himself against me. I hug him back and almost even laugh when he flinches at my cold fingers on his spine.

"Your socks are going to be so dirty," I say.

"I don't care," Wade says. "I don't care about the socks and I don't care why you're here. In a good way."

There's the Wade we know, Theo. He's always getting the sentiment right and the words wrong, but there's no getting mad at him because it's almost as if saying the wrong thing is his first language, and he can't quite shake it off. He stops hugging me but cups my elbows and I wish I wasn't wearing this coat right now so I can feel his palms against my flesh. "I want you to come inside, but I have to ask my mom first. I know that shit makes me sound like we're twelve again."

"Is everything okay?"

He sighs. "I'm on lockdown like never before. Long story."

"Short version?"

"I was skipping school."

"Why?"

"Wait for the long story." Wade walks back to his front door and is hesitant to go in, a lot like when we all went to Coney Island and he didn't want to go on the roller coaster, which I feel even more awful about today since I got to hold your hand while I was freaking out and Wade was forced to sit with a stranger. "You're going to be here when I get back, right?"

There's no saying no to that vulnerable, don't-break-me look of his.

"I'll be here," I promise.

His you're-piecing-me-back-together look says he believes me.

You've never seen this side of him, Theo, which makes sense because people reveal different parts of themselves to different people. I don't know why I could never see that before. How I was with you isn't how I was with Wade, and how Jackson was with me isn't how he was with you.

Wade returns to the hallway with a fitted white T-shirt that hugs his shoulders, and he waves me in. The apartment is very warm and smells like vanilla, which I mistake for a candle before quickly remembering it's probably the smell of his mother's flavored vodka floating around.

I walk into the living room where Ms. Juliette is half asleep and watching some game show. She says hi and asks me how I'm doing, but not in the same way everyone else has been, as if I'm a fragile piece of glass. The normalcy is almost a relief. Ms. Juliette asks Wade for water, which I hope isn't code for more vodka, but Wade fills a glass from the kitchen faucet, and she downs it in almost one gulp.

She announces she has a headache and is going to go to bed early and that I shouldn't stay too late because Wade shouldn't even have company in the first place. She's pissed for reasons I'll learn in a second, but she still kisses Wade on the forehead before retreating to her bedroom.

"The room has changed a little bit," Wade says, pushing open his bedroom door.

Understatement. His room looks like it's been robbed. There's an outline on the floor where his rickety home studio used to be and I wouldn't be surprised if the damn thing finally collapsed and he had to throw it away, except that doesn't explain what happened to his flat-screen TV or his Xbox. His laptop isn't in its usual spot on his desk, and his charger is nowhere in sight, either. The only things that remain are his bed; his chair and desk with a textbook currently open underneath the lamp; a bookcase well stocked with nonfiction books, which he rarely finishes because he gets over each subject due to "information overload"—the opposite of you; and his phone. It's sitting in the corner of the room and propped up at angle, his trick so his jazz acoustics are amplified.

"I'm really scared to ask where your mother hid your stuff. Please don't say she sold it."

"It's in storage somewhere."

"What the hell did you do?"

Wade pulls a stick of mint gum out of his pocket and chews it while sitting down on his bed and inviting me to do the same. I go for the chair instead. It's not very comfortable at first because I'm close to the small radiator, so I take off my coat, reminding myself I shouldn't become too exposed. The more exposed I am, the easier it will be to remove every last piece of clothing and lose myself in him—in front of you. Wade is confused, no doubt, but he doesn't pressure me because he knows me well enough that it might push me away.

Wow. Someone knowing me is supposed to be a beautiful thing and not something that prevents him from being open, right? I wish you were here to actually give me an answer.

"I was skipping school last week. Everything kind of fell apart after the library blowup and your choosing Jackson over me. Seeing you and Theo all over school didn't help make me feel less alone. Not in some ghost-seeing crazy way, but the memories sucked. The next morning I was going to school and forgot my damn tie, so I ran back home because I wasn't in the mood to stay there for detention. My mom had already left for work by the time I got there, and once the idea to stay home got in my head, it never bounced. I listened to music and played video games and napped. I did it again the next day. But on the third day, the school called my mom to see if I was okay, and shit hit the fan. She came home and I thought she was going to break her never-hit-me rule."

I nod. I understand. "Did she take all your stuff then?"

"The next day when I got home from school, yeah. She only let me keep my phone because it would've been irresponsible of her not to. I can't even use my laptop for homework, and she's forcing me to stay late at the library to get work done." Wade shrugs. "At least I have some games on my phone."

I can't even give him shit for any of this. "You could've just said you missed us, by the way."

"Say what?"

"When I asked you for the short version. You could've said you were skipping school because you were missing me and Theo."

"It took me a while to man up and say all that and you're judging me? You suck, Griffin."

I turn to the window because I can't "man up" and look him in the eyes. "I do suck, Wade. I've been really selfish, like my pain shadows everyone else's. I had Jackson to talk to, and you've had no one this past month."

"I have to ask," Wade says, and then asks nothing for a stretch of time. "You and Jackson . . . ?" He spits the words out and closes his eyes like he's behind the wheel of a car that's flying off a cliff. "Are you and Jackson together or something? Forget it, I don't want to know." He looks around the room, probably wishing he could turn on the TV and distract himself, but he's stuck here with me. Before I can say anything, he continues, "It doesn't matter anyway, it's not like we're dating. I mean, what the hell are we doing, Griffin? Is this just sex? I don't know if I can keep up with that if that's all it's supposed to be."

"I think we should just be friends again," I say.

"It's too complicated to attempt something more right now," Wade says.

"We shouldn't look at it like that. I think we're better off as friends, period. I personally don't want to be in a relationship again. Definitely not anytime in the near future. It's too soon."

"Okay," Wade says. "And I'm better off not knowing anything about Jackson."

The thing is, love doesn't make sense anymore, and I feel lied to. Love isn't this ultimate power that can make me feel unbeatable and all conquering. If I were truly in love with you, would I have turned to Wade? And if I were falling in love with Wade, would I have turned to Jackson? Maybe my self-destructive streak isn't so much about cheating on a single person as it is about cheating on love itself. Love, the hugest liar in this universe.

"I could really use a friend again," I say. "Can we be that?"

Wade nods. "Yeah, we can be friends."

"I'm so sorry, Wade."

So much guilt and anxiety has surrounded my evolving relationship with Wade that restricting ourselves to just friends feels like a disservice. It's something we both thought we had a shot at turning into more. But this is what will save us in the long run.

I tell him about California, leaving out all mentions of having sex with Jackson and the role I played in your death. I want him to know how we paid tribute to you, and I want to preserve who you were for everyone else. No one else needs to spend the rest of his life second-guessing how much they actually meant to you.

"I'm proud of you for making it to the beach," Wade says. "Both of you."

It wasn't easy. I couldn't admit it before because you were listening, but I really, really wanted Wade there with me and Jackson. He would've fought the ocean too. Thinking about it, I can't handle his compliment.

"I'm no longer talking to Jackson. We were a support system for each other for a while, but I think that was stupid and unhealthy. I should've been here with you and dealing with Theo instead of investigating more into his life with someone else. I'm sorry. Again." A second apology. An even number.

"Let's do that then," Wade says.

"Really?"

"Maybe you're Theo'd out, but I miss the guy."

Exchanging Theo stories is so exhausting—both good and bad—I wish I could crawl into bed beside Wade right now and fall asleep against his chest. But my dad is texting, telling me to come home before it gets darker, which is probably for the best because if I spend any more time here, I won't be able to stop myself from making a move on Wade.

"I got to go," I say, putting away my phone.

"You're not going to vanish on me again, right?"

"No." I hope I won't, at least.

"I'm thinking about visiting Denise and Theo's parents this week. You should tag along," Wade says. "I'm sure they could go for seeing some friendly faces this month."

"I'm not sure we should really be going to Theo's house together," I say.

"Why not? Griffin, you didn't cheat on Theo. Theo was dating Jackson and you were single. We did nothing wrong," Wade says. "Besides, we're just friends."

I want to hug him but resist. "Call me tomorrow and we'll figure out a day. See you, Wade."

He walks me out and something as simple as turning around when I step out the door feels like I've punched my own face. Back when he and I were just friends, I could tell him I'll see him later, get in the elevator, and go home without thinking about him for the rest of the day. Then he and I started hooking up, and there were times I couldn't even face him whenever I left his house. Then once—*once*—I actually turned around and kissed him at the door, guilt-free and excited for the next time I would get to see him.

Now I don't know what's appropriate. Wade is probably thinking the same thing, too, except he doesn't wait for me to decide and gives me a head nod when closing the door. This universe I'm stuck in gets worse and worse: all this history, and I can't possibly have a future with this guy any more than I can have one with you.

MONDAY, DECEMBER 19TH, 2016

WADE AND I ARE on Denise duty.

Ellen and Russell are about to run out to get their Christmas shopping done. Your parents not already having those presents wrapped and locked away in the chest at the foot of their bed is a big deal, though Denise is too young to realize this—but thankfully smart enough to know what's good about this Santa business because I'm sure Wade and I are bound to slip.

Your parents are looking better. Russell is clean-shaven but still smells of cigarettes, and I really hope to find a patch on his arm sometime in the near future. Ellen looks tired, understandably, and the gray in her blond hair has gone untouched, but she doesn't seem defeated.

"It's lovely to see you both, really," Ellen says, and I believe her. "Thanks for taking Jackson in, Griffin. He's family like you two, but hosting anyone during that time required fuel I didn't have. We're relaxing back to that point where we can trust our emotions a little better, I think."

"No worries," I say. She has no idea the role he played in her only son's death. The role *I* played in your death. I don't deserve to be here or anywhere near her family again. I'm sharp, I'm poison, I'm suffocation, and I'm fire. But going forward, I can be more careful with those around me. "Did the box with Theo's things arrive okay?"

Ellen nods. "Thank you for sorting through that with Jackson. Your love for Theo means more than I can find words for."

"No words necessary."

Russell and Ellen kiss Denise and rush out, hoping to be home at a respectable time. It'll be tough considering the time and store traffic this week, but Wade and I are here for as long as they need us.

Wade stands in front of Denise, arms crossed like a bouncer's, and looks down at her with a funny-serious glare. "All right, Dee, we are your minions. What do you want to play first?"

Denise runs into her room and returns with an armful of well-loved board games. I think she's going to make a move for Monopoly Junior, but then she opens the fifty-piece turtle puzzle we once did with her, and if she can be strong enough to piece back together this family of three turtles, then I can, too—then I will, too. Wade has always been more of an observer whenever it comes to puzzles, but I think he's surprising even himself when he begins participating, starting at the top right, which—spoiler alert—is the cave the turtles are headed to.

It's kind of cool, like Wade is making sure there's a home for the turtles Denise and I are creating.

Normally you lead the stories behind each puzzle. I'm ready to do so in your place, but Denise cuts in and her imagination is just as wild as yours. When the puzzle is done, Denise tells—excuse me, commands—us to put the puzzle away while she runs to grab another game.

"I never understand this part," Wade says. "Breaking apart the puzzle."

"Theo and I kept some," I say. Talking about you before, when Wade and I were doing our own thing, was legit awkward. Now that we're grounding ourselves, it feels natural to bring you up, although a part of me hopes it isn't making Wade feel a certain way.

"It's a waste of time if you don't. It's like sand castles that people just body slam their friends onto if you leave for a minute," Wade says.

"I don't think so. You still take some experience away with each puzzle. Puzzles are sort of like life because you can mess up and rebuild later, and you're likely smarter the next time around." I pull apart the edges of ocean and seaweed, then the fins, then the shells, and lastly the heads. I trust the turtles will come out to play again, maybe another time or two before Denise takes a shot at your harder puzzles.

Denise returns with her speakers and connects them to your mother's laptop and blasts the music from her playlist. "Dance party!" And then she's dancing with her eyes closed, so she's blind to how she's all arms and shoulders. I'm thinking I'm going to have to force Wade to be silly, but he's up before me and looking down at me with his serious-funny look. He extends a hand and helps me up, letting me go quickly. His head is bopping out of sync with the beat, but maybe he's lost in his head, a completely different song getting him through this little girl's dance party.

"Dance, Griffin!" she cries.

I do. I dance like I would with you, which just basically means a lot of hopping, and the three of us dance so hard we're probably pissing off the family downstairs. Even if they have the balls to come up here with some noise complaint, they're going to have to bitch to the door because we're not stopping. I'm not interrupting the happiness of a girl who's been missing her older brother, the happiness of a guy who's been missing the first love of his life, the happiness of another guy who lost his best friend, the collective happiness of three people in desperate need of happiness.

When the dance party finally winds down, Wade and I find your mother's iced tea in the fridge and get glasses for all of us, though who knows when Denise will get to hers since she's still doing handstands against the wall. We should've really encouraged her to go to bed by now, but if she has this much energy, I can't imagine she'll actually fall asleep. I hate to think about the thoughts she's thinking when she's stuck in bed alone.

My phone buzzes.

It's a text from Jackson: I bit my tongue twice today. IDK why. If you bit your tongue a third time, would you bite it a fourth time?

I don't know what the hell kind of message that's supposed to be, but it's certainly not a question I'm planning on answering. I throw my phone to the other side of the couch and tell Denise to choose a movie. Denise puts on *Peter Pan*, which makes me think of Jackson's former best friends in that play, but I shove Jackson to the back of my mind.

Halfway through the movie, Denise falls asleep on Wade's arm, and Wade is minutes away from completely passing out himself. It's early by his standards, so I don't know why he's so tired, but it definitely has me wondering what he's thinking about when he's alone in bed.

Once Wade is laid out, I get up from the couch. I walk to your room and wish there was a point in knocking. I open the door and everything is still in place, with the addition of the box Jackson and I put together from your dorm. You're the only thing missing. I don't have the strength to go in alone, but I'm happy to see your stuff still here and not suddenly abandoned on the sidewalk as the latest healing ritual emailed to your parents.

I turn around, and Wade's eyes are open now, watching me. I don't know why, but it stops me in my tracks. He's tired, but he also looks, I don't know, disappointed or annoyed. I mouth "What?" and he shakes his head gently. I don't believe it's nothing, but I'm not going to push this, especially not with Denise here.

I join them on the couch and kick my feet up on the coffee table. I try and concentrate on the movie, but it's not happening. I still can't believe you weren't actually immortal. I take a page out of Denise's book and close my eyes.

SUNDAY, DECEMBER 25TH, 2016

THIS CHRISTMAS IS EVEN more off than last year's. I know I said the same thing about Thanksgiving, but Christmas hurts more, as will New Year's Eve, as will your birthday, as will my birthday, as will every day you're not alive. If I'm really done with lying, I can't lie about that.

At least the day is moving by pretty quickly. We opened

presents at home, and now we're doing the family gathering at my aunt's. Dad promised me we won't be staying long, especially not after the showdown from Thanksgiving. I'm hiding out in my aunt's room to avoid my asshole cousin, but the sound of everyone's laughter carries over from the living room. I'm not even the slightest bit tempted to explore what's so funny, but it does remind me of how nice it was to leave my room this morning and find my mom and dad sitting on the floor beside our low-maintenance tree like it was their first Christmas together.

It's crazy how they're not tired of each other, or how it looks like they haven't even lost an inch of love for each other. Second-best part of the morning is when I joined them, and my mom modeled her pajamas for both of us from the living room to the kitchen and back, as if on a runway.

Mom brings my grandmother into the room, and I help out, holding her underneath her arm as we guide her to the rocking chair opposite the TV. Mom tells me that it was getting too loud out there for her, so she hopes I don't mind Grandma intruding on my "quiet time."

I put on the news, which she's obsessed with but can never actually absorb. I missed her ninetieth birthday last week in my brutal haze, but if I wanted to lie and tell her I spoke with her, she wouldn't actually know any better.

"Is Theo coming? I want to watch his movie with the flowers."

You're still alive for Grandma. You're still around making more films. You're still around to whip out your camera phone and play one of your videos for her. You're still around to hold my hand and kiss me good morning. I *know* you're not alive, but I know I don't treat you like you're dead. I know you're watching, but I know there's a chance you're not. I know you're not around to live, and I know you're always going to live through me.

I can't bring myself to upset her and tell her it's all over, because, well, I don't know, if I deny her the fantasy of your immortality, I don't know if it will ruin my mystery of where you are.

"Theo can't make it," I say. It's a truth hidden in the folds of a lie. "I have his video, though." I go through the album of videos on my phone and sit down beside my grandmother, feeling very vulnerable as I relive your creations with a woman who watches with the joy of someone witnessing magic for the first time.

Wherever you are, Theo, I hope you're having a Merry Christmas. I'll try some damn eggnog for you.

"I'M SORRY I DON'T have a present for you," I say, scratching my gloved palm and pulling at my earlobe the entire time I go up the steps outside the subway.

"I don't have one for you, either," Wade says. "We're all good." He walks over to my left, staying there. I shift over to reclaim my side, but he keeps messing with me. "I'm going to walk on your left for a minute."

"Nope. I'm going to walk on the left forever," I say.

"Entertain me."

"There's nothing funny about this."

"Exactly. This is serious, and you never treat it that way. I want to see what you're like on my right."

He's walked on my right side before, but only when you were alive and I was on your left, because you were obviously the more important one, so it didn't bother me as much in the grand scheme of things. Wade has never been on my right one-on-one, and allowing this feels a lot like a big deal, sort of like my first date with you. I was on edge despite knowing you for what feels like forever and trusting you with everything else I had to offer that the everyday person never experienced.

"It's not going to last long, but give it your best shot," I say.

The moment Wade takes a couple of steps back, as if the forces of winter have decided to blow him out of my life for good, I feel myself inching to the left to cut him off, but I remain firm until he reappears on my wrong side with freckles of snow on his shoulders and an anxious kind of smile on his face. "How are we doing?"

"It's probably better not to draw attention to it," I say, facing forward and refusing to turn to my left. It's almost impossible for my neck to shift that way. The moment I give in, this experiment falls apart and I'll disappoint him, which will snowball into something worse. "Tell me a story."

He starts right up about this Gatorade chugging competition he once got into with his neighbor. After he won, he went home to pee but his mother stepped out and he didn't have his own keys yet. So, yeah, screwed. He tried peeing at the bottom of the staircase, but someone started coming down and he ran away. It was daytime so he couldn't go pee in the corner or bushes without getting caught, and he didn't trust the outside neighbors not to snitch on him. His bladder hurt so badly, and he kept trying to distract himself but failed because puddles of water were around him and it began drizzling a little again, but not fast enough that it would scare everyone back indoors so he could pee outside in peace.

Right when he charged into the staircase for a second shot, his bladder decided enough was enough and unleashed "a fury" on his jeans, soaking them with a "never-ending piss" so great his eyes rolled back with relief before he could fully register how much this was going to suck once piss stopped running down his leg and into his sneakers.

We arrive at Wade's building and, sort of like his story, I've been holding in all my anxiety about his being on my left, except I didn't reclaim my side (or piss myself). I'm relieved once we get into the elevator and there are no more sides, just us standing opposite of each other. We get into his apartment and go straight to his room. He's been given his TV back for Christmas break because he already finished all his holiday assignments and college applications, but he'll lose it once school starts up again. I thought we were going to watch a movie or something and take advantage of his TV while he has it, but instead he puts on the *E.T.* soundtrack and sits on the bed while I relax into the chair. The first song ends and another plays.

"Wait, play it again," I tell him.

"Why?"

"It's relaxing," I say.

"That's not it," Wade says. "Maybe a little bit, but not entirely. You just want it on repeat. I know this game, Griffin. You must hate the radio."

"I don't hate it," I say. "But I wouldn't call myself a fan, either."

"Give me your phone," Wade says.

"Why?"

"I want to introduce you to the magic of shuffle," Wade says. I don't hand my phone over, but Wade isn't shy about going into my coat pocket and retrieving it. "We're going to play radio with your downloaded music. See, these are all songs you've chosen at one point or another and were all favorites for different reasons."

"So I'm still in control?"

"Not really. But you're in control of allowing yourself to be surprised."

"I can't control being surprised, that doesn't make sense."

Wade smirks. "Griffin, your comfort zone is maybe a little too comfortable, okay? It's like you've got a TV with surround sound and every video game and the biggest bed ever so all your favorite people can hang out with you. But that place isn't real and you should live somewhere a little more realistic." Wade crosses to the corner of the room and swaps out his phone for my mine for these better acoustics. "Stay in the moments."

He presses PLAY, and the first song that comes on immediately takes me back.

Then comes "Be Still My Heart" by the Postal Service. We listened to this on the walk home the day we came out to each other, sharing headphones. I feel like I've been thrown back to the beginning of time. I haven't listened to this song in so long, and I didn't even realize I missed it.

"All Night" by Icona Pop. I discovered this song with Wade the day after my birthday. It was a little after you called me to wish me a happy birthday, feeling the dumbest you've ever felt in your life when you realized you mixed up the days. Wade and I were walking to Duane Reade, the same one where my dad gave us all a sex talk, and this song blasted from some parked car's radio. It only planted itself in my brain for an afternoon, but I enjoyed my time with it—just like I am now.

"Take Me Out" by Franz Ferdinand: Another you song, though even I don't have to tell you this one. It's a little uncomfortable because I'm pretty sure Wade knows you and I listened to this on repeat after we had sex for the first time. It came up when we were all playing Guitar Hero, and everyone wanted to know why you and I busted out laughing and were so good.

"Hold On" by Wilson Phillips: Okay, this one is a bit of a downer, but it was something I really connected to in the months after our breakup. I know it's lame, but it allowed me to feel lonely and didn't force me to lie to myself about how I was really feeling. I understand putting on a tough face for other people but never myself.

"Carry Me" by Family of the Year: Wade's favorite song that isn't jazz or some film score. He shared this one with me because he knows I love songs with words, and, yeah, this one really stuck with me for a couple of weeks. There were times I didn't even want to be thinking about Wade and what we did together, but I couldn't keep myself away from this song, like it was oxygen.

I was right about not being able to control my own surprises, but I was wrong about how good these surprises could actually be for me. Every time a new old song comes on, I'm being resurrected. This is the true power of history. Old memories and feelings are being revived, and I'm not complaining. It's like I still have the fatigue that got me to quit the song in the first place, but I don't mind being woken up to it for a little bit.

Wade gets up and turns off my phone. "How was that?"

"Play another song," I say. "You only played five."

"I know."

"Five isn't one of my good odd numbers. It's one, seven, and any number ending in seven."

"I know. Three birds with one stone."

I feel tricked. At least I knew what the battle plan was with the walking on my left and playing different songs, but I didn't know he would make a move on my even numbers, too. But it's okay, I can make my way out of this; I've made my way out of tougher situations before, situations completely out of my control, situations that affected me as if they were my fault. The jazz song that played before Wade started playing my songs can count as the first and sixth, and it qualifies because it is a song I enjoy and a song I would've wanted played again.

As for his painful three-birds-with-one-stone comment, if I were desperate enough, I could say three plus one equals four, but that's not going to fly with me, so I need something else to settle me. Um, uh, okay, I got it. I'm going to go with the grouping situation, one group for the birds and another group for the stone.

"You okay?" Wade asks.

I take a deep breath.

"The world didn't end," Wade says. "You stayed in the moments."

He's right. The universe isn't eating itself up like some cannibal chewing on his own arm. It feels like the universe is at least nibbling, but I'm still here, I'm still whole. I know it won't last long, but knowing I could do three trials—three!—in one evening is a huge deal. And it's an empowering feeling I never felt with you, not with my compulsions, at least.

"Theo made me feel special," I say, which takes Wade by surprise. "With my compulsions, I mean. Sorry. I know they sometimes frustrated him, but I also couldn't ever shake this feeling that they made me stand out in his eyes. And, I don't know, I always believed Theo loved me but there was always this voice in me that convinced me to make sure I always fit with him. If I didn't change, I would never stop being special in his eyes. Almost like, if I started trying to do stuff like we're doing now, I might lose my spark and suddenly feel, I don't know, faded to him?"

"Your thing . . . it's not healthy," Wade says. "I don't understand what it's got to be like in your head, but you have to do what's necessary to not be your compulsions' bitch. It's limiting your life."

Not controlling. Limiting.

I try to believe it, but I can't. My compulsions threaten my health, physically and mentally. For example, I can't shake off the thought that I've had sex with three guys—three. Even though there's no one else I want to sleep with, I feel like I have to, otherwise the universe will close in on itself or something bad will happen to someone I love. I've tried making logic out of this, like how I only slept with two of the guys—Wade and Jackson—out of need, and not out of love. So Wade and Jackson are in their own category, far removed from the bubble you live in. But if I'm going to have a pattern here, the next person I sleep with needs to be out of love and not a need to feel something.

"I get it," I say. "I'll try these exercises some more." I can't bring myself to ask him for this great favor just yet, but I want him to help me, and that's the truth. And he wants to help me. I'm not trying to make it sound like I have to give him my heart or dick in exchange for his help, but I do have to give him friendship. He's given me some history back that I hadn't thought of in a while and was possibly at risk of forgetting forever. I have to be fully honest with him in return.

"I have to tell you something. I don't know how to do it delicately, but I just have to spit it out. I've messed up. I don't just mean that I messed things up with you and whatever you would say we were, but I did something stupid because I was just not in my best space." He knows what I'm about to say, I can tell from his face. But I can't cheat him out of the words. "I had sex with Jackson when I was in California."

Wade nods, over and over, pirate bobblehead–style. "I know."

"You know?" Impossible. I've told no one, and Jackson wouldn't reach out to him. "How?"

"Because I know you," Wade says. "It's what you do. Sorry, that sounds like you're a whore or something, that's not what I mean. You do things you know you shouldn't. It's like you're wired to make mistakes when you're not in your 'best space,' and it wasn't hard to guess that was going to happen."

"You don't understand. You know those kisses Theo and I used to do? Theo taught them to Jackson and it pissed me off, and I told Theo I wanted him to see me have sex with his boyfriend to get back at him, and—"

"You *told* Theo? I don't understand."

Shit. I can't lie to him and I can't omit any truths. I've said this to myself, to you, and I'm done being a liar. "I still talk to Theo."

"For how long? Since he died?"

"Yeah. Sometimes a little before that, like something I would want to say when we got back together. But since he died, I've been trying to get his forgiveness for things, except I couldn't even get myself to tell him what you and I did . . ."

"I can never win with you, can I? No matter what, best friend or . . . whatever, I will always be competing against a ghost," he says. "No, I'm not even competing. I don't have a fighting chance." Wade gets up from his bed and grabs my phone, handing it to me. "I'm kind of tired."

"Are you serious?" I ask.

Wade doesn't say anything else. I never thought he could push me away like this, but he has absolutely no interest in my being around him right now.

"There's more to this . . ." I thought Wade would be the first person I told about my involvement in your death, which should speak volumes to how much he means to me, but I refused to listen to myself. And I could go ahead and be an asshole and tell him anyway. But that's not a guilt he has to carry, especially not for a shitty friend like me. "See you."

I grab my coat and let myself out, head into the staircase and go down all twenty-seven flights. I should really stop blaming everyone and certain events for what's happening to me. *I'm* the worst thing that's ever happened to myself.

WEDNESDAY, DECEMBER 28TH, 2016

I TURN ON MY laptop's video chat and call Jackson on an odd minute.

It didn't surprise me that he agreed to chat, considering he's messaged me a dozen times since I left California. I'm only surprised he agreed to speak so early, considering it's seven in the morning in Santa Monica. Maybe he was also awake all night.

He answers on the fifth ring. The screen is still black, but Jackson's voice carries through the speakers: "Was that four on your end, too?"

I'm ready to tell him no, when he appears and, yeah, I'd be lying if I said I didn't miss him. I grew so used to seeing him around, hell, to even waking up close to him. There have never been any romantic feelings for him, which is the straight-up truth, Theo. No one's perfect, and Jackson is certainly not the exception, but I've never been drawn to him the way I was with you or even the way I was becoming with Wade. It's okay for two boys who are gay to hang out and not want to be with each other.

I'm learning. I'm adjusting.

"Five," I answer.

"Sorry. It was four rings on mine. I'll hang up and try again. I'll answer at four again, and then it'll be eight on my end and ten for you."

"Let's just move past it," I say. It's funny how you always played along and made similar adjustments, just as Jackson is trying to do now. I should ask Jackson how he's doing and how his Christmas was, but none of these things feel right—too friendly and, as we've learned, over and over, I haven't earned that friendship. "I'm sorry for cutting you off. You were really good for me, and I know I was good for you, too. But it got too messy."

"I was going to tell you the first night we hung out. It's why I wanted to meet," Jackson says. He shifts uncomfortably, and behind his shoulder Chloe hops onto the bed and rests her head on his pillow. "I wanted to rip you apart, but then we were getting to know each other, and I knew your pain was just as bad. I didn't want to sharpen that dagger."

He's a better person than I am.

"I'm sorry we had sex," I say.

"Me too."

"I'm not saying this to hurt you, but you should know why I made that first move," I say. I tell him about the series of kisses I shared exclusively with you, the series of kisses you passed along to Jackson, the series of kisses I never introduced to Wade, the series of kisses Jackson will never look at the same way again after this story. I take a deep breath before I finish. "I couldn't believe he shared something so personal with you. I acted out. It's not the first time I've done something like that. I started hooking up with Wade over the summer. It was turning into something, and that's why I called Theo that day."

"Whoa."

"Except Wade sort of hates me now. It's probably for the best. I'm not sure I can handle love again," I say. Being this honest about how fragile I am with someone who was my worst enemy a couple of months ago is an insane relief. Honesty is not history. I've learned that, too.

"I didn't know he was gay," Jackson says. "I know Wade and Theo had their nonsense going on, but I know Theo loved him and missed their friendship. One day I asked Theo when he thought you would move on. I never got a straight answer out of him."

"Did it sound like he wanted me to move on?"

Jackson nods. "But remember who he was talking to."

"He loved you," I say, which is the hardest and most honest

thing I could possibly tell Jackson. "I'm sort of a pro on what Theo looks like when he's in love."

"I'm happy for you if that matters," Jackson says. "I'm sure Theo would've been, too."

I believe Jackson is happy for me. Would you have been happy for me?

"It does matter," I say.

Jackson smiles. "I'm coming back to New York first week of January for a couple of days. Sometime after the flights become less crowded. I'm hoping to talk things out with Anika and Veronika. You too. It's totally okay if you'd rather not talk again."

"We better keep talking," I say.

"I'll be conscious of the time zone difference," Jackson says.

"I'm always awake. I'll try not to wake you up at seven in the morning again."

"This was a good reason to wake up."

We agree to talk again soon. I end the call, and the screen goes black.

It's suffocating how, like me, Jackson also doesn't have all the answers surrounding your life and death. Wade, Jackson . . . we all have questions and we can ask you as many as we want, but you'll never answer us. There's always going to be some mystery. And there are pieces to the puzzle I can hand over to Jackson. Our taboo kiss and the kisses you had no business teaching him. But maybe I can protect the history you two had so he doesn't pick apart the puzzle. I really want to protect the happiness he found in you. Maybe some mystery isn't a bad thing.

THURSDAY, DECEMBER 29TH, 2016

WADE STILL HASN'T RESPONDED to my text message yesterday asking if we could meet up. I really thought when I woke up from that four-hour "nap" after video chatting with Jackson that a message from Wade would be there. And I was even surer he would've responded by this morning, but nothing.

I think I really screwed up here, Theo.

FRIDAY, DECEMBER 30TH, 2016

I KNOCK ON WADE'S front door.

I can hear someone pressing their eye against the peephole, and considering how quickly they walk away, it's safe to guess that someone is Wade. I knock again and again until his mother opens the door to let me know Wade isn't home in the most unconvincing voice ever. I know she knows I'm not that stupid, but it's not her fight.

I back off and wish her a happy new year because it doesn't seem likely I'll be seeing her in 2017.

SUNDAY, DECEMBER 31ST, 2016

THERE IS ONE HOUR left in 2016. If Wade wants nothing to do with me by the end of the year, then this is where I'll leave him. I'll be Wade-less in 2017. These are the rules of New Year's Eve: out with the old, in with the new. I'm not sure about this newness I should look forward to, but I know this begins with me trying to become my own rock. I've leaned on Jackson for the better part of this past month and Wade before that. Being my own rock is promising, but it would be a huge lie if I didn't admit that becoming a mountain with someone else could be equally rewarding.

Maybe it's the cider—or the spirit of drinking with my parents—but I'm calling Wade one last time so I can leave him a voice mail and say bye the right way. I'm done with this texting nonsense, where he can't hear the honesty in my voice. I want him to know I'm not angry and how I'm just kicking myself for never giving us our best shot.

But Wade picks up.

"Hey," he says.

"Hey. I was actually calling to leave a message," I say, hurrying to my bedroom.

"Would you rather do that?"

"Not if you're okay with talking to me," I say. He doesn't say no. "What are you up to?"

"I'm home with my mom, but you know her."

"She's in bed already."

"She's not one for New Year's excitement."

"You should come over." To anyone else, this would be a casual thing. For Wade six months ago, this would be a casual thing. But everything changed before you even died, Theo. "Don't turn me down. We have food and bad music and we're going to watch the ball drop. You shouldn't have to do that alone. We can talk if you want to talk, or we can shut up tonight and talk later and—"

"You should definitely shut up now," Wade interrupts, and softly adds, "We can talk when I get there."

"Get here before the ball drops, please."

Recap: I called Wade to say goodbye and now he's on his way. There is one hour left in 2016, and this is the first time all day I'm actually feeling the high of possibilities and rebirth. And I didn't lie to make it happen.

I run and tell my parents Wade is coming over. They don't get why I'm so excited, but they're pretty damn happy to see I am. I rush back into my bedroom, cleaning clothes off the floor, making my bed, throwing my boots and coat in the closet, and doing other little things until the doorbell rings twenty minutes later.

I rush to greet Wade myself, opening the door to find him with a neutral face and panting. His lungs must be burning, and my hugging the hell out of him in the hallway can't be helping much either.

He catches up with my parents for a bit, but time is running out before the ball drops. I pull him away, dragging him into my bedroom and leaving the door open so he doesn't think I'm trying to use him for sex, and so my parents don't confuse the situation either.

It's been a long time since he's been here. Wade looks around, taking in every wall, every piece of furniture. There have been some changes, the biggest one being himself, whether he realizes that or not. You would probably say it's safe to assume he knows it, right? My persistence the past few days and tonight for us only to be friends would be really unfair, considering I know how he feels about me.

"Thanks for coming over."

"Thanks for the invite," Wade says, sitting on the windowsill.

I shake my head and reach out to him. "Come sit with me." Wade takes my hand and we sit closely, my knee against his thigh. "I should jump right in before it hits midnight. I don't want you starting off your new year wondering if I'm worth hanging around for or not." I take a deep breath. "I'm sorry my love for Theo has been a roadblock for you. It's been a huge one for me, too. But you should know the day Theo died I called him because I wanted to talk about you. I couldn't reach him, so I left a voice mail, which apparently put him in a mood that sent him walking into the ocean . . . I killed the person I've loved more than anyone because I was trying to tell him about my new feelings for our best friend . . ."

Wade doesn't wait until I'm finished before he hugs me, massaging my back. "There's no way this is your fault. There are one hundred things that could've gone wrong. Damn, dude, I didn't know you were carrying around this guilt." He pulls back. "I messed up, too. I knew you weren't actually trying to have some relationship with Jackson, but I got jealous anyway. It's not fun being the loser. I've spent the past couple of nights feeling like an idiot about our whole situation. If we never had sex, we wouldn't be sitting here right now trying to figure out if we're going to be in each other's lives next year."

This is true. "I want to give us a shot, I swear. But I can't rush this or we'll get it wrong. You have to understand though that I'm still carrying Theo around with me, and I'm sure you are too. But it's different for me. I know you're not Theo, and I don't want you to be."

I promise going forward I will never demote the love I have for anyone. I'm growing to hate the word *love* because it always sounds lame, but love shouldn't only count when there's a victory. Love was never the liar; I was.

"Do you trust me?" I ask.

"I guess." Wade kisses me on the forehead, which sends one of those cold shivers across my shoulders and down my spine. "Do you believe I want to be something more to you?"

"I guess." I kiss his cheek.

My mom calls for us; the countdown is about to start. We rush into the living room and put on stupid party hats and wear plastic whistles around our necks. My dad pours us cider in plastic flute glasses. I really wish you were here, not romantically, but to reunite the squad, back in full force like when we were younger, before everything got complicated. But that's okay. I'm going to try and have fewer regrets in the New Year. I'm going to move past what's already done and make sure I don't repeat my mistakes moving forward.

Ten. Nine . . .

Wade turns to me, smiling like his life has already been rebooted.

Eight. Seven . . .

I throw back my cider and put down the glass.

Six. Five . . .

Wade does the same, knowing he's about to need his hands, too.

Four. Three . . .

I'm getting ready to reintroduce him to the world.

Two. One . . .

My heart is out of control, but I'm not as I pull Wade to me, kissing him with the force of everything happy. A lot of that unexpected happiness is thanks to him. Once my parents pull apart from their own kiss, they'll be expecting to embrace me, and they'll find me in arms they were never betting on finding me in. I stay in Wade's arms because "Auld Lang Syne" comes on, and, damn it, Theo, last year was so impossible and trying, I don't know how I got out of it alive. But I know how I'll be surviving this year.

And I still know the hardest part of my survival is ahead of me.

WEDNESDAY, JANUARY 4TH, 2017

SHARING A CAB TO your house with your ex-boyfriend and my not-quite-yet-but-maybe-one-day boyfriend seems like the start to a bad joke. But the only thing funny so far is that Wade threatened Jackson, warning him to stay ten feet away from my dick at all times or Wade will chop his off.

That was all in good awkward humor, I think.

Jackson got here with good timing because I'm returning to school tomorrow. Luckily I'll have Wade by my side: Team Mountain. It sounds like Jackson isn't quite ready to return yet himself, and I won't fight him on that decision.

We get out of the cab and head straight upstairs to your apartment, where your parents are expecting us. Russell and Ellen give us the warmest hugs. They seem in good spirits. I'm sure it makes you happy to see them getting better and better every time, right? On a scale of happiness, no one wants them stuck on the unhappy side, unable to lift themselves up and move on.

Your mother prepares iced tea while Jackson and Wade talk to your dad and Denise tells me everything she got for Christmas. Every single gift . . . I'm rescued shortly because Ellen knows the conversation the three of us want to have with her and Russell isn't Denise-friendly and we don't want to upset her, so she sends Denise to her room to play her racing video games.

"So what's going on?" Ellen asks, crossing one leg over the other while sipping from her hot tea.

We—Jackson and I—tell your parents how we're responsible for your death. We tell them how if we hadn't been feuding, we possibly wouldn't have driven you so crazy, you needed to distance yourself from everyone. I tell them about the voice mail that sent you there, but not why I called you in the first place. Jackson apologizes for not being brave enough to save you himself.

"Oh my God," Ellen says, shaking her head. "No. No. You cannot do this to yourselves. Theo's death isn't your fault. Griffin, unless your voice mail was some sort of hypnosis trick where you convinced Theo to walk into the ocean, then you're not to blame."

"Right," Russell says. "Same for you, Jackson. No one ever expected you to go running in there to save Theo. He was in danger, and you could've drowned, too. Theo's death was an accident and unpredictable."

"We play the blame game, too, I promise," Ellen says. "What if we never sent Theo to school on the West Coast? What if we put him in better swimming classes when he was younger? We will drive ourselves crazy forever coming up with new what-ifs."

"Leave that insanity to us," Russell says.

"I don't think I'll ever stop feeling guilty," I say.

"That's because you love Theo, wherever he is," Ellen says. "All three of you. You know this already, but you have to live for him, and you have to love for him." Ellen eyes me and Wade, probably because we're significantly closer to each other than we are to Jackson, and there's so much space here that we could man-spread if we wanted to. "You're not supposed to be stuck. Do not feel guilty for falling in love again."

"It's scary and the last thing on my mind right now, but I doubt I'll ever be ready for that," Jackson says.

"Whenever you're ready, that's the right time," Ellen says.

"Might even happen before then," I say. I turn to Wade and take his hand in mine, locking fingers with him. I'm scared to look up, but he squeezes back and gives me strength. Both Ellen and Russell are grinning and nodding. Their approval means the universe to me, because I know they want what's best for you, and if they can see that me moving on is a beautiful thing, then I trust that's how you would've felt, too.

Ellen and Russell tell us how we're very much family. The three of us are their extended children, and we're all older siblings to Denise. We call Denise back into the room and set up her new Wii out here and play the racing game with her.

I don't know when I'll see your parents or sister next. Maybe next month around your birthday I'll stop by and bring something for Denise. But it's good to know I'll be welcomed back.

"I'M VISITING THEO'S GRAVE today," Jackson says after we leave your building. "I was planning on coming out for his birthday, but I think I'm going to stay home and try to figure out what's next for me. It'll be nice to have a little one-on-one time with him."

"Is that your way of making sure we don't invite ourselves to tag along?" I ask, wrapping my arm around Wade's.

"A little bit," Jackson says.

We try to convince him to have lunch with us, but he's dead set on having his Theo time before having to meet up with Anika and Veronika tonight to try and repair their friendship. Jackson invites the two of us out to California in April for spring break, and looking that far ahead in my almost-relationship and in general is sort of scary, but not overwhelming.

"Is it okay if I hug him again?" Jackson asks Wade.

"He's not the boss of me," I say, stepping into Jackson's arms. I hug him like the brother I never had, like the brother I would've never slept with if I'd known I'd one day be calling him a brother of mine. "Thanks for everything, Jackson. I don't even want to think about where I would be if I couldn't turn to you. That Alternate Universe Griffin is pretty fucking screwed."

"Well, that Alternate Universe Jackson isn't exactly living his best life either," Jackson says, stepping back. "If you don't stay in touch, I'm going to have to fly back out here and harass you, and I'm not sure if Wade is going to be a huge fan of that."

"He still won't be the boss of me by then," I say.

"That's what he thinks," Wade says.

"Go easy on Theo," I say. "And yourself."

"Back at you," Jackson says.

We hail Jackson a cab. With one last wave, he's gone. I really don't know when I'll see him again, but I promise you, Theo, that we'll continue taking care of each other, and that I'll never turn my back on him again.

SATURDAY, JANUARY 6TH, 2017

"I DON'T KNOW WHY I agreed to go back to school."

Thank the Creator of All Universes that Wade is a kind, bored soul who is spending his Saturday morning helping me catch up on missed assignments.

"I think we both know why," Wade says, pointing at himself. "Solid life choice, by the way." He is lying across my bed, finishing my math homework—don't judge me, I can't possibly do all of this by myself. Team Mountain, remember? His elbow touches my hip, and if this were us months ago, we would've shifted away. Now I inch closer to him.

I'm letting my playlist run wild, and after I put the finishing touches on my history report about World War II, I turn to Wade. "Done." I lie down next to him, knowing I can trust nothing too sexual is going to happen because we've left the door open. It sucks, but I'm happy Wade and I aren't having sex for a while.

Our beginning was pretty rocky, so we need a fresh start. This means earning our relationship.

"We should get going."

Not only am I going back to school this week, but I have a therapy appointment this afternoon with a new doctor. Dr. Anderson was fine and all, but I'm starting over with this psychiatrist my mom's friend recommended to her. Hopefully Dr. Fergesen doesn't make me anxious, or I'll walk out of her office too. I'll figure out my next move from there.

We throw on our coats and go outside, walking to the clinic.

"I know I've been lying to myself about how well I'm actually functioning, and I know I may not be able to scrub myself clean of all the impulses and anxiety completely, but I want to see if I can take some control of my own life back," I say.

"You're welcome," Wade says.

"I didn't say thank you," I say.

"I noticed. I thought I'd nudge you in the right direction."

"Thanks for forcing me to be honest with myself," I say.

"Anytime, champ," Wade says.

I smile at him before looking ahead. There's nothing wrong with someone's saving my life, I've realized, especially when I can't trust myself to get the job done right. People need people. That's that.

Even though I'm incredibly anxious as to how this session will go, I feel like I can do anything right now, like make snow angels in nothing but a T-shirt and boxers and never get sick, or race Wade up the side of a building, not giving a single damn about gravity.

I'm on his left, of course, but in the middle of his story about his earliest memory at the movie theater, I shift to his right and hold his hand, which does feel weird, I can't lie. But it feels good, too. I'm no longer waking up on the wrong side of my life.

HISTORY
SUNDAY, NOVEMBER 13TH, 2016

My closet is dusty and so are my clothes after burying some of Theo's things back there. I change out of my shirt and jeans, throwing them on the floor. I'm walking to my dresser when my phone rings. I'm a little nervous I'll now have to tell Theo about Wade, but it's what has to be done for everyone involved. Still sucks. But it's not Theo calling. It's his mother.

"Hey, Elle—"

She's crying.

Everything is blurring from there. She's lying about Theo drowning this afternoon, right? I don't know why she would do this, but there's no way it's true. But she's not lying. I'm crying with her as I run out into the living room, passing the phone over to my parents. My eyes hurt and I can't breathe and I need air.

I go outside and run as I hear my mom calling for me. I bullet down the stairs and almost trip several times and I don't care. Knock me out, Universe, I don't care. I get outside and it's freezing and it's the first time I realize I'm in nothing but my boxers and socks. My feet are wet instantly, but the cold isn't slowing me down from racing into the street. I don't want to do this; I don't want to live and be here without Theo. I see a car coming, and I can throw myself out from behind this parked one.

I'm going to do it.

I'm going to do it because he broke his promise.

The car is a few feet away, but I throw myself into a mound of snow behind me instead, shivering and crying. Theo wouldn't want me to hurt myself. But I also don't know how to be alive in a universe where I can't talk to Theo McIntyre.

TODAY
SUNDAY, JANUARY 7TH, 2017

I have to say goodbye to you, Theo McIntyre.

I'm kneeling before your headstone, my knees buried in the snow, and I hope you know this is what's best for me. My psychiatrist is treating me with exposure therapy for my OCD, and medicine because she's diagnosed me with a delusional disorder. I'm not convinced she's right, but I have to face a version of truth that's painful—you aren't actually listening to me. This thought gets me scratching my palm and pulling my earlobe, because if you haven't heard a single thing I've said to you since you died, then you died without knowing the truth.

But now that I'm here, where we buried you, maybe I can talk to you.

I haven't lost my love for you, I swear. I'm actually nervous I may never lose my love for you, as if I'll start dating someone else and while I'm piecing together that new puzzle, that new story, I'll find myself reaching for you-shaped pieces. This might be okay for two or four or six or eight pieces, but anything more than that, and I'll be left with a puzzle that has half your face, half someone else's. That's not fair to the guy who's expecting me to give him my all the way I did with you.

It's not fair to Wade.

You're always going to be my first favorite human. No one can steal that from you. But now I have to get it together and allow room for more favorite people, to trust that Wade and Jackson are worthy of their own crowns.

It's been rewarding to be this honest lately. I'm determined to stay this honest, as if lives depend on it, which I guess they sort of do. No one will die if I lie, but lives can grow and be fuller when I tell the truth. Being honest will end the fight I have with myself when I'm with Wade, and I can see him for himself instead of someone around to fill up the emptiness.

Maybe when Jackson was here he had this talk with you, too. It kind of makes me sick, like we're all abandoning you for something that wasn't your fault. But I guess the point of all this is, Jackson and I will always keep you close, but we're putting ourselves first, and we're going to move forward as we're sure you would want us to.

I promise I'll find happiness again. It's the best way to honor you.

I stand, shaking a little as I wrap your hoodie around your headstone to keep you warm. I don't think it's right for me to keep this around anymore. I wonder what will happen to it. I wonder if it'll miraculously be here the next time someone visits you, or if the wind will blow it off and bury it deep beneath the snow, only for some stranger to discover it later. This person won't know anything about how you gave it to me the afternoon we had sex for the first time.

But that's okay. History remains with the people who will appreciate it most.

I love you, but I can't stay longer.

It may be a while before I speak to you again. I'm so happy you were my first, Theo, and you were worth all the heartache. I hope I wasn't living in some alternate universe where I wasn't actually your first love, too.

But this universe is the only one that matters, and I have one last question for you: I didn't get our history wrong, did I?

Turn the page for new content,
including a postscript from Griffin, a letter from the
author and book group discussion questions.

YOUR HISTORY LIVES
WITH ME FOREVER
TUESDAY, NOVEMBER 13TH, 2018

I try to only talk to you while I'm at your grave.

That hasn't always been easy, I can't lie—I won't lie. I spoke to you all the time in my head after you died, sometimes out loud without realizing it. But through lots of work I mostly think of you as just Theo. The same way I think about anyone else. Like, *I really miss Theo today*. It's better than saying how much I miss you knowing that you can't say it back. And not knowing if you can even hear me.

Hopefully my words can find you, wherever you are.

It's been two years since you drowned, since the universe went dark.

I like being back here in the cemetery, just the two of us. I try to only come during special occasions, like your birthday or this awful anniversary. But I slip a lot. Sometimes I really need your company. Like when I feel lost about where I want to be in my life, or confused about love. Then I come here and I sit with you and we talk—I talk. I never hear your voice in the wind or anything like that because you're not just gone, you're gone-gone.

But you still help me anyway, just like when I'm with my therapist and she isn't saying anything or even nodding along, but I feel better and lighter after letting some words and truths fly free.

Thank you for giving me that space, too, Theo.

The grass above where we buried you is pretty beat today, like a parade of people have come to visit you. I don't know if that's true, but I know for a fact that your parents and sister spent time with you this morning. They left behind some pink tulips and yellow orchids, just like last year. I lay your favorite white calla lilies next to the flowers as I kneel before your headstone.

I trace your name—T-H-E-O M-C-I-N-T-Y-R-E.

Then I do it a second time. A third. And as much as I want to stop there, to prove that I don't have to do it a fourth time, I give in. I'm trying not to see everything through a lens of even numbers, and I've made a lot of progress. But, once again, I slip. That's okay. I was never going to be able switch off my compulsions overnight like some light switch.

I wanted to share all that with you because I think a lot about that day on the train when I told you I thought I was crazy. It was the first time I was figuring out my OCD, and talking about it with you made it more real with every word. You didn't fully believe me, and that's okay because even though you were always a genius, you were sometimes really clueless, too. But you came through when I needed you the most. I had confessed how scared I was that I might become too complicated for you to still be my friend, to put up with me. That was some vulnerable shit, Theo, and you made me feel safe when you said you were more worried about how zombie pirates might kill us than you were about losing me.

Four and a half years ago and I still remember that moment like it was yesterday.

How you scooted closer to me, your hand on my knee, then your hand in mine.

I may not talk to you all the time anymore, but I think about you every day.

It's hard not to while still living in New York, where memories of you are everywhere. I don't spend a lot of time in the Upper West Side Barnes & Noble anymore. I'm always in and out with a new book because it's too depressing to remember how we tried to come up with your memoir title, knowing now that you'll never be able to write one. Some friends from school invited me to Bonus Diner, but that's where we went on our first date, where I got to finally kiss you. And of course I'm not trying to relive the awkwardness of being caught buying condoms by my father in Duane Reade, though that doesn't have as much to do with your death.

The point is, it's hard.

Jackson Wright struggles with this, too, out in Los Angeles.

I'm honestly surprised by how close we've become since you died. I used to wince whenever I heard his name, even if someone wasn't talking about him. Now I call him just to say hi. I wish we could've been this close when you were alive, but you get how that was never going to happen, right? Jackson and I had to lose you to gain each other. Make no mistake, it's safe to say we both would've abandoned this universe if we could've slipped into one where you're alive and well. But we live here, where you've been dead for two years.

I was really looking forward to seeing him this week, but Jackson couldn't make the trip. I honestly think he's not ready to come back. He seemed really haunted when he visited last November for the one-year anniversary of your death. But later today he's going on the Ferris wheel in Santa Monica, something you did with him for the first time ever on your last day. He'll be alone this time and he's going to FaceTime later to let me know how it went.

See, Theo, it's been two years and no one is forgetting you.

Maybe that's more for me than it is for you. I hated feeling like we were all leaving you behind. Your parents have donated a lot of things from your room. Denise is coming to me like I'm her big brother. It doesn't always make sense to me, just like I don't get how people still go in the ocean even though it killed you. But it's the same thing I talk about with all your family and friends—that's life. It has to go on.

You're never going anywhere.

Your history lives with me forever.

But I've got my eyes on the future, too, Theo.

I still get really weird talking about Wade with you. It feels like the time for that has passed, but I'm also never going to get the chance to have the conversation with you in person. Not unless the fabrics of the universe split apart and you can walk back into mine. I've talked to you before about some of my struggles with Wade because that feels easier than bringing up the joy. Like that makes the fact that your first boyfriend and best friend are dating, or that we started seeing each other while you were in another time zine falling for Jackson, less of a slap in the face. And how we started seeing each other while you were in another time zone falling for Jackson. But I don't want to lie or hold back the truth anymore.

Wade Church makes me really happy.

He comes over and plays jazz albums on Spotify as we chill in bed and he tries to predict the future. He's wrong a lot, but it's just as fun as listening to you create alternate universes. He's still the only person whose right side I can walk on, but that's okay with me for now. Wade doesn't always have the right words, but he tries. I'm definitely not perfect either. Whenever I apologize for being self-destructive and pushing him away, he forgives me and holds me close. And when I'm grieving you so hard that it feels like a never-ending storm, he's my shelter. I'm his, too.

We will never forget you, but we're finding life beyond you. Like we're supposed to.

I've talked to you about being confused by love before, but today isn't one of those days.

It's been a journey, Theo, but I finally told Wade that I love him with all the confidence in the world. It wasn't a word that was being used as a dagger to hurt you. It naturally burst out of me on an evening when Wade was so patient with my compulsions. He gave me the time I needed and I thanked him with my full-on heart.

Sometimes it felt like I was never going to love again. Especially not someone who orbited so closely in our universe. But whenever I swear I would rather live in darkness, Wade pops up like a rising sun. He makes me feel like I could be brave enough to play in the ocean if he's holding my hand. Like I could even forget for moments, maybe even minutes why I hate the ocean so much. I feel guilty having those thoughts and gross for sharing them, but it's all true. It's one of many things I think you should know.

You died without me having all the answers, all the pieces to the puzzle. I don't want to leave you with any mysteries.

I want you to know that one day I'm going to beat my compulsions. It might not be in the next year or two or three or four, but I will win.

I want you to know that I'm ready to destroy any zombie pirate that shows up.

I want you to know that your family will always be a part of my life.

I want you to know that there isn't a day when this universe doesn't feel cold without you, but that warmth finds its way in, too.

I want you to know that my love for you didn't die because you did, but that my heart has found life again.

More than anything, I want you to know that I'm going to be okay.

And that's the promise for the future I'll leave you with today.

THE HISTORY BEHIND
HISTORY IS ALL YOU LEFT ME

Dear Reader,

Years ago I met my first serious boyfriend—another author, before I was one myself—at a book event. We'd had some social media exchanges and hit it off in person, hanging out on the streets of rainy New York until morning. But he didn't live in New York. We stayed in contact daily and it wasn't long before I was ready to move out of the city I called home my entire life to be with him. I came out to my mother and the rest of my family, packed an extremely large suitcase, got on a train, and left home. All was well for months with my then-boyfriend until I returned to the city for professional reasons. The relationship was long distance again, and what was once a source of happiness was growing into one of frustration for not physically being with each another. I ended things before it could turn ugly and knew we'd be better as best friends. Though I trusted we'd one day find our way back to each other.

Until he met someone else in a new city.

Watching my first boyfriend fall in love with someone else left me in this long state of brokenness because even though

I wanted happiness for him, I wanted him to find that in me. I became insufferable with my jealousy and insecurities, and suffered through hopelessness and strong suicidal urges (it wasn't the first time in my life, and it wouldn't be the last). One day he called to tell me he and his boyfriend almost drowned at the beach, and from then on, my already fragile state exploded into extreme paranoia that there was a chance I'd lose him forever, that I'd lose him before I could tell him I still loved him without interfering with his relationship. After a dinner in New York with my ex and his boyfriend—who'd slowly become a friend of mine—I was feeling hopeful again after I finally accepted that they were a much better match than we ever were. Maybe I wasn't screwed on finding my equal either. It wasn't exactly a happily ever after for me, but it was a promising new beginning.

I still had a lot to process and as is the case with all my books, a *What If?* question sparked a new idea.

What if my ex-boyfriend drowned that day?

And the rest is history.

Adam Silvera

BOOK GROUP QUESTIONS

1. Why do you think Griffin and Jackson are so immediately drawn to each other? Would they be friends—not to mention more—if Theo hadn't died?

2. When a break up occurs, what's the best way to move on? Reliving the history, as Griffin does, or forgetting the past? Is the latter possible for Griffin? For anyone?

3. How does Griffin's OCD manifest, and what are the misconceptions that surround that condition? Were you surprised by how this played out in the book?

4. Griffin says, "I'm not a big fan of secrets. Secrets can turn people into liars . . ." Do you agree? Or are secrets more often a way of keeping safe the ones we love? What are some examples of both kinds of secrets in the book?

5. Relationships, houses, and futures, among other things, are all described in the book as being completed or notably incomplete puzzles. What do you think is the significance of this recurring image?

6. So often in novels, particularly young adult novels, absent or negligent parents are a part of the plot. How does it change the novel that Griffin's and Theo's parents are all together and fairly happily married? Does their support detract in any way from Griffin's grief?

7. Would you have broken up with Theo when he left? Why or why not? Did Griffin do the right thing?

ACKNOWLEDGMENTS

My editor, Daniel Ehrenhaft, for believing in me very early on, whiplash-worthy edit letters, inhabiting Griffin's compulsions so thoughtfully, and losing sleep until we got everything right. My publicist, Meredith Barnes, for all the empathy she's shown toward my very particular mind. My agent, Brooks Sherman, for his super savviness and therapy when I'm doubting myself. My homie, Hannah Fergesen, an editorial wizard who's been right so many times my ego has suffered. My assistant, Michael D'Angelo, for bossing me around. My beautiful and brilliant higher-ups, Bronwen Hruska and Jenny Bent, and the hard-working champions at Soho Teen and the Bent Agency. When the time comes for the zombie-pirate apocalypse, I'm recruiting my publishing team first.

Luis "LTR3" Rivera, for being the best damn lifesaver in all the land, hosting me for a couple months so I could finish writing this book, epic *Super Smash Bro.* matches with the bros, and "a fourth thing." Corey Whaley, for sticking to my right, lion statues, history, and staying in my life. Cecilia Renn, for our psychic connection and checking me when I'm too stubborn to check myself. Amanda and Michael Diaz (and Ann and Cooper), who know my obsessive ways all too well—sorry-not-sorry for all those songs on repeat. Lestor Andrade, for the Carpool of Shame and many other Real Life moments.

Becky Albertalli, for making sure I didn't throw away my shot when things were at their worst. David Arnold(-Silvera), for the most epic fake-proposal in the universe. Jasmine Warga, for the greatest candy picnic in that swanky bathtub. (Team Beckminavidera forever.) Sabaa Tahir, a Jedi Master who can always sense when there's a disturbance in the Force. Nicola Yoon, whose generosity is nonstop. Victoria Aveyard, for never waking me up during every movie we see. Hashtag dope. Renée Ahdieh, for not outing me at Comic-Con when gum fell out of my mouth in the middle of our panel. Kim Liggett, for getting me out of the house to write this book and all the gossiping in-between. Lance Rubin, the worst rival ever because there isn't a bone in his body or word in his brain I could hate. Virginia Boecker, for too many laughs over too many unspeakable things. Dhonielle Clayton and Sona Chara-ipotra, wise forces on their own, world-changers together.

If I tried to name everyone in the community whose had a hand in my career, this book would weigh twice as much. Thank you all to the readers, bloggers (shout-out to Dahlia Adler and Eric Smith), writers, family (shout-out to my lovely mom for happy history), friends, booktubers, booksellers (shout-out to everyone at Books of Wonder), librarians (shout-out to Angie Manfredi).

And, most importantly, for all the Humans, named and unnamed, who've encouraged me to write my way into this life and helped me write my way through my depression. This one is for you—as are all the ones that will follow.